Airlis

Brian Willis

Edited by Irene Hunt, Drather B Reading

Cover Design by LaRen Thompson

author-brianwillis.blogspot.com

ISBN: 0692808094
ISBN-13: 978-0692808092 (Independent Publisher)

To miracles.

Warning

This may sound crazy . . . but what you're about to read might change the rest of your life. I figure I better get that on the table right now, so if your heart is touched and you find a desire for something more, you'll know who to give the credit! No, it's not me. If anything good comes from these pages, it will be because of the Grand Architect who molded the words and formed my life into everything I've become. Hopefully, God can touch you through my insane story—in at least some small way—like He has me.

Have you ever seen glimpses of eternity? Maybe you were in that fragile place between worlds; you know, when you can't tell if you're dreaming or not? And like a thick fog, you can feel and see glorious things, but no matter how hard you try, they always seem to slip through the fingers of comprehension. Oddly familiar, it's a place where limits and boundaries do not hinder your senses, a place full of people who love and live bigger than oceans!

As it begins to come into focus and make sense once again, the scene evaporates like morning dew under the bright sun of consciousness. What if instead of glimpses, you reached out and grabbed it in both hands! Even if only for a moment—oh, the things you could see. The places you could go! It would change your life.

I know . . . because during my senior year of high school, it happened to me.

I held eternity in my hands.

And now, my eternity will never be the same.

David Thorn

Tuesday, August 16, 2011

Yesterday

A small bead of sweat dripped from my nose to the grass. I could do this play in my sleep . . . actually, I *have* done it in my sleep! Zack yelled out the count, "Down. Set. Hut!" I exploded from my three-point stance and drilled the defensive end. Not only would it slow him down, but usually the outside linebacker would forget about me when I acted like a lineman. Tight ends can be deadly weapons if a coach knows how to use them. (That's right girls, a deadly weapon!)

A quick spin-move gave me the separation I needed, and I raced toward the sideline. The pass was behind me, but I reached back and pulled it in. Heavy footsteps were coming fast, so I quickly spun to the inside. The cornerback clipped my shoulder as I twisted, causing me to lose my balance slightly. As I planted my arm to get me back on my feet, BAM! I got drilled by the outside linebacker. An explosion of pain tore through my arm as it bent in a direction it wasn't supposed to.

Sitting on the practice field cradling my arm, all I could think was, *Not me. This can't be happening to me.*

Today

I'm sure if anyone ever finds this journal, my life will be over as I know it, but if I don't get this out of my head, I think it might explode. Today started with all the hopes and dreams a senior year can offer, but before the sun set, my life crashed—burned—and then I lost it as the ashes were scattered by the winds of insanity. Let me explain.

My life revolves around one thing, football. I don't think of myself as a star athlete, and I don't think others view me as anything special, but it's been my dream to play on the varsity team for as long as I can remember. Since junior high, I fought and clawed my way up the ranks, and by the time my senior year rolled around, I'd done it! David Thorn—Snowflake Lobos' starting tight end!

All summer, as we traveled to neighboring towns for passing league, I admit I was looking good. What seemed hard last year had gotten easier, the defenders had gotten smaller, and the coaches and I were excited for the upcoming season. A perfect way to begin my senior year. I was at the top of the world, with only bigger things on the horizon.

*　　*　　*　　*

Wasn't that nice? Wow, I didn't realize how much I missed writing! Okay, so maybe there's more to explain if you really want to know what's going on. This is where the blackmail material begins. My secret love is a pen and paper! I know, and I don't even get good grades in English. I used to jot down my daydreams of battling dragons until one day, in fifth grade, Brock Henderson swiped my notebook from my desk and yelled, "Hey look! David has a secret diary!"

Only a few people laughed, but I admit it bothered me enough to quit. Now I've got to unload somehow. If I don't, I think the alternative will end me in jail . . . so, I'm back.

Since I've already started throwing dirt, I might as well dig this hole nice and deep. That way, maybe it'll be quick and painless when I hit the bottom. Are you ready? I collect rocks. I love old bands like Simon and Garfunkle. I'm not only in choir because of the girls, I genuinely like music. And I'm a cowboy. Have you ever seen such a conglomeration? Confusing—yeah, I know. I have to live with it every day. Most people don't believe it when they see glimpses of the real me. Truthfully, it's because most people don't *see* the real me at all. It doesn't help that I try to hide it, though. At school I like T-shirts, loose-fitting pants, tennis shoes, and a ball cap. At home I wear tight wranglers and cowboy boots. Have you ever tried to ride a horse without them? As for the cowboy hat . . . well, I've never owned one actually. Here in Snowflake, the wind blows too much to keep one on very long. Besides, when I ride horses, the ball cap turns around for the high gears!

So there you have it, me on a platter. An eighteen-year-old, brown-eyed, dark-haired, 170-pound, screwed-up cowboy in disguise. But don't tell anyone about the cowboy part, or I will find you. Not sure what'll happen when I do, but I promise one of us will regret it!

*   *   *   *

Back to today and the end of life as it once was. It's our second week of school, third week of football, and our first game is next Friday against Holbrook . . . well, at least it will be for the rest of the team.

I couldn't control the cry of pain as I hit the turf hard. It didn't matter where the ball went or who had hit me, my mind was only focused on one thing. The coaches ran over and asked what was wrong. Between gritted teeth I cried out, "I think it's broke!"

They gingerly took my arm and began examining it. They tapped here and squeezed there, but nothing seemed abnormal. It looked straight, and I could move my fingers without a problem. There was only a deep throbbing in my forearm.

The coaches visibly relaxed as I began moving my arm around freely. *Phew! It's probably just a hyperextension or something*, I thought. I sat out for the remaining offensive plays, and then we separated for drills. The aching was still there, but nothing seemed out of the ordinary as the receivers began practicing overhead catches. Forcing myself to forget about it, I ran the drill. The moment the ball hit my hands, there was another explosion of fire, and I gasped in pain!

Coach saw my reaction and pulled me aside. "Thorn, you better go get that arm checked."

"But Coach, I think it's only a stinger."

"Better to be safe than sorry," he said without emotion, and I left feeling the same way inside.

Mom was standing behind the counter putting away groceries when I walked in. She must have recently gotten home, since she was still in her scrubs, her medium-length, brown hair pulled back in her usual pony tail. Her brown eyes filled with alarm when she looked up and saw me. "David, why are you home already? Are you hurt?"

That didn't take long, I thought. How do moms always know?

"Yeah, I got a stinger or something, and Coach wants me to get it checked out." My nonchalance didn't ease her worry. Mom knows more than anyone how much I love football, and besides, she's a mom.

She set up a doctor's appointment for today during third hour. A note from the office excused me from class, and Mom met me outside. Even after arguing I could take myself, Mom insisted she be there. I felt bad she had to miss work, but honestly, I was grateful she did. We sat silently in the waiting room. I played *Angry Birds* on my phone while Mom flipped through a *Home and Garden* magazine.

"David Thorn?" A middle-aged nurse with a pleasant voice stood in the doorway by the front desk. I don't remember much after that. Everything went slightly blurry until the doctor came back holding the x-ray—then it was as vivid as a fresh knife-cut.

"Yep, it's a clean break!" were the exact, slicing words. The doctor continued cheerfully, "If you look right here, about halfway between your wrist and elbow, can you see that thin white line on your ulna? That's where it broke." I sat there stunned as he continued to chat about the bone being set straight and that it'll only take six weeks to heal. SIX WEEKS!

Crashed.

When we got back in the car, Mom started crying. Usually mom's tears of concern carry healing qualities, but not today. We decided I wouldn't need to go back to school until after lunch and stopped by McDonalds. The Big Mac and fries didn't help either, and I couldn't finish the ice cream cone. *Six weeks* kept echoing in my head. Doc said I'd have to wait a few days for the swelling to go down, and then I'd get a cast from my hand halfway up my bicep.

"We'll check it in six weeks and see how it looks. I wouldn't recommend playing football even at that point, but we'll see." His words gouged into my mind like those on a gravestone.

I was late for fifth-hour Chemistry, but I was glad, because I didn't want to talk to anyone in the halls. Luckily, there aren't any football players in my class. I walked in as Mr. Fry was explaining something about the element table. Could he just let me come in and sit down? Oh, no. As the first tardy student of the year he had to make an example out of me.

"David, so glad of you to join us." He stared over his bifocals. "That'll be an hour of detention for tardiness." And then the straw that broke the camel's back. "Oh, and I'll take that hat. You know the rules. No hats in the classroom."

Burned.

When people talk about having a mental breakdown, I didn't realize things literally break! My emotions crumbled into a heap as I stared at Mr. Fry with dead eyes. Looking back now, I'm surprised I didn't get angry or cuss or something (Mom doesn't know I cuss), but that's not what happened. I simply turned around—and walked out.

Where do you go when you can't get far enough away? When I turned sixteen, Grandpa gave me his old Ford ranch truck, and fortunately, I had three-quarters of a tank of gas.

I hit Main Street and left a few black marks as I headed out of town. There's not much around Snowflake. It's kind of in a hole, and I mean that in more ways than one. When you climb out of the valley you find yourself surrounded by sage brush and cedar trees. Not much to look at, but, because of being raised on a ranch, I knew a few places I could hide.

Grandpa's ranch is east of town. It borders the city limits between Snowflake and Taylor and is roughly rectangular in shape. On the far-east side of the ranch is a natural, spring-fed watering hole called Lost Lake. All the others are manmade tanks that catch the runoff. The water is cool and clear, and the tiny lake is surrounded by lush grass, willows, and cottonwood trees. Literally an oasis when compared to the rest of the ranch.

It's a place of many great memories. My brother Josh and I made a swing there a few years back, and we've spent hours on its banks catching frogs and making rafts. But the thing I love the most about the place is its unusual rocks. Yeah, the weird side of me revealed, once again. I've spent hours walking around the lake, and all over the ranch for that matter, picking up arrowheads, pottery, and all sorts of different-colored stones. Anyway, this is where I was headed. I needed to be alone, and I wasn't sure when I was coming back.

I didn't think the school would contact Mom about my absence until tomorrow, but I turned off my phone anyway. I sat under the shade of a cottonwood I've always loved. It's the biggest around with perfect limbs for the swing we put in it. Swaying gently in the soft evening breeze, the old bicycle handlebar seemed to laugh, mockingly. What used to willingly transport me to a carefree world, now only drove despair deeper into my heart.

As crushing as it was to realize I couldn't even swing on a rope, the thing that bothered me the most was how football had become all that mattered in life. Now that it was gone, what was I left with? The question consumed me from the inside. I sat in turmoil watching the water ripple from unseen pond life.

Lost in thought, I picked up a stone and pulled back to skip it across the lake. Fire shot down my arm! Something snapped inside . . . and I lost it. I'm sure the ensuing tantrum made heaven's gag real: an eighteen-year-old kid crying in pain, screaming in anger, trying to throw oversize rocks with his wrong hand. One of them was much too large to get very far, and the splash covered me head to toe. I sat back down dripping and defeated.

Tears may or may not have started falling to the ground . . . I plead the fifth. But I will say, I've never hit bottom like I did today.

Have you ever heard the phrase, "a broken heart and a contrite spirit"? I had in Sunday School a few times, but today I got a whole new understanding of the term. As I thought about my broken life, this scripture popped into my head.

Religion has always been a part of me, just not a very big one. Mom's Mormon ancestors were partly responsible for founding Snowflake. Grandma said we've been members of The Church of Jesus Christ of Latter-day Saints since before the Mormon pioneers crossed the plains sometime around the 1840s. Although I've never known anything else, I haven't put much thought into it. I didn't need to. I had "more important" things, like football. Mom never gave up on me, though. As my thoughts turned to her, a memory sparked a valuable lesson she taught me years ago.

"You lost your book? Well, if you want help finding it, you should pray and ask God." Even though I was only seven, I remember my mother encouraging me, because after praying I found my book! It had fallen between the bed and the wall, and as I searched, the thought came to look there. Since then, I can't remember receiving anything special from God . . . but I needed Him now.

Sitting on the bank under that tree, I decided I would try asking again. With more incentive than I've had in the past, I began hesitantly, "Father in Heaven . . . I really need you right now. My life is falling apart, and I don't know what to do. Will you please fix my arm so I can play football? I've worked so hard for this all my life. In the name of Jesus Christ, amen."

Silence was all that followed. I didn't *feel* anything different, but then again, my arm didn't hurt unless I caught it wrong. Hopeful, I grabbed another rock. As I pulled back, the pain stabbed like a hot branding iron! I cried out and quickly cradled my arm in my lap. Even God was abandoning me.

Never had I felt more alone. I hate to admit this, but many unpleasant thoughts entered my head. *No one likes me, no one cares. No one would care if I ran away. No one would even care if I was dead.* Black feelings began to constrict around my heart. My shoulders sagged and my head drooped, but as I was about to deflate permanently, my gaze was drawn to my hand . . . and all I could do was stare dumbfounded.

The rock was gripped tightly in my fingers. It was about as round as a baseball but nearly flat, perfect for skipping. The curious shade of white swirled into a cloudy void within. It was there that the thoughts I had been thinking in my head slowly appeared as written words *inside* the rock:

No one would even care if I was dead.

And then the words vanished.

Blinking in disbelief, I quickly looked around. There were no cameras, and nobody snickering in the bushes. Shaking my head, I was about to write it all off as a hallucination when, to my utter amazement, I looked again and saw:

I care!

Lost it.

That's it, I've lost my mind, appeared in the rock as the thought entered my head.

That's too bad, was its reply.

What in the HELL is going on? Seeing my personal thoughts appear so freely turned my surprise into shock.

If you are not going to watch your thoughts, I will be happy to go, the rock replied. I can honestly say I was at a loss for words *and* thoughts at the moment. Not only was a rock talking to me, it was scolding me!

My muddled mind finally got back on track, and as I guided my thoughts to form a question, once again words appeared in the stone. Is this a joke? Or am I going crazy?

The rock replied, *I fail to see the humor, but I do feel overjoyed! As for you being crazy, I suppose that is yet to be determined.*

Great! I thought. Now I've got a sarcastic, reprimanding rock in my hands!

This is not a rock, it replied.

What are you talking about? I physically shook my head as the words kept pouring from my mind to my hands, involuntarily. And if you're not a rock, what are you?

I am a girl.

As if it wasn't confusing enough already. Oh . . . well that would explain the sarcasm. So you're a female rock?

*No silly, I am a female who is communicating to you **through** an Airlis!*

That was it, I set the rock down. My mind couldn't handle it anymore, and besides . . . this was madness! I looked down at the stone sitting by my leg. It looked normal enough. A bird hopped to the water's edge and snagged something from the moss. *What was going on?* I looked back down and it was still a plain old rock, kind of. Hesitantly, I picked it back up, hoping to prove I was only seeing things.

Are you going to leave me? asked the rock.

I purposefully thought my reply. I don't really have anywhere to go right now, so I guess not.

Good, because I have a million questions to ask you!

I responded without hesitation, Oh, crap—sorry, didn't mean to say that. Wow, it's hard to talk this way.

Have no worry, I will not leave . . . yet. But could you please control your thoughts better?

I um . . . I'll try, I thought sheepishly.

Thank you. Let us start over. Hi, I am Elli! What is your name?

I'm David.

David, I like that name. So David, where do you exist?

The question caught me off guard. Exist? Um, I guess I exist in Snowflake, Arizona.

The girl in the rock replied, *I have never heard of that. Is that the name of your world?*

My world? Are you an alien? I started getting a bit nervous.

What is an alien?

Well, that answers that question. I live on earth! Have you ever heard of it?

Actually, no.

What? I was stupefied. Where do YOU exist?

For now, I reside on Orantha; it is one of Father's worlds.

You ARE an alien! My heart started racing.

I am sorry, but I do not know what that is.

You know, green skin, antennae, large eyes . . . an alien!

Sorry to disappoint you, David, but I am not a grasshopper.

I wasn't expecting this response. You know what a grasshopper is? Confusion helped sidetrack my hysteria, at least for a moment.

Of course! Most inhabited worlds have the same basic creations, and I have never heard of aliens.

We call anything that comes from a different world an alien, and usually they don't come in peace.

9

Well under that definition would you not be an alien as well?

Again I was stumped. What? No! I was born and raised on THIS world. I'm beginning to think I'm actually NOT the one who's crazy here.

Wait a moment. When you first spoke, did you not say no one would miss you if you were dead? Are you mortal?

Huh? Of course! We're all quite mortal the last time I checked, except Superman.

Superman?

Never mind. You've done NOTHING to convince me yet that you're NOT an alien! My anxiety levels continued rising.

She ignored me and kept sharing her thoughts without hesitation. *So, if you exist on a mortal world, that can only mean you are either many galaxies away, or you are from the past!*

Hey ALIEN, what are you talking about?

I am not an alien, whatever that may be; I am a person! You know two arms, two legs, two eyes. The fact that we are communicating should be evidence enough . . . but wait . . . you have forgotten.

Forgotten what? I thought in exasperation.

Everything! You entered a mortal world without memories, correct?

Of course. Wait . . . you're human? A spark of sanity lit up my quickly unraveling mental state.

Yes, silly!

A flood of relief came over me, but I was still incredibly confused. Okay . . . that eases my mind a tad, but will you please explain what's going on?

Let me see. I recently learned about this in history, but how to explain. Oh! Let me ask you this, have you been taught why you are on your world yet?

Her weird questions kept throwing me for a loop. Yeah, they teach us in church about God's plan, but what does that have to do with anything?

Great! Now we are getting somewhere.

Um, do you have a frog in your pocket? I don't think "we've" gotten anywhere but more confused.

I will try to put it as simply as I can. I am a girl who is probably somewhere on the other side of the universe, or who is far into your future.

Oh that's better . . . clear as mud, I thought sarcastically.

Be patient, David, I am trying. Maybe it will help if I explain the Airlis.

Yes, PLEASE do. I am only seconds away from losing it!

Mortal worlds are created out of mortal material. Everything eventually dies, correct?

Okay, I guess so.

*An Airlis is probably the only thing on your earth that does **not** die.*

Um . . . it's a rock.

Yes, but all physical elements have different levels of spiritual matter. The spirit is what keeps the physical in order.

I don't **completely** understand, but keep going.

Your Airlis is made of the purest form of physical matter and contains one of the highest levels of spiritual life, as well. That is how it communicated to you and also connected to me. It can read our spirits.

I pondered for a second and then thought to myself, So, it's kinda like a high-tech cell phone, surprised again that my thoughts were speaking without my consent.

What is that?

How do you explain a cell phone? Wow, okay, it's a device we created **on earth**, and we can talk to each other through it.

Yes, precisely! It's like your cell phone except not only can we communicate through space, it also connected us through time!

My brain stumbled for a second before I could say, All right, I understand the space thing, but connecting us through time? And I thought chemistry was hard!

Wow, this is very difficult when you're trying to explain it to someone unintelligent. Oh, my! I am so sorry! I did not mean to think that.

You ARE human! I thought in surprise. Then I got facetious. Please remember to watch your thoughts, or I might have to leave you.

Yes, you are right. I am truly sorry. Will you please forgive me?

I guess so, but don't do that again! I teased.

I will do better, I promise.

Good. I smiled for the first time all day. Anyway, you were about to explain the "time" thing to me. By the way, I was just teasing you.

We are not accustomed to much teasing here. Sorry. It must be a mortal thing. Once again I was at a loss of what to think. She continued, *Somehow this mix of pure matter and spirit made the Airlis completely eternal, meaning it is not bound by time. That is how it is able to connect us to what seems to be the same moment, but could be thousands or millions of years apart.*

Woah. That's deep sh . . . stuff. I almost didn't catch that one.

Yes, even I do not understand how it works completely. Is it not amazing?

It's much more than amazing—it's *crazy*—it's . . . it hurts my head. I raised my arm to message my temple and yelled out in pain! OUCH! appeared and disappeared from the rock.

What happened? Does our conversation cause you pain?

I couldn't help but smile even though my arm was throbbing badly. No. I forgot about my arm and moved it again.

What is wrong with your arm?

Oh, nothing. I just broke it and ruined my life is all, I replied sarcastically.

I did not realize arms were so important in mortal worlds.

I couldn't help but say, You're very strange.

Sorry. If it makes you feel any better, I think you are quite nice for someone who moments ago wanted to be dead.

This brought me up short. Well . . . thanks for taking my mind off it for a while. Anyway, I'm not sure if it's better to be crazy or dead, but at least I'll have company in the loony bin, right?

I do not know what a "loony bin" is, but I would love to keep you company there!

I bet you would. So, Elli, let me see if I got this straight. From your perspective, I live a long time ago in a galaxy far, far away. And in this "Star Wars" fantasy, I happened to find an "Airlis" that connected me to you. How am I looking so far?

I have no idea why you would fantasize about warring amongst the stars . . . but I think you are understanding the rest. There might be hope for you yet!

Thanks. It's kind of like we're texting each other through time! This is CRAZY! The shock was wearing off, and wonder was sinking in.

What is texting?

Sorry, it's a cell phone thing. This made me think of something else. Speaking of which, can the Airlis send pictures?

I am not sure. I have only read about the Airlis, and they are rare enough that most people have never seen one.

So how did you get yours?

Honestly, I found it by accident. I was sitting at a bench in the garden and happened to notice it on the ground next to me. Captivated by its unique beauty, I had to pick it up! As I turned it over, soaking up its translucent aspects, I saw your thoughts appear inside, and I knew exactly what it was!

Okay, it's starting to clear up a little. I sort of understand how it may have connected to me when I picked it up, but how in the world did it connect us together?

I am not completely sure, but if I were to speculate, I would say the Airlis I found today must have been yours a long time ago. In our realities, we are holding two separate stones at different times, but to the stone, we are both holding it at the same time. Does that make sense?

Actually, not at all, but I get the concept, I think. So sometime in the future, you're going to find my Airlis, and SOMEHOW it will connect you back to me? This is insane!

You are exactly right! Somehow your stone has found its way to my world! Oh I would love to know its story.

I shook my head slowly in disbelief. This is heavy. Wow, I totally understand how Michael J. Fox felt now.

Do you name all your foxes?

This made me laugh. No, crazy head. He's an actor who went back to the future, and . . . oh, never mind.

Sometimes we do acting here, but it was not a talent I desired to improve.

Do you guys have movies, too? I thought curiously.

I am not sure what a movie is, but we do have performances.

That would be something to see, I thought in wonder. Even though it was still weird, I was beginning to get the hang of my thoughts becoming the voice to our conversation. So, Elli, if you don't like to act, what do you like to do?

Wait, I thought I was supposed to be asking the questions.

Sorry, but you started it, I teased back.

She paused for a second and said, *I guess it will not hurt to tell you. Actually, I love to paint. My family does not know about this, because I have only recently begun experimenting with the talent, but I enjoy it immensely!*

I know how you feel.

Oh, really? What is it you like to do?

Well, I guess it wouldn't hurt to tell you either if you truly are from the future—I want to be a writer someday.

I see! It would be very difficult to write with a broken arm.

Actually, that wasn't the reason I was upset.

What was it then?

Well, it ruined my future in football. Assuming she wouldn't understand, I continued, Football is a game we play here on earth.

You were going to kill yourself over a game?

The way she put it made it sound ridiculous. Yeah. Pretty pathetic, huh?

Yes, it is.

Her comment caught me off guard. Wait, are you teasing me? I thought you said you don't tease!

No, I said we don't tease much. Sometimes, the occasion permits for a little friendly banter. I believe this is a perfect opportunity with you being a Telestial mortal and all.

You know, for someone who comes from the other side of heaven, you sure are a smart aleck!

Oh, I am a smart aleck now, am I? What is that, another kind of green insect?

No, they're girls who mess with your mind and cut your heart open! Okay, maybe I was stretching the definition a little.

That is terrible! Are there really girls like that?

It seems like they're getting more and more common.

I am glad I still have time to get ready for my turn in mortality.

You're coming to earth? My heart vibrated with a flutter.

Not to your world. We exist in different times remember?

Oh, yeah, I forgot. The slight gust of emotion passed quickly, and my sails were left empty.

I believe your world, and you for that matter, are progressed far beyond a Telestial stage by now. Is it not strange to think about, though? Somewhere, out in the great abyss of space, you probably DO exist right now in some final state of glory!

. . . You lost me again.

She must not have been looking at the stone, because her train of thought ran right over my comment. *I will ask Father if he thinks there is any way I might be able to find you. Maybe you lost this Airlis and would like to have it back!*

Earth to Elli. What did you mean about getting your **turn** in mortality?

Oh, yes. Do you recall I mentioned I learned about you, or at least mortal worlds like yours, in History?

Yeah, I remember.

The reason we study history is because the process that allows spirit children to gain physical bodies, and eventually progress to immortality, has always been, more or less, the same. It cycles over and over with slight variations, depending on the decisions of the family within each individual realm.

This was one deep conversation. I pondered for a minute. Apparently, my thoughts wouldn't appear in writing inside the Airlis unless I actually formulated words in my head. Finally, I thought the question, So what you're saying is, the Plan of Salvation I learned about in church is basically going on in other places with other people?

I think so, and everyone is at different stages in that plan, and every plan is different depending on what the spirit children and their parents decide.

So are you a spirit child?

I am actually not considered a child anymore, but I once was. Are you a child?

Sorry. No, I'm not, and I didn't think you were either.

I am teasing you again, David.

You are definitely a girl.

A smart aleck, remember!

I laughed out loud before thinking, Yes, I remember.

I suppose, if you compare my growth and learning to other brothers and sisters, I would be considered a young adult spirit. It matters not. Father said we may all experience a mortal existence. It will not depend on the level of intelligence we have previously

16

achieved. The last time I spoke to Father, He told me He soon will present His plan of progression to us! We are very excited!

When you get to your earth, you're going to be a heart breaker for sure. I can already tell.

Oh, I would never break the heart of another person! Do girls actually do that? It sounds terribly barbaric!

Not all, I guess, but I haven't found one yet who has treated me otherwise. I was teasing, but there was also a strand of vengeful truth behind the statement.

I will be sure to be the nice kind, and I promise not to hurt your heart.

Okay, but I'm going to hold you to your word. Our conversation was all in jest, but the thought of actually meeting each other, even though it apparently was impossible, prompted another question. How old are you if you're no longer a child?

Of course, I am eternal—all matter is eternal—but we do monitor our spiritual growth. We calculate this by the cycles of our galaxy, and in my latest stage of growth, I am coming up on my eighteenth cycle!

Most of what she said flew right over my head, but I did catch the end. Cycles, huh? Well, I just turned eighteen, except we go by years on earth. Perhaps it was natural curiosity, but either way, the question transmitted from my head into the Airlis before I could take it back. So, do you have a boyfriend?

I have many friends who are boys. Is that the same thing?

Not exactly. I guess the question would be more like, are you seeing one special guy?

Do you mean, have I singled out someone who would make a good companion?

Yeah, I guess so. The weird way she kept wording things made me realize she probably was from a different world.

Not anyone in particular. I have focused a lot on increasing my intelligence and not much on companionship. But since our time to experience mortality is coming soon, maybe I should put more thought into it.

My mind was beginning to have dim flashes of comprehension. One of those bursts sparked a memory of the many times we'd watched *Saturday's Warriors* growing up, and I couldn't help but ask, So, if you can have companionships, is it possible to find your true love in a pre-mortal life and then find them again on earth? The concept of predestined relationships has been debated by many people, and I was curious to find out.

Possibly. In History, I've heard about people trying in past worlds, but I do not think it guarantees anything. Everyone still has their agency . . . well, all except for that one time.

What do you mean?

Once, a very long time ago, there was a plan brought to pass in a distant place where no one had agency. They were not able to make choices because they eliminated all opposition. They thought if they removed their freedom to choose between good and evil, everyone would be saved from consequences.

A world without agency? What happened?

From my understanding, something went horribly wrong. We do not study darkness in depth, but because of what happened, all plans since have used agency as their foundation. I know little else; I am still considered very young and immature when it comes to knowledge and wisdom.

I have never heard a girl confess that before. I'm going to write it down when I get home. Actually, I'm going to write ALL this down! My mind reeled from the amazement of this crazy conversation.

We document the things we desire to remember most. Do you wish to remember me?

I laughed to myself. I don't think I could forget you if I tried.

Then will you not mind if we remain friends for a while longer?

Of course not! This is the COOLEST thing I've ever heard of! I had a hard time keeping in my excitement. Besides, I have a feeling we didn't quite reach your million questions yet.

You are right! We still have much to talk about.

I looked up and noticed it was starting to get dark. Whoa, the sun is already setting! Mom is going to be worried sick.

I should be going, as well.

Well, Elli, I guess I'll talk to you later! How about trying tomorrow about this same time?

That would please me greatly! I am not sure how the Airlis works, exactly, but hopefully, it will keep us on the same time frame even if we are years apart.

Let's hope so.

It was a pleasure meeting you, David.

Same here, Elli. If we had been physically talking, I wouldn't have had the courage to say what I did next, but thanks to the Airlis, my voice didn't strangle my fear. By the way, I think I found out what you **really** are.

Oh, and what is that?

You're an angel.

There was a pause and she said, *At least that sounds better than alien. Take care of your arm.*

I will. Goodnight, Elli.

Goodbye, David.

I stood up and carefully put the Airlis in my pocket. Awestruck and overcome by deep feelings of curiosity and wonder, my eyes were drawn heavenward. A dark-blue canopy was chasing away the last tendrils of sunlight. Once my eyes began to adjust, I spotted two stars that had broken free of their daytime prison and then four. *An angel from across the universe, huh?* As I contemplated what had just happened, I realized I'd never look at stars the same again.

I'm not sure if I should have written that down or not. This has officially become my very secret diary . . . I'm such a girl. At least I have the insanity plea, right? Isn't that what everyone says when they've done something they don't want to be responsible for? Anyway, when I finally got home, Mom was wigging out as expected. The funny thing about it, though, was she actually found out from my friend, Frank.

Franklin Owens has been my best friend since our freshman year, even though I'm not sure he knows this. We're about the same size, he might be a half an inch shorter, but he has spiky, blond hair and blue eyes. His family moved into our neighborhood the summer before we started high school. Frank's my opposite when it comes to social status; he's the guy who is friends with almost everyone, and I'm not.

Frank decided when he moved in down the street that he was going to find out who I was, because no one in school really knew. Not that I'm a complete social reject. When I'm in football, I have friends in football. When I'm in choir, I have friends in choir. We talk and joke, but that's about the only time we see each other.

You see, on top of not being very talkative, ever since I moved to town I've had a job. We weren't even unpacked when Gramps first sent me to irrigate. He needed someone to help farm his hay fields and take care of his cows. Every day he finds something for me to do. There's no such thing as a holiday for farmers. The few times I actually got invited to go do something, I was either hauling hay or on a horse herding cattle. People eventually stopped inviting, and I kept working. I'm the guy everyone knows *of*, but nobody knows *about*.

That bugged Frank, so one day he showed up at my house.

"Hey, David, I'm Frank. We moved in down the street, and Mom made some cookies for you guys." He held out a plate of sugar cookies with pink icing.

"Um, thanks. Mom loves sugar cookies." I took them stiffly.

Not one to fear social stumbling blocks, Frank smacked my shoulder and said cheerfully, "We should hang out sometime!" Then he walked away.

I suppose I should've invited him in. Honestly, I didn't know how to react when someone came to my house. Even though I was awkward and seemingly unfriendly, he never gave up on me, for which I'm very grateful. It was Frank who eventually got me to ask girls out on dates, even after I'd sworn to hate them. And it was Frank who had my back the day I had my mental breakdown.

"You should've seen the look on Mr. Fry's face!" His animated voice was loud, and I had to pull the phone away from my ear. Mom told me to call him after she got finished chewing the other one off. I guess he called the house about twenty times looking for me. He kept on jabbering, "Yeah, when he asked for your hat and you just walked out, he had no idea what to do! He was so stumped, he never even marked you absent! And don't worry about the rest of your classes. I told the teachers you went home sick, so all you'll need to do is get a note from your mom, and you won't have detention for ditching." Luckily, we have all the same afternoon classes together. "What happened to you, man?"

"Oh . . . I had a bad day," was the only thing I could come up with. Ever since Lost Lake, I hadn't been able to think clearly. It was like my mind was chasing two twisted rabbits. One had a big set of teeth and sharp claws, the other had a huge set of wings that could fly me to impossible adventures. Does that help explain my state of mind?

Frank's my best friend, but how do you tell someone you've been talking to an angel through a rock? You don't, unless your friend's a lot crazier than you. Perhaps I should've told him about my arm, but I don't like people feeling sorry for me. And besides, my mental anguish was still too fresh to be aggravated by conversation. After I got off the phone, I decided to write this all down and didn't finish till after 1:00 a.m.

Did I imagine that? Last night I kept trying the Airlis, but my thoughts never appeared like they did before. Elli told me she'd try again tomorrow, but I couldn't resist. *Was she asleep? Do angels need sleep? What does an angel do for fun?* Unending questions slowly churned my thoughts into restless dreams.

Mom caved in pretty easily and gave me a sick-note, and it wasn't far from the truth. Mentally disturbed is a sickness isn't it?

School was hard, and not just because I was tired. I met Coach in his office before first hour to tell him the news. He was discussing the team's strategy for our upcoming game against Holbrook with the offensive coordinator. My gut twisted in pain as I told them my arm was broken, and I was out for at least six weeks. They looked at each other with disappointment, and Coach said, "Sorry to hear that, Thorn. I wondered if that's what happened. It's too bad." Without missing a beat, they started discussing Joe Carter as my replacement.

That's it? Just swap me out like an old pair of cleats. A new, debilitating pain seized my struggling heart, and emotions that were barely treading water began to sink. I turned and walked out of the office unnoticed.

Somehow I made it outside and found myself sitting on the brick wall in front of the gym. Kids were coming and going. Some said hi as they passed, but no one had a clue I was drowning inside. As I struggled to find air, ironically, what pulled my head above water was a small rock on the sidewalk.

Elli.

What would she say about this? I couldn't resist a small smile. *She'd probably call me silly and tell me to get over it.* The thought of talking to her again was the lifeline I needed to keep me from falling apart. The bell rang, and I managed to drag myself to class.

Sleep was the only thing that helped the day go by faster. I got yelled at a few times, but I didn't care. In English I fell asleep and almost tipped out of my chair. Miss Spencer made me move to the front row. During lunch I checked the stone, but nothing happened. When I went back to Chemistry, Mr. Fry acted like I wasn't even there. Now that's something I could enjoy all year. It's a good thing he wasn't looking at me, because I could not keep my eyes open.

I was glad no one knew about my arm except Mom and the coaches, because I didn't want to deal with a thousand questions. That's also why I didn't go to practice. I've never missed and didn't know what to do with myself. We live across the street from Grandpa, and I didn't want him to see me, because I knew he'd find something for me to do. It wouldn't matter that I only have one arm to do it with. He's an old timer who'd probably break out a team of horses if his tractor quit. Grandpa is a great man, and I hope to be more like him someday.

I drove around town for a while and eventually found myself back at the practice field watching the team. I didn't stay long; it hurt too much. Instead, I decided to drive. I know a lot of back roads around Snowflake and some good places to go four-wheeling, so I went out and tore up the countryside. Something about horsepower and dirt can sure make you forget your worries for a while.

Mom was cooking dinner when I got home. She asked about practice, and I told her I didn't go. A few beads of sweat had formed across her brow, and using the back of her wrist, she wiped them away as she turned to study me. For a long moment her searching eyes probed gently into mine.

"What are you gonna do now?" Her voice was soft and full of concern.

That was the million-dollar question, and I didn't have an answer for her. All I could do was shrug my shoulders and look away.

A gentle hand gripped my arm. "I'm sure you'll figure it out, son." Her confidence and love was exactly what I needed to brighten my dark day.

Now it's 12:15 in the morning, and I still don't have an answer.

I've been staring at a stupid rock every fifteen minutes for the past three hours. I finished some homework in the meantime and wrote this in my journal, but I'm beginning to think I just got stood up. I should've expected this; hadn't I already learned not to trust girls? Sometimes things don't get past my thick skull.

You know, you never realize how much you need something until you break it. I can still write, but I have to be careful not to move my arm too fast, and I've figured out exactly what sparks the pain. It mostly comes when I try to press downward, and holy CRAP did my arm ache last night! I've never broken a bone before and wasn't expecting the horrible throbbing. On top of everything that's happened, I now get to look forward to a night of pain. It wouldn't have ended any other way.

Thursday, August 18, 2011

I got my cast today. Mom set my appointment for lunch, so I wouldn't have to miss school. The Doc told her it wouldn't take very long because the bone was already set, and he was right. I was in and out without getting a shot or a sucker, and now I've got a blue club. It could be quite the weapon if only it didn't hurt to bump it. Coach must've told the team, because the questions bombarded me all flippin' day. I don't know how many times I repeated my story, but hopefully, it was enough to get the word around.

Frank was mad I didn't tell him what happened, but he didn't hold a grudge long. I think the cloud of melancholy that hovered over me curbed his anger. By the time we got to Chemistry, we were friends again, and I'm glad, too. I needed him to bump my desk to keep me from nodding off. It's hard enough to stay awake in there without being sleep deprived.

I also decided to go to practice. What else was there to do? While everyone was dressing out, I went into Coach's office and found a schedule of this year's games. Running my finger down the Fridays, a spark of hope ignited in the smoldering ashes of despair as I realized six weeks isn't as long as I thought it was. Actually, it's only HALF the season!

If all goes well, I could be dressed out when we play Winslow. I don't know why I thought it was such a complete disaster before. When the crap hit the fan, I guess I couldn't see straight. I made a new plan right then and there. If my right arm was going to be weak, I would work my legs and my left arm to be as ready as possible when the cast comes off. Changing into my gym shorts, I ran onto the practice field.

I came home in a much better mood than I'd been in days. I told Mom what I'd found out, and she almost started to cry again. She's such a great mother. I wanted to tell Elli, too, but like last night, there were no thoughts coming or going. Even though I'm ecstatic about my new discovery, exhaustion keeps dragging my eyes shut. Having the weight of despair removed has really helped my peace of mind. I'll see what tomorrow brings.

Sunday, 21 August, 2011

I tell you what, having a cast sure gets a lot of attention. Anyone who hadn't heard about my arm could not resist asking— like vultures to road kill. After I got over being annoyed, I decided to start a game. Now every time someone asks, I make up a completely different story and see how long it takes them to realize I'm pulling their leg. I've been having a blast! Sydney Flake is a blonde girl in my Sunday School class, and I mean completely blonde. Today, when she asked about my arm, I told her I roped a beaver swimming down the irrigation ditch, and as I was pulling it out, I fell and snapped my arm! There are probably punishments for lying in church, but I couldn't resist. I'll set her straight in a few days, after she starts the rumor all over school.

Oh, and of course, everyone's had to sign it. I admit it's opened conversations with girls that probably never would've happened before. The only bad thing is, it gave Chelsey Rogers another reason to hover into my space. She made sure her name was the biggest and brightest. Chelsey has had a crush on me since junior high, and as much as I've tried to avoid her, I can't be mean when she corners me. She's good at it, too, but I've also improved at evading her.

Too bad my cast didn't catch the attention of Lexi Dupree. Wow! She's one good-looking girl. A blonde-haired junior from Southern California, her family moved here at the beginning of the school year, and she was immediately put on the varsity volleyball team. If the mystique of being the *new girl* wasn't enough to snare whatever guy she wanted, I think those deep blue eyes would've done the trick single-handedly. It wasn't a week before she was going out with Zack Whipple.

Since our sophomore year, Zack has been the starting quarterback, a starting forward in basketball, and a starting pitcher. He's always had the skills, the looks, and the ladies. I think he's full of himself, and I know he chews and drinks in the off-season, but somehow that only makes him more attractive.

Oh, the madness of high school. If it weren't for football and Mom insisting I get my education, I would've dropped out and worked for Grandpa long ago. Gramps told me he would give me the ranch someday if I want it. I can't think of a cooler way to make a living. Rose, Mom's only sibling, lives in the Valley and has nothing to do with the ranch. (For all you strangers interested in my pathetic life, the "Valley" is slang we country bumpkins use for the Phoenix/Mesa area.) Aunt Rose has four girls, and they would rather go to the mall than get their hands dirty. I don't see them very often.

I really love the ranch, and technically, I don't need a college education to run it, but Grandpa suggested I learn more about running a business first. I was hoping to get a football scholarship somewhere, but now I'll have to wait and see what happens.

It was interesting that today's Sunday School lesson was about the Plan of Salvation. I couldn't help but think about Elli as we discussed leaving our Father in Heaven's presence to come to earth. What would it be like to be a spirit preparing to go to a mortal world? I sure paid a lot more attention than I ever had before.

This evening at dinner, my scrawny, good-for-nothing brother, Josh, told Mom I was losing my mind. We share a room because our spoiled ten-year-old sister, Sarah, gets her own. He noticed I was spending a lot of time staring at a rock. I thought I was being more discreet than that, but not much gets past Josh. He's thirteen and neck deep in the know-it-all stage of life. Luckily, I never went through that one . . . yeah.

Anyway, Josh told Mom I was losing it, but she told him to leave me alone. Mom understands better than anyone what I'm going through, and it's comforting to know she's got my back. But I confess, since my insane experience at Lost Lake, I can't help feeling I seriously might be going crazy. I haven't heard from Elli in five days, and I'm beginning to wonder if it wasn't a spurt of . . . scits-o-phrania? Skits-o-mania? Whatever that stupid word is, but hopefully you get my drift. Maybe it's a good thing my imaginary friend isn't talking to me through a rock. That must be a sign I'm getting better, right? We'll see.

Tuesday, 23 August, 2011

This week started like normal, except for the extra weight of depression wrapped round my arm. I've been working my butt off in practice to help me not dwell on it too much. Yesterday, Coach told me about a player he had a few years ago who broke his wrist. The guy was still able to play as long as he could flex his elbow, and they wrapped the cast with a half inch of pad. This only fanned my desire to get back in the game, and my spark of hope ignited into a hot flame.

When I got home from practice last night, I begged Mom to call the doctor at his home to ask when he thought I could get a shorter cast. He said he could possibly change it in three weeks! If it works out, I might be playing in our third season game against Blue Ridge! Life is getting better and better. And to top it off, my angel answered back!

Even though it had been a week, I couldn't stop trying. Right after dinner, I went to my room at about 7:30. Since Josh was watching TV in the family room, I locked the door and picked up the Airlis and immediately saw my thoughts, Oh Elli, where are you? My heart skipped a beat as the words faded away.

I am here, David. Did you miss me?

Yes! Wow, that was a little too eager. Oh crap! Shut up, David! My thoughts poured out in written words like water through a broken dam. My ears got hot from embarrassment.

Ha! I missed you too, she replied. I could imagine the smile she must've had on her face. *It is definitely harder to hide things when we can see each other's thoughts, is it not?"*

Yeah, and I promise to do better. Sorry, Elli.

That is all right. It is a relief in a way that we have to be this honest.

I guess so. I just hope I don't accidentally share things you wouldn't want to hear.

Oh, like what?

You don't want to know, I promise. This was heading downhill fast. A guy's mind is a bad place for any girl to be.

Why do you say that?

It's hard not to have bad thoughts when you see beautiful girls. Wow, did I think that out loud? My hands began to shake nervously.

You have bad thoughts about girls?

I gulped. Yes. I mean, no. Well, sometimes. Oh, this isn't fair!

Why? I think it is pretty revealing, she said. The smile I pictured for her turned to a smirk.

Okay, then why don't you *reveal* something you don't want anyone else to know, and see how it feels?

I already did. I do not want people to know I am learning to paint.

That doesn't count, I retorted. Why don't you tell me who you have a crush on?

A crush?

My mind had to work a second on how to rephrase. Who are you the most attracted to?

Oh, I understand. If you must know, I actually am quite attracted to Jared.

Ha! I thought with satisfaction. How does it feel now that you've shared your secret with me?

It is not really a secret, she replied. *We have been friends for a long time. We study history together, and we often have long, uplifting conversations.*

Oh, I give up. You really must be an angel if you have never had a bad thought before.

I do not know if it would be considered bad thoughts, but sometimes Jared brings up topics that make me uncomfortable.

Really? I paused awkwardly. Forgetting again how the Airlis works, I asked myself, What would make an angel uncomfortable? and of course the Airlis grabbed it faster than I could take it back. At least this time it wasn't such an embarrassing remark.

She replied, *Remember how I told you about that plan without agency? He has been studying it in depth with a group of students and a few instructors, and when he tells me about it, I get a nervous feeling inside. It is not pleasant.*

I blew out my breath. That's not what I thought you were gonna say.

And what did you think I was going to say?

Nothing! Oh, nothing. Just more bad thoughts. Sorry.

You sure have a lot of bad thoughts.

Sometimes I do, I confessed unwillingly. In an attempt to pass blame somewhere else I quickly added, Satan knows how to put the worst thoughts in your head, and it can be hard to control them.

Oh, yes, I forgot. Satan must be your tempter, correct? I never thought about how that would work before. You still have the choice to control your thoughts, do you not?

Beads of sweat were gathering on my forehead. Yes, if I try *REALLY* hard.

Then do it! Because I have many questions to ask you, and I do not want to hear your bad thoughts. She sure didn't dance around the point much.

Thinking to myself, the words came out, I just got put in my place by an angel . . . again. I was feeling about as big as an ant. This is the most unusual conversation I have ever been in.

Yes, I would have to agree, she replied. *How is your arm?*

Doing a little better, I answered, grateful for a change of subject. I found out I'll be able to play football sooner than I had hoped!

That is good, I guess. I can tell it means a lot to you. Forgive me for not understanding. We view games so differently here.

Really? The idea of angels playing games was rather strange. What do you mean?

We only play games that increase our knowledge or bring us happiness. To center your life on games—to a point that nothing

29

else matters—must be a mortal ideal. It is completely unheard of here, and it seems foolish. Oh, I am deeply sorry! That is something I would never say in person.

Ha! Doesn't feel so great, does it? I couldn't resist the opportunity to "help her" see things from my perspective.

No it does not.

Now I started to feel bad. You are probably right about the games, but down here there's a lot of good that can come from sports, too. Some people use them to help pay for education, and some play them to make lots of money.

That is interesting. From that perspective, I hope you use it for good.

Yeah, I hope I get the chance. My thoughts began to fade from words into fuzzy dreams of touchdowns and trophies. I shook my head, and once again the Airlis came into focus. An angel was waiting on the other end of that stone, and I was daydreaming. Anyway, how was your week, Elli?

A week? What is that?

Here we call seven days a week.

Seven days? Oh, how terrible you must feel! I am so sorry. It has only been one day for me.

My hidden, bitter feelings of being forgotten turned to guilt. I had assumed the worst. That would explain it, I thought. One day for my seven. Wow, you must have a lot longer day than we do.

I would guess it is because we are on a much larger world than you are.

Really? That's insane. How do you grow anything if you have darkness for such a long time? Having lived on Grandpa's farm for the last few years, it was the first thing I thought of.

There is no darkness here. Living in the presence of Father, there is always light!

That is so cool, I thought in wonder.

Actually, it is quite warm, unless it storms.

I couldn't help but smile. No, no, I mean "cool" as in "amazing." You know, if we can work on your earth lingo we would be able to communicate a lot easier.

Yes, I am beginning to see that. Besides your strange definitions, you also blur many words together, but do not worry, I'm a fast learner.

Good! Doesn't that flow better? Remembering the jab she made in our first conversation, I added mockingly, Hey, there might be hope for you yet!

Oh ha ha, you are very humorous, David. She had understood.

I learn from the best!

Quickly turning it back on me, she said, *I talked to Father about you . . . for a long time.*

My mood changed immediately from teasing to concern. Uh . . . what did he say?

He said that mortal "guys" with bad thoughts are not to be trusted.

My mouth dropped, and the only word that appeared on the Airlis was, Oh.

Just teasing, David! I made that up.

Relief loosened my white knuckled grip. Chuckling to myself, I thought, You think you're REAL funny don't you?

Did you fall for my joke?

Actually, you got me pretty good, I confessed. But you realize, I don't get mad, I get even.

We shall see. But I did talk to Him about you, and He had some very interesting things to say.

You can't taunt me like this and not tell me, I said.

All right, but you better be nice.

I will if you will, I countered.

Agreed. When I asked Him if He knew who you are and where the Airlis came from, He sat for a while pondering then turned to me and said, "Elli, all will be revealed in due time. Let it suffice to know that the Airlis has been placed in both your paths to help you through trials that will shortly come." In parting, He added something I do not quite understand. "Remember, Elli, what once was yours will return to you again." Very much cool, isn't it?

You got close, but don't quit your day job. It jumped right out of my head.

Hey, I thought you were going to be nice? Perhaps it's time for me to go!

Sorry! No, please stay. I'll do better, I promise. She couldn't leave me hanging like that. Does your dad *really* know who I am? A shade of fear crept into my mind.

Of course He does! One step in reaching Godhood is to become **omniscient**.

I jolted in shock. Wait a minute . . . your dad . . . is God?

Yes, silly! Well, He is MY God anyway, and whoever your Spirit Father is, is YOUR God. Only as a perfected, immortal being can you create spirit children. I thought you would have known that if you have learned about your Plan of Salvation.

My thoughts were getting all jumbled now. I do. I mean, I have. It's just . . . I never put two and two together. My heart started racing in anticipation. He doesn't want to interview me or anything does He?

I could probably arrange something if you would like.

Oh, no, no it's fine . . . I'm fine . . . I'm good. Thanks, though. Maybe some other time. I'd never stuttered my thoughts before, but I was stuttering now.

Are you nervous?

Heck yeah I'm nervous! He would probably zap me with a bolt of lightning just for speaking with you! My heart was still pounding hard.

I'm not sure about the lightning, and He has already said this is for both our benefit, but if you do not behave yourself, I might persuade Him otherwise.

32

My heart stopped. You're kidding again, right?

I guess you will never know. Be good, and there will be no problem.

I'll be good, I swear. And I meant every word.

Good. My first question for you is this: I was wondering where you stand when it comes to choosing between your God and your tempter? What did you call him? Satan?

Wow. You sure get right to the point. I was stunned. (So—reader of another man's journal—how would *you* answer that question? Yeah, not as easy as you thought!)

She continued, *Of all the questions to be asked, this is the most important for you and me both.*

I guess I choose God's side? It came to mind more like a question than a statement, and that's how the Airlis showed it.

You mean you have not chosen?"

I could imagine her shocked eyes staring into my heart. Defensively, I replied, Oh, I believe in God, and most of the time I try to do what's right, but often I fall short.

That would explain your bad thoughts.

It felt like we were dueling and she had a sword and I had a spoon. Hey, it's a lot harder when you're down here being tempted every second of every day and not just reading about it in some history book.

*I am sorry David. You are right. I do not know what it is like . . . what **it's** like . . . and it's hard for me to understand. It seems that it would be such a simple decision to follow God, but I have not forgotten everything, either.*

Well it's NOT simple, and frankly, sometimes it's even hard to believe there is a God. The truth of my confession hit hard. I had never faced my own lack of faith this openly before.

How can that be?

I tried to explain. All we have are some old books that tell us what happened a long time ago, and a bunch of old leaders who only talk to us twice a year.

And that isn't enough? she countered. If I thought I was getting hit hard before, this comment knocked the wind right out of me. *What about your Redeemer? Has He already come to pay for your transgressions and save you from death?*

Supposedly, our Savior came about 2,000 years ago, and sometimes that's how far away he feels. My head bowed in disgrace. I was getting a clear glimpse of myself for the first time, and I was disgusted with who I saw. I've claimed to be a Christian my whole life, but I've never really known who Christ is.

You have been taught the Plan, your Redeemer has already come and fulfilled His part, but you do not believe it yet? Her accusations were almost too difficult to face, but I couldn't set the Airlis down. My eyes were glued to it. It was like watching a wreck in slow motion and not being able to stop it.

I do believe . . . but I guess I'm not sure yet. I've been taught my whole life—I've never had reason to doubt—but I've never really found out for myself. Even when confessing my worst sins, a more humbling conversation I'd never had.

You need to find out, now! she stated, and I swear I could feel her intensity through my hands.

Why?

Your life is only a short moment, David. And what you do in mortality will affect you for eternity! What if you die tomorrow? Would you be prepared to return to your God?

My first response was, People my age don't die. As I realized that wasn't true, I started seeing it from her perspective. I mean, I guess they do. Honestly, I've never thought about it like that before.

Well, you had better START thinking about it. Besides, I know it will help you find the happiness you are searching for.

Her comment brought my wandering thoughts back to focus, and I asked, How do you know I'm not happy?

It is visible in your thoughts, David; and not only the ones I can read.

I sat there for a long time. It felt like my soul had been pried open before my eyes, and I didn't like what I saw. *Thanks for the advice. I'll keep it in mind. You know, I probably better get some sleep.*

I did not mean to upset you. I simply want to help. I realized she *could* see deeper than the words.

It's okay. You just got me thinking about things I haven't put much thought into before. It really is getting late for me, too. I don't know if I could have continued a conversation anyway.

After a pause, she asked, *Will we communicate again tomorrow?*

Sure. Did you want to try your day again or mine?

I would hate to miss you. Maybe we should simply try again like we already have.

That'll work. I'll talk to you next week, then. The thought was depressing, but I was slightly relieved. Our conversation had really roughed me up, and I wanted time to figure stuff out before we talked again.

I hope so. Take care of yourself, David.

I'll try. Good night, Elli.

I set the Airlis on my night stand and let out a long breath as I slumped back against the wall. My mind strained against a weight it had never tried lifting before. It felt like I suddenly woke up in the middle of a strange city built of ideals and beliefs, and I had no idea where in the heck I was. Lost in myself, I struggled for direction. Before I could find a foothold, Josh pounded on the door demanding entrance. After a short battle of words, Josh turned off the light and slipped into bed. It wasn't long until his breathing slowed.

Soft moonlight fought its way through our thin curtains. As my eyes adjusted, faint outlines began to appear. Answerless questions bounced around in my head as I watched dim shadows creep across the room. When I realized I wasn't going to fall asleep easily, I flipped on the bed lamp and reached for my journal.

You know, I'm really not sure if what I've been taught is true. I mean, I believe, but I don't *know*; and that's what bothers me most of all. I've heard Mom talk about going to her knees in prayer to find answers, but I've never tried it. At least not when it comes to finding out what's true, and what's not. Sure, I enjoy church most Sundays, and I feel good when I'm taught the gospel, but I can't honestly say the Spirit has ever told me anything. How could a man, even if He is God's son, be able to take away my sins? How could He break the bands of death? How can He forgive me for what I've done? How can He forgive someone like my father?

Wednesday, 24 August, 2011

The combination of complete exhaustion and an unsettled mind landed me in detention today. Elli, if I flunk my senior year, I'm blaming you! But I was able to catch up on my homework while I was there, so it wasn't all bad. Miss Spencer is a no-nonsense teacher, and when I fell asleep for the third time in her class, it was the last straw. Coach didn't really care that I missed practice. All I've been doing is running and studying plays on the sidelines. Tell you what, though, I don't even think football would've eased my mind today.

Still distraught after a sleepless night, I headed to my seminary class hoping to find some solace. Usually having a religious boost in first hour helps me through the day, but that wasn't the case today. This year we're studying the Old Testament, and after our lesson got over early, Bro. Sanderson shocked the class by opening the rest of the time for students to share their testimonies.

After a long, awkward silence, Ashley Dunn, a junior, stood and walked to the front of the class. Since she rarely makes comments, I was quite surprised when she got up. She stood for a second, arms folded timidly across her petite frame. Her hazel eyes scanned the room nervously. When she finally spoke, she didn't say much, but I felt every word.

"I don't know why I felt like I should get up, but I want to tell you something. For some reason, I've been really questioning lately if God is real. But something happened on Sunday." Her eyes glistened with the first sign of tears, but that didn't keep them from penetrating right through me. Softly, but with staggering conviction, she said with a radiant smile, "He answered my prayers! And I *know* He will answer yours."

Her words slammed into me, shaking me physically and spiritually right to the core.

She walked back to her chair, her red hair falling over her face as she stared at her shoes and sat down. I can't remember who else got up or what else was said. Her words kept echoing in my head, competing now with Elli's words, *You need to find out, now*! These thoughts battled for my attention all day.

When I got home from school, I waited till I found a moment alone with Mom. I know Mom believes in God, and it amazes me that she's found peace after everything she's been through, but I couldn't remember her telling me *how* she knows. As we were preparing the table for dinner, I asked, "Mom, how do you know God is real?"

Her hand froze midair as she was trying to place the silverware. She couldn't hide the surprise on her face. Too late to take it back, I continued placing the plates as if it was no big deal. Slowly setting down the fork, she got a far off-look in her eyes.

"Well David, first, I had to want to know for myself. Sadly, it took me a long time. I reached a point in life where I realized I *needed* God, I needed a Savior; and without help from a power beyond my own, I was lost. It was very humbling, and it took a lot of study and prayer, but I didn't give up. On one especially difficult night, he finally answered me." Her eyes became misty for a moment, "and now I know."

We finished setting the table in silence.

As mom went back to the stove to grab the pot of homemade macaroni and cheese, she called out, "Dinner's ready!" We listened as Josh and Sarah fought their way to the kitchen. Mom settled the contest with a glare, and we blessed the food.

Dinner seemed quieter than normal, and after a while, I realized it was because of me. My serious state of pondering caused an uncommon ripple in our usually boisterous dinner scene. Afterward, I tried to stay out of Josh's way and didn't fight for my turn to watch TV. I decided instead (since I was caught up on homework) tonight would be a good time to crack an unfamiliar book.

For seminary we've been asked to individually read the whole Old Testament as we study it in class. It's been almost two weeks, and I haven't even started. I went to my room and locked the door. Propping myself on my bed, I turned to Genesis chapter one. We had already studied the creation of the world in class, but as I started over it again, suddenly things began to connect. This wasn't *just* the creation, it was the beginning of God's plan!

The earth was organized; land and water, light and darkness, the plants and the animals. Lastly, God created Adam and Eve, giving them dominion over all things. As the meaning of the last verse sank into my mind, it dawned on me, *God created all of this—for us!* I've never felt the scriptures open up to me like they did tonight. How else could the creation have happened? A huge explosion and everything spun into perfect order like they teach us in school? Then how would you explain our ability to choose between right and wrong? Choices and consequences? Why is there guilt and happiness if there is no law and no God? Simple truth was flooding into my mind. As I finished chapter two, I read about Eve being formed and how a man should leave his father and mother and cleave to his wife. As good as the thought should've made me feel—anger started boiling inside.

I've never spoken or written much about my father. I guess I hoped if I forgot about him, everything he did would go away, too. After he died, I tried removing bad memories by getting rid of anything that reminded me of him, but when that didn't work, I put everything I had into football. Many times it saved me from losing my sanity, but no matter how hard I practiced, at the end of the day, there was always a "Thorn" I couldn't extract from my life.

As the memories darkened my mind, I literally felt bitterness drive all good feelings from my heart. The difference was like night and day. Stunned, I realized, *This is why I'm not happy!* All these years I thought God had abandoned me. Now I understood— it was *me*. I'd shut God out with everyone else. My shaking hands could no longer keep their grip, and the Bible rolled onto the bed.

He answered my prayers, and I know He will answer yours. Ashley's words brushed against my mind. Struggling for hope, I grasped my hands tightly. As the meaning of what she'd said came into focus, inside my chest a spark flickered and began to burn. Bowing my head, I poured out my heart to God.

"Father in Heaven, I'm *sorry*. I've hated my father for so long, I've forgotten how to be happy. I don't know how you can help me, but I believe you can . . . I *hope* you can. Will you please take this hatred from my heart? Please help me forgive my father."

Words can't be found to describe what happened next. If you've never had a soul-crushing burden suddenly lifted from your shoulders, then there's no way to explain how it feels. Have you ever been washed clean after years of wallowing in filth? Have you ever been able to see after being born blind? If you have, then you know! I can't think of a better way to explain the miracle I experienced.

Have you ever wept for joy? I did tonight.

God *is* real!

<u>Thursday, 25 August, 2011</u>

Do you remember when Aladdin freed the Genie from the lamp? That's exactly how I felt last night and still do today! I'm FREE! I didn't realize how much weight I'd been carrying around until God took it from my shoulders. The minute I crawled in bed and my head hit the pillow, I was out like a light. When my alarm went off, I woke up singing, and I can't remember the last time that's happened. Mom noticed something different and asked why I didn't wake up on that side of the bed more often. I guess it even showed at school, because as we walked to Choir, Frank asked me what I'd eaten for breakfast. I laughed and told him it wasn't what I ate, but what I got rid of. He looked at me strangely but didn't have a chance to ask more about it. It must've bothered him a lot, because he found me at home when I finished football practice.

"Dude, what's going on with you?" Leave it to Frank to get right to the point. He cornered me in the living room and waited until we were alone. "Last week, you were angry enough to kill someone, and today I could've sworn I heard you whistling in Chemistry!"

"Huh? You know what, Frank, sometimes you're crazy." It was a lame rebuttal, but I honestly didn't know what else to say. "And I wasn't whistling, I was humming."

"Okay," he paused calmly for a second and then yelled, "Why in the HECK were you HUMMING in CHEMISTRY?"

Shrugging, I said, "I don't know. Maybe it's because our first game is tomorrow."

"You're not playing, remember? You kind of have a broken arm. Did you meet a girl and not tell me about it?" The shock of him nailing it right on the head left me stuttering a few incoherent words. Frank's reaction was swift. "You DID! You sorry sack of trash. Why didn't you tell me?"

"I didn't meet a girl, Frank. Well, I mean I have, but not like you're thinking." My mind raced to find an out without revealing too much, and then I thought about Ashley and decided to tell part of the truth. "I mean, I guess you can say I've *noticed* a girl, but I have no clue if she's noticed me."

"Trust me, friend, the girls notice you." This was said as a side note, then his eyes got big as he asked mockingly, "Wait, you actually noticed a girl?" He threw his hands in the air and yelled, "Well, it's ABOUT TIME!"

"Oh, shut up, Frank. I notice girls all the time. I just don't date ALL of them AND their sisters!" Frank has had lots of girlfriends, and he considers himself a pro. I admit he's got a lot more experience than me. It's been his goal to hook me up with someone ever since I told him I'd never had a girlfriend. Judging by his determination, you'd think he'd bet money I'd have my first kiss before I graduated!

"So, who's the lucky girl?" he asked. I knew I had to cave in some, or I would never get him off me.

"Ashley Dunn, from my seminary class."

He weighed the information for a moment, and nodding his head in acceptance replied, "She's pretty cute! Kinda quiet, but not a bad choice. Are you going to ask her out or just keep 'noticing' her?"

"I don't know, man, I just saw her in class, okay? I'll think about it, and maybe I will."

We chatted a while longer, and eventually, he headed home with a smirk on his face. All right, a small truth about me if you must know. I don't think *I've* asked more than three girls on a date in my life, and all of those were by much persuasion and long suffering on Frank's part. I've been on more dates than that, but Frank always set them up. Yeah, it sounds lame, but I have my reasons. I might explain later, but I don't have time to dive into that can of worms right now.

Our conversation sure took an unexpected turn with Ashley, but I didn't want to tell him about my experiences with Bo, and I definitely wasn't telling him about Elli. Maybe someday I'll confide more, but he's been so obsessed with getting me a girlfriend, it was an easy way to change the subject. And truthfully, I really *do* like Ashley! I have for three years. She first caught my eye my sophomore year when I passed her every day walking from Spanish to Geometry. I might have said hi once or twice, but that's it. When I found out we were in the same seminary class this year, I was excited! But it faded fast, because I've been too much of a wimp to even talk to her. Now it's more of a torment.

Okay, maybe I'll open that can a little bit so you won't think I'm a spineless wuss. My petrification (Do you like that word? I might have made it up, but hopefully you get the point.) of girls started when I was in first grade in Thatcher. Her name was Jodi Burrow. Both Jodi and her cousin Amy were in my class and got in a habit of chasing me every recess. They teased me with giggles about being cute, and threatened if they ever caught me, they'd kiss me! I was scared to death.

One day I left the playground before the bell. Our classroom was the first door on the left, but since the teacher was still outside, and the room was locked, I leaned up in the corner of the hallway to wait. I thought I'd ditched the girls when suddenly they ran through the doors. I was trapped! Without a second's hesitation, Jodi caught my face in both hands and planted a huge kiss on my lips! Laughing and cheering in victory, they bolted outside as I dropped to the floor and covered my head. Within five minutes, the whole school knew I'd been violated. I was completely humiliated and permanently scarred. Sadly, later in life the wounds would only get deeper, but that's another story for another day. Girls are evil.

Friday, 26 August, 2011

We won! It was difficult to stand on the sidelines and watch my team play, but I was excited we annihilated our first opponent of the year. Holbrook has been known to have some great athletes, but they usually don't have enough of them to be very competitive. We ended up beating them 61 – 0! In spite of being a jerk sometimes, Zack really is an amazing quarterback. Not being on the field only made my game jitters worse! I kept running back and forth, whoopin' and hollerin'. People probably thought I was crazy.

We play in Alchesay next week. They're a lot like Holbrook with a few good players but not enough to compete against the bigger schools. I'm not too worried about it; not that I should be worried—I won't be playing. One more week, baby! The Tuesday before we play Blue Ridge I've got a doctor's appointment to get my short cast, which means I'll be able to practice most of that week in pads! I can't wait!

Saturday, 27 August, 2011

After watching film of our game this morning, I hurried home to help Grandpa haul hay. When he called yesterday to see if Josh and I would help, I reminded him that I had a broken arm. All he said was, "If you can go to practice and throw a football around, then you can lift these light bales no problem." They aren't quite the same size, Grandpa. Anyway, Josh and I ended up hauling about 200 bales and were exhausted afterward. For being thirteen, Josh is a tough kid. He had to do more than usual because of my handicap, and he held his own pretty well.

I tell you what, I'm really beginning to dislike this cast. Even though I had on a long sleeve shirt, hay still got everywhere—including down my cast. I don't only hate it because of hauling hay; simple things like writing and taking a shower are now huge ordeals. I have to tape a plastic sack around my arm before I get in the shower, or if I'm in a hurry, I hold it outside the curtain. Because there's no way to clean inside the cast, it's starting to smell pretty bad, and it itches like crazy. Have you ever had an itch you couldn't reach? Yeah, you should try having one for two weeks straight! I figured out the best way to ease the torture is to turn a flyswatter around and run the metal handle inside. Oh, it sent goose bumps clear to my toes!

Josh wanted to go swimming down in the creek when we were done, but I held up my cast in exasperation. We had sweat and hay everywhere, and a cold dip would've been heavenly. Instead, we settled for ice cream from McDonald's and the first three *Star Wars* movies from Rent-a-Flick. Even though Josh and I have our fights, we also have some good times together.

Tuesday, 30 August, 2011

I've been looking forward to this night all week! A lot has happened, and I found myself craving conversation with a girl! That's a strange new experience for me. Apparently, the years of calluses I've built up toward these demons don't apply to angels. Angels . . . David, are you listening to yourself? You are using a rock to text a girl in the future . . . you're definitely *crazy.*

I'm crazy.

Great. Now I have proof! Not only am I talking to myself out loud, I'm also writing my conversation with myself in my JOURNAL! Please don't tell anyone.

After dinner, around seven o-clock, I went across the street to Grandma's house. Instead of fighting for some private space tonight, I decided to go find a spot somewhere else.

My grandparent's place is old. It probably was one of the first structures built when pioneers settled the valley. The house is made of sunbaked adobe bricks, and over the years, slow cracks have snaked their way up the walls like decaying vines. Inside, the doors and windows are all constructed of weathered lumber. The ceilings are high with rounded corners, and the ancient pictures and decor give the impression that you've walked into a living museum. It's peaceful there, but it doesn't have the same effect as the old barn out back.

Something about the wooden beams and knotted boards takes you instantly back to a day of simplicity. Old workhorse harnesses line the granary walls, waiting patiently for time to slow back down to their pace. The shelves are still filled with ancient tools and supplies that years ago lost their relevance. Josh and I used to spend hours searching them for hidden treasures. Every now and again we still feel the enticing pull of *Peter Pan*-like adventures, and find ourselves building forts on the loft as we discover new ways to enter imaginary worlds. It sounded like the perfect place for me tonight.

The east side of the loft has an opening that overlooks the fields down to the creek. You can see the whole valley from there. Grandpa throws hay through the window down to his horses in the corral below. Pulling the Airlis from my pocket, I plopped myself down and dangled my legs over the edge.

It took a lot longer for Elli to answer tonight, but that was fine; I enjoyed watching the world slowly prepare for the night. After about a half hour, I looked down to see my thoughts appear, Hello? Elli, are you there?

Hi, David, how are you today?

I'm doing pretty good! How have you been?

I have had a splendid day, thank you. Maybe it was *my* emotion, but for a second I could've sworn I felt *her* happiness.

Oh, what happened?

We studied history today. We have been studying the world Father went to when He was experiencing mortality. Since meeting you, I've been soaking it all up like a dry cloth! Afterwards, I helped tend some of the animals. Now—my favorite part of the day—I come to my garden and visit with you!

Really? I didn't know I was *that* interesting, or is it my good looks? A smirk crossed my face.

I'm not sure it's either.

Oh. Smirk was gone.

I'm teasing you!

I let out my breath. She got me again! Why you dirty rat. You sure seem spunky today.

Ha! Thanks, I guess. You seem happier, as well. What happened in your, um, is it week?

Yeah, a week, and a lot of good stuff happened! I said excitedly as images of all the big events flashed through my mind.

I cannot wait to hear about it!

First off, I want you to know I choose God's side. I hadn't made the declaration mentally or vocally yet, and to see it in words made me feel great!

David, that is great! How did you make up your mind?

Starting with my sleepless night, I told her about seminary and my talk with mom, and ended with the night I finally realized that the problem all along was me. It was interesting how the feelings of my heart portrayed themselves through the thoughts in my head. The words came so smoothly, I had a hard time believing they were mine!

Oh David! My heart is swelling with happiness for you! Even though I'm only reading about your experiences, I am positively overflowing with joy!

My heart stretched as it, too, began to fill. As good as it was to share my experience, the thought of it being with a girl suddenly made me very self-conscious, and I clammed up.

David, are you there?

Yeah, I'm still here.

Is something wrong?

How do I talk to girls? I shifted nervously in the window. Sorry Elli, that wasn't supposed to come out.

Girls? I thought you were staying away from them. Wait, are you interested in the girl from your seminary class?

How did she figure it out that fast!? I mean, yes, it is the girl from seminary. Now will you stop reading my mind?

Sorry, but I only read what you willingly give. What is her name?

Ashley Dunn, but it's not what you think. I haven't even met her yet.

Wait, I do not—I mean don't—understand. Is she not the one who spoke to you in your class?

Yes, but it wasn't directly to me. She was talking to the whole class. To tell you the truth, Elli, I'm just scared of girls. Growling in exasperation, I almost threw the Airlis into the corral. Looking back down, I watched as—I HATE this stupid ROCK!—disappeared into the stone.

This is hilarious! You really are scared of girls!

My shoulders sagged as I thought, You can say that again. Before she could tease me further, I asked, You're a girl, right? How should I start talking to her?

Usually, when we are approached by our brothers, they start by saying hello! Have you tried that? I could swear she was mocking me.

You should call us "guys" it sounds better, and yes, I think I said hi once last year, but nothing recently. Wow, I'm really lame.

I'm not sure how to help the state of your extremities, but when it comes to communication, it's a good start for "guys" to say hello.

Not that kind of lame, Elli—oh never mind. I think I can manage a hello, but it's not knowing what to say afterwards that scares me. What do I say then?

She paused for a second then said, *I don't know. Talk to her like we are talking. Ask her about her day. Find out what she likes to do. Engage in thoughtful conversations about things around you, like the rivers and the flowers and what makes them grow.*

A smile spread across my face. I'm not sure girls are the same here as they are in your world, but you have some good ideas.

Try it with me!

Huh?

Act like I am Ashley, and you are meeting me for the first time.

Oh, I get it. I paused a moment. Um . . . Hi. My mind went blank.

Hello.

What are you doing? I started feeling awkward for some reason. Why now? We had been talking just fine.

I'm sitting here in my garden painting.

Really? What are you painting?

I was attempting to paint the flower I am named after.

Really? My curiosity erased all nervousness, and I even forgot that we were role playing. What flower is that?

It is called Ellinthim, but Mother always calls me Elli for short.

Really? What do they look like?

I hope you don't keep saying "really" when you talk to Ashley. She might think you are a little odd.

This snapped me back. Oh, right, sorry. I'm just a bit surprised.

Surprised that I am named after a flower?

Yeah, well, I realized there's a lot about you I don't know, and it's intriguing.

Good! That's exactly how you should approach Ashley. You do that, and you will be fine.

Perhaps. I tried to imagine myself tapping Ashely on the shoulder and talking to her. My heart started racing just thinking about it. I wish I could talk to her as easily as I do to you.

This is quite funny! You don't seem shy to me at all.

She was right. I thought about it for a second and said, That's because you're different.

How is that?

Well, I don't have to look into your eyes for one thing. It was all I could think of.

If you are scared of her eyes, contact her in a different way, she replied. *What about in writing?*

No. I won't do that again. A jolt of embarrassment and pain shot through me.

Why not? What happened, David?

It's nothing. My mind pulled up painful memories I'd tried to bury.

If it is still an issue of concern, you must face it, or it will prevent your progression!

Oh, and telling will fix it? I thought sarcastically.

I think it might help.

I pondered it for a while and said, I guess you won't be telling anyone I know, so it won't hurt too much. I took a long breath. (Not sure why I needed it to think, but I guess it helped.) I had a bad experience in junior high with the most popular girl in school, Andrea Marks.

And what happened?

A friend of mine talked me into writing her a note asking if she liked me. He took it to her before I could change my mind. After our next class, I happened to be walking behind her down the hall—she didn't know I was there—and I overheard her talking with her friends about how a dumb loser asked her if she liked him in a lame note. Something died inside me that day.

Oh, David, that is heartbreaking. Girls really are mean in mortality.

It felt good to finally get that out. Elli didn't mock or laugh; in fact, she seemed almost as disgusted with the situation as I was. Not all of them, I replied. But some girls can be.

It sounds like Ashley is a nice enough girl, and if she has chosen God, too, I think she will have a more peaceful spirit.

Her kind words bolstered my courage, and I found myself contemplating another attempt into the dangerous realm of women. Yeah, I think you're right. It's probably time to move on.

You can do it, David. I know you can. Think of Ashley as being me, and you will do fine.

Thanks, Elli. You are a sweet person. I mean nice.

I actually understood that one. And thank you. You are a good person too, David. Ashley will be lucky to have you as a friend.

I looked up to see the sun had set, and stars were dotting the sky. I better get home; it's getting pretty dark here. Thanks for helping me out.

Anytime. I really enjoy talking to you, and I cannot wait till tomorrow.

You mean next week, right?

Yes, at least for you. I will talk to you next week. Good bye, David.

Good night, Elli.

I swore I would never put my heart in a girl's hands EVER again, and up till now I've done a pretty good job. I've found comfort hiding behind my barriers, but I realize I can't keep myself locked up forever. Isn't this sad? A vicious, dragon of a girl attacked and drove me behind walls of stone, and it took an angel riding in on a white Airlis to save me . . . my life is the most screwed up story I've ever heard. I can just see the title when it hits Broadway: *David, the Damsel in Distress*. I'll make you a deal. If you promise not to tell anyone about Andrea—or Jodi for that matter—I promise I'll man up and talk to Ashley. But if you squeak a word, I will hunt you down and beat you with my cast! I hope you feel sufficiently threatened.

You know, I'm starting to get the hang of this whole writing thing. Are you enjoying it so far? If not, I hope at least you can learn from my mistakes. As good as it has felt to forgive my dad and be rid of that weight, someday I'll need to forgive Andrea, too. I'm sure she won't care either way. I know it's wrong, but I'm not finished hating her yet.

Thursday, 1 September, 2011

You would not believe what happened today! To back up, I almost talked to Ashley yesterday. Do I get points for trying? When we left the seminary building on our way back to campus, she was chatting with a group of friends, and I chickened out. In seminary today, I had a hard time paying attention. I kept watching her out of the corner of my eye. As soon as the closing prayer was said, I put my scriptures away and made sure I was behind her as we left the room. We walked outside, and I was about to tap on her shoulder when her friend Tracy brushed by me and said, "Hey Ashley, have you heard about Jessica getting asked to Homecoming by Troy Sorenson?" There went my chance, again. Tracy jabbered on and on about how Troy had asked her with a "super cool" scavenger hunt.

Depressed and deflated, I realized my chance was shot again. But then I happened to overhear a part of their conversation that put new wind in my sails. See, I had no idea what I would say once I got past, "Hi." I was hoping I could wing it, but when they started talking about Homecoming, I overheard Tracy ask Ashley if she'd been asked to the dance yet, and she said no. Of course, that was it!

All during my second hour History class, I tried to think of a way to ask her. I was so preoccupied, I completely missed the homework assignment. I had to stay after to get the details from Mr. Walters. He's an older gentleman who doesn't know the meaning of haste, and I ended up leaving his room as the tardy bell was ringing. I ran to my truck, which is usually parked behind the auditorium, and threw my books onto the front seat then sprinted around the east side to the back door. As I rounded the corner, I almost ran over a girl picking up spilled painting supplies. It was Ashley Dunn.

All my limbs seized up. Ashley blushed bright red as she stammered, "Oh, I'm so sorry." Tears were threatening as she scrambled to gather paint bottles, brushes, and papers that were strewn everywhere.

Her hurried motions snapped me out of my disbelief. "Here, let me help," I offered and knelt and began gathering scattered pages.

"You don't have to do that," she said. "You'll be late for choir." Fumbling with the papers, I looked up in surprise. How did she know I was going to choir? I had no idea when her classes were, let alone that she liked to paint.

After a stunned second, I replied, "Oh, don't worry. Mr. Walters already made me late. Besides, we always have like twenty minutes of warm-ups, so I won't miss much." She smiled shyly and started putting her brushes in a bag.

Without looking up, she said, "I didn't have my tray balanced when I tried to open the door, and once things started falling, everything went."

"Yeah, I'm not a fan of gravity, either," I replied.

She glanced up, and I pointed at my cast. She smiled, and I smiled back. As I piled the papers in a stack, I couldn't help but notice how real-life some appeared. One was a partial mountain setting surrounded in deep sunset colors. The next was a pencil sketch of a young girl holding a flower. "Are these yours?" I asked in astonishment.

Ashley smiled again and said, "Yeah, but I've only been working on them a few weeks."

"These are *really* good!"

"Oh, I've got a long way to go before I deserve that compliment." She nervously brushed her hair out of her face and bit down on her lip.

"I don't think so. This one looks like a real black-and-white photo!" I held the drawing of the girl a bit closer, marveling at the fine detail.

"Thank you," she said in a calmer voice. "That's my little sister."

"It's amazing! How long have you been drawing?"

"I've been doodling for as long as I can remember," she replied. "It used to drive Mom crazy. Every book we own has some kind of coloring in it."

"I bet she doesn't mind it as much now," I smiled.

"It depends," she said with a grin. "Sometimes I get distracted with my painting, and it gets me in trouble, especially when it comes to chores and stuff."

"Been there, done that," I said without thinking. Then I quickly corrected, "Not with painting, my distraction is television. Mom thinks when I turn the TV on, my brain turns off."

A soft chuckle brightened her eyes and she said, "I would be lying if I said that doesn't happen to me, too." We laughed again and started placing jars of paints on her tray. Luckily, they were made of hard plastic, and none had broken.

As we finished picking up the last few things, I remembered the testimony she shared in seminary. Nervously, I cleared my throat. "By the way, thank you for what you said the other day in seminary."

"Oh, that?" she asked in surprise. "It wasn't much. I just had the feeling I needed to get up, but thank you."

"I'm glad you did." She would probably never know how much she had helped me.

She started blushing again and quickly placed the bag of brushes on the tray next to her paints and stood up. I handed her the stack of drawings as I reached for the door. "Let me get that for you this time."

She gave me a slight curtsy and said, "Thank you, kind sir," and stepped through the door, holding the tray securely in both hands.

"No problem," I said, and we began walking down the hall together.

After a few silent steps, she glanced at me for a moment before shyly looking down. "Thanks for helping me clean up my mess, David." Her gaze reconnected with mine, and she grinned. "You turned a catastrophe into a pleasant experience."

I returned the grin and said, "Glad I could help. I guess you could say I was in the right place at the right time."

She laughed. "Well, maybe I'll have to drop my tray more often."

I smiled but couldn't think of anything else to say. I nervously realized this was the moment. I had five more steps to find my courage. Four. "Hey, uh . . . Ashley?" I gulped. We were at her classroom door, and she turned to look at me with those hazel eyes. I went for it before I changed my mind. "Would you like to go to Homecoming with me?"

Her mouth dropped open slightly as the shock wave struck, but she quickly pulled it back into a beautiful smile. "Sure! That would be fun!"

Now it was my turn for a shocked expression. "Great! Thanks!" My hands began doing some animated gesture of excitement, so I quickly forced them to open her classroom door. "I guess, I'll uh . . . catch you later then?"

"Yeah, see you around!" She gave me a sweet smile and stepped through.

They were finishing some scales when I floated into class. As all eyes turned to me, I quickly walked around the back and slid into my chair next to Frank. He stared at me with a look of confusion. I couldn't sing a word; I think I was experiencing a mild state of shock. When the warm-ups were over, Mr. Thompson said, "David, thanks for showing up today," and he changed my status on the roll. He's a cool teacher, and unless you do something way out of line, he tolerates quite a bit.

Frank leaned over, and with his mouth pulled awkwardly to the side, he whispered, "Dude, what happened? You look pale."

After a few seconds of indecision, I whispered back, "I just asked Ashley Dunn to Homecoming."

You should've seen the look on Frank's face. It was priceless! He didn't know what to say, and that doesn't happen very often. The choir started singing, but I was gone—dancing on cloud nine. Frank's face finally brought me back; it was contorted with torture. It was all I could to do to keep from cracking up! It was killing him not knowing what happened.

We only had a few minutes between classes, and I didn't want to be late for English with Miss Spencer, so I told Frank I would fill him in at lunch. He would have ditched in a heartbeat, but I was already on Miss Spencer's bad list and wasn't willing to chance it.

"I can't believe it! You DAWG!" Frank was still in shock two hours later. We sat across my kitchen table eating Ramen Noodles.

"I can't believe it either. It just sorta happened." As I sat twirling the same noodles around my fork, Frank kept shaking his head with a stupid grin smeared on his face. "Frank, do you think she'll think I'm lame? I mean, I didn't exactly ask her in a 'super cool' way."

Frank got serious. "No way, dude. Sometimes girls like things to be out of the ordinary, and the way you asked her was definitely not 'ordinary', so I think you're good. Wow! You actually did it, man!"

The double date was partially planned by the time we headed back to Chemistry. Before now, he had been so busy trying to find me a date, he hadn't found someone for himself, but he wasn't worried about it.

As we got in my truck to head back to school, Frank said, "Hey! I'll ask her friend, Tracy! She's cute, and maybe Ashley will feel more comfortable." I agreed and his mind was made up. "You know what?" His eyes lit up. "I'll ask Tracy the same way you asked Ashley. We'll set a new trend!" That's Frank for you. Out to set the newest trends. Me, I've always been so behind, it seems impossible to catch up. I'm just happy I actually asked her!

Oh, by the way, we had our game against Alchesay tonight. For some reason, we played Thursday instead of Friday. Not sure why. Alchesay is on the Apache Reservation, and even though they usually don't excel in football, they have one kid on their team who really knows how to hit! Last year, he gave our slotback a concussion, and he was out for the season.

I hate standing on the sideline. It's not too bad when it's an easy victory, we won 49 – 8, but I can't wait to get my shorter cast on Tuesday! It was such a wild day. I think I'll be up all night . . . again.

Ashely looked at me today! Wow, that makes me sound like I'm back in grade school. Sorry, but you're going to have to deal with it. Some of my social skills are a little below the normal curve. I found myself looking at her off and on throughout class, and the third time she caught me in the act. Smiling shyly, she quickly looked away. My ears got hot, and I tried harder to pay attention. We were studying the Ten Commandments in Exodus, and I was probably breaking a commandment for not paying attention while studying the commandments. I'm sure it's in there somewhere.

After class, I found myself a few people behind Ashley and Tracy as we returned to school. Tracy kept glancing back and giggling. The world must have gotten the news.

Frank was waiting for me by Fish Hall as I walked toward History class. Tracy and Ashley entered a few people in front of us. As soon as we stepped in, Frank pulled me to the side and said, "Hey, man, watch this." All I could think was, *Oh no, not here,* but I wasn't fast enough to stop him.

The girls were about halfway down the hall by now, and Frank yelled, "Hey Tracy! Wanna go to Homecoming with me?" Everyone stopped, and the hall went silent.

It's a good thing Tracy is as outgoing as Frank, because the embarrassment would have killed most girls. After only a slight pause, she turned and yelled back, "Frank? You're a dork!" Everyone started laughing as the girls turned and kept walking down the hall. Frank's jaw went slack as his feet quit working. I'd never seen him knocked out in round one before!

He turned to me and tried to say something but couldn't. From the other end of the hall, we heard, "Hey, Frank!" Everyone went silent again. "Yeah, I'll go with you, but you better pay for everything!" Once more, the hall exploded with laughter. Popular Frank had just been outdone by a girl. I couldn't help but laugh, too. I'm sorry to admit, but I kinda enjoyed seeing Frank eat some humble pie.

It took him five seconds to start functioning again. When he finally found his wits, he jabbed a finger in the air and yelled, "I

WILL!" Not the most graceful comeback. Frank shrugged it off, and we joked as we made our way to second hour, because we knew the whole school would hear what had happened before we got there.

Saturday, 3 September, 2011

Josh and I rode horses today. Grandpa runs around 150 Brangus cows, and it seems like we're always giving chase to wayward bovines. I can't think of a better way to spend a weekend! The ranch is about 20,000 acres. Gramps has it split into six pastures, and we rotate the cows over them periodically throughout the year. Today we gathered the Webb pasture and moved the herd into the Swale pasture.

Grandpa has four horses: B.J. is a two-year-old Gramps gave to Josh, and there's Dallas, Lucky, and Frosty. Josh spent hundreds of hours this summer training his stupid horse. It wasn't long before he had B.J. halter broke and would lead him all over the neighborhood. I might've felt jealous, but I'd devoted so much to football, I wouldn't have had time for a horse, anyway. I think Grandpa knew this.

I usually get to ride Dallas. He's a three-year-old sorrel that's full of crap. About every other time I ride him, I end up in the dirt. Earlier in the summer, Dallas decided it was getting too hot, so he walked into the middle of a tank and lay down in the water. There went my new phone; I could've killed him! I had to ride for two hours in wet clothes, and the rashes were not pleasant.

I didn't want to chance hurting my arm again in another "eventful" experience with Dallas, so I decided to ride Frosty today. He's a twenty-eight-year-old, dark-bay horse with a white star on his forehead. He was born on a cold morning in early spring, and the tips of his ears froze, so they're all crinkled up. Even though he's getting up there in age, he's still our best horse. Gramps rode Lucky, a beautiful, thirteen-year-old dun, and Josh, of course, rode his precious BJ.

Things went pretty smoothly. The cows are trained to head to the next pasture when we start gathering them, but there was one old bull that didn't want to go with the herd. Come late fall, early winter, the bulls start going off by themselves. I guess they can only handle being around the ladies for so long. It must be a universal condition.

We split up to cover both sides of Mike Ridge, and when we met at Mire's Well, of course Josh was flaunting a beautiful arrowhead. I wasn't really upset, but I told him I was going to beat him up and take it away for not looking for cows.

"I did look for cows!" he shot back. "You're just jealous because you never find anything." I couldn't think of anything else to say, because we both knew he was right. The little fart is always bringing some kind of Indian artifact home, and I hardly ever find a thing. I would blame it on bad luck, but I think the problem is I'm usually more interested in rocks.

By the time we got home and unsaddled the horses, we were all sun-worn and dirt-ified. Gramps decided to give us the rest of the day off. I called Frank, and he came over so we could make some better plans for our homecoming date.

"Hey, we could take our dates horseback riding!" Frank must've felt inspired by my report on the day's activities, but I wasn't sure it was a good idea. Only a few people know about my secret cowboy life, and I'm scared to death what a girl might think if she finds out who I *really* am.

"We only have two horses I would trust, so we would have to ride double." I thought this would be a deterrent, but it had the opposite effect.

"Perfect!" he said excitedly. "Now you're thinkin'."

At first I didn't like the idea. It was too close, too fast. But the more I thought about it, the more I began to feel like maybe it was time for me to take a risk again. Even though I'd been hurt, I couldn't shut myself away forever. "Okay," I said. "I'll ask Gramps."

Frank pumped his fist and called for a high five. I shoved him instead. We planned a while longer and decided to celebrate our accomplishments by heading for Show Low. It's the only town for miles that has a theater, bowling alley, and Walmart! When we got in his car, Frank asked, "So, are you going to talk to Ashley again before our date or what?"

"I don't know," was all I could come up with.

"Dude, you should ask her out to lunch or something. Get to know her better before we go on our big date. It'll help if you're hoping for a good night's kiss." He gave an exaggerated wink. I rolled my eyes. Even though we've been through this fight many times before, I have to admit, there's a small part of me that would like to test those waters.

We ended up going to Wendy's for some chicken nuggets and a frosty. Afterwards, we stopped by Walmart and looked at their five-dollar movies. Frank picked out *Monty Python and the Holy Grail* since his older brother talked about how funny it was. We headed home to finish the weekend with a bowl of freshly-popped popcorn and a movie so stupid we couldn't stop laughing!

Tuesday, 6 September, 2011

Hi, David! How are you today? I was walking to the barn with the Airlis in hand when Elli contacted me. Reading her words jolted me out of mental attempts to ask Ashley to lunch. So far I haven't built up the courage to move me to action.

Doing good, Elli, how are you?

I'm doing fine, thanks. How was your week?

My thoughts instantly transmitted the reply, It was great, thanks to you.

You talked to her! How did it go? I swear I could sense her excitement.

I guess it went fine; she agreed to go on a date with me!

"A date? she asked. Sometimes I still forget we're worlds apart.

Yeah, like a planned activity you do together, I said. I couldn't think of how else to put it.

I understand. That's great, David! I knew you could do it.

Thanks for the encouragement and advice. I honestly don't think I would've done it without your help.

You would have figured it out, but you are welcome.

What have you been up to today? Are you painting flowers again?

No, not painting. I don't have the peace of mind to keep my hands steady, and I don't think I could pick the right colors.

What happened?

It's Jared. He asked to visit with me after our elements class, so I walked with him a while. He tried to talk me into going to a study group with him, but I'm not sure.

What's wrong with study groups? I wondered.

Nothing usually, but the group Jared is talking about is specifically studying the Plan that failed; the one without agency.

Oh yeah, I remember.

What should I do, David?

She was asking for advice from me? I started stuttering again, Well . . . um, I guess . . . I don't know. Would you give me a minute to think about it?

Sure, but don't think anything bad.

Very funny, I replied. I knew she was smiling again. I set the Airlis down and began digging deep through a jumble of thoughts. I don't have experience helping a friend who's going down the wrong path, so I thought instead about the path being offered—no agency. One of the first things that came to mind was my dad. I can't really explain much else without filling in some blanks, so here goes:

Bo Thorn was an abusive drunk. I'll skip the black and blue details and give you a watered-down version. I guess dad was a heck of an athlete in high school. His sport was baseball, and because of this I never wanted anything to do with it. Bo grew up in a small, southern Arizona town called Duncan. Even though it's easier for good athletes to shine when there's less competition, he was still good enough to have recruiters come watch him. Mom said he was an amazing pitcher. Anyway, he ended up with a full-ride scholarship to Eastern Arizona College where mom was studying for a nursing degree.

Bo was born into The Church of Jesus Christ of Latter-day Saints, but he wasn't a very good Mormon. He fell into his fame too deep and ended up making decisions that prevented him from serving a mission. You see, those who want to serve missions are required to meet certain standards of worthiness. Bo got into drinking and had a serious girlfriend, and when it came time to either straighten out his life and serve a mission or play baseball in college, I don't think it was much of a choice. He loved his life too much to give it up.

When he met Mom, he fell head over heels for her. Mom loved him, too, but she wanted to marry a man with strong faith in the Lord. Bo came back to church, and for a time he straightened out his life. It was enough to convince Mom, and she agreed to marry him. They got married civilly first, with goals that in a year or so they'd seal their marriage for time and all eternity in the Mesa Temple.

That was in the summer of his junior and mom's sophomore year in college. By the end of the fall semester, things started falling apart. Bo lost his scholarship because he failed one of his classes, and was kicked off the team. I believe it was the same week Mom found out she was pregnant. Now with no baseball, no job, and a kid on the way, Bo was forced to find work.

After a few hard months, he finally got hired to work in the Morenci mine. It's a good forty-five minutes from where they lived, and Bo worked hard hours. It wasn't long before he started drinking again. Mom had to work too, so they could afford her schooling. She found an easy job at the town library, and before they knew it, I joined them in their small world.

At first life wasn't too bad. For a while Bo quit drinking, but by the time I was three, he was back on the bottle and growing angrier every six pack. Some nights he would come home and rant and rave about dinner not being ready or it being too hot, and sometimes he would slap Mom with his open hand. Occasionally, he would hit me, too.

I learned to avoid him as much as possible. I could usually sense his mood in the first few seconds of him getting home. The abuse got more frequent until Mom found out she was pregnant again. The beatings slowed to only a couple times a week, which we were both grateful for, but his yelling got worse.

Josh entered our lives, and I only pray in thanks that, for some reason, Bo never took out his anger on him. Mom put me in t-ball hoping it would give Bo and me something constructive to do together, but it backfired badly. He forced me to stand at the plate and swing at his fast ball. If I didn't hit it in a few tries, he would pitch the ball at me instead. Even though t-balls aren't as hard as baseballs, I had many painful bruises and swollen body parts.

Things escalated once more when Mom got pregnant a third time. Bo was not happy. He kept yelling about how he thought this wouldn't happen, and how were they supposed to feed another mouth. He hit Mom across the face really hard, and she fell to the floor. He stomped out of the house and peeled out of the driveway. I listened from beneath the covers in my room, and when I heard him drive off, I tiptoed downstairs to find Mom unconscious, her face lying in a pool of blood. I was only seven, and didn't know what to do. I tried to wake her up. When she didn't budge, I decided to get a rag and clean off her face. Finally, after about five minutes, she groaned and woke up. When she came to her senses, she pulled me into her arms, and we cried for a long time.

We crawled into Mom's bed and tried to find comfort, though we were deathly afraid of what would happen when Bo came home. We were awakened around five-thirty in the morning by a knock on the door. Suspiciously, I followed Mom to the living room. I knew it wasn't Bo; he never would have knocked, but I was still so afraid. Mom opened the door, and there stood a sheriff. "I'm sorry to inform you, ma'am, but your husband was killed in an accident last night."

It turns out, he went to the bar and got wasted. Trying to drive home, he swerved and hit a telephone pole. It was probably bad, but a flood of relief came over me when the sheriff told us the news. I was almost happy he wouldn't be coming back anymore, but Mom sank to her knees and started crying. I never understood this, and still don't. Her love for him must have been bigger than the bruises, but mine wasn't.

As you know, I carried that anger for a long time. Not only was my life horrible while Bo was alive, but my feelings continued to fester for years after he was gone. As I reflected on this, the negative memories began to weigh down on me again, and truths I once knew began to get fuzzy. *How was any of this a good thing? Is agency really worth it?*

As my mind wandered through these mists of doubt, I had an impression to look back again, but this time to focus on the good. I decided to give it a try. Suddenly, I began to see my life differently than I ever had before.

I saw love! The trials Mom and I had passed through forged a bond stronger than steel; stronger than the pain and tears. I saw determination. Even though I was driven by pain, I used it to accomplish great things. Mountains did not stand in my way. I saw knowledge. Addictions destroy people and families. Anger infects and love cures. But most important, I saw faith. It took years, but I *finally* opened my ears to hear the sweet song of God's redeeming love. He answered my prayers! He forgave me for my bitterness and healed my broken heart. Now the peace that fills my soul is so much greater than the pain.

I picked up the Airlis, my thoughts very clear now. They're wrong Elli. We *must* have agency. If there isn't opposition—if we can't choose between right and wrong—there can be no happiness. I told her the whole story of my dad, the good and the bad.

David, it feels like my heart is . . . stretching? I have never felt this before. I hurt deeply for the pain you have suffered, but at the same time, I rejoice in the great truths you have learned. I don't know whether to laugh or cry.

I smiled as I replied, Please don't start crying. There's enough pain in the world without the tears of an angel falling on it. Instead, use it as motivation to find a way to reach Jared. You've got to help him change his mind!

I will try, but what do I do? What do I say?

Tell him about me if you have to. Tell him my story, or let me talk to him.

I would, but I'm afraid we might lose our connection. I'm not sure how the Airlis works, but once it connects to someone else, I might never get you back.

The thought of losing Elli that quickly and permanently, frightened me. In that case, I'll take much greater care of it.

As I said, I'm not positive, but I would not want to chance it.

Right, I replied. So go ahead and tell him about me, and see if that helps.

I will, she said. *Thank you for sharing your story with me. It must have been unpleasant to revisit such terrible memories.*

No worries. They're in the past, and life is infinitely better now that I've got friends like you. I blushed as I realized how personal my comment was. I didn't mean to share my feelings, but it's what I thought, so that's what came out.

I'm glad we are friends, too. It is nice to have someone who will listen, and in whom I can confide.

I guess it helps to be able to listen without hearing, I thought with a smile. Probably makes things a little easier.

I think it does, Elli replied.

To my astonishment, I noticed for the first time there was a slight glow emanating from the Airlis. It must give off light when it's in use, and I didn't notice it before. But even with the slight glow, it was getting hard to read her comments now. Once again, the time has flown by, and I've got to get home, so I better say goodbye for now.

Yes, time seems to shorten when we talk.

Just be open with Jared. The truth seems to be working well with us, anyway, I thought with a smile.

You know, I think you are right! Maybe I'll give it a try.

Goodnight, angel.

Good bye, David.

Wednesday, 7 September, 2011

Sorry, I completely forgot to tell you about what happened to me yesterday! When I got home from visiting with Elli, I immediately wrote down our conversation, but my mind was so absorbed with her, I forgot to fill you in on my day. Here's the rest of the story.

I went to the doctor and got my short cast yesterday morning! My skin felt weird and tingly when he cut the old one off. That was short lived, but I'm not complaining. The AWESOMENESS of having movement back in my elbow makes the new cast much easier to accept. I can tell my arm is a lot weaker; it even looks smaller, but at least I can dress out in pads for football practice now! It takes about fifteen minutes to tape the padding around my cast, but it's worth it. Coach didn't want me to do much yesterday, but I did get to run a few plays today! I dropped the first pass, but the next one I sprinted in for a touchdown! The guys cheered when I trotted back to the huddle. It felt great! At first Coach was hesitant about letting me play on Friday, but after practice today, he said with a smile, "Okay Thorn, maybe we will throw you in for a few offensive series."

Oh, Blue Ridge. They've been one of the top teams in our division for years. They and Show Low seem to always be neck and neck for number one. Sometimes, when we have a good year, we can knock one or both of them off, but it doesn't happen very often. But this is our year! We've got great athletes in every position, and we're certain we can make it to State. The last time the Snowflake Lobos brought home a golden football was in 1993, and the time has come for that to change. I am pumped for this game!

Friday, 9 September, 2011

I sat on the sidelines and watched as Blue Ridge slowly ate away our Defense. Offense was just as bad. Coach let me play all of three plays, and two of those were runs I only blocked for. I got one pass, and of course, I dropped it. In my defense, the ball was thrown way behind me. I had to reach back with one hand, and the tip of the ball hit the strip of cast that runs through my palm. But either way, coach never put me back in. The final score was Lobos 7, Blue Ridge 24. Not exactly how I dreamed my senior season would begin.

For as bad as the game was, the night did end on a good note. That's right, I did it! And you thought I lacked the guts to ask Ashley out to dinner. Well, you underestimated the power of the dark side. Ha! I think my *Star Wars* reference fits the situation pretty well, actually. Whether you compare it to girls in general or to my decision to re-explore their world, I have succumbed to the influence of those creatures of the night.

Yesterday, Ashley and I ended up meeting on our way to third hour. I guess she usually walks by the front of the auditorium on the north, and I go around the south where I park my truck in the small lot between the football field and auditorium. That's why I never noticed her going to art before. As I came out of South Hall, I saw her coming down the steps of Fish Hall.

"Hey, David, how are you?"

It only took a half second for my shock to turn to delight. "Good! How are you, Ashley?"

She smiled and said, "Besides recovering from the scene Frank made the other day, I'm doing great."

"Oh, Frank," I said, shaking my head. "I tried to stop him, but I was too slow."

We talked and laughed the whole way to my truck. I don't know why I was ever scared. Her easy-going nature and fun personality made conversation natural.

I didn't realize she'd changed her usual course to make our paths collide until, to my delight, she was waiting for me outside of South Hall again today. I thought to myself, *Now, this is a habit I could get used to!*

The road that runs through the high school is 2nd West. The auditorium with all the music, drama, and art classrooms is on the east of that street with the football stadium; the rest of the school is on the west. We chatted as we crossed to put my books in my truck. As we made our way around the back of the auditorium, I asked, "Are you going to the game tonight?"

"I don't know." She cocked an eyebrow as she grinned. "Will it be worth going to?"

"Heck yeah! Blue Ridge is going down."

She was unconvinced. "Are you going to be able to play?"

I shrugged my shoulders. "I think coach might put me in a few times."

"In that case, maybe I'll come. But if we lose, you owe me dinner."

I smiled and held out my hand. "I'll take that bet."

She shook it briskly and said, "Deal." By this time, we were standing in the hall between our classrooms. She turned and pushed open her door. "See you tonight then?"

"Yeah, see you tonight," I replied. She gave me a bright smile and stepped inside.

Okay, okay. Maybe I'm not as big of a stud as I made myself out to be, but I should at least get credit for speaking to her, right? I stepped into the choir room, and as I made my way to my chair, I noticed a scowl on Chelsey Roger's face. Usually, I hate that nothing goes unnoticed in high school, but for once, I was glad to have made an impression. Frank was already excited about us walking together, but when I told him about the dinner bet he whooped out loud in the middle of warm ups! Mr. Thompson glared, but luckily it didn't land us in detention.

After the game, I dressed out quickly. We lost tonight, but I couldn't help feeling excited about it. It was a weird combination of emotions. My head didn't know whether to tell my heart to be crushed for having a horrible game or to be excited about going out with Ashley. Dinner and a date tipped the scale. I ran out of the locker room before most of the team had removed their pads.

Stepping quickly through the door, I rounded the corner fast and collided hard with a girl coming the other way. Throwing out her arms to catch her balance, a bag of M&M's flew from her hands. When it hit the sidewalk, candy shot everywhere. We both started apologizing, but when I looked up, my words died mid-sentence. It was Lexi Dupree! I stuttered something about buying her another bag, but she assured me she was almost finished and not to worry about it. I felt like such a dork, told her sorry again, and we parted ways. She must have been on her way to meet Zack coming out of the locker room.

Running over Lexi didn't help the nerves, but I gathered myself together and went looking for Frank. During warm-ups, I saw him sitting next to Tracy and Ashley, so I figured if I found him, I would find them too. They were all waiting in the courtyard between the concessions and the locker room.

"I think this is the first time I actually feel bad about being taken out to dinner," Ashley said with a grin.

"Not me," Tracy interjected. "You guys played like crap."

Frank jumped in, "Couldn't you guys tell David was *trying* to throw the game tonight?"

They all started laughing. I punched Frank as hard as I could with my left hand. Didn't hurt him much. "Yeah, real funny, Frank." I had to smile though.

We decided on Denny's in Show Low, not that we had much of a choice. It's the only late-night restaurant on the mountain. Besides, I love their 2-4-6-8 menu! Turns out, Tracy and Frank actually make a pretty good pair. There was never a dull moment, and if anything, I'd have to say Tracy won the battle of wits tonight. Ashley and I did a lot of listening, but that was okay with me. We all had a great time.

Back in the school parking lot, we dropped the girls off at Ashley's car. As she climbed in the driver seat, Ashley smiled and said, "Thanks for dinner, David. I hope you lose more often."

"Tell you what," I replied, "if we lose to Show Low next week, Frank will make you dinner. But if we win, you owe us ice cream."

Frank back-handed my shoulder and yelled, "Hey!" The girls laughed.

"You're on!" Tracy shouted from the passenger side. The giggles faded quickly as the car gunned it out of the parking lot.

Frank turned and looked at me in astonishment. "Dude, you're getting pretty smooth!"

"Whatever, Frank," I shot back, but I knew what he was talking about. I haven't been this open around girls, ever. "You better get your cooking skills warmed up just in case," I warned. It was, by far, the best bet I'd ever lost.

Tuesday, 13 September, 2011

An annoying mosquito was my only companion as I sat waiting in the barn tonight. I should've taken my homework with me, but Elli had been so reliable, I didn't think I'd need it. A little after nine o'clock I finally headed home. I wonder what happened. I don't think it could've been anything bad. Do bad things happen in heaven? I'll have to ask her later. Hopefully, I'll get the chance. After what she said about the Airlis possibly reprograming to someone else, there's no telling what could've happened.

Things with Ashley have been going great! Ashley, Tracy, and I have started walking together after Seminary. I didn't really know Tracy that well before, but she's a firecracker! We never have a dull moment, but I like talking to Ashley between second and third hour without the distraction. I've been trying to take Elli's advice and get to know her better. She loves to paint, obviously, but she also plays the violin in orchestra. In the back of my mind, I think I knew this, but I'd forgotten. They perform the week of Homecoming, like we do for choir, and she invited me to come listen to them. My only memories of orchestra are from junior high, and it sounded terrible, so I'm hoping they've improved since then.

Speaking of Homecoming week, I better start practicing my duet with Sydney Flake. I don't think I told you yet, but I'm in TWO choirs. Honor Choir and Madrigals, the hardest group. Somehow I made it my sophomore year as a bass, and I've really enjoyed it. Sure, make fun of the choir boy if you want, but do you have any idea how many trips we go on each year? It's a blast— especially with the girls. ☺ It's ironic, I know, but being scared to death of girls doesn't mean I'm not attracted to them. The curse of puberty.

Anyway, the Madrigal Homecoming concert is one of the funnest performances of the year. (And yes, I know "funnest" isn't a word, but dang it, it should be!) We perform a few numbers as a group, but unlike other concerts this one is mostly solos and small ensembles, and we're all expected to participate. A few weeks ago, I overheard Chelsey Rogers say she wanted to sing a duet with someone. That was motivation enough to volunteer myself enthusiastically when Sydney asked for help. Luckily, she'd forgiven me for the roped beaver story (which took her a good week to figure out, hee hee). It's a good thing, too, because, honestly, I'm probably the only guy in class who knows who Chicago is. Even though I'm familiar with "It's Hard to Say I'm Sorry," I won't lie, I'm a tad nervous.

Friday, 16 September, 2011

Football practice went really well this week. My arm was feeling fine, and I convinced coach to let me start against Show Low tonight. They're the defending state champions, ranked number two in the state right now, and they have a very good returning team. We're somewhere around eight or nine.

It was a beautiful night for a football game. We won the coin toss and chose to get the ball at the half. Coach put me on the kickoff team because I'm one of the fastest guys, and we lined up on the forty-yard line. If you've never been on the field for a Friday night football game, you are absolutely missing out. The smell of fresh-cut grass, the lights, the roar of the crowd; it all combines to create an atmosphere of AWESOMENESS! Sorry, but I can't think of a better way to describe it.

We kicked the ball deep and sprinted down field. I could see the wedge they were creating, so I aimed right for the middle of it. I lowered my shoulder and plowed into their lead blocker. I didn't aim to take him out, but glanced off him and broke through the line to find myself face to face with the ball carrier. He feinted to my left, but I didn't bite, and as he shot to my right, I aimed for the big "23" on his chest. I was a tad slow and barely caught him with my right shoulder and arm. My cast hit his thigh pad and bounced off as he ran right through my arms, around the wedge, and seventy-eight yards for a touchdown.

It wasn't exactly how I intended starting my first full game back. Coach was visibly upset but didn't say anything. I didn't tell him, or anyone, but it kind of hurt my arm. I didn't think it was anything serious, but I asked him to replace me on the kickoff team, anyway. I told him the guy bounced off my cast, and I didn't want to chance it happening again, which was mostly true.

On offense it didn't matter as much if my arm was hurting as long as I could catch the ball and outrun the other guy. After their first score, we battled back and forth; no one else scored in the first quarter. We finally got on the board in the second quarter when Zack faked a pass and took the ball in from twenty-four yards out. We scored again with only a minute and a half left before the half to put us up 14 – 7. Show Low marched back down the field to around the ten-yard line. With only seconds to go, they sent their quarterback in motion and hiked the ball straight to the fullback. It gave him enough of a jump to punch it in for the score. They faked the point after and got the two-point conversion. That put them up 15 – 14 at the half.

The locker room was very subdued, but coach told us he believed in us and was not going to let us give up. He kept getting louder and louder, and then, to our surprise, he grabbed his shirt and literally ripped it from his chest! Beneath the shredded remains of his collared coach's uniform were big white letters on a tight blue t-shirt that read: LOBO PRIDE. We jumped to our feet and burst through the locker room doors. Show Low never scored again. Our defense was unbelievable! Zack earned his medals today, too, as he carried the offense twice more into the end zone. When the final buzzer sounded, the Snowflake Lobos were victorious, 28 – 15! If we had played like this last week against Blue Ridge, it would've been a different story. Show Low did have some mistakes, but that's part of the game. The locker room could hardly contain the energy of our celebration! Someone started blaring the song "Eye of the Tiger," and Zack began dancing on top of a bench. Everyone was laughing and cheering. It was a moment none of us will ever forget!

My arm never gave me much of a problem after that kickoff return, for which I'm very grateful. I had another long catch in the third quarter that got us in the red zone, but I also dropped a touchdown pass two plays later. It's a good thing Zack was on his A-game tonight. The next play he tucked the ball and ran it all the way in from fifteen yards out. The bitter with the sweet, I guess. To top it all off, after the game, I got ice cream. McDonalds was packed with celebrating teenagers. It was so loud, we had to yell to have a conversation! I'm surprised they didn't kick us out. What a day!

Tuesday, 20 September, 2011

David, are you there? I'd been sitting in bed for about twenty minutes and was about to fall asleep when I saw a slight glow coming from the Airlis. I quickly wrapped my blanket around me so the light wouldn't wake up Josh. Tonight was our Madrigal concert, and so I missed our usual seven o'clock meeting time. When I got home at a quarter to nine, I tried a few times to get ahold of Elli but had things I needed to do and couldn't walk around the house holding a rock.

Where have you been? I shot back. I've been worried sick I might've lost you!

You missed me? That's good to know, she replied—was it with a sense of smugness?

It's not funny, Elli. Have you ever lost a friend for fourteen days without knowing what happened to them? I really thought you were gone! I didn't mean to come across harsh, but my emotions overrode my control for a brief moment.

Oh my, I keep forgetting about the time change. Sorry. It's kind of sweet that you care, though.

What happened? Or did you forget about me for a few days? I was still mad enough I didn't care if I jabbed her a little.

No, I didn't forget about you. I forgot what time it was.

I began to calm down. Sorry. At least you're back. I'm just glad I didn't lose you. There was more sentiment in my words than I hoped to share, but it was how I felt.

I was actually having a good conversation with Jared if you must know, she confessed.

A tinge of jealousy filled my chest. Looking back now, I wonder why I would feel that. Elli lives on a different world and in a different time. "Out of my league" doesn't even begin to describe my situation. I quickly bagged those feelings up and threw them in the bin of wishful thinking. That's great, Elli. It must have gone pretty good, then?

It went very well, thanks to you. Her comment caught me off guard.

What do you mean?

When Jared approached me yesterday, I decided to be open with him. I told him I didn't think studying the Dark Plan was a good idea, and it made me feel uneasy.

The "Dark Plan"? The phrase sounded too earthy to be coming from her.

Sorry, that's what we call the plan that failed—the one without agency.

Does that have anything to do with "the Dark Side"? I couldn't resist.

The dark side of what?

Oh, never mind. I didn't feel it was the right time to correctly indoctrinate her on the awesomeness of *Star Wars*. Instead, I decided to change the subject. So, what did he say after that?

He apologized and promised not to bring it up again now that he knows how much it bothers me.

And you forgot about me in that short of time? I said teasingly.

No, afterwards we sat and talked for a while. I think he likes me, David. Jealousy chewed at me again, but I quickly brushed it off.

That's great. I tried to force some enthusiasm, but I don't know why. I realized how silly it was, since she was only reading words. Without feeling the emotion behind them, words can mean many different things.

Elli interrupted my epiphany by saying, *Ever since you asked me if I had a special companion, I have been thinking a lot about it. In spite of our different views, I realize I have strong feelings for him, too.* My attention snapped back to the conversation. As my mind raced to digest this information, I couldn't help but think about similar sensations I've been having toward Ashley.

Before I realized what I was thinking, the words appeared, Life is a lot better when you have a girlfriend. A girlfriend. I would be lying if I said it hadn't crossed my mind, but I haven't dared approach the topic with Ashley, yet. It freaks me out thinking about it.

Elli asked, *Do you think I should pursue a companionship with Jared?*

Yeah, was all I could say. My emotions were all tangled at the moment.

How do I become his girlfriend?

The idea that anyone would ask me for relationship advice was so funny I started laughing out loud. Josh rolled over and slurred, "Hey, w-what's going on?"

"Oh, nothing." My mind quickly raced for an excuse. "I was just laughing at something that happened today."

Josh replied sleepily, "Oh." I waited for a second, and when I thought he had gone back to sleep, I looked back to the Airlis.

David, are you there?

I reverted back to communicating by thought. Sorry, Elli, yeah I'm here. You kind of caught me off guard with your question is all.

Oh, sorry. It was a silly question, I know.

It's not that. I was laughing because I'm in exactly the same predicament with Ashley, and I have no idea what to do next. I've never had a girlfriend before.

If that's the case, what is the traditional way on your world to become a serious couple?

I pondered her question for a minute, and was surprised to realize I had no idea. The only thing I knew for sure is that you are not supposed to ask them in a note, at least not after grade school. I'm not really sure, was the only thing I could say.

Then I suppose we will have to face the unknown together!

Yeah, I'm going to need all the help I can get. For me it's usually extremely difficult to admit my weaknesses, but with the Airlis, confessions jump out of my head of their own free will! Having your soul exposed to an angel is a very humbling experience.

Elli changed the subject by asking, *How has it been going with Ashley?*

It took me a second to convert from humble to happy, but once I got going, the words poured out. She didn't say much until I started describing our plans for Homecoming. I've got another small date tomorrow night watching her perform in the orchestra, and a few days after that, we'll go to Homecoming!

And what is Homecoming?

It's the original date I was talking about last time; the first one Ashley accepted?

Oh yes, I remember. What is so special about Homecoming?

It's kind of a week-long event. We have activities, and competitions, and a parade for the whole community. There's a big football game Friday night, and Saturday is when we have our date. We usually do something fun during the day, then dinner followed by a dance in the gym.

It sounds amazing! Have you decided what you will do for fun yet?

Actually, we're planning to ride horses during the day, and that's all Frank and I have come up with so far. It hit me that we were running out of time to get everything else figured out.

That does sound like fun! I absolutely love horses. They are such majestic animals.

You have horses, too? Her comment piqued my curiosity. What else do you have on your world?

Ha! Now that is a heavy question if ever I heard one. You might have to be more specific.

I guess I'll start with animals, since we're already on the subject. Apparently, you have horses and grasshoppers, but what other kinds of animals do you have?

We have all of them, she replied vaguely.

Now YOU might have to be more specific, I thought back mockingly.

If you want details, we might be here for days. There are millions of species! Maybe this will help you understand.

Everything that's created on a mortal world, is first created spiritually on a world like mine. In short—we have all of them.

The idea was astounding. How do you have room for all of them?

We don't keep them all here, even though we could fit a lot of them. Ours is a very large world. There are worlds upon worlds, and some are specifically created as homes for lesser creations. People who have a great love for animals will live with them, to act as stewards and keep order, but usually, there are not many humans.

What type of world do you live on if it's not an animal one?

Ours is a world created for Father's spirit children as a place for learning and growth. We have schools and universities, grand buildings, and small homes. We also have beautiful gardens and working stables. The whole world is one large community of brothers and sisters.

I tried to picture our world as one large community. It's hard to imagine such a place, I told her. An image of people covering the whole globe crossed my mind, and with it came a new question. Do you have deserts and mountains? Or snow and seasons?

I have read about all these things, and I've seen small glimpses of them while visiting other places, but no, we don't have them on our world. Here, the climate is very mild with soft rains, and everything is beautiful and green, like one enormous garden.

Wait. You visit other worlds? She stated it so nonchalantly, I almost missed it. My mind stretched to contemplate the notion, but I felt like a tadpole trying to take on a monsoon flood. How is that even possible? Oh, let me guess. You have circular, flying machines that transport you at the speed of light?

No, we don't have circular machines, she said, and I sighed with relief. I was almost convinced at this point that she wasn't an alien, but I hadn't ruled out the possibility. *We travel much faster than that.*

Oh, was all I could say. I waited for a second to hear a "just teasing," but when nothing came, I asked, Are you joking?

No, I'm not joking. It would not be possible to travel the immensity of space if you were limited to the speed of light. How to explain this? We travel more at the speed of thought, meaning it is nearly instantaneous.

I sat there in stunned amazement as the flood waters of endless possibilities kept rolling me over and over. I was finally able to get out one shocked word, How?

I'm not exactly sure. I told you, I am still very young when it comes to knowledge and experience. This type of traveling is something only the greatest ones learn. I've only been able to travel this way when accompanied by someone else. The only thing I understand is that it requires great spiritual power along with complete knowledge of the principle. Both things I hope to achieve someday.

Whoa, this is crazy. My mind was reeling with thoughts of space travel, and I thought of Superman, and I had to ask, Can you fly?

Like a bird? No, but I will be able to move through open space as soon as I learn how. The knowledge of elements and forces and having power over them, is a course I will be able to take when I progress far enough. When you achieve this knowledge, then yes, you can fly—more or less. It's a different type of flight—not the propulsion and lift that comes from a set of wings.

This is unbelievable, I thought. Why in the world would we ever want to leave such a place to come to a world like this? My mind filled with a thousand images of wars and riots, floods and fires, the pain and suffering we live through daily is sometimes unbearable.

Have you not understood what you have been taught? Do you not see the eternal importance of the Plan of Salvation? Her questions seemed to stab at me. I dug through the memories of all I knew and tried to find what I had missed. What was it about the Plan that was so important we would leave such a wonderful place to come and go through such hell?

I'm not sure. I can't remember, I thought guiltily.

Well, you will need to find that out for yourself, too, was all she said.

Won't you tell me? I pleaded.

I can't. That was one of the things Father admonished me not to do. He told me it is of the utmost importance that you build your faith and knowledge on your own, at least when it comes to your God and your Plan of Salvation. Your experience must be kept a test of faith. If not, it could stunt your spiritual growth.

I don't understand. Why not?

Trust me, David. Some things you have to learn on your own. But I can tell you this; the pathway to truth is just as rewarding as the knowledge itself.

Oh, okay. Well thanks for the riddles, anyway. I said it with a twinge of sarcasm, but I knew she was only trying to help.

Don't give up, David. Seek out the answers, and I promise you will find them.

Deflated, I replied, *I guess I'll have to.* Glancing at the clock, I sat up with a jolt. *Holy Smoke! It's past two thirty in the morning! I really should be sleeping right now.*

I'm sorry, David. I've read it's important for mortals to get enough rest, but we don't have to worry about that here.

You don't sleep, either?

A question to be answered another day. I should be preparing for my next class, so I will also say goodbye for now.

Well, try not to forget about me tomorrow okay? I said jokingly.

I promise I won't. I hope you have a great Homecoming!

Thanks. Me, too. Goodnight, Elli. The dim light went out of the Airlis, but thoughts kept tumbling around in my head. It was late, but I knew I wouldn't sleep, so I decided to write it all down. I know I've been taught the gospel, and I know it's true. I know God is real, and that Christ is my Savior, but I don't know everything. I started to see tonight that there's so much more to learn.

Wednesday, 21 September, 2011

Today was camouflage day at school. I participated by wearing my camo hat. Usually, I try to stay inconspicuous in public. Some people don't mind attracting attention, and I admit, they make me jealous. I wish I were a little more open and carefree, like Frank. He came decked out with EVERYTHING camo. He had the pants, shirt, socks, boots, sunglasses, hat; he wasn't even ashamed to admit he borrowed camo underwear from his younger brother. I don't know how he got them on, his brother is only eleven.

It was a fun day. I asked Frank if he wanted to go to the orchestra performance with me, and he promptly turned it into a date by asking Tracy to come, too. The band and orchestra perform on the same night, and I was shocked to find they actually sounded like a band and orchestra. For the last number, they performed together, and to my surprise, Ashley had a solo. She did an amazing job. Even Frank had nothing but compliments for her after the performance, at least until we got outside. "And I thought violins were only good as torturing devices!" he quipped. Leave it to Frank to break up a nice compliment with a wisecrack.

Afterward, Frank came to my house, and we made some final preparations for our date this weekend. Homecoming isn't a formal date in Snowflake, so usually couples wear matching shirts for the pictures. This freed up our day a bit, since the girls wouldn't need as much time to get ready. We decided that not only would we ride horses, but we would impress our dates by cooking them dinner over a campfire. Even though I'd never taken anyone besides Josh out to Lost Lake, it was the perfect spot for our date.

"So this pond is pretty cool, huh?" Frank asked, as we finished making plans.

"Yeah, you're going to love it," I replied.

"I can't believe you've never taken me out there before."

"Well, if I wasn't working, I was playing football; and you were always out chasing girls." I tried to turn the blame back on him.

"I guess better late than never," he said with a shrug.

I wasn't sure I wanted to talk to Frank about it at first, but I thought, *what the heck.* "Hey Frank, how do you ask a girl to be your girlfriend?"

"Ask?" he replied with astonishment. "Brother, you don't ask, you just do, and the rest of the world will tell you if you're going out."

I thought about this for a while, and when I couldn't figure it out, I said, "What do you mean?"

"You'll find out soon enough," was all he replied with a smirk on his face. "Don't worry, you're doing fine. All my training has finally paid off." He leaned back in his chair and put his hands behind his head, soaking up my achievements as if he owned them.

"Oh, shut up," I shot back. "If you had half my good looks, you wouldn't have to *do* anything! The girls would flock to you like bees to honey." I kicked his chair and sent him sprawling onto the living room floor.

He landed flat on his back with a grunt, and I could tell it knocked the air out of him. He groaned then mumbled, "And pride shall be thy downfall." Slowly, he rolled onto his hands and knees. "Just don't forget the hand that's fed you all these years."

"Yeah, fed me a load of crap," I teased as I reached to help him up.

He slapped my hand away, and with embellished pride he spat, "I can get up *myself*, thank you very much." He forced out a grunt as he began to stand up . . . very slowly. He groaned like an old geezer all the way to an upright position.

I snorted with exaggerated disappointment, "Frank, you're an idiot."

"Perhaps that's true." He put his hands on his lower back and stretched, grimacing in exaggerated pain. He pushed out his belly to an abnormal size, and while picking his nose, he said, "But the ladies can't resist my charm! You see my young padawan, *that,* is why you fail." He pulled his finger out of his nose and started shaking it at me. "It's not what's on the outside, but the inside that counts," and he stuck his finger in his mouth.

"Watch out girls, the Neanderthal has left the cave," I said flatly. "I can't believe you quoted *Star Wars* and *Aladdin* in the same breath. That has to be crossing moral boundaries somewhere."

We joked a while longer, and then he had to get home and finish some homework he'd procrastinated. I still don't understand what he meant when he said the world would let me know. I guess I'll have to wait and see.

Friday, 23 September, 2011

We played St. Johns tonight, and even though they're in a lower division, they came ready to kick our butts. We knew they were a tough team, but as it goes, we underestimated them. Winning last week against Show Low didn't help. We felt like we were untouchable.

I don't remember much, because in our second offensive series of the game, I slipped and re-broke my arm.

It was a simple corner route, but as I faked inside and turned to cut for the sideline, I lost my footing and went down. Of course, I threw my hands out to catch my fall, but the weight of my body was too much for my weak arm. The pass went flying over my prone body into an empty field.

It must have re-broke the original fracture, because the pain was awfully familiar. There was an initial shock of fire, then only a slight throb until I tried to push down with my hand. I lay on the ground for a mere second before jumping up and jogging to the sideline. I didn't want Mom to come flying out of the stands to see what was wrong. I told coach what happened, and he just shook his head. I watched the rest of the game in silence. *How could this happen to me again?* I absolutely could not believe it. I'm supposed to get my cast off in one week!

We ended up winning—barely. I think we were behind at halftime, but I can't remember for sure. We were able to come back in the fourth quarter, with a final score of 21 – 15. After the game, I dressed slowly and spoke as little as possible. Most of the team didn't even know what happened, and of those who did, only a few cared. When I came outside, Mom was waiting with arms folded and eyebrows knit together in worry.

"What happened, son?"

There was no way to sugar coat it for Mom. "I think I re-broke my arm," I told her, devoid of emotion.

"Oh, son. I'm so sorry." Her eyes began to tear up, but Mom is strong, and she quickly got it under control. Seeing her strength actually helped ease my burden more than the tears. "Do you need to go to the hospital?" she asked.

"No, it's okay. Just get me some Ibuprofen, and I'll be fine."
Isn't that supposed to fix everything? Mom gave me her worried
look but didn't badger me.

After a few seconds of scrutiny, she asked, "Are you coming
home, or will you be going out tonight?" Usually, the
Homecoming game is followed by fun activities, but we hadn't
planned anything. Besides, I really didn't want Ashley to see me
all sweaty and in a bad mood.

"We might, but I'm not sure," I replied unconvincingly. I
backed it up with, "I need to shower, either way."

She gave me a gentle hug and asked, "Will you be able to
drive home okay?"

"Oh, yeah," I said in a reassuring tone, and moved my arm
through a series of convincing motions. "It feels like it did the first
time I broke it. It only hurts when I try to push down. I'll be fine."

She gave me a brief, questioning look, and after a slight pause
continued, "Well, I'll see you at home then." With a gentle squeeze
to my shoulder, she headed to her car.

I'm glad my truck was in the opposite direction of the stands
and crowd; I just wanted to get out of there. I grabbed my pads and
ducked into the dark parking lot. As I reached for the truck door
handle, I heard footsteps behind me. I didn't want it to be Ashley,
but at the same time I hoped it was her.

"Hey, are you okay?"

I turned to see her walking toward me alone, surprised she
also had noticed my injury. "Hey, Ashley. Yeah, I'm all right."

"What happened? Is your arm okay?"

Looking down at my arm, I started to rub it slightly. "Oh, I
hurt it again, but I think it'll be fine."

With deeper emotion than I was expecting, she said, "David,
I'm so sorry." And before I could react, she put her arms around
my neck. It happened so fast all I could do was stand frozen in
shock! I'd never been hugged by a girl before—besides Mom and
maybe Grandma. The emotions that hit me were so new, and
strange, and wonderful all at the same time, for a moment I
actually forgot about my arm. The smell of her hair and the
warmth of her arms on my neck disconnected my brain from my
body for a moment. I tried to move my right arm around her, and

was abruptly returned to reality. She jumped back as I gasped in pain.

Sucking air through clenched teeth, she said, "Oh! I'm so sorry!" Watching her concerned face twist into guilt snapped my gloom into bite size pieces of humor, and I couldn't hold in a chuckle.

The horror on her face softened when she realized she hadn't maimed me. The release that came from laughing—along with her hug—was like cold water on a fresh burn. Grinning nervously, she asked, "What's so funny?"

Smiling, I replied, "I never realized a hug could hurt that bad."

Even though she'd let go of my neck, her hands were still on my shoulders. At my comment, she quickly dropped her hands. "Sorry." This time she said it with contrition.

"Oh, it's okay," I replied quickly. "I think your hug was the only thing that could've made me feel better tonight. Thank you."

She relaxed and smiled. "You're welcome." After a brief pause she asked, "So will you have to get another cast?"

"I don't know. I'd rather not have another elbow cast if I can help it. Actually, I would rather not have a cast at all. They're terrible! Have you ever had one?"

She gazed off in the distance for a second. "Mom said I broke my leg when I was five or six, but I don't remember much except that it itched *really* bad."

"Yeah, it's horrible," I agreed. "It's a good thing you can't remember it very well."

With a soft grin, she said, "Yeah, it's probably better I don't." A look of concern chased away the grin. "Will you be okay to go on our date tomorrow? If you're in a lot of pain, we can do something else or even go another day."

Shaking my head firmly, I said, "No, I'll be fine. I don't think it'll bother me much to ride tomorrow."

She got a mischievous look and asked, "So, we're *riding* are we?" I'd forgotten we were keeping it a surprise. "Should I expect exotic animals or motorcycles?"

This got a good laugh out of me. "Well, I'd hate to ruin the surprise any more than I already have, so you'll have to wait and see."

She gave me a that's-not-fair look and asked with pleading eyes, "Can you at least tell me if I need Wranglers or a leather jacket?"

"Sorry, if I tell you anymore, Frank will kill me. But it probably wouldn't hurt to bring both."

"Well in that case, I'll look forward to seeing you tomorrow!" A sweet smile radiated from her face as she turned to leave.

"Thanks again for the hug," I said as she began walking away. "It brought more joy than pain, I promise."

She turned back with that same pretty smile, and replied, "I'm glad I didn't do more damage."

Somehow I got home. I don't remember the details. After pulling in the driveway and shutting off the truck, I sat for a while and numbly contemplated the last few hours. *I'm sure I re-broke my arm. Where will that leave my football career? Ashley hugged me! She noticed I was hurt when most of my own team had no idea. I think she likes me—I like her, too. My arm hurts. I don't want another cast.* The thought of six more weeks with another cast made me cringe. *And I was supposed to get my cast off for good next Tuesday!* The weight kept getting heavier and heavier. That's when a rank aroma filled my nose . . . and I made up my mind.

I walked over to Grandpa's place. It looked like they were asleep, but I didn't care. I entered his garage and flipped on the light, searching through the tool box in his truck until I found some tin snips. I sat down on his tailgate and cut off my cast. Oh, it felt so good to have that gone, but the smell was rancid! That was the deciding factor. I didn't want a cast, or that smell, clogging my life another second. The relief of no longer having the weight on my arm was euphoric, but only on a physical level. Sure it felt good, but sitting on the tailgate next to me was not only a shredded cast, but a shredded dream.

Mom was sitting at the kitchen table going through a stack of papers when I walked in. Her first glance was quick, but the second one locked on my arm in shock. There was a quick intake of breath. "Where's your cast?"

Fidgeting with my helmet, I said, "Mom, if I go to the doctor on Tuesday, he'll cut my cast off, anyway, so I saved you from paying for a doctor visit—you're welcome." I tried to make it sound like I was doing her a favor.

"What do you mean 'if' you go to the doctor?"

I set my pads on the floor and walked over to the cupboard and grabbed a cup. "Look, I've thought about it a long time. If I didn't re-break my arm, all the doctor will do is cut my cast off, and I'd be wasting his and my time. But if I *did* re-break it, the bone must be fairly straight, because it feels and acts the same as before. I can't handle another six weeks with a cast, Mom." I filled the cup at the sink and took a drink. "Besides . . . I'm not playing football anymore."

The words were harder to get out than I expected. I'd thought them, but vocalizing made them real—and that hurt. I watched my tears race down the drain along with all the dreams they'd been carrying. I couldn't look up. Besides not wanting to see any more pain on Mom's face, I didn't want her to see me cry. She didn't say anything for a long time. After a moment, I heard her walk to the pantry. When I glanced up, I noticed she was wiping her eyes, too. "Would you like some popcorn and hot chocolate?" she asked over her shoulder. Mom knows this is my favorite. We've spent many nights watching movies with a bowl of buttery goodness and a cup of heaven's nectar.

"Yeah, I'd like that," I sniffed.

"If you aren't going to do anything tonight, we could catch up on a few episodes of *Prison Break*," she suggested as she put the popcorn in the microwave.

"That sounds like a great idea," I replied.

I love my Mom. We've been through so much together, and have always had each other's backs. Even if she doesn't say it in words, she says enough with a bowl of popcorn and a cup of hot cocoa.

Saturday, 24 September, 2011

I'm starting to feel like a girl. If something extraordinary happens during the day, I can't sleep until I write it down. I don't know one guy who has this problem. It's definitely remaining a secret. Crap! That sounds girly, too! I need to go run over a cat or something. I'd try cow tipping again, but I had to fix a half-mile of fence last time . . . another story for another day.

Frank and I spent the morning getting things ready for our date. We decided on tinfoil dinners and Dutch oven peach cobbler as our surprise meal. We both grew up going to Scouts, and because of our many campouts, we felt comfortable with our open-flame, culinary abilities. He borrowed his dad's four-wheeler, and I hooked up Grandpa's four-horse trailer to my old Ford. We caught the horses in their pasture by the creek and brought them to the barn. After feeding them some hay, we loaded our stuff and headed for Lost Lake.

If you're ever in Snowflake and you look east of town, about ten miles out, you can see a series of high plateaus. Not large enough to be considered mountains, they're taller than most hills in the area. If you climb to the top, you can see for miles in every direction. These hills are almost smack-dab in the middle of Grandpa's ranch, and Lost Lake is in the valley behind them.

"Wow! Those are a lot bigger up close than they look from town." Frank had pulled up beside me on his four-wheeler as we stopped at the base of the largest plateau.

"If we have time, we should take our dates up there," I replied. I hadn't thought about it before. "It has an amazing view."

"Oh, I see," he said with a wink. "A better make out spot I've never seen!"

I rolled my eyes in mock disappointment. "Frank, to you everywhere is a good make out spot."

He nodded his head with pride, and said, "Now you're getting the picture! So, where is this pond of yours?" I led the way around the hill. Crossing the valley on the bumpy ranch roads took us about five minutes.

"This is freakin' cool!" Frank said, as we pulled up to Lost Lake. "I can't believe you haven't brought me out here before."

"If you weren't so busy chasing girls and wanted to have some real fun, I might have!" I shot back accusingly.

"Hey, at least you're finally figuring out how to have 'real' fun and girls at the same time." I had no comeback for that one, because suddenly, I was completely agreeing with him.

We parked the truck and trailer under the shade of a big tree. Besides needing a way to bring all our gear out, we wouldn't have time to ride the horses home after dinner and still make the dance. We jumped on Frank's four-wheeler and headed back to town.

Ashley came to the door wearing Wranglers and a plaid, button-up shirt. In her arms, she held a leather jacket. I let out a friendly laugh and said, "Well, I can honestly say you're the first biker cowgirl I've ever met."

"I wasn't sure what to expect, so I thought I'd be prepared," she replied with a smile.

Tracy was with her. Apparently, while we were getting the food ready, they were getting themselves ready. Tracy must have hoped for a Harley ride, because she was decked out in a biker outfit—down to leather gloves and black lipstick.

She looked at Frank and said with attitude, "You better not disappoint me."

Frank laughed nervously and said, "It might not be what you expect, but you won't be disappointed, I swear."

"Good!" she snapped. "Now let's get this show on the road." I have to laugh every time Tracy walks all over Frank. He had no idea what he was getting himself into.

On our way back to Frank's car, I told Ashley, "You look nice as a gothic cowgirl."

"Thank you, sir," she tried to say in a Western drawl. "You don't look half bad either as half a cowboy." Frank had gone all out from the boots to the cowboy hat, but I came dressed as I usually do: Wranglers, boots, T shirt, and ball cap.

I felt pretty self-conscious, but since I was trying to turn over a new leaf, I shrugged my shoulders and said, "Yep, this is me; at least when I go riding."

"Really?" she asked in slight astonishment. This was the moment. Once again, I put myself in the hands of a girl, like I swore I'd never do. "I kinda like it," she said and smiled that soft smile. My whole body relaxed. She looked down and noticed my arm. "Your cast is gone!" she exclaimed in surprise. "It's not broken?"

"I'm not exactly sure, but it's been feeling fine. I just couldn't take it anymore. The cast had to go."

"You cut it off?" she asked in surprise.

"You would've too, if you'd smelled it. It was horrific!"

"Are you okay to ride?" she asked thoughtfully.

"I'll be fine. Besides, camels steer with voice commands." I tried to keep a straight face.

"Oh, really?" she asked with a grin. "Is there an oasis nearby I haven't heard of?"

I smiled and answered, "Actually, that's exactly where we're going! You better quit asking questions, or we won't have any secrets left."

She playfully narrowed her eyes, and asked, "How many secrets are you hiding?"

My cheeks reddened, and I stuttered, "C-can't tell you any more. You'll have to wait and see."

Before we picked up our dates, we saddled the horses and tied them to the fence in the barnyard. From the road we couldn't see them, but when we walked around the barn, Frank pointed to Frosty and said, "Tracy, I'd like to introduce you to your steed. This is Widow Maker; the meanest set of teeth on four legs this side of the Mississippi. He can go 0 to 15 in three seconds flat, and his horse power is without equal!"

Tracy couldn't hide her smile as she started petting Frosty on the nose. "He sure looks like he's been in a bar fight or two." Her smile turned to an impish grin and she asked, "Where's your horse?"

This rattled Frank for a second, but he recovered quickly. "No ma'am, we'll be riding together, so I can keep you safe from harm."

Tracy looked back to Frosty and said, "Well, if this is my horse, then I get to drive," and she swung into the saddle with apparent skill. Frank was dismayed. He'd been imagining her arms wrapped around his waist for the next hour, not him holding on for dear life. She reached her hand down, and with a look of victory she said, "Are you coming or not?"

Frank was a good sport, though. Straightening up, he tipped his hat, and in his best John Wayne accent said, "Yes, ma'am!"

Ashley and I were both laughing at this point. I turned to her. "Your camel, my lady."

"He's the cutest camel I've seen, that's for sure."

"His name is Lucky." She walked over and patted him on the nose. To avoid the same scene Frank made, I asked, "Would you like to be driver or passenger?"

Ashley looked down a little embarrassed. "Since I've never really ridden a horse before, maybe I better be passenger today."

"You've never ridden a horse before? And you live in Snowflake?"

She kicked in the dirt and replied, "I know, pretty crazy, huh?"

I thought for a second and said, "Tell you what, you ride in front like Tracy, and I'll teach you how to steer. It's really easy, and Lucky's a good horse. Besides, we wouldn't want Frank to feel left out."

Frank was sitting behind Tracy at this point and reacted to our teasing by resting his hands behind his head and saying, "Hey, I don't know what y'all are talking about. I *love* making the woman do all the work." He closed his eyes and acted as if he were going to sleep. Tracy kicked Frosty, and he jolted forward a few steps. Frank's hands shot around Tracy's waist before he toppled over backwards. For a moment he had a very serious look on his face that said, *Oh CRAP!*

"You better hold on tight, Frank," Tracy smirked. "This might be a bumpy ride."

Frank never let go of Tracy, she made sure of that. She turned out to be quite the opposite of a biker. We found out later, she rides horses all summer at her uncle's place in town. They rode circles around us as she jumped Frosty over small washes and wove through cedar trees.

Ashley picked it up quickly, to my utter confusion. After I swung on behind her, I instinctively put my arms around her to demonstrate how the reins worked. I didn't realize the situation I was in until the smell of her hair hit my brain. I was sitting close . . . really close. My heart began thumping like a jack hammer, and I started sweating. Hurriedly, I showed her the basic steering maneuvers and sat back stiffly. Since Jodi attacked me in first grade, I hadn't been that close to a girl. It was nerve-racking and exhilarating all at the same time. My desires began battling my fears and the result was petrified stupefaction. (Yes, that's a word, and it's exactly how I felt!)

In spite of my obvious problems, Ashley seemed to absolutely love the ride! If she hadn't been so engrossed with the horse, she most likely would've noticed my awkwardness. Gratefully, with each step we took, my old walls began to break down. By the time we reached Lost Lake, almost two hours later, I was honestly hoping she would drop the reins, so I would have an excuse to reach around her again!

Ashley gasped as we rode our horses over the bank. "You weren't kidding!" she exclaimed with wide eyes. "We really *have* ridden our camel to an oasis. This place is amazing!"

Tracy dismounted leaving Frank to fend for himself and walked down to the rope swing by the water's edge. She grabbed onto the old bicycle handle bars, walked backward a few steps, and let herself glide out over the water. With a smile of wonder, she said, "If I had known about *this*, I would've come in my swimming suit!"

"Yeah, me too," added Frank, almost in disgust. I'm sure he would've loved an excuse to get our dates in swim suits.

"Sorry, I didn't think about it," I replied. "We planned the date when I still had my cast on, and I knew I couldn't swim. Besides, some September days can be pretty cold."

It would've been perfect today, though. It was nearly eighty degrees and very calm. Pointing back to a large limb about ten feet off the ground I said, "Usually, my brother Josh and I swing from there. It launches you way out into the lake."

Tracy's eyes glinted, and I could tell she was calculating something devious. Frank looked in amazement and said, "You swing from up there?"

"How deep is the water?" Tracy asked.

"Around twelve feet, I think," I replied. "Deep enough that we never hit bottom."

Turning to Frank, Tracy said, "I'll make you a deal. If you go off the swing, I will too."

Frank looked at her in surprise. "You'll go off that?" he asked, pointing to the limb.

"Yep," she replied. "Come on, are you chicken?"

"No!" he shot back. "I just don't think you'll do it."

"What? You don't trust me?" she asked with exaggerated innocence.

"Nope," he retorted flatly.

"Okay, if I don't go . . . I'll let you kiss me tonight."

Frank's eyebrows shot up for a moment, but quickly narrowed. Scrutinizing her with a dagger like stare, he asked, "Do you have ten bucks?"

In shock Tracy replied, "Ouch. You would rather have my money than a kiss?"

"Let's call it insurance, in case you get cold feet later."

Tracy gripped her heart in mock pain and said, "Oh, that hurts." But not wanting to pass this up, she quickly agreed, "Okay, fine," and reached into her leather pants and pulled out a few bills. "All I've got is seven. Is that enough to buy your courage?"

"Courage?" Frank laughed. "It's not my courage on the line here; it's your honesty!"

Tracy looked him straight in the eye and said, "Prove it."

"I will! I'll prove you wrong, too! I don't think you'll swing, and I don't think you'll let me kiss you!" Frank walked over to her. "But to make sure I get something besides the satisfaction of proving you wrong, I'm taking this," and he snatched the money from her hand. Tracy just smirked at him. He walked over to me and started emptying his pockets. "Will you hold this? And make sure Miss Sassy Britches doesn't take it back when I'm not looking." I nodded my head.

Ashley and I stood there not knowing what to do or say as Frank removed his shoes, socks, and shirt. He stomped over to the tree and climbed the ladder of old boards we'd nailed to the trunk. When he moved out on the limb, I tossed him the swing. Even though it's only ten feet from limb to base, the bank slopes down about ten more feet to the water's edge. When you stand on the limb, it's a LONG way to the water. Balancing with one hand braced on the trunk, Frank stood motionless; the white-knuckled grip of his other hand discernible from where we stood below.

"What did you say about courage?" Tracy taunted.

Frank's look grew determined. He grabbed the handle bar with both hands and jumped. He flew by us with a *Swoosh*! At the peak of his swing, he let go nearly twenty feet in the air. On the way out, his momentum twisted him around, and coupled with a clumsy release, he ended up being nearly horizontal when gravity took over. His arms and legs flailed wildly trying to gain a better position, but it wasn't enough. He landed face first with a loud "SLAP!" We all gasped in unison. I knew what that felt like. The first time I tried a back flip off the swing, I did something similar but landed more on my side. When you hit the water from that high, it feels like concrete!

Tracy started laughing so hard she fell over. Ashley stood there, both hands covering her mouth. Her eyebrows were raised high over laughing eyes. I was about to go in after Frank when his head shot out of the water with a gasp. A look of extreme pain covered his face. He slowly swam to shore where he pulled himself onto the bank and rolled onto his back with a groan.

Tears were running down Tracy's face, but when she saw his chest, she gave an honest effort to tone it down. Half laughing, half coughing she said, "Oh, Frank!" and scooted over to where he'd collapsed on the bank. His chest and the right side of his face were bright red, and there were even a few specks of blood on his right shoulder where the vessels had broken. She softly touched where the blood was seeping through the skin in tiny beads and said, "Now, that was a stupid thing to do!"

Frank didn't say a word, but slowly turned his head and gave her a look that would have stopped a charging bull. Sputtering in self-defense, Tracy argued, "I never said you had to belly flop!" Frank rolled his eyes. "But I have to give you credit," she continued as a smile crept back onto her face. "That was, by far, the best belly flop I have **ever** seen!"

We couldn't hold it in any longer. Ashley and I burst out laughing! Tracy laughed too, but not as hard. Frank even chuckled slightly, at least until the pain stopped him. He wrapped his arms around his red chest in an attempt to ease the torture, and said, "Stop it! You're making it hurt worse."

We sat a while longer. Of course, Tracy wanted nothing to do with the swing after seeing Frank's amazing stunt. I don't think she was planning on it in the first place. She teased about it being the best seven dollars she ever spent. Frank glared, and in a soft but direct voice, he said, "You haven't finished paying, yet."

"Maybe," Tracy replied, her sassy attitude back in full color. "You better behave yourself, or seven dollars and a lot of pain is all you'll get out of this deal." Frank accepted the threat with narrowed eyes but decided not to press the issue.

The sun was just starting to touch the tops of the hills by this time. I knew we'd need some coals soon, so I set about gathering wood while Frank, very painfully, tried to pull his shirt back on. I thought he was exaggerating a tad, but it had the desired effect. Both girls jumped to help him. That guy soaks up attention like a dry cow turd in the first summer storm.

I got the fire going about the same time Frank finally got his shoes on. He stood with a groan and shuffled over to help get stuff out of the back of the truck.

"So, what's for dinner, Señor Chefs?" Ashley asked with a Spanish accent.

"It's a surprise," I answered, as we set the cooler on the ground. "What, you don't trust us?"

Before Ashley had a chance to reply, Tracy cut in, "Nope, not yet." She was leaning over the fire, torturing a small cedar branch in the flames.

Frank was pulling out a few camp chairs and without turning to look at her, he snorted and countered, "I definitely think it should be *us* not trusting *you*." Tracy smiled in response. I think she knew he was right.

It felt good to finally relax in a chair. Without being able to brace myself in stirrups, the horse ride was more taxing than expected. We watched flames dance on dry cedar limbs for a time, content with the silence. There's something calming about a fire. The sun had dropped behind The High Hills, but I could tell by the light in the sky it hadn't gone down yet.

I turned to the girls and said, "Hey, it's going to be a while before the coals are ready. Do you want to ride to the top of that hill and watch the sun set? It's a pretty amazing view." The idea of another adventure, snapped them out of their fire hypnosis, but to my surprise, Frank sagged deeper in his seat. His day hadn't gone quite as planned, and I don't think he wanted to get back on the horse. It wasn't exactly a pleasant ride out.

"Come on, Frank, it'll be fun!" Tracy said as she reached for his hand.

"Yeah, that's what you said about the last activity," he replied suspiciously. He didn't deny her help though, and she pulled him reluctantly to his feet. The ride back to the west side of the valley didn't take long, but by the time we reached the top of the hill, the sun was almost gone. Our horses were pretty winded after the climb, so we dismounted to give them a breather. Ashley and I found a spot to sit on a gnarled stump, and Tracy and Frank moved about twenty feet away to an outcropping of rock where they sat with their legs hanging over a small ledge.

"Wow! You weren't kidding about the view!" Ashley said in astonishment. We could see for miles in every direction. With magnificent mountains to the south and stunning valleys and ridges all around us, there was more to see than days of gazing would allow. But for all the stunning variety in the landscape, our eyes were automatically drawn heavenward. Mild pinks and soft reds reflected in breathtaking arrangements from thin clouds, frozen majestically on a canvas of purplish-blue. Arizona is famous for some of the most stunning sunsets in the world, and today we were not disappointed. In spite of all the beauty above, in the final rays of light that skipped across the land, I found myself looking down.

The tops of all The High Hills are covered in an amazing assortment of rocks, and I couldn't help but notice when the light glinted off a small stone, completely white and smooth. I picked it up and turned it over in my hand. My thoughts went to a similar rock sitting under my bed in an old ammunition box. *Elli. What are you doing right now? Are you sharing a similar evening with Jared?* As my mind went to a girl probably a million miles and a million years away, I briefly forgot about the girl sitting right next to me.

"That's a pretty rock." The comment jolted me back to reality, and I was suddenly embarrassed. I turned to see Ashley looking at me with amusement. "Is that some kind of rare gem?" she asked teasingly.

"Oh, it's not a gem," I replied sheepishly. I sat for a second not knowing what else to say. I've never told anyone about my fascination with rocks, and my first reaction was to hide, but she hadn't shunned my Wranglers, so I thought, *what the heck.* "I've been collecting rocks for as long as I can remember."

"Really?" she replied with astonishment. "I keep learning *new* things about you, David. Is there anything *else* you're hiding that I should know about?"

"Maybe," I said with a smile. Glancing around as if nervously searching for spies, I leaned toward her and whispered, *"But if I tell ya, I'll have to kill ya."*

Without blinking she leaned in, too, and whispered back, *"My dad warned me about guys like you."* She gave me a paralyzing grin.

My heart started thumping again, and this time, I think she heard it. Her eyebrows rose slightly as if daring me to lean closer. A strong, warm, tingly feeling began sucking me in! In a flash of panic, I sat back hard and looked quickly down at the rock in my hand. I kept rolling it nervously over and over again. That was my chance . . . and I blew it.

In a last ditch attempt to drag my shamed ego out of the pit of awkwardness, I said, "This is actually one of my favorite kinds. It always amazes me how, in the middle of all these different rocks, you can find one that's completely white. And how did it get this smooth?" I left the question hanging.

"Huh," was all she said. I turned to see her looking down as well. When she turned to me again, she seemed genuinely surprised. "I've never looked at rocks before. They're all different colors!" She reached down and picked up a dark brown stone that appeared to be swirled with yellow paint. "How'd they get like this?"

"I don't know," I replied, some of the tension leaving my stiff back. "That's what's amazing about it."

She turned to me with a smile and said, "Thank you. I've tried painting a lot of amazing scenes, but I've never noticed the beauty of rocks before." Her compliment helped lift me from my rapidly decompressing self-esteem.

I smiled back and said, "You're welcome. Here, why don't you keep this one? Now you can start your own collection." Ashley took the stone and held it protectively.

"Thank you. Maybe I'll do that." As she placed the rock in her pocket, I noticed for the first time it was completely silent on the hill. I looked up to see Frank sitting with his back slightly turned to Tracy, a very impatient look on his face. Tracy was oblivious to anything except her phone. Her fingers were flying over the keys as she texted something that, apparently, was more important than rocks, a sunset, and even Frank. Poor guy couldn't get anything to go his way today.

Frank stood up quickly and said, "We'd better get back to the fire if we want to have time for dinner."

"Oh, okay," Tracy responded nonchalantly. Turning to Ashley with a look of shock, she said, "Did you hear Jessica told Troy last night she wasn't going with him to Homecoming?" and the whole way back to the fire we were filled in on the latest town gossip. Frank sat behind Tracy with a sullen look on his face.

Dinner went well. The tinfoil dinners were slightly burned, but the cobbler turned out great, and that's the most important part. We packed up and got back to town around 8:15. Frank had picked out neon-green shirts from Walmart for all of us, and the girls said they would only need about forty-five minutes to get ready. Of course they were late, and by the time we waited in line to have our pictures taken, it was almost 11:00. We danced a few slow songs, but most of them were fast. I didn't move around much for either, but at least I got to hold Ashley's hand during the slow ones. Frank was off balance all night. He wasn't his usual carefree self at the dance, and I could tell something was bothering him.

We left around 11:45. All of us had the midnight curfew and didn't want angry parents joining the party. We took Ashley home first, since she lives the closest. As I walked her to the door, I told her what a great time I had and thanked her for going with me.

"I enjoyed it too! It was fun getting to know you better." She turned and smiled up at me, "And thanks for my gem."

I smiled back and said, "You're welcome."

We reached her front door, and my heart rate began to increase. People always talk about kissing goodnight on the doorstep, and Frank told me it was perfectly okay since we had technically been on a few dates already, but I was still freaking out. She stood there for a moment . . . I stood there for a moment . . . then she said, "I hope we can do this again sometime."

"Yeah, I hope so, too," I replied. There was another long, awkward silence, and Ashley got a mischievous grin.

"Would it hurt if I gave you a hug?" Her eyebrows shot up again, daring me to accept.

I let out the breath I didn't realize I was holding and smiled back. "I don't think it'll do *too* much damage." She wrapped her arms around my neck, and I hugged her back, taking special care not to hurt my arm this time.

"I really did have a great time," she said as we pulled apart. "Thank you."

"You're welcome. I had a great time, too."

She turned and opened the door. Looking back she said, "Good night, David."

I managed a nervous, "Good night," and walked back to the car disappointed with myself.

When I slid into the back seat of Frank's car, I noticed the soft clicking noise of cell phone buttons. Tracy was in the front, texting again, and Frank was staring out his window.

We pulled onto the street, and Tracy said in exasperation, "Sorry, apparently there's a lot more to the story with Jessica and Troy than I thought." When neither Frank nor I asked about it further, she decided to change the subject. "So, what did you think about Zack and Lexi's outfits tonight? I thought she should have been kicked out for immodesty. That shirt was cut **way** too low!"

Frank got an evil grin. *Oh no*, I thought, but all I could do was cringe. He shrugged his shoulders and said, "I don't know, I thought she looked fine."

"You think Lexi is pretty hot, do ya?" Tracy snapped back.

Without pausing, Frank replied, "Heck, yeah!" It sounded too enthusiastic. I think Frank saw an opportunity to take a jab and was anxious to start throwing punches. "What, Tracy? Do you think Zack *isn't* good looking?"

"Zack is a self-centered jerk, and I bet he carries a comb in his back pocket!" Frank's head drooped. His last attempt to get an ounce of satisfaction from his day, even if it was with cruel intentions, deflated like a popped balloon. Tracy didn't know Frank carries a comb with him everywhere he goes. "Besides, Frank, I've heard Lexi has two boyfriends in California. I see her texting everywhere she goes." Apparently, that was evidence enough to convict her of immoral crimes.

Frank's game had been way off all day, and this was the last move into check mate. He slumped in his chair, all wittiness and charm reduced to dust. I'd been watching the comedic battle all day, but now I was beginning to get worried. Tracy must have noticed something wrong, too, because after a pause, she asked, "Frank, are you okay?"

"Oh, I'm fine," he said with a shrug. "I'm just not feeling very good." It was a bad attempt at hiding the truth, and Tracy could tell.

"Is it from your spectacular belly flop today?" she asked while trying to conceal a smile.

"Yeah, I think that's part of it." We had pulled up to Tracy's house at this point. Tracy didn't wait for Frank to come open her door. It's just as well. Frank probably wouldn't have done it even if she waited. I watched them walk slowly to the front door where they stopped to continue their conversation. To my surprise, Frank started getting more and more animated with what seemed like anger. Tracy folded her arms and stood expressionless for probably a good thirty seconds. All of a sudden, she seized him by the front of the shirt, jerked him in close and kissed him square on the lips! For a brief second, Frank went completely rigid, his hands frozen in mid tirade. Before he realized what had happened, she shoved him backward hard. He stumbled a few steps and almost went down. She barked one last thing, walked inside, and slammed the door. Frank staggered back to the car and flopped in the seat. His hands hung limp by his side as he stared blankly through the windshield.

"What . . . happened?" I asked in astonishment.

He kept gazing forward with the same comatose stare and quietly said, "I'm not sure." His head shook slowly side to side in a daze. Turning to look at me, suddenly a huge grin cracked open his face. "But I think she likes me!"

For the second time today, I exploded with uncontrollable laughter. Holding my stomach, I started gasping for air. Dreamily, Frank put the car in drive and pulled onto the road, the same stupid smile stuck on his face. I had just witnessed twitterpation first hand. When I finally caught my breath, I asked him to tell me what happened. Apparently, she kept asking what was wrong and wouldn't let it drop, so Frank decided to tell her the truth. He told her how he had tried repeatedly to impress her and act cool to make her like him, but she kept stealing his punch lines and making fun of him. Later, when he attempted his moves for a romantic kiss on the hill, she wouldn't put down the stupid phone! It was right after this comment when she attacked. The last thing she yelled before slamming the door was, "Now we're even!"

Still chuckling, I told him, "I don't know, Frank, she looked pretty mad."

He shook his head confidently this time, and said, "No. You didn't feel that kiss, man. What a woman!" I laughed all the way home.

Even though there were some ups and downs, it ended up being a pretty good Homecoming date after all. As I wrote all this down, I couldn't help but start laughing again. Looking back, I actually couldn't tell who had a more awkward date, me or Frank. That made me feel somewhat better about all my inadequacies. Even though I wasn't brave enough to get my first kiss, I'm kind of glad I didn't. I've never felt such strong emotions. When she started pulling me in with her secret mind powers, luckily, shock engaged the flee button instead of attack! Either way, I had no control, no defense! Yeah, I know—*David, you wuss, it's just a kiss!* But for me it was more than that. Without personal boundaries what would keep me from going too far and doing something I'd regret? I passed a milestone I thought I'd never reach, and now I realize I've no idea how to proceed. I have to figure some things out, but maybe another time; right now I'm completely exhausted. It's been a very good but very *long* day.

Sunday, 25 September, 2011

Sometimes I'm glad for Sundays to get here, and other times I get bored out of my mind, but today I needed a day of rest. A lot has happened this week, and I haven't had time to really sit down and think about it much. I slept in as long as I could and almost missed church, but I'm glad I went. I've been enjoying it a lot more since I found Elli. Her comments have been digging under my skin and churning up a curiosity I've never felt before. It seems like I'm finally learning things for the first time that I've been told my whole life. Even so, I still can't figure out what she was trying to say the last time we talked. She made it seem like I was missing the whole picture! Well, at least when it comes to why I'm here on earth. She accused me of not seeing the eternal importance of life, and I couldn't disprove her. I had Homecoming week with all its activities, I re-broke my arm and lost my dream all over again, and as if life weren't screwed up enough, I go and throw a girl right in the middle of it!

After we got home from church and had Sunday dinner, I found myself sitting outside on the front porch. One of the first things Mom got when we moved to Snowflake was an old, wooden swing. I helped Gramps put it up, even though I probably wasn't much help back then. It's our favorite spot when we're in need of some peace and quiet. Mom keeps a few flowers growing under the window and insists we mow the grass every Saturday so the lawn is nice and trim for Sunday. Across the street, to the east, is Grandma's house. The barn and corrals sit to the south, and the fields run behind their place down to the creek. It's a beautiful view.

I wasn't sitting long when Mom came out and asked if she could join me. I scooted over to make some room. We slowly swayed back and forth, our only intrusion was the high creaks of the swing chain. After a few minutes, Mom finally broke the squeaky silence. With a knowing smile she said, "You've had quite an eventful week."

I guffawed in exaggeration, "You can say that again."

She paused for a few more swings and added, "Ashley seems like a really nice girl. How was your date?"

"It was great! Yeah, she's pretty cool." My answer was vague, but girls are a topic we'd never breached, and neither of us knew what else to say. In an awkward attempt, I said, "Did I tell you she's never ridden a horse before?"

Mom looked a little surprised. "No, you didn't. Did she enjoy it?"

"Yeah, she got the hang of it *really* quick," I said sadly. My mind flashed back to the brief moment I had my arms around her. "I think she liked it a lot."

As I replayed the main events of yesterday, I began to laugh. Mom watched me quizzically, and when I caught my breath, I described in detail the world's worst belly flop. My eyes began to water when I reached the moment of impact. I'm not sure if Mom was laughing more at me or Frank, but I loved the sound of it. It was a precious addition to an already unforgettable memory.

After some time, the chain once again dominated the conversation. The world was at peace and at the peak of its majesty. Birds played in Mom's peach tree, and everything seemed to be merrily soaking up the warm rays in preparation for a rapidly approaching fall.

"How's your arm, David?"

I studied it while maneuvering through a handful of motions. "It hasn't been bothering me as much as before, but I still feel pain if I'm not careful."

She thought for a minute and asked, "Have I ever told you my experience when your father asked me to marry him?"

This caught me off guard. Mom rarely talked about Bo. "No, I don't think so," I replied.

"After your father asked me to marry him, I was very confused. You see, I loved Bo very much, but I knew he had weaknesses. I didn't know what I should do, so I took a trip home. I told Mom and Dad my situation and asked for their advice. I'll never forget it. They looked at each other, and then Dad looked me in the eyes and told me to figure it out on my own. I was crushed! I expected them to fix my problems or take them away. Mom suggested the best way to figure things out was to come up with an answer myself, make a decision, and ask God if it was right. She told me the most important thing was to get direction from God.

Then, no matter what happened, I would know I did the right thing."

"So what happened?" I asked, intrigued.

"I stayed for a few days and did a lot of pondering and praying. In the end, I felt like I *should* marry Bo. I went into my room and knelt by my bed and asked God if this was the right course. I still remember my answer as clear as if it happened yesterday. In my heart I felt comfort and peace, and the thought came into my head to ask Dad for a blessing."

In case you're not familiar with blessings, I'll quickly explain. In the Church, any worthy man can be given the Priesthood. This gives him authority to perform ordinances like baptism and give blessings of healing and counsel, like Christ did. Grandpa was given this priesthood long ago, and so he's able to also give blessings. Back to Mom's story.

She continued, "Of course, Dad was happy to give me a blessing. I remember a great feeling of calm come over me as he started to speak, and though I don't remember much of what he said, one thing really stood out. He told me the Lord supported my decision, and though I would experience much pain, my joy would be *far* sweeter."

I knew about Mom's pain. We had experienced much of it together, but I had never considered her joy. In my confusion, I asked, "Have you had more joy than pain?"

She smiled tenderly and replied, "More than I could have ever hoped for. He gave me three of the greatest joys in the world."

I knew she was talking about us kids, but I still didn't understand how it was possible. Being somewhat ornery, I said, "Even when we fight and knock your favorite mirror off the wall?"

"Well . . ." she teasingly rubbed her chin as if in deep thought, "some days are less *joyful* than others, I guess." She smiled softly and said, "but I wouldn't trade them for anything." We sat a while longer staring across the valley. After a few minutes, she got off the swing and started for the front door. Pulling it slightly open, she stopped and looked back at me. "I love you, son."

"I love you too, Mom." The door closed with a soft thump. As I chewed on what she said, I chuckled at her "eventful week" comment—a small description for such big experiences. Sure it had its high moments, but in the end, it left me with more questions than answers.

Football. I love the sport. I've given my life to it . . . now what? I thought about Ashley and girls in general. How ironic to find out now how hopelessly attracted I am to the sneaky critters. It scares me, because the feelings are stronger than my control. It's like I got thrown on a wild horse without a bridle or saddle. No wonder I jumped away! And there was Elli's comment. What's so important about our messed up existence that we would *want* to leave Heaven to come down here? Without answers to cool down my mental struggling, my head began to overheat.

It was nearly dark, so I jumped down and walked back inside. Josh and Sarah were watching *The Prince of Egypt* . . . again, so I sat down on the couch. Mom prefers we watch church-type movies on the Sabbath, and we only have three of them. Sometimes we can convince her to let us watch a Disney, as long as it teaches good morals.

After sitting restlessly for a few minutes, I went to my room and slid the old ammunition box from under my bed. Gramps said I could keep the cool treasure after I discovered it under a pile of used windmill parts. The latch opened with a clank, and I pulled out the Airlis wrapped in an old beanie. No matter how brightly my hope flickered, it could not change the inevitable. The stone remained silent.

Letting out my breath in exasperation, I flopped on the bed and began rolling the Airlis over in my hands. The smooth surface and uncommon coloring made it easy to start the bad habit. Turning the rock slowly in my palms, I found myself doing the same thing with my thoughts. Maybe answers would come if I looked at matters from a different angle . . . but all it did was churn everything into one confusing lump. Finally, I decided I was going to need more help if I wanted to get anywhere. I set the Airlis down and slid to my knees.

It was a short prayer, but I meant every word. I simply asked God to help me find answers. There was no voice or mighty impression, but I wasn't necessarily expecting that. I simply wanted help, and so I returned to my pillow, picked up the Airlis, and started rolling things over again. My thoughts kept returning to Mom's story and how she felt impressed to get a blessing. The idea gnawed at me, and the more I pondered it, the more it felt right. I decided it would be a great place to start, and I put on some shoes.

Our front screen door banged closed behind me, and I sauntered across the street. As always, I knocked once and walked in. Grandma was in the family room watching the news and crocheting something in blue yarn. Gramps was sitting next to her reading a thick book.

"Hello, David," Grandma said in her soft voice.

At only 5' 4", she's the sweetest little grandma I've ever seen. Years of life have left its mark on everything except her short gray hair. Always arranged in a stylish poof, somehow it continues defying gravity!

She gave me a wrinkled smile and asked, "How are you, dear?"

"Hi, Grandma. I'm good. I came over to see how you guys are doing." It wasn't exactly true, but I wasn't sure how to ask Grandpa, and I was stalling, searching for the right moment.

"Oh, we're both fine and dandy," she said. "How was your date with the Dunn girl?"

"We had a great time. Thanks for letting us borrow the horses, Gramps."

Grandpa glanced up for a moment then looked back to his book as he said, "I'm just glad no one got hurt."

Grandma set her work in her lap and looked off into the distance. "I remember when I used to teach her mother in Primary. Debby was such a cute little thing." After a moment lost in her memories, she picked up a long hook and returned to a rhythmic motion.

"Yep, sure does," I answered without really thinking about what I was saying. The silence that followed revealed the soft tick of a clock. Apparently, that was all they needed to remain content with their slower way of life.

I don't know why it's hard to ask Gramps for things, but I decided if I didn't speak up now, I would likely never do it. "Grandpa, do you think you could give me a blessing?"

He stopped reading, set down his book, and took a long look at me. "Sure, David. Why? Are you sick?"

"Well no, not really. I don't know if Mom told you or not, but I think I might've re-broken my arm Friday night."

Grandma gasped, "Oh, David! No, she didn't tell us. Are you okay?"

"Yeah, I'm fine. It only throbs a little—unless I put a lot of weight on it." I thought about all the other reasons I wanted a blessing, but I couldn't find the courage to confess my mental struggles, too.

Grandpa stood up and started for the formal sitting room. "Of course I will, son. Come in here and take a seat."

He stood at the door and motioned me inside. As I sat down, he asked if I would be willing to wait a few minutes while he rounded up another elder to help administer the blessing. I hadn't realized I'd be such an inconvenience, but it was too late to turn back now. Gramps called our neighbor who happens to be the second counselor in the Bishopric, and he came right over. Brother Lowry anointed me with oil, and Gramps sealed the anointing and gave me a blessing.

I've had a few blessings before but not in a long time. After opening the prayer, Gramps paused. Instead of healing my arm, or even hinting to a speedy recovery as I thought he might, he said something else.

"David . . . if you have faith in Jesus Christ and believe that through Him miracles can happen, you will regain the use of your arm for the fulfillment of all your goals and dreams. Though you might experience some pain, if you put your trust in the arm of the Lord, your arm will not fail." To my greater surprise, right before he closed, he said, "Also, if you will seek out the principles and guidelines the Lord has given the youth through his modern Prophets, you will find the answers and the joy you seek."

His words astounded me. I could feel them settling in my heart. Peace came over me like a warm blanket. I thanked Brother Lowry and gave Gramps a hug. He's the kind of man I'd like to be someday. It's amazing how God, having billions of children and worlds without number, is mindful not only of my broken arm but also my concerns about girls. It's hard to fathom, but somehow, it's true.

On my way home, I kept staring at my arm and rolling my wrist around to see if I could feel anything different. As far as I could tell, nothing had changed. He didn't say it would be healed directly, but that it would heal according to my faith in Christ. *Oh great*, I thought. *I wonder how far that'll get me.*

I wasn't ready to go in the house, so I sat on the front swing again. When I broke my arm before, the motion that always brought pain happened when I'd ball my hand into a fist and push down. I clenched my fist and slowly pushed against the swing in anticipation. At first I didn't feel anything, so I pushed a bit harder. A shot of fire ran down my arm and made me grimace. Disappointment covered me like a dark, heavy shadow. My faith must be pretty weak indeed. But as doubts began filling my mind, I thought about a story we'd learned in Seminary last week.

Most people know about Abraham, but in case your memory is a little rusty, I'll give you a quick re-cap. Abraham and his wife Sarah tried for years to have children, but at last gave up hope. In their old age, God blessed them with Isaac. Not many years later, God spoke again to Abraham and commanded him to take Isaac into the mountains and sacrifice him. It's hard to believe God would ask this of him, but Abraham decided he would be obedient. He took Isaac and climbed to the top of a mountain where he built an altar, then tied up his son and placed him on it. He picked up the knife and was about to kill him, when an angel appeared and stopped Abraham. You see, it wasn't until after he'd done all this that God sent an angel to stop him and tell him he had passed his test of faith.

Now I know my meager trials in life don't begin to compare to Abraham's, but I think we're all given tests. We all have mountains that stand between us and a better life. The question we must ask ourselves is: Am I going to climb it? Am I going to give it everything I've got and put my faith in the Lord, or am I going to turn back and say it's too hard?

Reflecting on Abraham and his trial of faith was the faint ray of light I needed to make my decision. No matter how much it hurts, I'm going to give football my all! It feels good to have a goal and a dream to fight for again.

When I excitedly shared my experience with Mom, she was so overcome by my sudden change, I couldn't tell if it was harder for her to get words out or keep tears in! After a few seconds, she said, "Son, I am so *proud* of you," and she gave me a hug.

Moms sure know how to make you feel better. It must be a special gift they have. Maybe it's part of a girl's secret powers. First they use it to lure in the husband of their choice, and then it morphs into a healing agent once they become mothers. Who knows? I doubt they'll ever tell their secrets.

Speaking of girls, after I finished visiting with Mom, I went to my room and found my "For the Strength of Youth" pamphlet. It's a booklet of guidelines specifically for the Church's youth that covers topics from how we should speak and dress to what we should read and listen to. It also talks about proper standards for relationships and dating. Bishop gave it to me when I became a Deacon at age twelve, and admonished me to read it. We've gone over most of it in Sunday School, but I've never read the whole thing myself.

It took me over an hour, but I finally got from cover to cover. It's crazy how much these guidelines differ from the way the world views moral standards. Sadly, I'd forgotten many, and there are a few I've not been living very well. Again, I thought about what Gramps said. I figured if I'm going to give football all I've got, I'd better not hold God's standards with any less enthusiasm. Even though I know a few of them will be pretty difficult (like watching my language and keeping my thoughts clean), it's my new goal to live them as closely as I can. I've found a mountain to climb!

Monday, 26 September, 2011

I surprised coach today. I guess he was expecting the worst about my arm, and when I came running onto the field for practice, he did a double take, "Thorn? What are you doing in pads?" I told him it must've been a stinger or something, because my arm was feeling a lot better, which was partly true. I dug up an arm pad out of the "spare parts" bin in the locker room and slid it over my forearm. It helped ease my mind, but my arm still felt pretty vulnerable.

It didn't take long till I got the first trial of my faith. It was a seam route straight down the field. The ball was thrown perfectly, just over my head, and when it hit my hands, I felt a sharp pain shoot down my right forearm. I didn't drop the pass (and I didn't cuss!), but I did grit my teeth as doubt filled my mind. Forcing myself to recall Grandpa's words, I thought, *If I put my trust in the arm of the Lord, my arm will not fail.* This gave me the hope I needed to keep going. With every pass, the pain got less and less, and my faith grew more and more. Why does God care about me? I'm only one person in billions. I don't know how He does it, but somehow He really does care for each one of us. It's very humbling to get a glimpse of God's love, and oh, how amazing!

Switching to the funny side of the day, let me fill you in on what happened to my dear friend, Frank. Walking back from Seminary with Ashley and Tracy, I couldn't help but notice the topic of Frank was being avoided. Later, as Frank and I were leaving English on our way to lunch, we happened to run into the girls heading to Ashley's car. Frank tried to say hello, but Tracy flipped her hair and looked away as if he didn't exist. She can give a vicious cold shoulder. I looked at Ashley and she shrugged, not knowing what to do or say.

After a brief, awkward silence, I asked, "So . . . do you guys want to get some lunch?"

Tracy answered. "Oh, that would be great and all, but Mom's already expecting us." Ashley mouthed the word—*sorry*—as Tracy dragged her to the parking lot by the elbow.

"Some other time, then?" Frank called out in a last ditch effort for acknowledgment. The question was as flatly ignored as his greeting.

I slapped him on the back and teased, "What's wrong? Have you lost your A-game?"

Shaking his head, he put his arm around my shoulders and said, "Oh, David, the best trophies are the ones you have to work the hardest to get."

"I think you've got it backward, Frank." I shoved him away. "She's got you shot, skinned, and stuffed!" He looked back across the parking lot at where the girls were getting into Ashley's car. I continued sarcastically, "You prove my point. Bambi."

He whipped around and almost shouted, "Oh, and *you* have room to talk? I'm not the only one twitterpated here, **David**. I've seen you wait by Fish Hall, so you can sneak off behind the auditorium with your *girlfriend*."

This caught me off guard. Fueled by embarrassment and anger, my ears began heating up. I hadn't realized how it might appear to other people. I defensively replied, "You know nothing happens, Frank. We barely have time to make it to class, and sometimes we even have to run so we're not late!"

"Oh, *that's* why you come into choir out of breath," he said with a Cheshire grin.

"Oh, shut up!" I sputtered. "Let's go to lunch."

"Sounds good to me," he said with a shrug. We walked to my truck in silence and climbed inside. As we drove off, he smirked and said, "You realize, if I'm Bambi, that makes you Flower!" and he busted up.

"Now you're hitting below the belt," I replied, and as embarrassed as I had been, I couldn't help smiling. "Oh, what would those girls think if they heard us talking about *Bambi*. We should be ashamed of ourselves."

Frank's face filled with mock pain and he asked, "What's wrong with *Bambi*?"

Tuesday, 27 September, 2011

After dinner tonight, I grabbed the Airlis and a blanket and sat on the front swing. Elli probably wouldn't contact me for a half hour, but I needed time to have my thoughts to myself. Last Tuesday seemed so long ago. A lot happened while we were worlds apart. Ha! Who would *ever* use that phrase literally unless it was in a *Star Wars* movie? Crazy. Anyway, I thought about my date and how much fun it's been getting to know Ashley. My injured arm has been like a bad roller coaster ride, but things are finally looking up. It seemed to hurt even less today. At times I almost felt back to normal. With each pass, my faith in God grows. It's such a strange experience to be learning spiritual lessons and football plays at the same time.

David?

Elli! How are you? It was weird, but I could've sworn I felt the Airlis . . . activate? It was the reason I looked down.

I'm well, thank you—that was strange.

What happened?

I was sitting down on the bench when something in the Airlis stirred. For a moment I thought you were trying to speak, so I looked down. Instead of seeing your thoughts, the outline of an image began to appear. But as my mind spoke your name . . . the cloud vanished, and once again I saw only words. Hmm, very interesting.

Yeah, strange. Well, I'm glad it's still working!

Yes, I am as well. How was your date? I've been curious about it all day!

I took a mental breath and dived in. Elli asked few questions, content to let me ramble on. It must've taken me thirty minutes to give her all the details.

Oh, what a wonderful time you both must have had! I only wish I could have been there to experience it with you.

Yeah, I wish you could, too, I replied with a bit more longing than I expected. To take an angel on a horseback ride, now wouldn't that be something. I focused back in my thoughts and asked, How are you and Jared?

Our relationship seems to be blossoming, as well! He came by to walk with me on our way to History, and it's a long way out of his usual path.

I know how you feel, I thought with a grin. I hope things continue to go well for you guys.

Thank you. I have high expectations they will. Changing the subject, she asked, *How about your arm? Has it completely healed?* Once again, I found myself going off on a long-waved tangent. (I tried to use *long winded,* but realized . . . my thoughts don't breath! ☺) I told her all about the re-injury, the hug of pain, the battle in my head, the emotional cast removal, and finished with Gramps blessing and the miracle from God.

The Airlis was blank for a few moments, and then Elli replied, *David, you have no idea how amazing your experiences truly are. It is phenomenal to see your growth first hand!*

What do you mean? I asked confused. I'm just a normal guy going through a normal life.

Okay, to you who stole my journal and are reading it without my consent: between you and me, maybe I'm not exactly what you'd call a "normal" guy, but she doesn't know that, and I'm not about to describe all my social failures to an angel. The point I was *trying* to make was down here I'm nothing special, and even though I think she understood, I wanted to make sure you were on the same page, too. Capeesh?

She replied, *No, you're not normal, at least not from the studies I've done, and I think it's great!*

Oh, I thought deflatedly. And yes, I know, I made that word up. It fits—get over it. It's how you think when an angel tells you you're not normal. What do you mean? I asked after my deflatedness.

How to explain . . . to grow spiritually when you are a spirit, takes a very long process. Habits, talents, and even hobbies like painting take years to create and change. The hardest of which is the expansion of light and intelligence. In a mortal world, with

118

mortal bodies governed by agency, the same process is magnified when used correctly. What would take me years to gain as a spirit would come much faster if accomplished with a physical body.

Huh? How is that possible?

I'm not sure exactly. I was told it has something to do with the power of faith. When your faith in your God is tested to extremes and you combine that with self-control over the natural desires of your mortal body, the results are staggering!

Huh. I guess I'll have to take your word on that one.

Trust me. It may be unclear from your perspective, but for me it's like gazing into a pure lake of water.

I did feel like I learned a lot this week. I might have even grown a bit, too, I guess.

Believe me, you did. And I am very happy for you!

I jokingly replied, At least, for once, it seems like I'm moving in the right direction.

Changing the mood, she warned, *Be careful. We have studied this very subject recently, and as fast as you climb in a good direction, you can fall away much faster.* Her words brought to mind some kids I know in school who are sliding down the wrong path and others who have jumped rather willingly.

Thanks for the advice, I said sincerely. Yeah, I don't want to fall either. Besides, I can tell this upward climb really has been making me a lot happier.

Watching you change has filled my heart with joy as well. Please don't give up. I could not bear to see you fall back into darkness.

I won't, I promised, and I meant it. I kinda like this path I'm on. You know, Elli, I'm really glad I met you. This last thought sorta slipped out, but I was all right with that.

I'm glad I met you, too. You are a good man, David. Sorry, I mean a good guy.

Ha! You're really catching on quick! Well, I better get to bed, Elli, but I can't wait to talk to you next week!

I'll be waiting!

Thursday, 29 September, 2011

Girls are funny. Yesterday, as we walked back to the high school from Seminary, I noticed Tracy was quieter than usual. We were about to split up and head to our second hour when, all of sudden, she turned on me with eyes full of fire and asked, "Is Frank going to ask me out again or what?"

My body's natural fight or flight responses simultaneously went in opposite directions. The end result was a stupor of thought. Ashley started giggling, and I realized my mouth must've dropped open. Tracy didn't break a smile, though. Instead, she folded her arms impatiently, and asked, "Well?"

I shrugged my shoulders. The movement helped jar my lips back to life, and I said, "Honestly, I think you've got him scared. I've never seen him act like this before."

The stern muscles in her face twitched briefly. It looked to me like a smirk. "Good!" she said and started walking toward South Hall. Before she entered, she turned abruptly and said, "We're going to have lunch at Bits today. We'll meet you guys there, unless Frank's too chicken."

Her comment was dripping with sassiness, and I couldn't help but smile. "Oh, we'll be there," I replied.

As soon as I got out of Mr. Tate's history class the next hour, I told Frank about our lunch challenge at Bits and Pizzas. He pumped his fist and yelled, "YES!" The melancholy Frank suddenly disappeared, and the old full-of-crap Frank said with a glint in his eyes, "Dude, I've got an idea."

We made a mad dash for my truck, stopping first by Frank's house then mine before going to Bits. The pizza/movie store was packed full of kids, and everyone went dead silent when Frank stepped through the door. I told him it was a bad idea, but he was determined to make an entrance, so of course, I let him go in first. Between our two houses, we were able to find my football helmet, a Roman breastplate and shield (from an old Halloween costume), and a light saber.

No one moved a muscle. Frank scanned until he found his target and began creeping toward the table where Ashley and Tracy sat in shock. Somebody snorted through clasped fingers, and like an opened gate to a herd of cows, laughter burst free in a stampede. About this time, I stepped in, and it wasn't until the girls saw me that they realized who the nutjob was in the ridiculous outfit.

"Frank, is that you?" Tracy asked in astonishment. This was Frank's cue to whip the light saber from behind his back and strike a fighting stance. The laughter roared again. Tracy tried to hold it back, but she couldn't resist a huge grin. "What in the HECK are you doing?"

Frank spoke in a deeper voice than usual. "I just wanted to be prepared in case this was a trap!"

Tracy leaned her head back, rolling her eyes dramatically. "Frank, you really *are* a dork." But she said it with a smile. The noise in the room slowly died as people turned back to their pizza with loud, gossiping voices.

Frank held his pose. He looked at me from the corner of his eye and said, "David, you might want to check the chairs before we sit down," and he nodded toward them with his head. In a whisper loud enough for all to hear, he said, "*They might be booby trapped*! I'll watch your back."

I walked over to Ashley and sat down. "This one isn't. But I'm not sure about that one," and I pointed to the seat next to Tracy. He walked up and poked it with his light saber. Then he tilted it over and looked underneath.

"Oh, sit down you psycho!" Tracy's arms were folded and she was shaking her head. "I won't bite-cha . . . this time." She raised one eyebrow. "Unless you don't take that stupid helmet off, and then I might!"

Frank slowly, cautiously removed the helmet and held it in his lap. Ashley grinned and said, "Why don't you two *guard* our table while David and I order pizza?"

Frank whipped out his light saber again and said, "We'll do our best!" Tracy rolled her eyes again.

I stood up and followed Ashley toward the cash register. As we got in line behind five other students, I said, "Thanks for getting me away from the dueling duo."

She laughed and said, "Yeah, there's not a shortage of excitement when you get those two together."

Looking back, Frank was waving his hands as he talked excitedly, and Tracy was laughing. "It's good to see Frank back from his depression," I said.

Ashley grinned as she let out a loud breath. "Tracy, too! She's been a little cranky the past few days." She glanced over her shoulder toward them. "It's good to see a smile on her face."

We turned back to the line, and after a moment of silence, Ashley peered through the display at the buckets of ice cream and asked, "So what's your favorite kind?"

I thought about it for a second and replied, "You might think it's weird, but the best ice cream in the world is Grandma's homemade peach ice cream."

"Ooh, that sounds delicious! I've never had peach ice cream before."

"Come to think of it, we haven't had it in quite a while. Maybe I can talk her into making it again soon."

"Well if *you* don't ask her, *I* might have to," she grinned.

I smiled back and asked, "What's your favorite? At least until you try Grandma's."

She laughed. "Up till now my favorite has always been this." She pointed through the window to a blue bucket. "Bubble gum ice cream! I used to do extra chores to save enough money for a double scoop! I don't eat it as much anymore, but it's still my favorite."

"Huh, I've never tried it," I said.

She raised an eyebrow and asked tauntingly, "Are you feeling brave like Frank?"

I laughed, "Sure, what the heck." Along with our slices of pizza, we both got a scoop of bright-blue ice cream peppered with colorful gumballs We made it back to the table and sat down in the middle of a *Star Wars – Star Trek* argument. Apparently Tracy is a Trekkie and Frank's a Jedi.

"Didn't take you guys long to start arguing again," Ashley stated flatly.

Tracy turned in shock, "Frank thinks the Millennium Falcon is faster than the Starship Enterprise." Ashley's blank stare turned Tracy in my direction. "You seem to have some common sense, tell Frank how ridiculous this is!"

"Sorry, Tracy, but I'll have to agree with Frank on this one."

Tracy huffed and muttered something under her breath about being under-educated.

Frank gave me a high five, raised his light saber over his head, and declared, "May the force be with us!"

Picking up her pizza, Tracy turned back to Ashley. "This goes to show you what *Star Wars* will do to a person," and she pointed at Frank.

Frank examined his outfit and turned back to the girls defensively, "What?"

We all started laughing. Frank spent the rest of lunch valiantly justifying his attire. It was good to see him back to normal. As we were about to head back to school, Frank asked, "So, shall we have another friendly wager on the football game tomorrow night?"

Tracy replied, "I'm in if there's another swing involved!"

Frank ignored the comment and said, "I was thinking if the Lobos win, YOU guys have to make US dinner Saturday night!"

"And if we lose," Tracy leaned toward Frank, "YOU take US to Charlie Clarks!"

Frank met her challenge with narrowed eyes. In a deadly serious tone, he stated, "You're on." He held out his hand and they shook on it. Oh, and by the way, the ice cream was disgusting, but I tried to act like I enjoyed it so Ashley wouldn't feel bad. Gum and ice cream are two things that should never be mixed. Please don't tell Ashley I said that!

Saturday, 1 October, 2011

Happy October! Today was a great day, and it started last night . . . that doesn't make sense. Oh well. I went into the locker room around five thirty to get taped up for the game. I think half the team needs at least one appendage wrapped. Coach likes us to come in early so we'll be ready before warm-ups.

My arm has been feeling great! Coming into the game last night against Winslow was the first time all season I felt I was back 100%. Even though I've been doing well in practice, I don't blame Coach for not putting me back on the kickoff team. He hasn't liked me playing very much defense, either. That's all right. I'll play there if I'm needed. My true love is that spiraling long bomb! Joe Carter really stepped up in my place as defensive end and has been doing a killer job.

Oh, it was a fun game! Not to brag or anything, but it was the best game I've ever played in my life! We scored on almost every possession. I don't remember all my receptions, but late in the first quarter, Zack hit me on a corner route, and it was a perfect throw. The safety was close, but I easily pulled away from him for a thirty-four-yard touchdown! I caught two or three more fifteen-yard passes, and the first play of the fourth quarter we had the ball on our own forty-two-yard line. Coach called a seam route, which is my favorite. Zack was forced out of the pocket and had to scramble to the far sideline. He let her fly a half second before they laid him out. By that time, I was well behind all the defenders. I danced untouched into the end zone! That put us up 38 – 0, and coach sent in the second string for the rest of the game. No one else scored.

After the game, Coach congratulated me on being back and told me I had over 150 yards passing with two touchdowns! *Finally,* years of practice collided with growing skills to lift me out of mediocrity. I had never flown higher! To top it off, my arm never hurt once! What a miracle it has been. I'm so grateful for answered prayers.

Now back to today. Gramps wanted Josh and me to make a trip around the ranch and put out salt. Cows, like us, have to have a certain amount of salt and minerals to stay healthy. At each tank,

Grandpa has old tires with plywood nailed on one side. Oddly, he calls them salt boxes. We loaded the bags in the bed of the old Ford, grabbed two of grandpa's .22 rifles, and headed out.

I have to admit, Josh is an excellent shot. He got three rabbits to my one, and he even hit a few cow pies as I was driving. We stopped at an Indian ruin, and the fart found two more arrowheads. He was struttin' around like a rooster in a hen house until I found a fossil! It's kind of oval and almost as long as a Twinkie. The top looks like a regular rock, and I would have passed it by if it hadn't reminded me of one of my favorite treats. When I turned it over, the bottom was completely flat with a perfect fossil of what looked like dinosaur skin! It's really cool. I've found smaller fossils of shells and stuff but never of an animal. It made my day! I was happy to see it flatten Josh's feathers a little, too.

After lunch Gramps had us take the horses out to the Jay Tank pasture and ride the fence to check for holes. We'll be moving the cows there in a few weeks, after we wean the calves.

I don't know why I don't ride more often. Josh and I always have a blast! If we aren't racing across a flat, we're chasing coyotes or climbing hills. Once we even tried to rope a deer! It was all fun and games until Josh got wiped off by a tree. Fast horses and thick cedars don't mix well. Oh, the world's so much simpler when you're the man from Snowy River! Even if it's only for an afternoon.

We got home about a half hour before sundown. I had barely enough time to get cleaned up before Frank came by to take me to Ashley's house. The girls seemed excited to make us dinner. I won't lie, I was kinda worried; not only because I feared our grub might be laced with Ex-Lax, but I was extremely nervous to meet Ashley's family.

You know how sometimes you anticipate what something will look like before seeing it? Well, my exaggerated assumptions of the Dunn family were way off. To my surprise, when I walked through their entryway, instead of a living room they had a remodeling war zone. Her father is a partner in a construction business. At the moment, Greg is in between jobs, so he decided to tear into home projects. He's a happy man and made us feel welcome from the get-go.

Ashley's mother, Debra, is a sweet, quiet lady who smiles a lot. Even though she's soft-spoken, a fun side emerged when we started playing Rook. Ashley has one younger sister who is seven. Her name is Elisabeth. I recognized her from Ashley's drawing. It turned out to be a very accurate depiction! They also have an older sister and brother who are both grown.

They wouldn't tell us what was for dinner until we had no hope of escape. When Ashley pulled the lid from the pot, steam billowed out in swirling clouds. "We call this, porcupine meatballs!"

Frank glanced at me nervously. Tracy snorted at his reaction.

A savory smell filled the room. My nose was automatically convinced I had nothing to fear. I leaned over to get a better look. Large meatballs packed with rice were smothered in a tasty-looking sauce. My eyes put the vote strongly in favor with my growling stomach. Even though I'd never heard of it before, with my first bite I knew immediately I had a new item on my list of "favorite foods." I was very impressed!

The list got longer after Debra brought out hot apple pie. I found out later, she did most of the cooking, but my taste buds didn't care who made it. My favorite word of the week is definitely, à la mode!

Dang it. My mouth is salivating again!

After dinner, we played cards with Ashley's whole family. Frank couldn't resist an attempt at center stage, but it backfired when the Skittle wouldn't come out of his nose. Remember what I told you at the beginning? If you get nothing else from this journal, hopefully you learn from our mistakes; don't ever try to impress girls by putting candy up your nose. At first, Tracy was furious with Frank, but by the time we realized he needed help, we were all dying laughing! Debra eventually had to round up tweezers to complete the extraction. I actually think Frank got embarrassed. It was great!

All in all, the weekend was fantastic. The only thing I would change, if I could go back in time, is I wouldn't have turned down seconds on the pie, no matter how stuffed I was. What was I thinking?

<u>Tuesday, 4 October, 2011</u>

It's strange how, in the matter of only a few days, you can go from one extreme to another. Life really is one big roller coaster. I think tonight is the closest I've ever been to beating someone to a pulp. When I opened the ammunition box this evening, the beanie was empty. The Airlis was GONE!

My heart stopped beating. If someone took it, someone touched it; and if someone touched it, I might have lost Elli forever! When I could start thinking again, I *knew* the only one who would've done this was Josh.

I went flying through the house screaming his name. When I got to the family room, I noticed *Mythbusters* playing on NetFlix and the back door standing wide open. He knew I was going to kill him, and he had fled for his life—the coward. I sprinted through the door just in time to see Josh disappearing around the corner of the house. By the time I made it to the front, he'd locked himself in the van, a large smirk smeared from ear to ear.

Sprinting to the car, I instinctively grabbed for the door handle. Of course it was locked. I looked up. Josh was laughing hysterically.

I snapped.

Anger boiled inside as I raised both hands above my head and smashed my fists into the window. It shattered and fell into the van as extreme pain shot down my right arm.

That got rid of the smirk, all right. Josh's mouth hung open, and his eyes filled with mortal fear. The impenetrable barrier that was keeping him alive was now lying shattered in his lap. But he didn't have anything to worry about now. Excruciating pain extinguished all other emotions. I cradled my re-broken arm in my other hand and slowly backed away from the van. The empty hole where once my anger raged now filled with shame.

The next thing I knew I was curled in a ball on the loft in Grandpa's barn. I was pretty sure I hadn't hurt Josh, but what if the window had been down? Would I have restrained myself? Even though, looking back, I think I was just trying to get inside the van, I'm not really sure what my intentions were once I got my hands around his neck. I was FURIOUS! As I lay on dusty boards in pain and despair, two questions kept ricocheting inside my head: *Am I turning into my father? Did I lose Elli?*

If I thought life was bad when I broke my arm the first time, it just multiplied by ten. Sadly, the pain had become familiar. But stronger than the pain of broken bones was the horrifying reality I had just become my father. And as if that weren't enough, I might have lost Elli forever. Darkness surrounded me and seemed to steal away the very air I breathed. These thoughts swirled, dragging me further and further into an abyss. It was then that a rather vivid memory of my father sliced open old wounds.

It was my favorite possession. When I was around six years old, we went to visit Bo's mother. Nanna was a very sweet woman, and I loved going to her house, because it was stuffed full of trinkets in all shapes and sizes. I always tried to stay out of the way of the adults and found myself meandering down the hall, fascinated by the shelves and shelves of endless treasure. A colorful glass turtle caught my eye, and I stopped, leaning in to see the details. It was kind of flat and looked like a small plate. It was intricately formed with a combination of mellow colors. To me, it appeared to be molded from the shards of a stained glass window.

I didn't realize Nanna had come up behind me. "Do you like that turtle?" she asked sweetly. I shyly nodded my head. Lifting it off the shelf, she handed it to me. "If you can promise to take care of old Ralphie, you can have him."

Nodding my head in wonder, I gently pulled it to my chest.

When I walked back into the front room, Bo scoffed when he saw what I was cradling. "Thanks, Ma, for giving my son an ash tray." It always hurt when he made me feel stupid, but somehow the glitter of my new gift gave me strength. I held it gently all the way home and safely stowed it away on my top shelf.

Nanna passed away not long after that. Looking back, I think it was part of the reason our life with Bo got worse. A few weeks later, I was out back "practicing" baseball with Bo. He was hitting the ball at me, trying to teach me to stop a grounder, when the ball bounced hard and hit me in the face. I started crying and ran to my room. He yelled for me to stay put, but I didn't listen.

The door flew open, slamming hard against the wall when he barged into the room. Jabbing a finger at me, he yelled, "If you're not going to listen, I'll REALLY give you something to cry about!" He yanked me off the bed and kicked me hard. The backhand that followed sent me sprawling onto the floor. Sadly, the pain was nothing new. But then I watched in horror as Bo ripped that precious turtle off my shelf and hurled it against the wall. My heart shattered into a hundred stained-glass shards that flew all around the room.

Old barn boards creaked as I flinched from the sharp stab of the memory. "No!" My cry sliced through the darkness and reverberated through the rafters. Sitting up with a jolt, I yelled, "I will NOT be like my father!" This declaration seemed to clear my mind, but that only made the colors of my transgression more distinct. I rolled to my hands and knees and began to pour out my soul—pleading for God's forgiveness—but no amount of begging could pry open those sealed doors.

"I'm so sorry. What can I do?" In spite of the silence, I didn't give up. Time watched pitifully as my prayers persevered. After about my twentieth attempt, something shifted, and in the stillness that followed, I finally got an answer:

Repent.

The word stabbed through my mind and pierced my heart and with it came a reflection of many Sunday School lessons. Slowly, painfully, I began mentally reviewing those familiar steps.

First, recognize you've done something wrong. Yes, I'd done that one. *Next, feel Godly sorrow and ask for forgiveness.* I'd been begging God to forgive me but realized there were others I'd hurt, too. *Finally, do all I can to correct the wrong.* That was it! Bo would ask for forgiveness sometimes, but he never tried to change. I would not make the same mistake.

I pushed myself off the floor with a determination to do whatever it took to become someone different from my father. When I got home, Mom was outside taping a trash bag over the window. As she turned toward me, I saw a flash of fear cross her eyes, a look I'd seen before. Something crumbled inside of me. I'd always relied on her trust; I needed it to survive, and the realization I might've damaged it in any way was more painful than all my broken bones combined.

Tears began to form again. "Mom . . . I'm sorry." She looked down at the shattered window as precious drops fell from her eyes. Seeing her weep those kind of tears because of me crushed my heart. Voice quivering, I said, "Mom, I promise you, it will never happen again." She wiped her tears and looked up at the stars that were now starting to cover the night sky.

"I'm just glad you didn't hurt anybody," she sniffed.

I looked down at my feet and watched the tears roll off my nose and soak into my shoelaces. Mom's arms gently found their way around my shoulders, and we hugged until the pain went away.

"I'll get the window fixed tomorrow, Mom," I told her as we pulled apart.

"You'll have to wait until Saturday, because I'll need the car for work," she replied. I nodded my head and helped her finish taping the window.

When I got inside, I found Josh lying on his bed throwing a ball at the ceiling. He glanced my way then quickly stared back at the ceiling.

"Hey . . . I'm sorry I got mad at you." The words were hard to get out.

He paused to look at me again and shrugged his shoulders. "It's all right. I'm sorry I took your rock." He reached behind his pillow and tossed the Airlis to me. I caught it gingerly with both hands and looked at it with deep concern. "I thought I'd get you back for finding that fossil," he smirked. "Ha! The joke was on me." He smiled, and I did, too. "So, is Mom mad at you?"

"No, actually," I replied a little astonished. "I think she's as shocked as I am."

"Yeah, and me!" Josh said with a grin. "I really thought you were going to kill me for a second."

I shook my head. "I don't know what got into me. I've never lost my temper like that before."

Josh sat up with a serious look. "It's a good thing, too." He smiled and tossed me the ball, "Or we'd have to replace a lot of windows around here." I smiled and threw it back.

I feel a lot better now. I know I'm on the right path, but I still have consequences to deal with. I'm not too worried about the window. It might cost a bit, but I've got a couple thousand dollars saved from working with Gramps. I never really had much to spend it on. My hands are tender where I hit the glass, and my arm hurts more than ever, but the worst pain of all—it's now after midnight, and I haven't heard a thing from Elli.

Saturday, 8 October, 2011

Sorry, but I haven't felt like writing till tonight. To catch you up, I'll start with Wednesday. The pain in my arm didn't ease up much, but greater than that was the unrest in my head. As the experience tumbled over and over again in my mind, it kept disturbing me more and more, and I couldn't figure out why.

I told Coach I injured my arm again, and asked if it'd be all right if I didn't go with the team this weekend. It takes over three and half hours to get to Page, and I didn't want to suffer any more than I already was. He wasn't too upset. Page isn't very good this year, and we actually ended up beating them pretty bad. I think the final was 47 - 0, and that was with the second string playing most of the time. Instead, I decided to go camping.

Wednesday, Frank noticed something was wrong and asked me about it. I told him I injured my arm again, and I wasn't going to be playing football for a while. He's the one who reminded me about our Scout camping trip to Hawley Lake this weekend. The more I thought about it, the more I wanted to go.

Out of the eight priests in the ward, seven of us went. Tyler Sorenson is a defensive back and was gone to the game. Friday was a half day of school, so we met at the church at one o'clock. Brother Brimhall and Brother Peterson are the Priest Quorum Advisors, and we had to cram all our stuff into a minivan and a four-door Silverado. Somehow, we got our gear and ourselves loaded and headed to the Apache Reservation.

In Snowflake things are backward. North you travel *down* to hot, treeless plains and South takes you *up* high into the White Mountains. We skirted around Show Low and passed through Pinetop-Lakeside. The flashing lights of the Hon-Dah Casino marked the entrance to the Apache Nation. In spite of our prodding and begging, Brother Peterson did not pull in. We continued up the 260 and passed through the small town of McNary.

After a few more miles, we turned south off the main highway and drove for what seemed like an hour up a winding road. You wouldn't think there'd be a large body of water so close to the crest of the mountains, but our continuous upward climb eventually led us to a beautiful, serene lake.

We drove around until we found a nice campsite. Frank brought a four-man, dome tent for us to sleep in; we claimed a spot upwind of the campfire ring. Sleeping upwind is one of the many things we learned in Scouting through trial and error. Four of the Scouts and Brother Peterson quickly grabbed their fishing gear and headed to the lakeshore.

Brother Brimhall is the youngest of the two leaders and prefers to go by Brad. He's very athletic and wanted to play Frisbee golf. To try and make it fair, he let Sam Morrey, Frank, and me be on one team. We each would throw, then he'd let us pick the best Frisbee to continue from. At first we thought he wouldn't have a chance, but quickly changed our minds. He ended up beating us by five in a nine-hole course! After our game, it was about an hour from sundown, so we got the fire going. Along with our tinfoil dinners, we enjoyed a bountiful catch of fresh fish and Brother Peterson's Dutch-oven apple crisp. Every belly was stretched to capacity.

As we sat around the fire waiting for our stomachs to make room for a roasted marshmallow, Brother Peterson asked us all a general question. "So, what's everyone going to do with the rest of their life?" We sat in silence for a minute, contemplating the loaded question while flames danced on sap-filled pine logs. "Come on, surely somebody has a plan in mind."

Of course, Frank broke the silence. With a look of deep contemplation, he said, "You know, Brother Peterson . . . I've always wanted to be a professional whistler." He tried to hold a straight face as guys around the fire snickered.

"Frank, I don't think anyone expected anything less," said Brad with the shake of his head.

"I suppose someone has to do it," replied Brother Peterson. That's when Frank decided to show off his skills, but he was so horrible, no one knew what song he was trying to mimic.

Brad cut in, "You know, Frank, if I were you, I'd probably stick with basket weaving." We all got a kick out of that. Even though it had been a few years, no one forgot about the summer scout camp when Frank was adamant he get his basket weaving merit badge.

After the chuckling died down, Brother Peterson turned and said, "What about you Sam?" Sam's a quiet guy who loves to play guitar. People say he's pretty good.

Sam thought for a second, and to my surprise he said, "When I get home from my mission, I want to become a chemical engineer." I knew he was taking chemistry, but I hadn't realized he enjoyed it that much.

"That'll be a great career," said Brother Peterson with obvious approval. "What about you, David?"

My back stiffened as the pressure of his abrupt question slammed into me. Until a few days ago, I thought I had a pretty good plan. I'd play football to pay for an education in business . . . but now I wasn't sure what I was going to do. There's no way I'll be able to afford college on my own, and Mom can't pay for it—and what about a mission? I always thought I'd go, but it didn't hit me until last night I hadn't made that decision yet.

Brother Peterson must have seen my turmoil, because he asked, "If you don't have a solid plan yet, how about your goals or dreams?"

My head shot up, and I stared at him in surprise. Gramps had mentioned my "goals and dreams" in the blessing he gave me. He told me if I have faith, I could accomplish them. I ducked my head and nervously picked up a small twig. I no longer had any dreams or the faith to make them happen, and it deeply disturbed me.

I looked back at the fire and threw in the stick. "I'm still trying to figure that one out," I replied vaguely. After a slightly awkward pause, he moved on to the next guy. Everyone had a plan except me. After hearing everyone's confession of greatness, the noise simmered back down to just a crackling fire.

Blank stares covered deep thoughts until Brad's voice broke the silence. "It wasn't long ago that I sat around a fire much like this one and told my big plans." He paused and we all looked at him. Picking up a stick, he snapped it in two. The small end he threw in the fire, and with the other, he began to scratch something in the dirt.

"I'm not sure if any of you guys know this, but I played professional baseball for three months." If he didn't have our attention before, he had it now! He continued, but this time it was tinted with sarcasm. "Oh I was a *great* outfielder, and at Mt. View

High School I set a new record for the best batting average in a single season. I had scouts looking at me when I was a sophomore. I was flying high."

The same words spoken by someone else would've been dripping with bragging rights, but he kept drawing on the ground. The only face lit by our fire that wasn't radiating surprise was the one looking down.

"I dreamed all my life of going pro, so when an opportunity came to play in the minor leagues, I went for it. I didn't think I needed college, and I was worried a mission would cause me to miss my chance, so I decided not to do that either. I rose quickly through the ranks, and one day I got 'the call.' They wanted me to play right field for the Boston Red Sox. I figured the time couldn't be better to ask my high school sweetheart to marry me, and she accepted. We both thought we'd get sealed in the temple someday, but it wasn't a big priority. Everything was going perfectly. Then three months and four days later, I went sliding into second base and SNAP! My baseball career was over.

"I quickly found out that without baseball, I didn't have much. Actually, if I wouldn't have had my Becky, I wouldn't have had anything. I thank God every day she decided to stick with me and get through it together."

He looked up from his sketch and glanced around the fire, pausing when he got to me. He tossed his stick into the flames and watched as it quickly burned. "I tell you this, because I hope you can learn from my mistakes. Now, I'm not saying sports are evil or anything, but what I am trying to say is I hope you can get your priorities right the first time. I wish I had. I missed out on a lot of things I'll never be able to get back."

I didn't stay by the fire long after that. My mind was too heavy for campfire stories and jokes. I lay in my sleeping bag staring at the stars through the mosquito-net top of our tent and pondered on goals and dreams.

My night was very restless. Mix a disheveled mind with a thin sleeping bag on hard ground and you get about twenty-eight minutes' worth of sleep. Finally, a hint of gray crept onto my starry canvas, and I could tell dawn was getting closer. Quietly, I unzipped myself from the sleeping bag and pulled on my shoes. The crispness of the cold morning cut right through my hoodie, so

I threw some more wood on the smoldering coals. When the fire didn't jump to life, I decided to go for a walk to help warm myself up.

When I got to the lake's shore, the sun was still about thirty minutes away from breaking the horizon. Fog had rolled in and settled across the lake, shifting in slow curving patterns, pushed by unseen hands. About four hundred yards to the east was a herd of around twenty cow elk. They were leaving the water's edge when they stopped to calculate the danger of my sudden intrusion.

I found a nice boulder along the shore and sat down. With the twitch of an ear, they shared a unanimous decision—even though I wasn't a threat, it was clear we could never be friends. I watched as they slowly disappeared through the thinning fog. The glassy-smooth surface of the lake rippled occasionally as the trout began their morning runs. Something about the scene connected to my soul. Like this lake, my life was beginning to get less foggy— revealing a far grander picture than I ever dreamed possible.

For the first time in my life, I feel like I'm *finally* setting goals that will lead to lasting happiness—I've found a dream that can't shatter with broken bones.

Tuesday, 11 October, 2011

I wouldn't have thought it possible to change the course of my life 180 degrees in three days, but I did. After church on Sunday, I went over to visit with Gramps. You see, my new plan in life is going to require a change for him too, and I wanted to ask not only for his advice but also for his permission.

As I lay on the hard ground watching the stars appear and disappear through the tent roof the other night, I couldn't help but wonder if one of those stars is actually the beginning of the galaxy where Elli will someday live. I thought about her excitement to come to an earth like mine for the opportunity to experience a mortal life. I thought about my own experiences: the bitter pain, and the even greater joy when the Savior took it all away. I thought about the numerous people who live on the earth with no idea who their Savior is or how to find peace in His loving arms. Suddenly, an overwhelming desire to go and share *that* with everyone filled my heart! That's when I made up my mind. I AM going to serve a mission. As I mentally declared that to the world, the stars standing as my witness, the comfort and peace of the Holy Spirit confirmed: *YES! This is what God wants you to do!*

The feeling was amazing! Not just because of the sweet sensation only the Holy Ghost can give, but also because, for the first time in my life, I truly have a dream and a goal worth climbing for.

The rest of the night, and all through the next day, I pondered excitedly on my new course correction. Slowly, I began piecing together an outline of what I'll need to do to get on a mission. One dilemma of serving a mission for the Church of Jesus Christ of Latter-day Saints is, you are expected to pay for it yourself. I've heard from other guys who are also getting ready to go that it costs over $10,000. After my $140 window replacement, I'm down to $3,785 in the bank. Yeah, that one hurt. Anyway, I calculated my normal school-year revenue from helping Gramps, and I was shocked to see, by the time I turn nineteen on the 13th of May, I'll be about $3,500 short.

I shared all of this with Gramps and told him I was thinking about getting another job. Besides paying me 1960's wages, during the winter months work slows down, so he usually has to *find* things for us to do. I explained to him that Josh is now big enough to do most of the work, and I could probably still help on the weekends. He thought about it for a while as I sat and listened to their old clock ticking, and then he said, "You know, Brother Lowry was talking to me just the other day. He mentioned he was getting behind in his work and could use an extra hand."

Brother Lowry owns his own handyman business. He used to be a contractor down in the Valley, but when the housing market crashed, he lost his job and his home and ended up moving in with some family here in Snowflake. He's a hard worker, and since he was able to keep most of his tools and one old work truck, he started hiring out to fix anything and everything. He called his business, "Mr. Fix-It Man." Before long, the word got out and business took off. He now has his own place next door to Gramps and can't keep up with the demand.

The idea of learning the skills of a fix-it man was intriguing, and when I expressed my interest to Gramps, he picked up the phone.

"Brother Lowry?" Gramps asked. "My grandson David would like to speak with you," and he handed me the phone! This caught me by surprise, and after stuttering a few seconds, I finally was able to ask if he still needed help.

"It's funny you called, David," Brother Lowery said with a chuckle. "I was actually planning on putting an ad in the paper tomorrow to find an extra hand. My only concern is I was hoping to hire someone who could work more like thirty hours a week, and I need the help as soon as possible. With school and football, you'd only be able to work on Saturdays."

I thought about that for a minute, doing some quick calculations in my head. "Can you give me till tomorrow to see what I can do?" I asked.

"Sure, David. I'll wait till Tuesday to put my ad in the paper."

"Thanks, Brother Lowry. I'll call you tomorrow." After our goodbyes, I told Gramps I had to see if I could change some things around first, but I'd let him know if it worked out. I thanked him and went home and sat on the front porch for a while. Looking down at my arm, I was surprised to realize it hadn't hurt all day. I did a lot more thinking and a lot more star gazing.

Monday morning I asked Mr. Thompson if I could leave Madrigals early so I could go to the office. Madrigals is a zero-hour class, meaning it happens the hour before regular school starts. Mr. Thompson said it was no problem as long as I had the lines memorized for the Silent Night number by the next morning. That'll be easy enough.

In the front office, I asked to see the school counselor. Mrs. Phisher is as friendly as she is round and has helped me with my class schedule before. I asked her what would happen if I dropped my afternoon classes. Pulling up my records, she found that if I dropped Chemistry, P.E., and Weights, my grade point average would drop from a 3.7 to a 3.5, but I didn't need any of the classes to graduate. She said usually I'd need Mom's signature, but since I'm now legally an adult I didn't have to. That made my chest puff out a bit, I won't lie. She informed me the only thing I had to do was fill out a form and have Coach Fuller and Mr. Fry sign it. The air whooshed out of my lungs. I knew I'd have to face Coach sometime, but it didn't make it any easier.

The form that would change my schedule and my life felt as heavy as an anvil. Even after stuffing it under some books in my truck, it still left a constant pressure on my mind. Ashley noticed my sullen demeanor in Seminary, and as we walked back to school she asked, "Hey, are you okay?"

I shrugged my shoulders. "Yeah, it's just . . . oh, I've got some things to do today, and I'm not looking forward to it."

Her eyebrows bunched together. "Well, that's a little cryptic. Are you planning on hurting someone?"

I looked at her in surprise. She was grinning at me. It was amazing how quickly my sunken spirits began to float again. This brought a much-needed smile. "No, I'm not going to *hurt* anyone—I don't think."

"Oh, okay. I thought I'd make sure," she teased. Her face went smooth as concern chased away the smile wrinkles. "You just look really sad today."

It had been a while since we did anything together besides walk to class. Actually, I hadn't talked to her much since I broke the van window. North Hall was getting close by, so I turned to her and asked, "Can I meet you somewhere for lunch? I'll explain more to you then."

Her look of concern didn't leave. She tilted her head slightly and said, "Sure, David. Where do you wanna go?"

"I've got to do a few things first." My mind quickly ran over the few places to eat in town. I didn't want to deal with the lunch crowd at any of them. "Can I meet you at the park?"

This made her smile again. "Oh, do they have good food there?"

I smiled back, "Depends on what you bring." The tardy bell started ringing, so I began walking away.

"Anything you want in particular?" she asked while holding the door open for the rush of late movers.

"Don't worry about me," I yelled over my shoulder as I began to jog to my History class. "I have a feeling I'm not going to be very hungry." Her look of confusion only deepened, but she didn't have time to pry out any more answers.

The lunch bell rang, and instead of jumping in my truck and running away (like I wanted to do), I grabbed the form and dragged myself to Coach's office. I found him kicked back with his feet on the desk, eating some kind of homemade sandwich and watching game film of the Round Valley Elks.

He looked up and smiled. "Hey, Thorn! How's the arm feeling?"

"Well," I had no idea how to sugarcoat this, so I just spit it out. "Coach, I'm not going to be playing anymore."

His mouth froze open in mid-chew as he stared at me in disbelief. After his brief imitation of a stunned statue, his feet hit the floor with a thud. "What happened? Is it broke? Where's your cast?"

I didn't know how to respond exactly. Truthfully, my arm had been feeling okay, but how would Coach understand? "I didn't see a doctor, so I'm not sure, but I really don't think my arm can take anymore. Besides, I really need to get a job."

His face scrunched in confusion as my words sank in. "You didn't . . . you need a job?" The questions began running together.

I bolstered up some courage and plowed ahead, "Yeah Coach, I need a job. I found a good one, but I'm going to need to drop P.E. and weights—and football."

"But son, you're on a path that could lead to scholarships! I've never seen you play like you did against Winslow. We *need* you if we're going to take State this year!" He was pleading with me now! I couldn't believe it, especially after how he'd moved on so quickly after my first injury. He shook his head, not able to understand, and asked, "What do you need a job so bad for, anyway?"

I felt like David from a different time, but I swear my Goliath was bigger. He looked ten feet tall, and he was still sitting in his chair! I gulped some air, looked him in the eyes, and said, "I need the money so I can go on a mission."

Coach threw his hands up and let out a guffaw. "Oh, you Mormons are something else!" He sat back hard in his chair. Coach doesn't go to church. He only moved here a few years ago and was still getting used to the way us "Mormons" live. Shaking his head slightly while staring at me, he asked, "You would give all this up to go on one of your missions?"

"Yes, sir," I said with a lump in my throat. I'd always been intimidated by this man, but as I faced him, something started growing inside; a warm strength that calmed my thudding heart and shaky knees.

To my surprise, he sat up and reached for the form. "Sometimes I don't understand you guys, but I admit you're sure a dedicated bunch." I smiled and handed the paper over. "The team is really going to miss you, David."

"I'm going to miss it too, Coach, believe me." This comment added a new flavor of shock to his YOU'RE CRAZY! look. If I hadn't been so nervous, I might've laughed. Instead I said, "But I really don't know how my arm will do anyway, especially the way I keep hurting it. And there's no way in heck I'm getting another cast!"

This finally solicited a smile out of him. "Can't say that I blame you. I broke my leg skiing when I was about thirteen, and I still remember how horrible that cast was." He stood up and reached out his hand. As we shook firmly, he said, "You're a good kid, Thorn. I'm glad I got to know you."

"Thanks, Coach," I replied and left his office for the last time.

Under a huge cottonwood tree next to the playground area at the park there's a picnic table and a grill. Ashley was waiting there with a McDonald's bag when I pulled up. Pioneer Park is a beautiful, simple park on the north end of town, and in spite of being in the opposite direction of all the fast food, we weren't the only ones sharing a lunch there today. I wasn't too upset, though. The three other high schoolers were occupied trying to eat pizza and swing at the same time.

"Is this seat taken?" I asked as I pointed to the bench next to Ashley.

"Nope. Saving it for you," she smiled. "Would you like a chicken nugget? Or are you still too sad to eat?"

I laughed and sat down. "Sure, what the heck. Nothing like sweet and sour sauce to brighten the day."

"Thought you might," she said with a grin, sliding the box over to split the distance between us. "That's why I got a twenty piece."

"And you even got extra sauce!" I said with an impressive nod. "You must've read my mind." I peeled back the container and grabbed a golden nugget of goodness and plunged it in deep.

As I plopped the whole thing in my mouth, Ashley added slyly, "Oh, and by the way, for payment you have to tell me why you've been acting so down today."

I stared at her for a moment then pulled the nugget out and acted like I was going to put it back in the box.

"Hey!" she yelled, slapping my hand.

"Just kidding!" I laughed and threw it back in my mouth.

She smiled and leaned back to a comfortable position on the bench. After swallowing the first nugget, I said, "I'll tell you as soon as we finish eating." She scowled and folded her arms. With exaggerated slowness, I picked up another nugget, dipped it three times, and inched it toward my mouth. This time it wasn't a slap, but a full on punch! "Ow!" I squawked and grabbed my arm.

"Well, at least you seem to be feeling better now," she said and grabbed another nugget. She dunked it once and tossed it in her mouth. In a muffled, very un-ladylike fashion, she said, "Vere, u haffy?"

This made me laugh out loud. "Okay, okay," I conceded, and as I reached for another nugget I told her, "I quit football today."

Her jaw went slack as a thousand questions poured from probing eyes, but her mouth was still too full to speak. I couldn't help chuckling at her. She quickly chewed and gulped. As soon as her airway was clear she gasped, "What happened?"

It took the rest of the box of nuggets and three fourths of the fries to cover the whole story. Well, not the whole story. I intentionally left out the part of "how" I re-injured my arm, but for the rest I was pretty thorough. As I concluded with my David and Goliath meeting with coach, she looked at me in wonder.

"Wow. That must've been pretty hard." I looked down and nodded my head, not knowing how to respond. To my surprise, I felt her hand rest on the back of mine as it lay on the table. "I think you're doing the right thing, David, and I'm proud of you."

The touch of her hand sent a shock clear through my body. It reminded me of the adrenalin rush I got on the opening kickoff, but it was also very comforting. I looked in her eyes and could sense her genuine care and concern.

"Thanks," I replied. She smiled that soft smile, and our eyes locked for a few more seconds. Wow. I could get lost really fast in those hazel eyes. Right before she hypnotized me with her powers, her eyes ripped away from mine at the same time her hand shot up. She looked at her watch and yelled, "Oh, crud! We're LATE!" I snapped back to earth, and we quickly shoved our trash into a bin and sprinted for the parking lot.

It took me three blocks of speeding to realize—*Wait, I no longer have afternoon classes!* The side effects from our little "moment" sure rattled my brain. Dang those super powers! Guys try *so* hard to have a skill, a sport, or a trait that might—by some slim chance—catch the attention of a passing girl, and all a girl has to do is look at you. It's not fair!

After slowing down, collecting my thoughts, and doing a dance of joy for not having chemistry anymore, I decided it was a good time to empty my football locker and turn in my pads. There was no way I'd be able to do that with anyone watching. It was a soul-crushing moment. Standing in an empty locker room, staring at my empty locker—it was a vivid and symbolic reflection of how I felt inside. Even though I understood that in order to rebuild something new the old must be torn down, all "tearing" does is leave a hollow place for you to store the pain.

On a happier note, I got the job! As soon as I got home, I called Brother Lowry. He was surprised when I told him I'd dropped my afternoon classes and quit football. It took him a moment to calculate my proposition, but we figured if I worked after lunch and maybe some weekends, it would be the thirty hours he was looking for. I start tomorrow, and he said he'll pay nine bucks an hour! It might not sound like much, but it's almost twice what Gramps pays.

When Mom walked in from work, I realized I probably should've asked her before I went and changed my whole life around. Guilt overwhelmed me as I confessed the activities of my day. She didn't take it well at first, slumping breathlessly onto the couch. I think she was too stunned to speak. I saw a whole range of emotions cross her face. Confusion, anger, concern . . . but after some time the shock began to wear off, and surprisingly, her eyes began to tear up. She began crying and smiling at the same time. I'm not a hundred percent sure what that means, but she did tell me she supported my decision and that she loves me. Have I told you I have the best mom in the whole world?

Now do you see what I meant when I said life has changed? I was going one direction, now I'm going another. Not just a simple 180 degree turn; things have also been going up and down like a bucking bronco! Changing classes, facing Coach, holding hands, hypnotic stares, getting a job; it's been CRAZY! Now, as the final hours of the day creep by, minutes of silence keep piling up to confirm the fear I've been trying to ignore: *Elli you can't be gone. I still need you.*

<u>Saturday, 15 October, 2011</u>

What a week! After the wild ups and downs of Tuesday, things started climbing out of the hole that had become my life. I hit a few bumps on the way out, but nothing that won't be set right in time. To start, Frank was pissed! Apparently, when you become good friends with someone, it's expected you don't go making life-changing decisions without running it by them first.

Tuesday afternoon, as soon as he found out I wasn't in Chemistry, he sent me a text. Over the course of the next FOUR hours we had a huge war of words! For me to change my schedule, quit football, and get a job without telling him really ticked him off, and I still don't understand why. He tried to explain all the moral laws I'd broken, but I'd never heard of the "unwritten laws of friendship." The conversation ended in a stalemate of harsh words, and the next day he avoided me completely. Sometimes, Frank, you can be such a girl!

Speaking of which, the other bump in the road had to do with me and Ashley. Come to find out, the little "moment" we had at the park was not only being observed, but photographed! The stupid jerks who I thought were just eating pizza were secretly watching every move we made. Cell phone pictures of us holding hands and gazing dreamily into each other's eyes were texted around school with the title, "Should've seen what they were doing in the car!"

I swear it spread to every cell phone on campus before I returned to school on Wednesday. I couldn't believe it! The bad thing about rumors is you can try to put out the flame, but some people only hear what they want to hear.

That same day, Mom even heard about it at the hospital! When I got home from work, the first thing she asked was, "David . . . can you explain *why* I heard from Cameron's mom today that Ashley is pregnant?"

My mouth hit the floor! "Whoa, whoa, WHOA!" I held my hands up in defense, trying to use my puny arms to stop the massive force of the gossip train, but I was way too late. Throwing my hands in the air, I shouted, "I can't BELIEVE this! We haven't even KISSED!" I quickly explained what had happened and how things must've gotten blown out of proportion.

"I knew it was absurd," she said with the shake of her head, "but I still couldn't believe I was hearing about it at work!" It's a good thing I didn't get a clear view of those kids at the park, because I think I would've hunted them down right then and run them over with my truck! I fumed for an hour, my tension mounting as I fidgeted around the house. As if by miracle, the doorbell rang, and it was Frank!

When I opened the door, the first thing he said was, "Oh man, you've got yourself in one MELL-OF-A-HESS!"

With a breath of relief, I flat out begged, "What do I do, man?" I needed help!

"First things first," he said somberly. Before I could flinch, he pounded me with a vicious right hook! This made Ashely's punch feel like an affectionate love tap.

"OUCH! What the heck?" I yelled as I grabbed my dead arm.

He shoved me into the house and said, "THAT'S for leaving me out of everything." He brushed past me and plopped himself down in the recliner. "Now for starters, how about you tell me what *really* happened, because we both know Ashley is NOT expecting your baby."

For the second time today, I sat on the couch and confessed every detail. I didn't leave anything out, because the last thing I wanted was Frank getting the wrong idea. His fingers drummed on the arm rests for a minute before his stern-thinking look turned into a huge grin. "Dude, you're getting pretty dang smooth!" His head tilted back as he let out a laugh, "HA!"

My cheeks flushed from embarrassment. For a second I almost smiled, but reality swung its own right hook. "You call it smooth that the whole town thinks I got Ashley pregnant?"

"Well, it's not exactly how I would've done it," he shrugged, "but some say it's best to jump in the deep end, and you're in up to your eyeballs!"

"But what do I do?" I pleaded. "When we try to tell people what really happened, they don't believe us!"

"That's why I came over," he pointed out. In a slightly sarcastic tone he added, "See, this is how you're *supposed* to treat your friends."

"Okay, okay, I'm sorry," I conceded. Jokingly I continued, "From now on, I'll let you know every time I need to take a dump!"

"Well, it's a start," he said in acceptance. "Now, back to your dilemma. When it comes to gossip, I've been at both ends more times than I can count, and I have an idea."

At first I wasn't sure about his plan. It seemed like it could backfire horribly, but on the other hand, I didn't have any better ideas. Now, the only problem was convincing Ashley to help. I called her up and told her Frank's idea of how to set things straight. She was hesitant at first, but Frank grabbed my phone and talked her into picking up Tracy and meeting us at the park.

The next day Frank met me at the end of Madrigals, and with a bit of persuasion, we solicited the help of twenty-three other cell phones to get the new gossip going. By the time lunch hour hit, everyone had pictures of at least two different scenarios of what "happened" in Ashley's car that day. We were only going to take one picture, but we were having so much fun thinking up new ideas, it ended up being an hour-long photo shoot.

It worked GREAT!

We took one picture of us fighting, and Ashley was rolling my head up in the window. We took one of us standing on top of the car with sunglasses and fake microphones, as if we were singing karaoke. In another one, we draped a Twister game across the back seat; I held the spinning pad with a thumbs up while Ashley winked at the camera. That was my second favorite, it looked hilarious!

Toward the end of the school day, Frank got the Student Council to help him send out "What *really* happened!" It was a picture of a very guilty-looking Frank leaning over Ashley in the back seat, as if they got caught making out!

Tracy, the makeup artist, went all out on this one. She dolled up Ashley with dark eyeshadow and bright lipstick and messed up her hair to make the scene look authentic. For a final touch, she put the lipstick on and planted bright-red kisses all over Frank's face. She grabbed his shoulders and said, "This is JUST for the picture." and smacked a hard one right on his lips!

He stumbled backward a few steps, and with slightly slurred speech replied, "Oh, I'm not complaining." We were all cracking up! He was in a complete daze the rest of the night.

We heard that kids all over school were bursting out in the middle of class as our texts made the rounds. Quite a few even got their phones taken away. It was a day to remember. If fame in a small town were measured by degrees, we just became SMOKIN' HOT!

Frank saved our lives. In a small town, your reputation is remembered for years and years. I'm mostly glad for Ashley's sake. It would be terrible to have a big black mark when you're such a good person. I'm grateful to have amazing friends.

Friday was a hard day. No matter what I did or how hard I tried to focus I kept finding myself fantasizing about the game. I won't lie; I had an ongoing battle in my head all day wondering if I'd done the right thing by quitting football.

Scott could tell I had something on my mind when, for the third time, I handed him the wrong wrench. He was stuffed under a sink repairing a leaky valve. "So . . . is she beautiful?" he asked.

"Huh?" I replied in confusion.

"The girl you're thinking about, is she beautiful? You've handed me the same wrench three times." Then he started laughing.

"Oh, sorry," I said embarrassed and handed him a half-inch wrench. "No, it's not a girl this time. I was thinking about the game tonight."

"I see," he said thoughtfully. "I remember those days. Don't worry, it'll fade in time."

"Oh, that makes me feel a LOT better," I said sarcastically.

He continued, "The trick is to fill the emptiness with something else you love."

I pondered this for a minute and asked, "So what sport were you in love with?"

Sighing deeply, he said, "Badminton." The word was foreign for a second, but as it registered, a loud laugh exploded from my mouth. "I'm serious," he retorted, "I joined the badminton club when I was a junior."

"They have a club for that?" I asked in surprise.

"Not here. I went to high school in California, and it wasn't *just* because I liked badminton; there was also a cute girl . . ." The sentence trailed off as he traveled down memory lane.

I laughed again. "Well, that's a different scenario."

"I don't think so," Scott said with a grunt. He must've been tightening up the water lines at that moment. "Love is love, whether it's for an object, a game, a person, or even a combination of things. But true happiness can only be found in how much *they* love you back."

Feeling mischievous, I said, "Are you a handyman or a philosopher?"

He laughed. "Even a handyman can learn from his mistakes. The real question is, what will you put in the place of football?"

"Well, I am doing all this so I can go on a mission?" It ended as a question, because I wasn't sure what he was looking for.

"Then I suggest you focus more on your new goals and less on the ones you've let go. You won't find any more happiness there, anyway."

He was right, and I knew it, but I still couldn't erase football from my head. It would probably take time. I asked him with a smile, "So . . . did you have to give up badminton or the girl?"

He let out a long breath and replied solemnly, "Both. But it was for the better. I decided to go on a mission instead of run off to college with her, and because I did, not only did it change my life, but when I got home, I found a woman TEN times what she was. The empty space now overflows with greater things."

The rest of the day I thought about what Scott said. In spite of my reconciliation, I couldn't bring myself to drive over and watch the game. Instead, Frank invited Ashley, Tracy, and me over to watch a movie at his house. At first he put in *Star Wars*, and you should've seen the fit Tracy threw. He was pulling her leg, though, and we decided on *Sahara* instead. I had seen it once and liked it, but neither of the girls had. As I sat on the couch next to Ashley, I wondered if perhaps someday she would fill more of that space Scott was talking about. Almost on cue, she scooted closer and offered to share her bowl of popcorn. It was a very pleasant movie.

I do have one confession. After the movie, I got in my truck and the highlights of the football game happened to be on the radio. I sat in our driveway for almost an hour listening to how we won 34 – 6, but all it did was make me realize how big a hole football had left.

On a side note, my new job is awesome! I worked a few hours today, but Scott said we usually won't work on Saturdays. It was an emergency call for a heater unit. He said I can call him Scott now, instead of Brother Lowry, since we'll be working a lot together. I've already learned how to frame in a window and hang drywall. I've also had the pleasure of unstopping a plugged sewer and learning how NOT to check if the electricity is still running to a broken light switch. The shock went through both arms, and felt like I was grabbed by a professional wrestler and shaken like a chocolate milk bottle! I'm lucky the fuse blew so I didn't DIE! It was the weirdest type of pain I've ever experienced, and afterwards I could taste all the fillings in my mouth. That's why you always turn the breaker off BEFORE you try replacing the light switch. Hopefully, this goes on the list of things I only have to learn once. (See, I'm teaching you all kinds of things NOT to do!)

Tuesday, 18 October, 2011

Three weeks! I haven't heard a thing from Elli since our conversation before Josh's "stunt," and it's driving me crazy. It's like those stories you hear about soldiers missing in action. Most of the time they end up staying lost, but my hope is resting with the one in a thousand who get found in a POW camp a year later. But I *really* hope it doesn't take a year.

I think I've finally gotten over my occasional flare-ups of anger toward Josh. I thought those would all disappear after I asked for forgiveness, but every time I'd think about losing Elli forever, I could feel my temperature start to rise. I should've known better than to expect immediate results. Tonight was the first time I was able to hold the Airlis without getting riled up. It wasn't his fault. He would never have done it if he knew the circumstances, I'm sure. Now instead of anger, I get a hollow feeling, like someone I know just died. But still I cling to a faint glimmer of hope.

Tonight, in an effort to get a response at any cost, I decided to try Josh as a guinea pig. Since he touched the Airlis, I wondered if my connection broke and it reset to him. He was sitting at his desk working on a model airplane from World War II. The only reason I knew that was because it was in bold letters on the box next to the trash can. Bo made an old model jet once when he was young and kept it on the shelf next to his trophies. When Dad died, Josh wanted that jet for some reason. Now it hangs from the ceiling over Josh's bed with a collection of others he's added since then.

"Hey, Josh, what do you think this looks like?" I didn't know what else to say. I walked over and handed him the rock. "Here, do you see that coloring? Does it remind you of anything?" I was fishing for things now.

Josh gave me a look like I'd lost my marbles and glanced down at the Airlis. "It looks like a rock," he said, not trying to hide his sarcasm. He raised his eyebrows at me questioningly.

I glanced at the Airlis, half expecting to see something like, *My brother's crazy!* reflected in its depths, but nothing happened. "Oh, I was just wondering what you thought," I said with a shrug.

"It's definitely a pretty rock," he said and handed it back to me. He must've seen the slight disappointment on my face, because he added, "You don't see many that color." He usually doesn't try that hard to be kind. I could tell he was still a little skittish.

"Yeah, it's definitely one of a kind," I answered. *Oh, if he only knew.*

He went back to his model, and I flopped back on my bed. My hope was fading.

We had Fall Break yesterday and today. Why they didn't let us have vacation at the end of the week, I'll never know. Scott was glad for the extra help, though. He decided to tear into a roof replacement when he realized I was available two full days. It took us most of Monday to rip off the old asphalt shingles before we put on the new ones. Luckily, it wasn't a very large house. The fiberglass in those old shingles is nasty; made my arms itch all day!

Ashley and I have gotten into quite the texting habit lately. Last night we stayed up till almost midnight sending messages back and forth She was in the Valley with her mom and sister on a "girl's getaway". I heard all about her exciting shopping activities and how they later went to Castles and Coasters. They were staying with an aunt, and Ashley was bored out of her mind, because all they wanted to do now was play Scrabble. So she sat out by the swimming pool and we texted.

Her favorite color is mauve? I don't know what that is. She tried to explain it to me, but that didn't help. Her favorite movie of all time is *You've Got Mail*, and her first crush was Phillip Tate, but I'm not supposed to tell anyone. That was shocking, because Phillip and I are two very different people. I suppose most of the girls in school had a crush on him at one time or another. Now he hangs out with the skaters and smokes marijuana, or so I hear. I had to give her a hard time over that one.

The only problem with gaining all this information is she required payment in return. Reluctantly, I gave in.

~U had a crush on Andrea Marks??!!!

-Don't worry . . . it didn't last very long.

~LOL! Oh, you've got to let me tell Tracy! She HATES Andrea!

-Nope. Part of the deal remember! No telling!

~Fine. So was she your first kiss?

This question caught me by surprise. Not just because I'm ashamed of that story, but because Ashley was the one asking the question! I don't think she would've asked me that face to face. For some reason, texting makes you feel less accountable and more brave. I laughed thinking how different it would be if our phones read our thoughts and posted them whether we wanted them to or not.

-That's a long story, and I'm not a very good texter. It'll require a good hour and an extra-large root beer.

~It's a date then! ☺ What about tomorrow @ 6 after your work @ our "secret" picnic table?

-Make it a root beer float and I'll be there!

~You got it! Gotta run. Can't wait to hear the rest of the story! TTYL

Her last text message arrived at 11:59 pm. I assumed she must've reached her curfew. As neutral as I am with most desserts, a root beer float has never sounded so good.

Wednesday, 19 October, 2011

Today dragged by. School was boring and work was slow. It didn't help that I kept salivating for a root beer float. Ashley didn't have much to say at school. She actually seemed subdued, but when I asked her what was wrong, she smiled and said jokingly, "Can I meet you somewhere for a root beer float? I'll explain it to you then."

I smiled and said, "How about the park? Let's say around six o-clock?"

"It's a date." But there was still something in her eyes that made her smile look almost sad. I chewed on this all day.

This time I got to the park first and claimed the table under the large cottonwood. There were two young children running around the playground, and I assumed it was their parents watching from a blanket on the grass. People were also playing racquetball in the second court, but I couldn't tell who it was, because there are no windows in the building. The racquets would "pop" back and forth, and after a short struggle, I'd hear a shout of victory or a cry of despair—sometimes both.

Fifteen minutes passed, and I couldn't wait any longer. I thought I would be funny, so I brought chicken nuggets, but they were getting cold, and my stomach was growling. As I finished off the first one, Ashley pulled up.

"Is this seat taken?" she asked slyly as she neared the table.

Smiling, I said, "You know I'm getting an awfully big sense of *déjà vu*, and last time it didn't end so well."

Her face saddened as she sat down and said, "No, it didn't . . ."

I started to really get concerned at this point. Pushing the nuggets toward her, I said, "At least this time, I won't make you eat all of them first."

She smiled weakly and grabbed one, staring at it as if it might relieve suffering, but no comfort came. "David, I can't go out with you anymore."

"Huh?"

She kept her head down, and I could tell she was struggling to hold back tears. "My sister was looking through my phone on our way home from the Valley and made a comment about all our text messages. Mom asked if she could read them, and I couldn't say no; especially after everything that happened last time." I sat like a statue. Her words were spilling out now, and as much as I wanted them to stop, my voice had frozen along with my heart.

"Even though we didn't talk about anything inappropriate, Mom was furious. She couldn't believe we'd go right back to the same park and the same situation that started so much gossip in the first place. She said that even if nothing ever happens, giving Satan a toehold is a recipe for disaster; being alone at the park leads to being alone in a car. Mom went off on me the rest of the way home about how my standards should be higher than this, and if I really want you to make it on a mission . . . I would quit going steady with you."

Frank was right—the world would let us know. How ironic that the moment I realize we're going out, she dumps me. Bitter tears began running down her cheeks. Now it was my turn to try to find comfort from a cold nugget clenched in my hand.

"I'm sorry, David." Her bottom lip quivered, and she stood up quickly. With shaky hands, she sat the root beer float she'd been clutching, along with the dry nugget, on the table. "I truly hope we can stay friends." She wrapped her arms tightly around her chest and hurriedly walked away.

I sat stunned. *What the . . . why did she . . . did that just happen?* My heart was in such great pain, my thoughts couldn't think straight. Not a muscle twitched as I watched her pull out of the parking lot. My mind couldn't make any sense of what happened. I thought things had been going so good! I had a flash of anger toward Ashley's mom, but like a bolt of lightning that's too far away, the thunder never came. I knew it was my fault, and as responsibility of the ruined friendship landed squarely on my slumped shoulders, the anger vanished to reveal a new friend: shame.

I knew Ashley was a good person who tried hard to keep her life on the straight and narrow. Wasn't it only a few weeks ago that I read the standards for the youth of the Church? We're advised to never single date and to avoid steady dating until we're old enough to marry, because it leads to a comfort in relationships that Satan uses to lure young people into sin. If I wasn't going to follow this advice for my own convictions, I should've at least applied these principles for Ashley's sake. Now I've chased her away.

The nugget squished between the fingers of my tightening grip. Whipping around, I hurled it as hard as I could. It flew apart and didn't get very far . . . just like our relationship. My stomach knotted, and suddenly, I was no longer hungry.

I stuffed everything in the trash, including the root beer float—especially the root beer float—and headed out of town.

Darkness was getting thick when I pulled up to Lost Lake, but I didn't want the comfort of the sun, anyway. I sat down in the same spot I had a little over two months ago. *Two months. A lot has happened in two months.* But I wasn't angry this time. I was in need of a friend, and this was as close as I could get to her.

I lay on my back and gazed up at the stars. There was no moon, so millions of pinpricks of light danced uncontested across the night sky. The Milky Way was out in dazzling color, stretching from horizon to horizon. I wondered how many worlds were in our galaxy alone, and to think there are hundreds of thousands, if not millions of other galaxies! I started to feel very small . . . and alone.

Saturday, 22 October, 2011

And just when I thought life couldn't get much worse. You would think, since God wants me to go on a mission, I might get more support from above, right? Ha! You remember the hole Scott talked about? Well, mine just got a lot bigger.

It's been cold all week, and I'm not talking about the weather. Not only do Ashley and I awkwardly avoid each other, the whole school is chittering about the "breakup." I'm glad I only have to deal with it for half a day. As soon as the lunch bell rings, I'm gone. I'm starting to get sick of high school.

Frank was as stunned as everyone else. He tried more than once to get me to talk to him about it, but I flat out told him no. I think this hurt his feelings, because I haven't heard from him since. Sad to say, I don't care right now. I partly blame him for pushing me toward Ashley.

Oh, but the news sure made someone's day, and how did Chelsey celebrate my new single status? By asking me to the Halloween dance—and it isn't even a girl-ask-guy dance! I came out of History on Friday already upset. There was a long pep assembly for the football team that morning before they left to take on the Mingus Marauders. That put me in a foul mood, and Frank has been purposefully ignoring me, which hasn't helped. I got to my truck to find the cab filled to the ceiling with popcorn. I yanked a note off the window that read, "Somewhere in this 'maize' of fun, you'll find the name of only one; her joy and happiness will overflow, if to the Halloween dance you will go!"

It might have brightened my day, or even made me smile, except I recognized the handwriting—Chelsey Rogers. I could feel myself slipping into another mental breakdown. What was I going to do? Gratefully, there weren't very many people in the parking lot yet.

I opened the door, and popcorn poured onto the ground. I made a mental note to lock my door from now on. I didn't spend time searching for her name; I just jumped in and sped away. What was I going to do with all this popcorn!? I decided to drive out in the boondocks and kick as much out as I could. Afterward, I went to the car wash and drove around back to the vacuums. Fifteen dollars and half an hour later, I got my truck back. Halfway through my silent cursing, I found the package under my seat. It was a beautifully wrapped box, and inside was a pink and purple handstitched pillow with the name Chelsey Rogers across the top with a heart underneath. At first I was confused why she would leave such a big space below the heart, and then it dawned on me. It was the space for my name. Words cannot describe . . . at least not any appropriate ones.

Oh, but the day kept getting better! I was late for work and didn't have time to eat lunch. Scott was in a hurry to head out of town. Past White Mountain Lake, off Bourdon Ranch Road, we had another backed up sewer. Of course we did! Scott wasn't excited about it either, and I could tell he was a bit short tempered, so I didn't bother him with my problems. I was content to let them fester.

The project went into the night and overflowed onto Saturday, and no, I'm not trying to be funny. We ended up replacing the sewer line from the house to the septic tank. It was an old clay pipe that disintegrated when you touched it. This morning the smell got so bad Scott and I both lost our breakfast. I honestly didn't know how we'd ever finish the job until the old man came out with a container of Icy Hot. I was still cleaning throw up off my mouth when he walked up and said, "Here, wipe this under your nose."

We didn't have to think twice. I've used Icy Hot before, but never on my face. The sensation was weird, but it worked! The burning aroma of the salve was enough to neutralize the fetid sewer stench.

I turned to the old man and said, "This works great! How did you know this trick?"

His eyes glazed over as he looked off into the distance. In a monotone voice he said, "It also covers the smell of a rotting corpse."

Scott and I both froze. We looked at each other, and I could tell he was thinking the same thing I was—*How fast can we get the HECK out of here?!*

Just as we were about to engage the flight mode, the man turned to us and smiled, "I was a fire chief in Santa Barbara for twenty-five years. Death was a weekly occurrence, and sometimes the bodies had been there for days."

We both let out a loud hoot of relief. He played us good! It was the first dose of anything besides pain I'd received for days, and it felt nice. The project went by much faster when we weren't being gassed to death.

I got home and decided it was time for a movie marathon. I asked Josh if he wanted to join me in watching some kind of trilogy. He thought for a second and snapped his fingers, "I know! We haven't seen the *Bourne Identity* movies in a long time!"

I quickly evaluated them in my head: *Almost everyone important dies except the main character, and he kicks butt!* It was exactly what I needed.

"That's a great idea!" I told him. "I'll go rent the movies if you'll get out some popcorn."

I wasn't paying attention when I walked into Rent-A-Flick, but I wish I'd noticed Zack's Jeep in the parking lot. I stepped inside as Zack was walking out carrying pizza and a movie.

"Well, look who it is!" Zack said with his boisterous voice. "How ya been, quitter?"

"Oh, I've had a pretty *crappy* day, let me assure you." I replied dryly. I tried to step to the side to let him pass, but he wasn't finished with his verbal abuse.

"You missed a hell of a game, Thorn. Everyone thought we were going to lose. Ha!" He leaned toward me and half playing, half serious, poked me in the chest. "You're lucky we won. You would've been blamed for it if we hadn't."

I gulped. "What do you mean?"

"Colton sucks at tight end, man! I swear he dropped every pass I threw at him. Luckily, we were able to take the lead back right at the end. I've never seen such a *sweet* catch!" He put his pizza and video on a table and began to reenact the play with animation. "It was third and long. We were on our own thirty-yard line with only thirty-five seconds left. Coach calls for the streak. DOWN! SET! HUT!!" Zack took an imaginary football and started backing up. "They stunted both inside line backers, so I had to scramble. One got a little close, but I shoved him down and rolled to the outside!" He ducked and weaved his way through the tables. "As they closed in, I pulled back and let her FLY! They were on Brett like flies on [bad word], so he jumped as high as he could to catch it. The defender tripped! Brett's hands snagged the ball, but

his feet were knocked out from under him, and he fell on the DB.
But the crazy kid sat right on his BACK! His knees NEVER
touched the GROUND! He jumped up and sprinted—untouched—
to the end zone! It was CRAZY MAN! The crowd went WILD!"

"Really?" I asked in disbelief.

"Yes, Sir! Final score was 32 - 29! Oh, you missed a good
one, man." He slapped me on the back and picked up his stuff.
"We're going to take it this year, bro! Too bad you won't be there
with us. See you around, dude. I'm off to celebrate with my girl."
He winked at me as he walked out.

I wanted so badly to hate him, but he's such a likeable guy, it
was impossible to hold onto anger very long. I watched him jump
in his nice Jeep and speed away. My life had been shriveling all
day, but this was the gash that instantly deflated me into a wrinkled
mass of failure. A long breath escaped my lungs, and fortunately
my body decided to suck one back in. At the moment, I didn't care
either way.

Sunday, 23 October, 2011

Even though it was late last night when I wrote that last entry, my restless mind wouldn't allow me passage into dreamland. I lay there a long time weighing, calculating—trying to figure how to fill the growing hole in my life. The only conclusion I came up with was . . . I had no idea.

A reflection of a memory caught my attention, and I remembered a story Mom told me once when she was looking for answers. In her struggling, she'd decided to fast for extra help. The reason for her fast was fuzzy, because my attention was drawn to the part when she said she received a miracle. I've never been a very good faster (that doesn't sound like correct English, but I'm not sure how else to say it), but I really needed a miracle.

If you've never taken the opportunity to fast, I would normally say you're not missing much. But I learned today, if you do it right, it can bring great rewards. Our Church fasts once a month, usually the first Sunday. We go without food or drink for two meals, and it's suggested to "donate generously" to help those in need. That's about the extent of the guidelines, and we're encouraged to follow them to the best of our ability. That's how I always viewed fasting. But more important than the starving and the giving is the part I often overlook: the asking.

Mom tries to remind us about Fast Sunday the night before, and she always includes the advice to think of something to fast for. Usually this means to ask for answers to any questions we might have or a special blessing for someone who's ill. I've tried most times to do as she asked, but I couldn't remember ever really pursuing it to a successful outcome. I think the main reason was I never really had anything personal to fast for—until now.

Today wasn't Fast Sunday for the ward, but that didn't matter. I rolled onto my knees sometime around two in the morning and told God I really needed some extra help. I wasn't sure quite how to ask but decided to be honest about the desires of my heart. I told Him I had two requests. First, I asked if He'd help me find ways to fill the emptiness my course change had caused. Second, I pled, if possible, that He'd somehow reconnect me with Elli. This would be the focus of my fast for the next day. It wasn't until after I crawled back into bed that I was finally able to get some rest.

I didn't have to try hard to avoid breakfast, because I was almost late for church. The missionaries who serve in our ward spoke, and it seemed like they were talking directly to me. They told story after story of experiences they were having and the joy they felt as they helped people come to Christ.

In the Priest's Quorum, Brad taught the lesson today. He talked about missionary work, too, which I found surprising, because he didn't go on one. He told of a few experiences he had during his baseball career to share the gospel, but he admitted he wasn't the best example then. The focus of his lesson was on how he'd decided later to try and be a member missionary all the time. He spent the rest of the hour telling us experiences he'd had at work, on vacation, in the store, and even at church, where he has been able to answer questions and share the gospel with people around him.

After he finished, Bishop thanked him and added, "A reminder for those of you who are getting close to nineteen, the Mission Preparation class is every Sunday evening at six at the Seminary building."

His words seemed to thump me on the head. I'd never thought about preparing for a mission before, but all of a sudden I became excited to start. I got a soft impression it was a step in the right direction, and it brought a smile to my lips.

The Mission Prep class had fifteen guys and three girls. The girls can't serve missions until they're twenty-one, so they were all a few years older than us. I recognized most of the guys, and they all welcomed me with warm handshakes. The instructor was a younger man who recently returned home from serving his mission in upstate New York. His smile was big and his energy contagious.

I didn't know what to expect. I guess I was thinking we'd have manuals and lessons, but I was wrong. The first thing he did was ask for half of the class to volunteer. I, being a little hesitant, didn't raise my hand. He had the volunteers all stand against the white board, and then he turned back to us. "Okay, today we're going to discuss service, and as an object lesson I'm going to need you to be the gracious recipients of a service these guys are going to do for you. Do you accept?" I nodded my head. What option did I have?

"Great! Now if you'll please remove your shoes." Everyone looked around at each other nervously. "Go on! Our volunteers will be massaging your feet for the next ten minutes. We've got odd numbers, so some will have to take turns."

It was an awkward moment for everyone, but the teacher was persistent, and he started assigning massagers to feet. I was hoping I wouldn't get a girl, but Brother Woodside kept it mission appropriate and had the girls only rub other girls' feet. But when he asked 200 pound, nothing-but-muscle-and-manhood John Bryant to rub mine, the girls started to look very appealing.

I wanted to crawl in a tiny gopher hole. It was a humbling experience for everyone, but it was a very effective lesson. I never realized that being able to *accept* service could be so hard. One of Brother Woodside's main points was, in order for service to be the most beneficial, it must be received as well as given. In spite of the extreme discomfort of the moment, I learned a great deal from the class.

When I got home, I went into my room, so I could end my fast with a prayer. After locking the door, I sat on my bed and slowly reviewed the day. A comfortable grin landed lopsided on my face as a thought popped into my head. Maybe it's because of the farmer's blood that runs through my veins, but I felt like God gave me a shovel today. And next to it, a large pile of hope so I can start filling up my life's void. I also got the impression that *service* will have a lot to do with getting that hope from the pile into my heart. With great anticipation, I dug out the Airlis from the ammo box and held it gently with both hands.

I formed clearly the words in my head, *Elli, are you there?* But nothing happened. I tried three more times without success. With a sigh, I placed the Airlis back in the box. I didn't allow myself to give up hope, though. If God can part the Red Sea, I'm sure He can help me find Elli again. I consoled myself by deciding it must not be the right time, and I left it at that. Even though it wasn't the miracle I was expecting, it was more than I could hope for. God didn't move any mountains for me, but He did show me where to start—one shovelful at a time.

<u>Tuesday, 25 October, 2011</u>

I sat bolt upright in bed so fast my English book went flying off my lap and skidded across the floor. I'd been lying there reading my homework assignment when all of a sudden I felt a sensation coming from my right hand. With great anticipation, I looked down, and sure enough, the miracle had happened.

DAVID!

"ELLI!" I shouted out loud. Luckily I was alone at the moment. The Airlis still understood, and my captured thought appeared briefly before fading into the rock. My heart expanded until my eyes began to burn with tears.

Oh David! You don't know how GLAD I am to hear from you!

Actually . . . I think I do, Elli. A realization of *what* I'd felt through my hand hit me like a ton of bricks. The Airlis had not only portrayed her words but also how she *felt* about those words. Elli—I can *feel* your happiness!

I can feel you as well! How AMAZING! Her wonder flowed through the Airlis. *You are filled with such joy! It's almost more than I can contain.*

I could tell she was stunned. I thought I really lost you this time, Elli. I haven't heard from you in a whole month.

You're angry, too!

It was only a small twinge of anger, but I had felt it surface briefly. This is crazy! How is it doing this?

Father said the Airlis has potential to grow, but I didn't understand what he meant until now.

The Airlis grows? I asked in surprise.

Yes! But he never explained how.

A new thought overpowered me and almost put me in shock, You're real . . . . You are really, REAL!

Yes, silly! I thought you already figured that out?

Sorry, it's just . . . I had hoped, but . . . you know, my thoughts started jamming up.

I DO know! I can sense your confusion!

This snapped me back, Oh man, I'm going to have to be even *more* careful now.

I understood that, too! And yes, I agree. I must be more careful, as well.

I sat in a semi-shocked state for a few seconds. As much as I wanted to set the Airlis down to collect my thoughts, I didn't dare. I did *not* want to lose her again. Instead, I decided to change the subject. So where have you been?

Oh, have I got a story to tell you!

Just one? I thought in surprise, I've lived a whole life in the last thirty days. How long has it been for you?

Let's see, the last time I talked to you was the day before our Grand Council, so that would have been four days ago. Did you say THIRTY days? Oh my stars . . . I've forgotten how much time changes between us.

Well twenty-eight days to be exact, but who's counting? I replied sarcastically.

YOU have been, and I would have too if it had been that long. Oh, David, I can feel your despair. It's terrible. We don't experience that emotion much here. I am extremely sorry.

It's not very pleasant, but we are back together now, and that's what's important. What's a Grand Council, anyway?

The Grand Council is when Father invites us all together for important announcements and discussions, and oh, this was a grand one indeed!

I marveled again at feeling the sensation of pure excitement coming through the Airlis. You're ECSTATIC! I said in surprise.

YES, a fine choice of words! Father gathered us all together and told us that the time has come to move forward! David . . . WE ARE GETTING A MORTAL EXPERIENCE!

The shockwave of pure joy nearly knocked me off the bed! WOW! You better tone it down a notch, or you might give me a heart attack!

That did the trick. Her feelings mellowed abruptly and she began apologizing again. *I'm sorry. I can't help it! Two plans were presented, and Father admonished us to ponder and study which we'd prefer, and to be ready to choose our Plan of Progression in thirty days' time!*

That . . . took you FOUR days?

I can feel your sarcasm! This is so EXCITING!

Uh huh.

OH, how amazing! No, it only took two days. On the first day I tried to contact you, and an interesting thing occurred. When I picked up the Airlis, I saw the words, "David is going to kill me!" But when I asked who it was, there was no reply.

It took me a second to realize what happened. That must've been my brother, Josh! and I told her the whole story of that night.

Elli replied, *We are lucky he didn't erase our connection.*

An emotion of gratitude and relief flowed from her to me, and I returned the feeling with the words, Yeah, me, too.

I'm not sure how to describe what happened next. Things . . . intensified for a moment. We didn't share any words, but I'm positive she felt something, too, because a slight flash of embarrassment was followed abruptly with the words, *I think when we reconnected through the Airlis, it must have grown to channel our feelings as well!*

This snapped me out of it, and I replied, That would make sense. Whatever the reason, I'm glad it did.

After another short pause, she said, *Yes, I am, too.*

To avoid another quick dive into uncharted waters of emotion, I asked, So, you had a pretty good council then?

It was marvelous! Words can't do it justice. Our joy overflowed, and we rejoiced with song and dance for days! Most of my brothers and sisters are still rejoicing now, but I wanted so badly to tell you what happened, I left early to come back home.

Her concern for me was felt through the Airlis, and I wasn't sure exactly how to understand it. Was it genuine care for me or something else? I'm sorry you had to cut your party short, I said, but I'm very glad you did.

It was worth it. Besides, it's good to be thoughtful of others.

Her words filleted me with one quick stroke. Frank. Ashley. Tracy. People I considered last week to be my best friends, now I haven't spoken to them in days. Yeah . . . it's good to be thoughtful.

David what's wrong? You're . . . in pain.

I smiled, Like I said, I've lived a whole life in the last twenty-eight days. I've gained friends and lost them, lost dreams and gained new ones, and I've changed the whole course of my life along the way.

Your words are bursting with emotions. Do tell me what happened!

I let out a long breath, then thought, Do you have anywhere you need to be, because this might take a while?

Our regular schedules won't begin again until after our day of rest, so that gives me a whole day. I'm all yours!

I laughed, Ha! Time won't be a problem then. Good. Now let's see . . . where did we leave off? Do you remember?

Oh, yes! You had recently returned from your amazing date, your arm was feeling better, and you were back to playing your football! Does that help?

Yep. That brings it *all* back, thanks. Her excitement vanished.

Sometimes your words and your feelings seem to be in contradiction. Why is that?

Well, it's called irony, because I lost the girl, re-broke my arm, and quit football. I felt what I assumed was a gasp, because I didn't actually see any words. At that moment, the door handle turned, and I shoved my hand under the blanket. Josh came in and threw a pile of clothes on his bed. He glanced at me and said, "Mom's got a pile for you, too," and he started stuffing clothes in his drawers.

I didn't know what to do besides get up and go get my clothes. I went to put the Airlis in my pocket, but before I did, I thought,

Elli, can you give me a second? I need to grab some clothes from my mom.

I looked down and saw, *I'm not going anywhere, David. I promise.*

Not daring the chance to lose Elli so soon after getting her back, I kept my hand in my pocket, fingers clasped tightly around the Airlis. Mom was sorting through Sarah's socks when I got to her room. "Thanks, Mom," I said as I scooped up my basket in my left hand.

She replied, "You're welcome, and will you make sure Josh puts them away this time? I'm tired of finding washed and folded clothes in the dirty laundry basket!"

"Sure, Mom." I ran back to my room and threw the basket on my bed. I quickly sorted the clothes and threw them in the right drawers.

"You in a hurry?" Josh asked.

"Yeah, I've uh, got a friend waiting to talk to me . . . on the phone." Josh gave me a weird look as I hurried out the door. *Where to go?* I finally grabbed a blanket and went outside. The night was bitter cold. The wind was blowing, and I knew I would be an ice cube in seconds if I sat on the swing, so I climbed in my truck instead.

You still there, Elli?

I haven't moved a micrometer. You were talking with your mother?

Yeah, she had a pile of clothes for me to put away.

It sounds like she's very kind. Does she make all your clothes?

This made me laugh, Ha! No we buy our clothes from stores, but she does wash them for me.

That is very sweet of her. We're in charge of our own clothing from a very young age. It's one of the first responsibilities we learn. This again caught me by surprise. I never thought about what Elli's daily routine might be like. She interrupted my meandering mind and said, *But we stray from the* point; you were about to tell me what sounded like a terribly sad story.

Oh yeah, let's see . . . I started with the night I almost killed Josh, went through the struggle of quitting football and getting a job, and ended with the park, the gossip, the fun, and the breakup. When I finally finished my story, there were no words for a good twenty seconds, just a sensation I could only describe as confusion.

David . . . I've never cried tears of pain and joy at the same time before. Is mortal life always this complicated?

I chuckled, Yeah, I guess it is, but don't worry. I'm sure you'll be sent to a much better situation than I'm in.

I've never given it much thought. I don't know, your life is intriguing. If nothing else, I hope I have a caring mother like yours.

You'll be lucky if you do, I replied with a deep sense of gratitude. What about you, Elli? Tell me about this party. Was Jared with you?

Her emotions brightened instantly. It was wonderful! To finally have a day set for this momentous occasion, we were all bursting with joy! And yes, Jared was by my side throughout almost the entire celebration. David, he asked me if I would like to petition for 'Continued Friendship' with him. Most people let mortal life take its course, but some request to continue their friendships on earth in hopes it may lead to eternal union.

Wait, so he asked you to marry him?

Not exactly, the marriage ordinance can only occur after you receive a physical body. If the union is successful, and the two people continue in righteousness throughout mortality, they may remain sealed together for the eternities. If I accept Jared's proposal, Father will provide a mortal existence where our paths meet. If we still desire to continue a relationship, we may get married. If we make those covenants, and honor them to the end of our mortal existence, we qualify for eternal union. Does that make sense?

That's a lot of "ifs," but yeah, I think I get it. So, basically you'll be engaged until you go to your mortal world, right?

Engaged in what?

I smiled. Sorry. Engaged means. . . The humor disappeared as I struggled to find the words to explain. It means you're promised to each other, but you haven't actually made the promise yet. It really was confusing. No wonder she didn't understand.

Yes, quite similar to what Jared is proposing.

What did you tell him?

I didn't know what to say. It's such a big decision. I know it isn't permanent yet, but I'm sure the consequences will be nothing short of eternal. I asked him if he would give me until the next Grand Council to decide. He gave me a hug and said he would be happy to wait. He is a very thoughtful guy.

I think you did the right thing, Elli. Marriage isn't something you should jump into. It sounds like you have a lot to do in thirty days.

As far as deciding which plan to choose, I've already made my decision, but I'm concerned about Jared. He's becoming deeply rooted in the Salvation Side. That's what they're calling themselves now. Those of us who support agency are called the Freedom Side. My heart is made up, but I haven't made any verbal pledges yet because of Jared. I didn't want to cause any friction in our blossoming relationship.

Pondering this for a moment, I said, But Elli, you can't choose different sides and be able to continue your friendship on earth. You've got to convince him that his plan will never work!

I know. We've been trying to avoid the topic, but I don't think we'll be able to for much longer. You see, by the next Council, every person will have to voice which plan they are dedicating themselves to, so I only have a handful of days to persuade him.

I'll help all I can, Elli. If your plan ends up anything like ours, those who choose the Salvation Side will be cast out! He'll be lost forever.

My studies have confirmed that very point. Despair flowed thickly between us for a moment, but she quickly brushed it aside with a wave of hope. *Together we will find a way to reach him. Thank you, David. I understand now what Father meant. Your support and friendship have helped me more than I can say.*

I feel the same way about you. Our emotions collided, and for a second, I couldn't tell which were mine and which were hers. I probably better be going, Elli. I can't feel my toes anymore.

Oh, no! I didn't realize our conversations restricted your sensations!

I laughed out loud, Ha! No, no, I'm sitting outside, and the temperature has dropped below freezing. I just need to get back in the house and warm up a bit.

That makes more sense, sorry. I'm glad to be able to feel your happiness now. It helps me understand you even more clearly.

I'm glad to have you back, Elli.

Yes, I'm glad, as well, David.

After our goodbyes, I put the Airlis in my pocket. Strong emotions of gratitude began overflowing through my eyes. I couldn't help but be overcome by the miracle I'd been given, again! I bowed my head and poured out my thanks to God for bringing us back together. A friend is exactly what I needed. Even though my toes were tingling, I sat in the truck for a while longer and pondered some of the things Elli had said. Two things seemed to stand out: *I need to be a more thoughtful friend, and I need to be a more thoughtful son.* I decided to set some more goals. Helping Mom with my own laundry was the easy one. Besides, I'll need to learn how to do my own laundry soon enough. Rebuilding some crumbling bridges? That might be a little more difficult.

Thursday, 27 October, 2011

Yesterday, as I dragged myself through bland and scheduled motions, for some reason I began to examine my life from the outside looking in. Putting myself in other people's shoes revealed something that startled me—I'm not a very nice person. Take Frank for example. The guy has gone out of his way to be my friend, and all I've done is push him away. Ashley clearly has feelings for me, but when she faced the struggle of our relationship alone—a problem I helped cause—I sat and watched tears roll down her face without saying a word. She has no idea what I feel or think about her, and I still haven't tried to set things right. Even Chelsey Rogers deserves better. Every day she finds a way to hint about the popcorn or my truck, and all I've done is act like I didn't know what she's talking about. I was ashamed of who I saw. But how do I fix me? Where do I start?

Frank conveniently sits on the other side of the bass section during Honor Choir now, so I don't have a chance to talk to him there. I realized if something is going to happen, I'll have to take the initiative. I thought about it all afternoon at work and decided I need to face it head on.

I knocked on Frank's front door, hoping a family member would answer to cushion the enmity between us, but it was Frank. After a brief second of surprise, he got a smug look on his face and said, "Sorry, but we don't want any Girl Scout Cookies," and slammed the door.

"Frank, I come with a peace offering." Pause. "Come on man! I promise it's better than cookies."

He cracked the door, and with his right eye showing, he said, "That's too bad, some Thin Mints might have gotten you in."

"I have something better than Thin Mints," I held up the drink in my hand, "an ice cold, vanilla Dr. Pepper from Sonic."

His eye glanced down to my hand. "Is it extra-large?"

"Yep."

"Does it come with a heartfelt apology and a side of groveling?"

"I'm sorry, okay? I had a really bad week, and I shouldn't have taken it out on you." I held the drink up.

"And the groveling?" he asked.

I froze for a second, drink poised in mid-air, "You know, on second thought, I think I'll keep it." I pulled it back and took a long swig.

Frank yanked the door open and yelled, "HEY!" I acted like I was about to walk away then smiled and pulled out his real drink from behind my back. He snatched it, and with an almost respectful tone, added, "You sly dog."

He took a long drink, and I waited until he got the—*oh that tastes gooood*—look on his face before I asked, "Am I forgiven?"

He smacked his lips and said, "There's nothing like a good soda to cover a multitude of sins."

I laughed, "A *multitude* huh?"

"Yep, just covered 'em all up."

"Well, I'm glad, as long as you don't uncover them later at your convenience."

He shrugged and said, "That'll be up to you," and walked back inside. Glancing over his shoulder as I followed him in, he asked, "So what have you been up to lately, besides pulverizing girls' hearts?"

"Ha ha, very funny."

"You sure know how to be the center of attention," he chuckled.

"Believe me, it isn't on purpose." I sank into his sofa as he sat in the recliner next to me. "Did you hear who asked me to the Halloween dance?"

Frank almost dropped his drink, "The Halloween Dance? It's obvious she was responsible for the popcorn—she's been bouncing off the walls in choir—but I thought it was for Winter Formal!"

"I know! The Halloween dance isn't even an "ask out" dance, it's just a dance! Help me think of a way to answer her," I begged.

"Oh, sure." He took a long drink and said, "Tell her to go jump off a cliff!"

I backhanded him. "I'm serious man."

He grabbed his arm and warned, "Be careful, they aren't buried THAT deep. Wait . . . you're gonna go with her?" I nodded solemnly. "Dude, your life can't be *that* bad." He leaned toward me and rested his elbows on his knees. "Listen, if you say yes, she'll never let you go. She has tentacles, man!"

"I don't have a choice! I can't tell her NO two days before the dance."

"Oh, yes you can! Consider this a life or death situation."

I shook my head. "Then what do I do?"

"Like I said. I promise, there's no easy way down for girls like her. The faster she realizes there's no future with you, the quicker she'll hit bottom and move on."

"But it seems so harsh."

He replied, "Don't worry, your reputation right now isn't exactly shining. Speaking of which, what happened between you and Ashley?" I knew this was coming at some point, so I inhaled a lot of oxygen—I was going to need it.

When I finally wrapped it up, he said, "That's basically what Tracy told me, too."

"So are you two still going out?" I asked trying to change the subject.

"Yeah, we have our ups and downs, but we're still together . . . I think. You never know, right?"

I laughed, "Nope, you never know."

He sat back, deep in thought, and said, "So what you need is a prior engagement, something you supposedly had already committed to that you can't get out of." He sat up and snapped his fingers. "Dude, I've got it! The HAUNTED CORN MAZE!"

"At the Willis Farm?"

"Yeah! I know Kyle pretty good, maybe he'll 'happen' to need our help this weekend!" Frank immediately picked up his phone. Kyle's a senior this year, too. He's a tenor in choir, so I know who he is, but he plays soccer and hangs out with a different group of friends. I don't know him that well.

As I sat and listened to Frank's side of the conversation, my heart was in turmoil. It felt morally wrong to do this, but on the other hand, I could see how Frank was right. Chelsey has been stalking me forever, and I didn't want to put gas on THAT fire. After a short conversation he hung up and said, "Okay, we're in!"

"Huh?" My inner battle had not yet warred its way to a conclusion. "What about Tracy?"

"She'll understand. Maybe I can talk the girls into helping us." One glance at me, and he quickly amended his question, ". . . or not. Dude, you've got to talk to Ashley and smooth this over."

I looked down, "I know, but I don't know what to say."

"Just talk to her, man! You'll figure it out." I nodded in agreement. He continued, "K, now back to this weekend. Kyle said they need help with their 'hunting' section of the haunt. It sounds like a blast! They're using their laser tag equipment to turn half of their corn maze into hunting grounds. I guess the people will each get a gun, and they have to shoot targets or something as they work their way through."

It sounded like a lot of fun. The comparison of scaring people in a corn field or dancing the night away with Chelsey was pretty black and white. I just couldn't tell which way was black. "I don't know, Frank, I still feel terrible about turning her down. It was hard enough making one girl cry. I don't think I could do it again."

We sat in silence for a while longer, and then he snapped his fingers and yelled, "I've got it! To show her you're sorry, you'll buy her two tickets to come *through* the maze! That way you'll be showing your gratitude, and you'll get to scare the CRAP out of her, too! You win both ways!"

His plan actually sounded like it'd work. Once again, I was amazed at what this crazy guy could come up with. "Frank, you're the most devious guy I've ever known."

He puffed out his chest and put his hands behind his head. With cocky acceptance he said, "Thanks!" I couldn't help but laugh. It was good to have my friend back.

Saturday, 29 October, 2011

Coming into this weekend, there was a point when I thought this entry might end up being my obituary, but to my surprise and relief, it actually didn't turn out half bad. On my way home from Frank's Thursday night, I stopped by Kyle's house to pick up two tickets to the haunted maze. I wasn't exactly sure how it was all going to pan out, but at least I had some options now.

I wrestled with myself all night, but I couldn't commit to any road. Part of me really wanted to go through with Frank's plan, but in my mind, I kept seeing a fuzzy image of a girl. I couldn't make out her face, but I could feel her piercing gaze. I went to school the next morning with the tickets in my pocket, but no plan in my head. In Seminary, I tried to focus on the lesson, but my thoughts kept wandering to the pair of green vouchers burning in my pocket. About the time I reined my mind back to class, my eyes would catch a glimpse of Ashley, and I'd lose my grip all over again. As a distraction, I forced my hand to draw something. Before I realized it, a pretty horrible sketch of a bench began to appear on my paper. I thought to myself, *It's just missing the girl* . . . All of a sudden I understood. The girl I'd been almost seeing was Elli! Ignited by this thought, words began echoing in my head, *Besides, it is good to be thoughtful of your friends.* This is what sparked a crazy change of plans.

"Hey, Ashley! Wait up." She was already walking out the door.

She turned, slightly surprised, and said, "Hey David . . . um, how are you?"

"I'm still alive, I guess. How have you been?"

She looked at her feet and shrugged her shoulders. "Doing okay, I guess."

"Is it all right if I walk with you?" I didn't know why I needed to ask permission, but it felt like the right thing to do.

She looked up and smiled, and I felt the ice between us crack slightly. "Sure, but I better warn you." She took a quick glance around and whispered, *"This might end up on everyone's phone by the time we reach campus."*

This made me laugh, and the sound helped break the icy barrier. I said, "We wouldn't want that now, would we." She smiled again. It felt good. "I have something for you." I pulled the two tickets from my pocket and handed them to her. "They're tickets to the haunted corn maze."

Her face registered surprise and then gratitude with a twinge of confusion. "Really! What are *these* for?"

"Well, first off, I wanted to tell you I'm sorry for what happened. I should've realized I was putting us in bad situations."

She looked down and said, "I should've been more careful, too."

"And I was also hoping we could still be friends."

She looked at me for a second and smiled again, "Yeah, I'd like that."

It was good to see her smile. My shoulders relaxed as I grinned back. "I hoped you would."

She turned the tickets over in her hand and asked quizzically, "So . . . are these for us?"

The reason for her confusion suddenly became clear. "No, no, I mean I *would* go, but I was only giving them as a peace offering."

"Oh, I see. Well, thank you very much." Her gratitude was genuine.

Then I remembered the rest of my plan, "Besides, I might be working in the haunted maze this year, anyway."

"Really?" she asked in surprise. "I didn't know that."

"Yeah, it kinda happened last minute. I've got a few things to work out, but that's the plan."

"Well, it sounds like a lot of fun."

I replied vaguely, "Yeah . . . I hope so."

We reached North Hall and Ashley turned to me. Tilting her head slightly, she searched my face for a moment. I couldn't read her look. It was a mixture of emotions as far as I could tell, most of which didn't mesh. I thought I saw joy for things found, but there was also pain for things lost. There was great relief but also deep strain. Whatever it was, it was intense. I wasn't man enough to match it and looked away.

In a kind voice, she said, "Thank you, David. This means a lot to me."

I glanced back up to see her smile softly. "You're welcome." Then she walked inside.

I'm not sure what happened. Girls are so confusing! I *think* part one of my crazy plan was accomplished. At least now I feel better about us, but I'm not quite sure what "us" is anymore. At least I made it through; now on to part two.

When I tapped Chelsey's arm, and she turned and realized who it was, you would've thought the girl had won the lottery. I cleared my throat and said, "Hey, uh . . . can I talk to you for a minute?" We were walking on our way to Honor Choir and had just passed the auditorium.

"Oh, sure, David!" Her giddiness was so hysterical I almost started laughing.

I shook it off and pushed ahead. "So, I have a slight dilemma with the dance . . ." Her euphoria started evaporating quickly, so I hurried to spit out the rest. "You see, Kyle needs help scaring people in their haunted maze, so I talked to him after second hour and asked if our date group could come and help, and he said that would be great. They usually close at 10, so if we hurry out of there, we can still make it to the dance for an hour or so. What do you think?"

We had stopped walking by this time, and for a split second, her face went completely blank. I cringed. This was the moment her heart would either break or burst. As the information settled, a huge grin split her face, and she jumped in the air! "That would be AWESOME!" she exclaimed.

Her reaction caught me by surprise and made me jump. *Well, it definitely didn't break,* I thought, and I smiled in relief. "So, you're okay with it? I'd hate to ruin your plans."

"Oh, no, this is GREAT! I've always wanted to help scare people in the maze! Thank you SO much!" She threw her arms around my neck and gave me a big hug. Before I could lift my arms to accept or reject it, she pulled away and went skipping off to the choir room.

We had assumed our old seating arrangement on the back row, and after my whispered confession, Frank's mouth fell open. "I couldn't tell her no, Frank. At least this way, she won't have all night to dance cheek to cheek, and you won't miss your date."

He threw his hands in the air and whispered back, too loudly, "Well, it's your funeral, pal."

"I'm sorry, man. At least the tickets mended things with Ashley, right?"

This curbed his anger enough to un-ruffle his feathers. "At least you did ONE thing right. I'm glad I haven't told Tracy the date was off. You're probably right, though. She would've killed me."

I looked down at Chelsey sitting on the second row. She was jabbering a hundred miles an hour to her good friend, Andrea. I assumed she was one of the other girls in our group, and I was right.

There were three couples actually: us, Andrea and John, and their friend Sarah from Speech and Debate with her boyfriend Russ. I didn't know the rest of the group very well, but once we started playing games the awkwardness left, and surprisingly, I had a really good time!

It started today with a picnic at the park. The girls organized some fun games to play after we finished eating our turkey sandwiches. They made up a crazy three-legged-race obstacle course we had to do with our dates. The funniest part was trying to cross the monkey bars together. We also had to build our own dessert using chocolate, marshmallows, graham crackers, and whipped cream then eat it without using our hands!

After the park, we went to Chelsey's house and played all sorts of games. We started with the card game Apples to Apples and then Catch Phrase. We ended with a really fun group game I've never heard of, called Ninja. We stood in a circle, and on the count of three, we took some type of fighting stance. We had to stay completely frozen. To start, the chosen attacker had one fluid move to try and karate chop another person's hand. That person had one move to avoid getting their hand hit. At the end of the chop, jab, or slap, you had to freeze again in whatever pose you ended in. The person to the right got the next turn to attack. If one of your hands got chopped, it was out of the game. The last person with a hand in won. We played it for a good hour. It was hilarious!

The girls made us a delicious spaghetti dinner, and afterward, we all ran home to change into our camo outfits. Kyle asked us to meet at the Willis house around seven wearing as much camouflage as we could find. We made up quite the group. Some had hunting camo, some had army camo, and Andrea's was bright pink. Kyle explained we were going to be an ambush. He gave us each a three-foot swimming pool noodle and walked us to a spot deep in the corn field. You see, the people thought they were coming in to shoot at targets, but really, THEY were the ones being hunted! We hid in a circle and jumped out all at once to chase them with the noodles! We had an absolute blast!

Andrea was our distraction—since she was almost glowing—and when the group looked at her, we would attack from behind. It was the funnest date I'd ever been on! Every group reacted differently. Some screamed and ran, some tripped and fell, others tried to shoot us, but they had laser guns, and we had pool noodles. One guy ran and dove in the corn, completely disappearing. We couldn't help but join his group in laughing hysterically! Before we knew it, it was past ten and the last group came through. We decided our camo outfits were perfect costumes for the dance, and we drove to the school cafeteria.

People called us the Rambo group, and we were proud of it. After we waited in line to get our pictures, we only had time for a few dances, but that was all right with me. I can't dance worth crap, but it gets worse when the music speeds up, and that's all they seemed to play. John would get a little freaky, and the girls moved around pretty good, but I only swayed in place. Gratefully, we mostly stayed in a circle and laughed about the fun we had. Finally, the last song of the dance was a slow song, and Chelsey grabbed my hand.

"Thank you, David, for going on a date with me and for inviting us all to the maze. This was the best date EVER!" The lights were down low, but I could see the glint of small tears forming in her eyes as we moved in a slow circle.

"No, thank you, Chelsey. You guys thought of the coolest things to do. I had so much fun tonight. That game, Ninja? That was awesome! Where did you learn that?"

"My cousins from St. George told me about it. Yeah, it's a blast! The best was when Russ took out half the circle!"

"Yeah, that was hilarious!" I smiled at the surprisingly sweet memories we'd made together. Who would've thought?

"But scaring in the maze was a *really* good ending. Thanks again, David."

A stab of guilt hit me. I couldn't believe I had almost turned her down. It didn't last long, though, because fortunately, I'd made the right decision, and *that* felt extremely good. As the song ended, Chelsey gave me another hug, and this time I had enough sense to give one back.

Tuesday, 1 November, 2011

Hey, angel, how are you today? My message sent on the first try to my extreme relief. It wasn't as cold as last week, so I decided to bundle up in a blanket and sit on the swing tonight.

Doing well, David, and how are you?

You know, I'm doing *pretty* good, actually.

You do feel more at peace today. What has happened in your expanse of time?

I smiled at her peculiar use of words. A LOT has happened!

I can't wait to hear about it! I loved the sweet feeling of her enthusiasm.

It took a good half hour to send the details of the past seven days across the heavens. She asked a lot of questions, especially about my mended relationships. As I wrapped up the story of the unexpected fun I had on my stalker date, I said, Thanks, Elli, for all your advice. I may not have made the right decision without it.

It wasn't I. All good things come from our Fathers. You should give your gratitude to Him.

Her words sank into my mind. Thinking back, I couldn't remember if I had given thanks to God for the way things ended up or not. I made a mental note to be sure to tell Him tonight.

There you go again, giving more good advice. You're absolutely right. God has blessed us with a very unique relationship, and I'll be forever grateful for that. But you didn't have to be my friend. Thank you, for not giving up on me.

There was a slight pause, and with a deep sense of humility, she said, *You're welcome.* Her emotion suddenly intensified into what I could only describe as affection. *But remember, David, true friendship grows from two directions. Thank you for being my friend, as well.*

Even though there was slight discomfort at sharing such personal feelings, it was getting easier to handle. Not that I had much choice. It was the price I had to pay to talk to Elli, and it was worth every embarrassing emotion. All I could do was try to change the subject when intense moments came up. So, Elli, tell me about your day.

My day has been wonderful so far. Today is our day of rest, and it was well needed after the long celebration.

Oh, yeah, I forgot about that. You guys must be party animals! I teased.

Her emotions brightened briefly, and then there was a hint of sadness. *If only you could remember, you'd understand why it was such a glorious day.*

She was sad for *me*! I turned the humor down a bit, and replied, I'm sorry, I shouldn't have teased you about that. I've read in the scriptures that we shouted for joy the day we got the news, but that's about all we know of our pre-mortal existence.

Believe me, it was a day you anticipated for millennia.

I sat back in shock. Do you think my spirit could have been that old?

It's very possible if your spirit was organized at the dawning of your God's creations, but that is nothing when compared to eternity. You won't remember until you return to Him again. My oldest brothers and sisters are way beyond millennia, and their spiritual progression has reached levels of Godhood. I can only imagine the anticipation they must have felt to hear the announcement of our upcoming mortal existence.

Huh, was all I could reply as big gears began grinding in my head. I've heard of these things, but I've never really thought about them in depth before. It's hard to grasp eternity when everything we know has a beginning and an end, and sometimes they don't last very long.

It's just as hard for me to understand things of a mortal nature, but I'm excited to find out! Her enthusiasm was still as intense as it had been last week.

So, what do you do on your "day of rest"? I asked curiously.

We rest, silly!

No, smart aleck. I figured that much. I mean, do you do anything else? Do you go to church in heaven?

What is church?

Well, that answers my question, but as for your question, church is where we go to learn more about God and take the sacrament.

In that case, I suppose we have a similar thing. On the Sabbath, we meet together, and we also have sacramental ordinances, but mostly we rest from our labors. Sometimes Father comes and teaches us himself, but a majority of the day is spent enjoying family and the beauty of creation.

Wow, I thought in amazement. To be taught at the feet of God is something very few people get the chance to experience here. And it's interesting you also call it the Sabbath. I wonder why our worlds are so similar?

From what I understand, principles of truth are still true no matter what galaxy or time you live in. Resting is one of those eternal principles. Everything needs a time of rest. The Sabbath is another truth. It represents a holy day where we learn the principles and perform the ordinances that increase our spiritual progression.

This is crazy! That's exactly the same thing I've been taught! And it makes sense, too. Why wouldn't there be a universal order to things spiritual when there is such perfect order to everything physical. Once again, you stun me with things I've never thought about.

A sensation of guilt flowed through the Airlis. *I'm sorry.*

What for? It's amazing!

No, not that. Do you remember how Father told me to be careful of what I divulge? If I say too much, I could damage your mortal experience.

Oh, I forgot. Half kidding, but also half serious, I asked, Do you think I'm damaged?

I felt what must have been a laugh, *I don't believe so, but it depends on your definition of "damaged," I suppose.*

She was teasing me! HEY! Angels aren't supposed to make fun of people! But no worries, it's *only* my eternal salvation on the line.

I know, and I'm sorry. You're right, it's not a laughing matter, but I couldn't resist.

Well, I'm glad you're at least a *little* concerned about it, I replied sarcastically.

I desire to talk with Father again anyway, so I'll ask him for more details. Cutting short your struggle of faith and depriving you of eternal blessings is not something I desire to have on my conscience.

Yes, please ask him. We both remained thoughtless for a moment. Ha! Not that kind of thoughtless. No, I mean we were too deep in thought to form words for conversation. After a time, I asked, So, what do you think we *can* talk about?

Let's see, I'm pretty sure we may discuss my relationship with Jared without eternal consequences.

You're only "pretty sure" about that? I gulped. Well, I'm "pretty sure" I would hate to lose my eternal happiness if you're wrong!

I don't think it's like that. The strength of her feelings of confidence helped sooth my anxiety a little. *It has something to do with learning truth too quickly without having a struggle of faith. I'm not sure exactly how it works, but Jared will be a safe enough topic.*

If you say so, I replied hesitantly. What happened between you guys?

Not much, but we did spend a good portion of today in deep conversation. I remembered your advice and told him we should be as honest and straightforward as we can in our relationship. We decided over the next twenty-six days and before we declare our choice of plans, we will try to objectively hear each other's reasons for the side we support. We set some foundations for our discussions and both felt good about our arrangement . . . but I'm worried, David.

Why?

Jared is convinced of his path, and he is very well-educated. I'm afraid I won't know what to say. Her fear of failure pulsed through my arm and weighed on my chest, and it was *heavy*!

Elli, I'm not sure if I'll have many answers, but I'm here if you ever need me, okay?

The pressure subsided, and with a sense of gratitude she said, *Thank you, David. I feel your perspective is going to be most helpful if I'm going to persuade Jared.*

For a moment we didn't say anything. Strong feelings of affection were flowing through the Airlis again, but this time it was a two-way exchange.

Father was right.

About what?

We do need each other.

I chuckled to myself. I don't know about you needing me, but I've sure needed you. My ears began to burn. That one jumped right out before I had time to pull it back.

An interesting, beautiful sensation flowed through the Airlis. The only way I can explain it, is that I felt her smile. Then she said, *I need you, too.* We said our goodbyes, and I swayed back and forth on the swing for a time. In the back of my mind, an unfocused picture of a girl sitting on a bench came into view. Everything was still fuzzy, except now I had a clear image of her tender smile.

Friday, 4 November, 2011

Time for a football update, however painful it may be. I'll start with last week. With all the craziness that happened, I forgot to fill you in. They played Safford here in Snowflake and beat the snot out of them! Frank wanted to sit in the student section, but I convinced him to watch from my truck. I bumped over the curb and parked against the fence on the southeast corner of the field. I tried to listen to the game on the radio at the same time, but that's where Frank drew the line. If I was going to make him suffer, it would be with his choice of music.

We scored twice in the first quarter and two more times in the second to make the score 28 – 0 at half time. When we came back out and scored two quick touchdowns, Frank couldn't stand it any longer.

"Okay, that's IT! You KNOW we're going to kick their butts, David. They put in the fourth string! Come on, let's go to my house and play Guitar Hero or something." I wasn't easily swayed, but when he said he'd ask his mom to make some caramel popcorn, I gave in. We left with only a few minutes to go in the third quarter, and the score was 42 – 0. I found out later, we scored again in the third quarter, and Safford finally got on the board in the fourth to make the final score 49 – 7.

That was the last game of the season, and with that victory, I believe we ended up being ranked third or fourth going into the state tournament. With the higher ranking, we hosted our first-round playoff game against Window Rock tonight. I didn't think it'd be a game, either, and it wasn't.

Because of the torture I put him through last week, Frank demanded we go inside this time. As torturous as I knew it'd be to sit in a charged student section and watch my dream die over and over again, the only reason I was willing to face the pain was because I wanted to see Ashley. Things have smoothed over pretty well, but our friendship isn't quite the same. I hoped tonight would be an opportunity to find a better balance between us.

Tracy and Ashley were sitting right behind the band in the student section talking to each other. Frank jogged up the bleachers and plopped down next to Tracy. Ashley had her back to me as she chatted and didn't see me walk up. I tapped her on the shoulder and asked, "Are you saving this spot for someone?"

She turned and got a terrified look on her face. "Um, actually, I was saving it for Ben Harper." She cringed. "Sorry. I asked him to Winter Formal yesterday, and he wanted to sit by me tonight."

"Oh," was all I could say. I felt like an idiot. By the time I gathered my wits, the silence had already gotten awkward. "Cool. No worries." I didn't know what to do next, so I walked around the three of them and sat next to Frank. It wasn't long till Ben came bounding up the stairs in his flashy band outfit, toting a shiny trombone. I wondered why we were sitting behind the band section, but I quickly found it was so Ben could play between lame attempts at flirtation. It was torturous to witness, but couldn't be helped. When the band wasn't blaring, I could hear most of their conversations.

I tried to focus on the game, but that didn't help much. We kicked the ball off, and Window Rock couldn't do a thing with it. After three plays and no yards gained, they punted the ball. Our punt return guy, Trent Hancock, ran untouched all the way back for six points. It only got worse after that. We scored quickly on every possession, and at the end of the first quarter, it was already 29 – 0. The guys were having a blast out there! Being stuck between bad flirting and awesome football was like taking nasty cough medicine after gargling with vinegar. It only made me sicker.

In the second quarter, Coach started putting in the second string, but even they scored two more times before the half. The team danced their way into the locker room with a 43 – 0 lead. My emotions were at war. I was happy for their success, but at the same time, I was physically sick because of what I was missing . . . then I hit the end of my rope.

It was the last home game of the year, and the marching band had a special surprise. At the beginning of their final number, they had the announcer dedicate the song to Ashley Dunn. While playing a collection of 1990's love ballads, they marched out the word, "Yes!"

The crowd oohed, the announcer awed, and I was done. I leaned over and whispered to Frank, "Dude, I'm leaving. I'll catch up with you later."

He looked at me with surprise, "You're not staying for the game? How are you gonna get home?" Frank was my ride.

"I only live like four blocks away. Besides, I need some fresh air."

"All right, man, whatever you want." He shrugged his shoulders. "I'll text you the final score."

As I walked past Ashley, she asked me in a concerned voice, "Are you leaving, David?" She caught me off guard. I was hoping she wouldn't notice.

Scrambling for a convincing excuse, I said, "Yeah, I've gotta go. Steve wants me to start early in the morning. We're putting in a wood floor, and he wants to get it done tomorrow." This was mostly true. We were starting early, but seven wasn't earlier than any other Saturday we've worked. Is it being dishonest if you deliberately leave out certain facts to make people think something is different than it is? Probably . . . I'll repent later.

Shoving my hands in my pockets, I tried to hide the pain, but rubbing this on top of deep football wounds felt like salt in a knife cut. Forcing a stiff smile, I turned quickly and started down the bleachers.

"Oh, okay." She sounded sad, but I didn't care. Calling out almost desperately, she added, "I'll save you a seat at the next game, all right?"

Glancing over my shoulder, I said, "Sounds good." I wanted the reply to be nonchalant, but it came out with more pain than expected. Not trusting myself to say more, I walked away.

A storm of emotions hovered over me all the way home. Flashes of anger were followed by thundering thoughts of confusion. But as the rains of self-pity began to fall, my temper cooled into bitter acceptance. I guess I can't blame her for asking out someone else. We did break up, after all. But the thought did little to relieve the burning jealousy. Before tonight, I was still debating whether or not to drive down to the Valley for the quarterfinal game, but by the time I reached our front door, I'd decided I was going to be busy.

Tuesday, 8 November, 2011

David, what's wrong?

Huh? I thought in confusion. Without Elli's usual warm welcome, I was thrown for a loop.

I can sense that you're distraught. Did something happen?

I stared at the Airlis in amazement. You know, I'm not sure I like this new and improved Airlis. My feelings have nowhere to hide!

It does take some getting used to, but I think it helps us communicate more openly, don't you?

I smirked, We don't have much of a choice, do we?

Her reply was serious, *Of course we do! You simply have to learn to control your emotions.*

Is that all, Yoda?

Yes, and it seems like someone could use some more practice! If it weren't for the impression of jovial teasing, I probably would've misunderstood her meaning. She was right about it helping our communication. If only I could understand all girls this easily. *What's a Yoda?*

Oh, it's nothing, I laughed. Okay, smarty pants, I'll try harder. And, yes, something did happen this week. Ashley decided to go on a date with another guy.

The Airlis emitted pain. *I'm terribly sorry to hear that. You seemed happier when you two shared friendship.*

The flood of bittersweet memories of Ashley flashed through my head. Don't worry too much about it. I've decided I'm just going to stay away from girls until I get home from my mission. They're nothing but trouble, anyway.

There was a slight pause before she asked, *I hope you don't mean all girls.* Her comment was serious. She thought I included her in that category.

I smiled. Don't worry. I'm talking specifically about girls on *my* planet.

I felt a wave of relief as she thought, *That is the first good reason I've found for not sharing the same existence.* I understood the implications behind her words and blushed as I realized I wasn't the only one who wished we could meet in person. The thought brought with it a sudden desire, but it shriveled quickly into despair of what could never be. Hoping she wouldn't be able to read all these emotions, I quickly brushed them into a dark corner with all the rest of my girl-inflicted pain. I was beginning to accumulate quite a pile of it.

It's better this way, I thought with a smirk. If you were actually the girl next door, I'd probably scare you away.

I disagree. A wave of comfort flowed through the Airlis. *It would make no difference if I lived there or here, I'd still desire your friendship. You're a good person, David.*

Well, at least I've fooled somebody besides my mother, but she would probably love me even if I killed someone.

Elli paused, and with a feeling of embarrassment, she asked, *How do you "killed" someone? What does that mean?*

Laughing, I replied, When you kill someone, you end their mortal life for them. What a strange conversation. The second part of my "transmission" was unintentional, my thoughts had kept rolling, but luckily I don't think she was offended.

I understand; it's the act of causing death to someone. I've read about death, but it's not a part of this stage of our existence, so I'm not very familiar with all the terms. But what I don't understand is, if death is a step in our progression, why is it such a bad thing if you help someone take it?

To hear this point of view from her, an angel from another heaven, was so absurd—my mind completely jammed up. Well . . . it's just bad. I had to ponder on it for a while before I could form words again. First of all, it's a commandment. God told us not to kill, and the consequence for breaking that law is usually death. I think it's because it's the ultimate way of taking someone's agency from them.

That makes sense! If someone does not want to die, then it would definitely be against having agency to take that choice away! Yes, please don't kill anyone.

I laughed out loud again, as I thought, Don't worry, I won't. Sorry Elli, it was a bad figure of speech.

Oh, I see. Her emotions continued to churn. *"But David, what if they want to die?*

In English a few days ago, I think I heard a good word to describe my state of mind at this point: befuddled. If that isn't the right definition, then know it sounds like how my head felt. My thoughts stuttered. Um . . . I, ah, don't know. We just don't.

I'm sorry. I didn't mean to cause more distress. I should be trying to help you feel better.

Have you seen those cartoons where smoke starts coming out of someone's ears? That's how I felt. No, it's okay. It's just, I've never thought about it before. Elli was content to give me time to ponder, and I needed it.

After a minute, an interesting comparison popped into my head. When we try to grow sweet corn in Grandpa's garden, we never start pulling the plants out of the ground before they've produced corn. I guess you could look at killing yourself the same way.

Comprehension flowed through the Airlis again. *You are absolutely right! That makes perfect sense. Only your God would know when you have reached your highest potential.*

Yeah, and you might miss your biggest growing opportunity if you decide to end it all by pulling it out at the roots. Interesting how this whole conversation had turned.

Thank you, for your enlightening insights! There it was again, the sensation of a sweet smile. *But we digress from the issue at hand.*

And what issue might that be?

The issue of your broken heart.

My heart? I asked, confused. Then I remembered we'd been talking about Ashley. Oh, don't worry about me. Hearts break all the time down here. But thanks to friends like you, they usually mend. Well that was a little forward. That's when I smacked myself in the head.

Ha! She laughed jovially. *I'm glad I am of service! Speaking of broken things, how's your arm?*

Grateful for the distraction I said, My arm? I hadn't thought about it for days. You know, it has almost quit bothering me, come to think of it.

I'm extremely glad to hear that!

Thanks. I guess the blessing Gramps gave me worked after all. It didn't go how I first thought it would, but God must've known a better way.

She paused for a few seconds before continuing, *Yes, it has been obvious how much your God has been a part of your life so far, and what an amazing transformation to behold! I can't wait to see how your life will continue to change!*

The idea of having an angel as an audience to my life was humbling. Well, I hope I don't let you down.

You won't.

Thursday, 10 November, 2011

I hate being sick. I started feeling it in Honor Choir yesterday when I took deep breaths to sing and probably shouldn't have gone to work. Even though it wasn't hard hauling boxes out to the moving van, my strength faded fast. No, my job isn't always respectable carpentry work. Actually, helping the Williams family move wasn't even getting us paid. But sometimes, you do what you gotta do.

As we moved stuff from the house to the van, I started getting the cold sweats. Maybe it was triggered by the extreme temperature change. I swear they had their house set at ninety degrees. Scott must have noticed, because when I asked if I could go home, he only said, "I was about to suggest that. You don't look so good."

I went home, took a long shower and climbed in bed. Vaguely, I remember Mom asking if I wanted dinner, and all I could do was shake my head. Last night was absolutely horrible. I couldn't sleep because of the painful body aches, and today my throat burned away any desire to speak or swallow. Mom had no objections to me staying home from school. She even took off work herself to take care of me. Sometimes when it would almost get too much to bear, the only comfort I got was from her cradling my head in her lap and stroking my hair as we watched one episode after another of our favorite shows.

I have never been so sick in my life, and yes, I want your pity. I know you'll be reading this long after I recover, or maybe after I'm dead, but it's always nice to know someone cares. It doesn't matter if they live years away. I would know. It's funny how sickness can change your perspective on things. It definitely makes you more grateful, especially for mothers.

Speaking of pity—if my sob story didn't squeeze some out of you, maybe I'll get a drop when you hear—I didn't get asked to Winter Formal.

Part of me wants to be grateful I wasn't, because in my state of health, I would've had to cancel. But apparently, the bigger side of me must be pride, because it sure hurts thinking I wasn't wanted.

Changing the subject, do you remember how I conveniently got "busy" this weekend to avoid the game? Well, I've had a lot of time to think things over—a lot of time—and I realized I was doing it again! I was being a selfish jerk, and I was taking out my pain on someone else, undeservedly. As the sickness began to ease up this afternoon, I changed my mind and decided to make plans to go to the Valley on Saturday. High school is too short to spend it being miserable. Why not try to be "just friends," have a good time, and even date other people? The more I thought about it, the more I realized I didn't want to miss another moment of good memories like our date at Lost Lake or even my date with Chelsey for that matter. Right as I was about to get my hopes up, Gramps walked in the house.

"Well, son, you're looking a lot better."

Oh no, I thought. *This is* not *a good way for him to start a conversation.* "Yeah, I'm feeling a little better, I guess." I tried to make my voice sound as weak as possible.

"Josh told me there's no school tomorrow. Veterans Day I suppose, but with a three-day weekend, I think it'd be a good time to wean the calves." It was more like a friendly deportation than an invitation.

"Yeah, I guess it's getting to be that time of year again." I knew where this was heading.

"If you're feeling well enough to ride tomorrow, we could use you. If not, I suppose Josh and I could at least get them gathered, but we'll definitely need your help to work the cattle on Saturday." He gave me a brief moment to consider it and patted me on the shoulder as a token of his nonverbal acceptance of my unspoken agreement. "So rest up. You'll need your strength." He left me to fill in the blanks.

Just like Gramps to not even ask, and I know all too well the strength I'm going to need. This was the big round-up, when we wean the older calves and brand the young ones. Some bigger ranches have branding tables. It's faster and safer when you're handling big calves, but Gramps never saw much need in that. We do it all the old fashioned way: rope 'em, throw 'em down, grab their legs, and bite their ears! Grandpa says the best way is through blisters and sweat. Gotta love this old-time cowboy. (We don't actually bite them, ya city slickers.)

I was torn. This is one of my favorite times of the year. I get to be a real cowboy! But I still wasn't feeling well, and this time it was going to cost me a road trip with friends, a seat next to a pretty girl, and the quarterfinal football game. The balance of my personal desires teetered back and forth. I say that jokingly, because I hate doing anything that would make Gramps unhappy. The scale clunked solidly toward a weekend of sweat, blood, and most likely, tears.

Friday, 11 November, 2011

As much as I would have loved to ride horses today, and as much as Gramps wanted me to, I decided to stay home. Last night I finally started feeling better; I was able to eat most of my supper, which is huge progress compared to the last few days. I know most of the hard work is going to be tomorrow, and I figured I better prepare myself as best I can. I just hope I'll have the strength to survive.

Frank stopped by this morning to check on me. "Don't worry dude, you didn't miss much last night." Frank was spread out on our front room sofa. "The best part of the whole dance was when Principal Howard tried to show off his break dancing skills! It might've been cool back in the eighties, but everyone laughed at him."

"I'm actually glad I missed that," I joked. "I'm embarrassed for him just hearing about it." Frank filled me in on their group-date activities.

"It was SO boring! The girls made up a pretty cool scavenger hunt, but the other guys in our group were lame. Oh!" He sat up and with a mischievous grin continued, "and you might like to know, that whole date was rather unpleasant for a certain red-head!"

"Ashley?" I sat up "What happened?"

"Poor Ben, he was doing everything he could to win her over, but the kid was trying *way* too hard. Ashley was polite, but after walking him to the door and giving a stiff hug, she hurried back to the car and let out a big sigh when she got in the driver's seat."

"Ha!" I couldn't help it. My laugh was as much out of relief as it was out of humor. I leaned back and let a big grin spread across my face. "Well, I can't say I feel very sorry for her. She's the one who asked him."

Frank laughed, too. "Yeah, I don't think she'll make that mistake again. Speaking of mistakes, you've *gotta* go with us tomorrow! I won't survive being alone in a car with two girls for *that* long!"

It usually takes two and a half hours to get to the Valley, and if I remember right, the game is supposed to be in Scottsdale. That

196

would probably add another 45 minutes. "Sorry, man, I *can't*. I've gotta help Gramps brand tomorrow."

Franks eyebrows shot up. "Brand? You mean like brand cows?"

"Well, it's only the calves, but yeah."

He scooted forward on the couch and asked, "Do you need any help?"

I thought about it for a second. Grandpa doesn't like bringing new people when we work cattle. There's always an element of danger when you get in the corral with 1200 pound animals, and you never know when one might go crazy. Then again, I wasn't feeling anywhere near 100% and knew it would be really nice to have another set of muscles to wrestle the calves.

"You know, we probably could . . ."

"YES!" he cut me off.

"BUT," I interjected quickly, "I'll have to make sure it's okay with Gramps first." This didn't dim his enthusiasm one bit. He was more excited than a mouse in a cheese factory!

"This is going to be AWESOME! I've always wanted to brand baby cows."

"Calves, Frank, they're called calves, and don't get your hopes up yet. Gramps has never let anyone come out before who wasn't family." I was trying to let him down gently.

"Oh, I'm not worried about your Grandpa. If you can't talk him into it, let me at him. I'll convince him!"

I smirked. "What are you going to do? Show him your roping skills?"

"If that's what it takes!" He jumped up and started twirling an imaginary rope. "I'll make him jealous of my amazing lariat-wielding powers."

I shook my head and said flatly, "I'm sure he'll be very impressed."

Frank left on cloud nine, but before I could get back into my *Lord of the Rings* movie, he called my cell phone. "Dude, Tracy and Ashley want to come, too!"

"What?" I asked in shock.

He jumped in defensively, "Yeah, of course I had to tell Tracy why my plans had changed, and to keep her from getting mad, I told them they could probably come, too." Before I had a chance to retaliate, he pushed on, "But they're both super excited about it. Come on, man, it'll be fun!"

"Oh, it's not the fun I'm worried about." I let out a long sigh. "I'll see what Grandpa says, but no promises."

"Be brave, little lamb. Don't forget about our backup plan in case it doesn't work. I'll go find some cowboy attire and a lariat."

"Call it a rope, Frank, and trying to convince Gramps with your skills isn't going to work. Believe me on that one."

When Grandpa and Josh didn't get home till around two, I knew Gramps would be in a bad mood. I gave them enough time to eat their late lunch and get stretched out on the couches before I showed my face.

Josh was the first one to speak when I walked in the house. "Man, you missed a *fun* ride today." He sounded exhausted. "Someone drove through the ranch and left the gates open, so we had to gather all of the Swale plus the Webb pasture again!"

This wasn't good news. "Dang. But did you find them all?"

Gramps was laid back in his recliner in what appeared to be a peaceful nap. Without opening his eyes, he said, "We got 164 cows, and six of the eight bulls. The other two we'll gather when they decide to come out of hiding. We put them all in the T Bar pasture for tonight. It's not very big, so we'll be able to catch them easy enough come morning."

I wasn't sure if there would ever be a good time to ask, so I decided I might as well get it over with. "Gramps, do you think I could bring a few friends out tomorrow to help us brand?" He cracked an eye at me. "I'm still feeling a little weak, and thought it'd be nice to have some extra hands. Especially since you guys already had a long day today." I hoped I could use his exhaustion to my advantage.

He closed his eye and acted like he fell back to sleep. After the silence got fairly uncomfortable, he asked, "Who is it? Frank?"

Just like Gramps to go directly through the layers and right to the heart of the issue. If the ship was sinking, might as well sink it fast. "Yeah, and two girls."

This got both eyes open, and they were accompanied with a deep, questioning look. "Girls?" he asked in surprise. "Do you plan to have *them* wrestle calves, too?"

The thought made me smile. "Well, I think it'd be good for Tracy to get a little dirty, but Ashley will probably just watch."

After another second or two, he laid his head back and closed his eyes again. He sat there for a moment before saying, "It would be good for Frank to get dirty, too." I laughed at this, because I totally agreed with him. He added, behind closed lids, "Make sure to let Grandma know we're going to have a few more mouths to feed tomorrow."

I let out a sigh of relief, "I will! Thanks, Gramps."

Saturday, 12 November, 2011

Today was one of those days you wish you could put in a jar and keep on a shelf. That way, every time you walked by, you could pick it up and remember the details that made it one of the best days of your life. But since that might prove to be difficult, I suppose capturing it in words would be the next best thing. Hopefully, I can give it the justice it deserves.

To my surprise, the gang showed up pretty close to seven this morning. I would've lost a bet had I put money on it. The girls actually got here before Frank, which shocked me—at least until Frank pulled up. I don't know how he got his getup, but apparently he knows a friend whose uncle's cousin is a bull fighter. Some people call them rodeo clowns, and that would be more fitting for the outfit Frank was sporting. He had the boots, cowboy hat, and a red bandana tied around his neck. He stepped out of the car bowlegged, and with every step, he jangled giant spurs with a little more gusto than necessary. But what nearly gave Gramps a heart attack when Frank strutted into the house, was the bright-purple chaps. Grandpa's teeth about fell out of his mouth!

"What in tarnation?!" Gramps finally stuttered. "Frank you're going to scare every cow, horse, and tree in a ten-mile radius! Get those silly chaps off." Frank wasn't going to argue if it meant missing the day of his life. We all cracked up as he tied himself in knots trying to unfasten all the buckles. Eventually, we had to help untangle him.

As Frank and I loaded the truck with a few more saddles, Josh brought Lucky and Dallas from around the barn and put them in the trailer. We didn't have to worry about Frosty and BJ, because Josh and Gramps had left them at T Bar overnight.

Gramps has an older-style, four-door Ford truck, where the back doors only open if the front doors are opened first. With an unspoken agreement, Josh and I made sure to maneuver Frank into the front passenger seat. What Frank thought at first was a high honor, was soon revealed as our underhanded trick to make him the official "gate opener." Gramps always says the smart cowboy is the one sitting in the middle, but now I have an amendment to that old saying: The "really" smart cowboy is the one who sits in the back with two girls! And that was Josh. I was so focused on pulling a fast one on Frank, I totally missed it! Sure made Josh's day, though. He had a grin from ear to ear.

Near the center of Grandpa's ranch is a grassy valley. You can't see it until you've passed through most of the Bull Duck pasture and climbed the ridge on the far side. Once you top the crest, off in the distance is the faint outline of a lone cottonwood tree next to an old windmill. This is T Bar.

As you bump closer down the two-track road, a brown smudge to the side of the windmill focuses into a set of old wooden corrals, and the small, dark shape to the right becomes a tin-covered shack. The tiny building contains a small cook stove, an old bed, a round table with three chairs, and a tiny cupboard with enough dishes and canned food to provide an emergency meal. Gramps says he used to live here for weeks when he was younger. He would ride his horse out to keep an eye on the cows, but once he started doing more farming (and they got a truck) he would stay in town and drive out and back as needed. I think it's also a secret time machine, because when you step inside, you're instantly hurled back to 1950. The thing that has often made me wonder, but I've never been brave enough to ask, was where he went number two! There's no plumbing, not even an outhouse. God doesn't make cowboys like He used to.

You don't realize until you get much closer to T Bar that there's also a large watering hole surrounded by cattails. The windmill fills a twenty-foot drinker that runs over into a dirt tank. I'm not sure how the critters got started, but the tank is full of frogs and salamanders. It's easily a hundred feet across and about twice as long. The water is deep enough to swim in, but not as deep as Lost Lake, probably only six feet in the middle. This is where Josh and I tried making our first zip-line. Did you catch the key word in that phrase? "Tried" doesn't quite do the story justice, though.

It took us hours to run the cable from the top of the windmill to the bottom of a cedar post on the far side of the pond, and it would've worked great if the pulley hadn't been ancient. I'd only gone a few feet from the windmill when the bearings seized up. The pulley came to a dead stop, but my body didn't. As my feet swung up, the sudden and unsuspected g-forces ripped my grip free from the handle bars. The next thing I knew, I was stuck headfirst in about two feet of mud. I'm just glad I landed in the shallows instead of on the hard bank. If you ever want to see Josh pass out from laughing, ask him to tell you about it. I'm serious! I honestly thought I would have to give him CPR that day. There I was, stunned and disoriented with mud stuffed up my nose and crammed into my eyes, and when I finally got myself washed off enough to see through thin slits of blurred vision, I found Josh unconscious on the bank behind me. He laughed so hard he literally passed out! Yeah, that's not an activity we ever "tried" again.

I'm sorry. That's a jar of memories from a different day, back to the present.

When we got to T Bar we caught Frosty and BJ and threw on some saddles. Josh was eager to let us use his horse once Tracy started batting her eyelashes. Gramps wanted to use Josh to get the branding stuff set up, anyway. The T Bar pond provides water for two different pastures. One of them is a small, one-section holding pasture Gramps calls the T Bar pasture. It encompasses most of the small valley, and looking across the flat, the cows were spread out like black raisins on a golden piece of bread.

It only took an hour to round up the herd. Once we got the cows headed for water, they practically went on their own, for which I'm glad. Even though Ashley was on easy-going Frosty, she was scared to death to be by herself, so I stayed close beside her. Tracy did most of the rounding up, actually. As much as Frank wanted to be helpful, without having a rider in full control, Lucky followed BJ around like a lost puppy. It turned out okay, though. All the cows were gathered, everyone had a good time, and no one got hurt. You can't ask for more than that. But don't fret, the real rodeo was about to begin.

After locking the cows in the corral, we put halters on our horses and tied them to the side of the trailer. The first thing we needed to do was separate the calves. Because Gramps keeps a calm herd of cattle, we always do our sorting on foot.

When people have never been around cattle, they don't realize cows are somewhat predictable animals. If their eyes are calm, their mind is calm. If their eyes are filled with burning fire . . . you better believe you're about to get smoked! The calves, on the other hand, have no idea who or what you are and will usually treat you like a bloodthirsty monster. It didn't take long for an overanxious Frank to corner a wild-eyed, 200-pound calf. I could tell Frank was crowding it, and his angle was all wrong to turn it through the gate, but before I could say anything, the calf bolted between him and the fence. As it shot by, it jumped and kicked! Frank caught a back hoof square in the chest, and it sent him flying across the corral!

I ran over to assess the damage and was relieved to find him chuckling between gasps of air. I let out a breath of relief and began snickering as I pulled him to his feet. We turned to see the girls laughing hysterically! Tracy was sitting on the ground, and Ashley was doubled over in tears!

Dust went flying as I smacked Frank on the back. "So how does it feel to be a REAL cowboy?"

"Feels FANTASTIC!" he replied, rubbing his chest. He was genuinely ecstatic to have been laid out by a "baby cow".

Tracy hollered over the sounds of the jostled herd, "Well, no matter what else happens, Frank, you just made my WHOLE day!"

"Yeah, I sure got my money's worth," Ashley added with a smile.

Frank tipped his cowboy hat and drawled in his best southern accent, "Glad I could be of service, ladies!"

"Hey, rodeo clowns," Gramps shouted from the far side of the corral. "Get out of the gate!"

We realized we were holding up the herd and jumped back into action. Frank was slightly more timid about his approach this time. It took a few more minutes, but we finally got the calves all sorted away from the cows. Tracy went to close the gate, and when she turned, we noticed a fresh green streak across her backside!

Ashley pointed and cried out, "Oh, Tracy! Your BUTT!"

She froze in shock. "What is it?"

"You sat in COW POOP!"

Tracy's face went pale. She wrenched her head around and let out a blood-curdling scream! We lost it all over again.

After a moment, Gramps grinned and asked, "So how does it feel to be a real cowgirl?"

"NOT fantastic, that's for SURE!" Tracy shot back with a smile.

Frank jumped in, "Well, now YOU just made MY day!"

Gramps finally had to shake us out of our humor stupor by throwing a rope to Frank. "It's time to show me those roping skills I've heard so much about, Mr. Cowboy."

Frank snapped to attention and said, "With pleasure, sir!" That's when the fun really began.

We moved the calves into the circular pen. On one side, we had all our branding gear, and on the other, the calves were grouped in a bunch, but they didn't stay that way for long. When the ropes started flying, it was utter chaos. Frank, Josh, and I manned the ropes. Gramps guarded the branding stuff so it wouldn't get run over, and the girls were the self-designated spectators. They sat high on the fence with smartphones ready, and I knew they wouldn't be disappointed.

Once someone had a calf on the line, the other two would run over and dive on it, trying to wrestle it to the ground without getting the crap kicked out of them. Poor Frank, couldn't catch a break. He must've been nailed over twenty times before it was all said and done. I think from now on, anytime someone gets kicked, it'll be called "pulling a Frank."

Toward the end, he started getting the hang of his "lariat." He even had a few real throws where the rope actually left his hand, flew through the air, and lassoed . . . something. Sometimes it was a back foot, sometimes a front foot. He did catch one around the head, and the girls cheered. The rest of the time he ran around holding the rope out with his arm, hoping something would run into it. I don't think the girls ever stopped laughing. Frank really earned his spurs today. By the time we finished the last calf, we were all scraped, bruised, and out of breath, but Frank was ten times worse than Josh and me combined!

"Well, boys, it wasn't the prettiest branding job I've seen . . . but all in all, gentlemen, you did fine work." Grandpa's compliment caught me off guard. He doesn't give them often. I looked at Josh and Frank with a smile but then busted out laughing! I didn't realize till that moment how completely covered in crap and dirt we all were.

"Yeah, look who's covered in poop, now!" Tracy smirked from her safe perch on the fence. We tried to get the girls to come down and help earlier, but I think Tracy's encounter with the green stuff scared them both off. They were more than happy to be the official video-ers.

By this time, it was after 11:30 a.m. Gramps had us guys go over to the drinker and clean up as much as we could while he and the girls got lunch ready. Grandma had really outdone herself. We had marinated chicken, mashed potatoes and gravy, corn, and homemade rolls! And when we thought we couldn't eat another bite, Gramps pulled out a gallon of her famous, homemade peach ice cream from the bottom of the Igloo.

"Wow! You weren't kidding!" Ashley said with big eyes as she took her first bite of dessert. "I think I found my new favorite ice cream!"

"Yesh . . . thish is divine!" added Frank, not worrying about speaking with his mouth full.

"Frank, just because you look like a cowboy, doesn't mean you have to eat like one!" Tracy chided.

Frank's face lit up! He turned to me and said, "Did you hear that? She thinks I'm a cowboy!" He pumped his fist and yelled, "YES!"

Ashley and I started cracking up again. Gramps and Tracy shook their heads, and Tracy said, "Yes, Frank, you got the crap kicked out of you, *and* the crap kicked onto you! We're all very proud." This got Gramps laughing. I think he liked seeing Tracy give Frank a hard time. All in all, I've never laughed so much in one day in my whole life! And ironically, I didn't realize till now that my arm never bothered me once.

After lunch, we turned out the newly-branded calves with their moms and put the pairs back in the T- bar pasture for another week or so. The bigger calves we left in the corral so Gramps could haul them to town. They're the ones we branded in the spring, and now they were big enough to wean. We helped load eighteen of them into the trailer, and Grandpa and Josh headed to town with the first load. There were seven loads to make before the sun went down, so they had a pretty full day. To save having to make another trip for the horses, Gramps asked if we'd ride them back to town. Of course, the girls were more than willing. Frank on the other hand was starting to stiffen up from the beating he'd endured. He didn't like the sound of getting back in the saddle for another hour. It wasn't until Tracy grabbed his hand and begged with dramatic puppy dog eyes that he caved in.

"So you guys are still hanging out . . . but you're no longer going out?" We'd been riding for only a few minutes when this came from out of the blue. Leave it to Tracy to snoop around till she finds the elephant in the room and then jab it with a cattle prod!

Ashley's mouth dropped open in shock, and she glared at Tracy. It surprised me, too, but seeing Ashley's reaction helped absorb the shock.

"Yep, that's right," I replied. "We both think it's a good idea not to get too serious yet."

"Yet?" Tracy asked with a sardonic smile. "So perhaps sometime in the near future you might give it a try?"

I felt my cheeks turn red. I hadn't realized how that came out, but as I mulled it over for a second, I couldn't fool myself. A part of me hoped someday I'd try a serious relationship with Ashley. I looked up and saw Ashley giving me a very peculiar look. Anger, shock, surprise, hope? Why are girls so hard to read! I have no idea what it was.

I stuttered, "W-w-well, yeah. Maybe not in the near future— I'm planning on leaving on a mission as soon as I can, but afterwards I might give it a try . . . if it's okay with her, of course." Oh, I was in it deep now. I've never felt the hairs on my ears before, but now I could tell they were dancing in some extreme heat!

I turned to Frank for help, but apparently his mouth was only capable of gaping at the moment. He abandoned me at my time of greatest need.

"So, you like her?" Tracy was not holding back the punches at all. If anything, she was swinging bricks. Suddenly, I knew exactly how that poor calf felt; I was cornered, and I really wanted to kick someone! But Frank was too far away, and I knew Tracy would kick me back, so I resisted the temptation.

Ashley whirled around to face her again, but she was still too stunned to speak.

Swallowing dryly, I gathered up some courage and exclaimed, "Yeah, I do!" Such small words, but wow, did they carry some weight.

Ashley quickly twisted back around to look at me again. The look was different now. Her cheeks were redder, and the stupor was replaced with a warm smile.

I smiled back and quickly looked down at my saddle horn.

Finally Frank snapped out of it. "You DAWG!"

Thanks, Frank, for magnifying an awkward moment. I was just glad he finally decided to say anything!

Tracy boasted, "See Ashley, I told you he likes you!"

This snapped Ashely to her senses, and she blurted out, "Tracy, you're a menace! And David's right, we decided it's better to stay friends for now. Okay? And if it works out in a few years, then we'll see what happens."

She was looking at me when she said that. I felt myself getting lost again in those hazel eyes. Strong feelings went zipping around out of control in my chest! All with one look. You can't tell me that isn't a super power—and it scared the crap out of me, again. In that brief intense moment, I made a decision. *I'm not going to date her anymore. At least not till I get back from my mission.*

Yeah, you're probably thinking, *He's crazy! You can't tell a girl you like her, and the next moment decide not to date her anymore!* I already told you I'm not normal, but in my defense, have you ever been around someone who has lost control? I have. Sure, this is a different situation, but consequences always follow people who lose it . . . and it felt like I was about to lose it.

I looked away, but it wasn't fast enough to hide my turmoil. When I glanced back, her tractor-beam stare had changed to a look of concern. Luckily, neither of us had to be tortured by the situation much longer. Tracy and Frank started arguing about who liked who first in their relationship, the topic shifted to something else, and we rode on to town.

It's probably not the decision you would've made, maybe no one would have, but it was the right decision for me. I've seen disrespect and abuse, and I've experienced it. It was horrible. Because of it, I've made a personal vow to never—ever—be the kind of person who loses control. Well, I'm finding out there are more emotions than anger you can lose control of—strong emotions. That gravitational pull keeps getting worse, and I'm falling without a parachute! I know guys at school who are only concerned about getting some "action." I hear them boast triumphantly in the locker rooms about all the bases they've rounded, but I don't want to be that guy.

Do you know what I really want? I want to be a good husband and a good father. I want to be a dad my kids can look up to, not one they run from. I want to be true to my wife. I want to take a beautiful girl to the temple and be sealed together for all eternity! Is it Ashley? I don't know. But finding out someday will be an awesome adventure. Till then, these are the kinds of decisions that will get me there. These are the mountains I'm going to climb.

Sunday, 13 November 2011

Small towns like Snowflake take their fame seriously. Sadly, it usually isn't for positive things. Perhaps it's the nature of the beast; negative, horrible events attract attention, and we, like vultures, are inexplicably drawn to them. Today we were stunned to silence as devastating news ripped open deep wounds. Today, the heart of Snowflake stopped when we heard about the accident.

It started out a normal Sunday, better than normal actually. I was still riding the after-waves of yesterday, and I woke up in a very good mood. That only lasted until I got to church. It was the second councilor's turn to conduct the meeting, but Bishop Call was the one who came to the pulpit.

"Brothers and Sisters . . . I'm afraid I have some very bad news. Late last night, on their way home from the football game in the Valley, Zack Whipple and Alexis Dupree were in a horrible accident this side of Heber. Zack was *killed,* and Lexi is in critical condition. *They aren't sure if she'll make it.*" He was barely able to get the last part out. His whole frame started to shake as tears began flowing down his cheeks. It felt like I got hit by a truck—I couldn't move or breathe.

Zack's dead? It's been many hours now, and I still can't wrap my head around the idea that he's really gone.

Huddled in a close circle, our Sunday School class quietly listened as Sydney Flake filled us in on a few details. Her dad was one of the DPS officers first on the scene. He thought Lexi had at least one broken leg and a bad back injury. They had to medevac her to some big hospital in the Valley. No one has heard any more since.

I'm not sure who started the idea, but the message quickly spread that there would be a candlelight vigil for Zack and a prayer for Lexi at the Lobo Stadium at 7:00 pm. The field was absolutely covered with people; it was a humbling sight. The preacher from Calvary Church, where Zack sometimes attended, led the community in prayer. The feeling of love and support was overwhelming, and I've never seen such a unified gathering. The only mar on the evening was when two news film crews showed up. It felt like they were intruding on something sacred, but apparently our story was good enough to sell. They replayed it over and over on the evening news.

I'm sitting here on my bed trying to make sense of everything. This is different than my experience with Bo. When he died, there was so much hatred and fear, I never felt the pain of loss. It's sad to say, but it's true. Now that pain cuts deep.

It's interesting how one of the last things Elli and I discussed was death. We compared life to a garden and came to the conclusion that ending it prematurely would be like pulling out corn before it was ripe. It made sense to me. We shouldn't end our own lives before we maximize our potential—but what happens if God does it? Why an eighteen-year-old in the prime of his life? He had everything going for him. It's confusing. It hurts. It shakes faith.

These questions haunted me all day. This evening I went to my room early. I needed a quiet moment away from everyone to try and calm my troubled heart, but peace wouldn't come.

Minutes slowly piled into an hour. Finally, the struggle forced me out of bed and onto my knees. *Why Zack, God? Why did he have to die? Why does Lexi have to suffer?* As my emotions struggled with my thoughts, for some reason, the story of Job came to mind. We'd recently studied it in seminary, so the details were fresh in my memory.

According to the scriptures, God allowed Satan to take everything from Job to test him to see if he'd remain faithful. Job even lost his children. When all was gone, Job held fast to the only thing he had left—his knowledge! He knew when the worms destroyed his body, in his flesh he'd see God. His testimony of life after death, in peace after suffering, carried him through his trial. He never understood "why" while he was suffering, but by willingly accepting things on faith, he made it through! Not only did he become stronger because of it, in the end he gained more than he ever lost—much more.

As Job's story came to a conclusion in my head, soft words soothed my brittle heart.

Life is a test, David. Have faith. Death is not the end. Christ broke those bands forever! Zack will live again, and so will you.

Tuesday, 15 November 2011

I didn't feel like waiting in my room tonight, and it's getting too cold to sit in the truck without the heater running, so I told Mom I was going for a drive and wouldn't be back for a couple of hours. I grabbed a box of matches, the small can of lawn mower gas, and headed out to the ranch. Gramps once told me about a State-funded project to clear land that happened a few decades before I was born. Using two huge bulldozers, they attached a large cable between them and crisscrossed the country, pulling over the thickest patches of dense juniper trees. Some were piled and burned, but others were left as they lay, creating cedar bone yards! It's eerie to see trees standing completely upside down, their dead branches frantically searching the ground, as shriveled roots reach for the sun. Strange as it is, it's a perfect spot for bonfires.

On the edge of one of these areas is a hill we call Sand Hill. It's more like a pregnant ridge than a hill. The gentle slope on the south was once cleared of trees all the way to the top, and the north is one huge sand dune. Josh and I have spent hours playing here. Mom hates all the sand we track home afterward. From town it's only about a fifteen-minute drive to the top of the hill. Within minutes, I found myself sitting in a camp chair, trying to keep my hands warm by a nice-size fire as I held the cold Airlis. Not as tall as the high hills but still commanding a respectable view, it's a great place to spot cows from horseback, but I wasn't looking for cattle tonight. My eyes were searching the stars.

What a strange combination of emotions.

I looked down when my feelings began to stir. Why do you say that?

I don't know how to describe it, but you feel . . . unsettled. What has happened? she asked with concern. With a fresh stab of pain, I told her about the accident and Zack's death.

There was a long pause before she spoke again. *David, why does this hurt so much?* She was shocked. *I have never had to face loss before, and the feelings are . . . horrible.*

This actually made me smile, but I'm not sure why. I think it was a mixture of her innocence and the absurdity of not having to deal with death. Well, you better prepare yourself if your mortal experience is coming soon. It definitely isn't a walk in the park.

I think I understand what you mean. Father told me there is no way to fully understand what it will be like without experiencing it personally.

It certainly has its ups and downs. Speaking of ups and downs, how's it going with Jared?

I felt a mashed conglomerate of emotions as she replied, *I'm glad we agreed to be honest and open as we research both plans, because it has brought us to common ground*—her feeling of concern overrode the rest—*but I'm not completely comfortable with it.*

How funny, I thought. I had a similar experience with Ashley this week.

Really? she asked with delight. *Oh, please tell me!*

I described my whole weekend in detail. She wouldn't have it any other way. If she felt like I was leaving something out, she would interrupt and ask for more information. She was very curious about many things. What is a brand? Why would we do that? What is poop? That one caught me off guard. I couldn't help but laugh. I guess spiritual beings don't create waste. She knew about it, but was not familiar with the term. I didn't go into details. Some things she's better off learning from experience.

You told Ashley you care about her? I do know what that feels like, and it takes a lot of courage!

Yes, it does! I was very nervous, and when she looked at me I . . . well, it scared me. This is when I felt the weirdest thing through the Airlis. Are you laughing at me?

Her emotions jolted. *OH, my! I'm sorry, David.* The humor died down, a little. *Perhaps you are right. Maybe it's not such a good thing all our feelings are portrayed. I apologize, but the thought of a simple look delivering extreme fear was humorous to me!* I could tell she was still giggling, and I couldn't help but smile.

Well, at least someone finds joy at the expense of my pain, I said sarcastically.

I'm happy you're not upset with me. Her laughter faded into relief. *I really am glad I can sense your emotions. Your words are much easier to understand this way.*

Yeah, I suppose I'm glad, too. For a brief moment I was again amazed at this whole experience and unlikely friendship. I thought about all she had done to help me through the last few months, and I got an overwhelming sense of gratitude. Thank you, Elli . . . for everything.

There was a slight pause, and then a sense of her own gratitude and love warmed my chest. *I'm grateful for you, as well. It was not a coincidence we met, David, and I feel there are still things to come we'll need each other for . . . that I will need you for.* Our emotions melted into each other, and we sat for a long time enjoying the sensation.

When the dim light in the Airlis faded, I leaned back in my chair and gazed out into the starry abyss for a long time. The night sky never looked so big.

Sunday, 20 November, 2011

I was just informed, once again, I'm a horrible friend. For a few days now, Frank's been giving me the silent treatment—I don't know what in the CRAP for—but that ended this afternoon in double forte. He came to my house after church and literally cornered me in our front room.

"Dude, I don't see you anymore, you don't talk to me anymore, and when I wave, you look the other way! What's the deal? Are you too good for me now or something?" He was really pissed! I had never seen him like this before.

"Frank . . . CHILL!" I threw my hands up in self-defense. I honestly wondered if this was going to end in blows! "I've been busy man! And when did I ignore you waving at me?"

"It was after history on Friday! You were heading to your truck, and you acted like you never even saw me!"

"I'm sorry, Frank, but I really didn't see you! Wait . . . is that why you were so mad in Honor Choir?"

This caught him off guard. I don't think he was expecting an honest mistake. "Well, that still doesn't explain why you turned us down on Saturday!" His anger lowered a few notches, but steam was still coming out his ears.

"I promised Sarah I would take her to Rent-a-Flick, and we'd get a movie." This was mostly true. I may or may not have asked her *after* Frank invited me to double with Tracy and Ashley. Honestly, I've been too scared to tell him about my decision to not date her anymore. I knew he wouldn't understand, especially after I openly confessed to liking her.

"David, I think you hurt her feelings. She decided not to go with us either, so Tracy and I went to the movies alone." He was mellowing out now, and the anger was replaced with what almost looked like pain. I was hopeful at this point there wouldn't be violence. "You can't mess with her heart like that, man. That's pretty cold, even for me."

This is where I lost it. "What? Well, if *you* and your *girlfriend* would quit pushing us together, maybe none of this would've happened!" It was a low blow, but he didn't show up intending to play nice, so I felt justified. Then I spit it out, "I don't want to date her anymore, Frank!"

They say truth can be like a two-edged sword . . . well, it did the trick. He recoiled as if I had stabbed him in the heart. "Are you CRAZY, David? After all I've done to help you get over your social awkwardness, this is how you thank me? Well, GOOD LUCK figuring the rest out on your own." He stomped out and slammed the door.

Wow! I was not expecting that at all. Really, Frank! Because I didn't go on a date? This is such a stupid thing to fight over! I'm still fuming mad about the whole situation. I am so done with high school and all its stupid DRAMA! The gossip! The assumptions! I can't wait for it to be over. I'm ready to get out of here.

*　　*　　*　　*

Nothing helps clear your mind like swaying on the front porch swing. It's been a good half hour since I unloaded that last paragraph. I realize Frank views girls differently than I do, and I know he wants me to be like him, but I don't! I *can't*. My self-control over all these new and explosive feelings is too weak to be able to have a serious relationship right now. Perhaps in time, when I get a little more experience, but not now. Frank doesn't understand. I hope this doesn't ruin our friendship. He's the only true friend I've had—but I can't afford to bend on this one.

Frank and I will need some time, I think, but Ashley? Well, that's a whole different matter. To think I may have hurt her in some way gives me a horrible pain in my gut. She's an amazing girl; beautiful and smart, with a strong testimony of the Gospel and a genuine relationship with her Savior. The last thing I want to do is cause her pain, and I really want to stay friends . . . I'm going to have to talk to her.

No need to prolong it. The pain will only get worse and the situation harder to fix. Besides, having one person awkwardly avoiding me is hard enough to deal with. I don't think I could handle two. But how do I do it? It's hardest to talk in person, but writing can be easily misunderstood. No, I don't think I'll ever do that again. I thought about it for a minute and picked up my phone.

"Hey, Ashley, how're you doing?"

"Oh, hey, David, I'm doing okay. How are you?" Her tone was pretty normal. I had no idea what she might be feeling. I think I'd prefer an Airlis for this.

"I'm all right, I guess." My mind was racing. I should've put more thought into this, but it was too late now.

"You guess? Why, what's going on?"

"Oh, I think Frank's mad at me." *How much do I say?*

"I'm sorry. I don't think I'd *ever* want to have Frank mad at me." Her voice was filled with concern. "What happened?"

I told her about the fight, and when we got to the part that included her, I decided to tell the whole truth. "Frank thought I might've hurt your feelings by not going on that double date, so I wanted to make sure you knew it wasn't because of you. I think you're awesome, Ashley, but a steady relationship is not the right thing for me right now, and I don't think Frank understands."

There was a brief everything-is-hanging-on-an-edge silence and then a sigh of relief. "David, I'm so glad you called. I feel the same way!" My fear instantly evaporated. "I was worried sick I was going to have to tell you 'no' on Saturday, but when Tracy told me you had already backed out . . . well, at first I was relieved but . . ."

She trailed off as if she didn't know how to continue. I was pretty sure what she was thinking though, so I asked, "But you weren't exactly sure *why* I backed out, right?"

"Yeah, that's right," she answered in astonishment. "How'd you know?"

"It was partly a guess. When Frank said I hurt your feelings, I realized he was probably right. From your perspective, I imagine things were pretty confusing—and for that I'm sorry. Will you forgive me?" The words were hard to get out, but it felt good for them to leave.

"Of course, David." Her voice was softer now, more relaxed. A short silence was followed by her voice full of emotion. "Thank you. You don't know how much this means to me."

It felt good to smooth things out between us. For once in a long time, it seemed like I was back on solid ground, ready and able to move forward.

"Thank you for not hanging up on me," I said, trying to lighten the mood.

She let out a soft laugh and said, "It was tempting, but I'm glad I didn't." I could tell she was teasing me, which was a good sign.

"So, I guess I'll see you tomorrow, then?"

"Yeah, see ya tomorrow. Good night, David."

So . . . it wasn't in person. Sorry, but I wasn't feeling *that* brave tonight. I just needed to be free from those eyes. That's where the trouble starts. I can think a lot better when they aren't casting spells. At least I was able to mend things. She was right about Frank, though. I think I'd rather jab an angry bull with a hot-shot than be in his crosshairs. I have a feeling I'm going to need more than duct tape to fix that problem. Only time will tell.

Tuesday, 29 November 2011

Sorry, I haven't written in a while. It's been a long week. Where to start? I did talk to Elli last Tuesday, and that's about all it was—me talking and her listening. Where my life goes seven days to her one, I usually have a lot more to tell. Not much happened with her anyway. She had a few classes and a discussion with Jared about the Freedom Side. That's the plan that revolves around agency. Nothing new to her or me or Jared for that matter, but it was the common ground they wanted to start from. I guess his one rebuttal was agency brings risk into the plan, and he didn't like it. I think he's a pansy.

Work slowed down this week, but that was okay. Most people have plans for the holidays, and Scott and I were both leaving town. School was slow, and that was not okay . . . in fact, it was horrible. You know how it gets right before vacation: time crawls, and all the projects are due. I'm so glad I don't have Chemistry anymore, but I still had a five-page paper due in History. I decided to write on the United States vs. Native Americans. I didn't realize all the bad things that happened there, but I won't educate you today. If you want to know more—Google it. Isn't that where all truth is found now-a-days? Ha!

To add to the torment of creeping time, school has also become somewhat uncomfortable with Frank. The torture has upgraded from the *silent treatment* to the *deliberate avoidance treatment*. It's blatantly obvious, and now it seems the whole school has been gossiping about *our* breakup. Are you KIDDING ME?! I'm afraid my hatred for high school is turning into a time bomb. I only hope it doesn't explode before May 25th.

Ashley and I, on the other hand, have plateaued at a very comfortable "just friends" status. We talk often, but it's with no strings attached. She doesn't walk with me to choir anymore, and I no longer time my exit from Seminary so we leave at the same time. She's already been on a date or two (not that I've been counting), and I've been working. OH! But I *did* go on a date while I was on vacation! Do you remember my aunt Rose? Well, Grandma and Grandpa carpooled with us down to the Valley this weekend to spend Thanksgiving with Rose and Uncle Bill and their family. This is the first time I remember doing something with them for more than a few hours. Sure, their kids are all girls . . . and they love their dolls . . . and pink rooms . . . and fancy fingernails, but surprisingly, we ended up having a really great time together!

Lyndsay is in college, so we didn't see her much. Erin and Kaitlyn are twelve and ten, so they teamed up with our sister, Sarah, to terrorize Josh. But Meagan is a junior in high school now, and she was bound and determined to have me meet all her friends! Four months ago I would've locked myself in a room and refused to come out, but now I was actually excited to hang out with some "Valley girls!"

We went to her friend's house Friday night and played games with a big group of people. I was really nervous at first, but the kids were all chill, and it wasn't hard to fit in. One of the girls I met is named Brianna, and she's the one Meagan set me up with on Saturday. We went goofy golfing at Golf Land. This is the part where I have to confess something—I absolutely STINK at golf! I might've played it twice in my life, and "goofy" was about as good as I could get. And yes, every girl and guy in our group beat me . . . except Meagan, but I wasn't surprised. She's one of the bubbliest, funnest girls I've ever been around—and the most uncoordinated.

There is one hole near the end that has three big humps, like a dragon's back. Well, I kind of miscalculated my swing, and when the ball hit the first hump at ninety miles an hour, it went airborne, sailed right past my date's head, and disappeared into the swimming pool area! I wished I could've died. It was close enough for her to feel the air go by her ear! I am SO relieved I didn't hit her. Everyone was cracking up. If not for Meagan's natural talent to put people at ease, I probably would've keeled over. "Well, David, I knew you were strong, but not THAT strong!"

I joined in this time, and we all had a good laugh. I blamed my lost ball as the reason for my low score, but I knew there was no amount of "hole-in-ones" that could've saved me at that point.

It was such a nice break from everything going on at home. When Sunday rolled around, I was reluctant to pack up my stuff. Meagan pleaded with me to come down again, and I assured her I would. Brianna is pretty hot, and so are a lot of Meagan's friends.

You better believe I'll be back! I told Meagan if she ever wanted to come up and bring some of her friends, maybe I could talk Gramps into letting me take them horseback riding or something. Her face lit up with excitement. I don't know why they never visited much before. I think it was mostly circumstance, with perhaps a tad of Aunt Rose's hatred for dirt. But we seemed to be turning a new leaf as a family, and I'm hopeful our friendship will continue to grow. And if my girl cousins happen to bring some of their cute friends along . . . well, I think we could find room for them on a horse somewhere! ☺

When I finally reached Elli, I was pumped to tell her about my week. Have I got some stories to tell you!

Ha! I can tell. Her warm laughter flowed into me. It's such a peculiar thing to *feel*. If your heart could literally dance with the merriment of Christmas morning, you might understand. *I can't wait to hear them all!*

Delving into the details of our trip, I told her all about the family, our Thanksgiving meal, and of course the date! When I told her about Brianna, especially when I said how cute she was, I sensed a new emotion I hadn't felt from her before. Elli, are you jealous?

The feeling suddenly flashed to fear. *Jealous? Me? No. I mean, yes, but it's not like that. Oh my, how to explain . . .* I started to laugh. *Are you laughing at me?*

YES! I thought emphatically as I sat chuckling on my bed. Sorry, it's just, I've never caught you off balance before! I felt her shame, so I cooled it off slightly. I'm sorry, Elli, but it's nice to finally have our roles reversed. Usually, it's you laughing at me!

It's not as much fun having it the other way around. I didn't realize what it must have felt like to you. I'm sorry if I ever embarrassed you, David.

Oh, please, don't be. It's part of life. We have these kinds of experiences all the time! You'll see. You learn from them, grow from them, and then you laugh and move on. Your mortal life will be FULL of things like this.

She paused for a moment, her emotions finally returning to a more peaceful level. *I can only hope it will be as grand of an experience as you have, David. I really do.*

It will be, Elli. I have no doubt of that.

And just to clarify, she said with a slight smirk. *Yes, I AM jealous of you and your wonderful experiences. And, YES, I am jealous of the girls who meet you and get to know you . . . and see you.*

Her straightforwardness caught me off guard, but what stunned me the most was the feelings that came after. The sensation of hope dying as it longed for what can never be was all too familiar.

Yeah, I know what you mean.

Friday, 2 December 2011

Have I told you yet I hate school? Sorry, I'll stop beating that dead horse after one last comment: I hate, hate, hate . . . double hate . . . AND LOATHE IT ENTIRELY! At least that's how the Grinch would describe my feelings. I love that movie! Sarah has been watching it over and over again since we got home from Thanksgiving break, and honestly, it never gets old! She's been so excited for Santa this year. Sadly, most of her friends tease her for still believing in him. I'm not sure if it's strong will or a hard head, but I love seeing the shining glimmer of hope in her eyes. Some days, I wish I was still young and innocent.

Life is not full of many pleasant things at the moment. The situation has not improved with Frank. If anything, the hostility has gotten worse. Someone waxed the windows on my truck yesterday, and even though I can't prove anything, I have my suspicions. I think it's been bugging him that I don't seem to care. He throws his fits to try and get my attention, and I ignore him. Not that I don't care about him, but dude . . . GROW UP!

I know I should be more forgiving, but the last verbal jab Frank spat about me being socially awkward as he stomped out of my house really hurt. I guess the cutting blade of truth stabbed both ways. The thing is, he really has helped me. I'll give him one more week. If he doesn't crack by then, I'll get out some duct tape.

I went to the basketball game Tuesday night. It was the first game of the season. After the Star Spangled Banner, we were asked to remain standing and join in a moment of silence for Zack. A few of the guys on the team shed some tears. Nothing like a double barreled shot of emotion to help whoop the snot out of Round Valley! Final score was 80-36.

Speaking of Zack, I guess Lexi is doing pretty good. I'm not sure who found the details, but the word is out she'll be coming home soon. Both legs ended up being broken, and her back was smashed up pretty bad. She's in a wheelchair for now, but they're hopeful she'll be able to walk again. Poor girl. One broken bone is bad enough. I would hate to know what many feel like.

Saturday, 10 December 2011

Have you ever done something crazy, and you're not really sure why? I just did something really crazy . . . but to help explain, I'll need to back up. After Mom became a nurse's assistant, she applied at the hospital in Show Low, and was able to land a job there. It was a huge blessing for us. Not only was the pay good enough to support three kids, but the hospital was also willing to help her become a nurse.

Sometime on Thursday, Lexi came to the hospital to have tests done, and Mom happened to be the nurse who took care of her. As we ate dinner that night, I could tell something was on Mom's mind. After a silent minute, she said, "Lexi Dupree came by today. I guess she's staying in The Cottage." For a moment, she held her cheese sandwich midair and stared at a blank spot on the wall. Turning she asked, "David, does she have any friends?"

This caught me off guard, and it took a second to speak. "I uh, don't know." I tried to think back on what I knew about Lexi. She showed up out of nowhere on the first day of school this year. She was the hot, new girl, and before the first week was over, she and Zack were a couple. If she wasn't with Zack, she was on her phone. And like Tracy said, it was *assumed* she was very popular. So what was going on? "I never saw her hang out with anyone except Zack, actually. Why?"

Mom wrinkled her brow in contemplation. "Oh, she just looked really sad." I knew she couldn't say too much about her patients, so I didn't press the issue, and after a few more bites, the topic of conversation changed.

This gnawed at me all day Friday. It didn't make sense! And then karma struck. Scott got a job in Show Low on Saturday. It was a small shed repair he didn't think would take us but a few hours. He also needed to get some supplies at the store and stop in to see his parents. I guess they live in Lakeside, which is near Show Low. He told me I was welcome to join him, but if I didn't want to get dragged around all afternoon, I would need to drive up separately. So that's what I did.

As fate would have it, we took a left at the hospital and drove right past "The Cottage Rehabilitation Center" to get to our job. No matter how I tried, I could *not* get Lexi out of my head.

Scott cleared his throat, "Huh hmm!" Blinking, he appeared right in front of me, watching me queerly. "Would you like a little 'alone time' with that hammer?" Apparently I had been standing there in a daze with it gripped in my hands. I dropped my arms embarrassed, and he started laughing. "Go talk to her, David!"

His comment really shocked me! "I uh . . . who?"

"The girl you're daydreaming about. It won't go away until you man up and talk to her."

Laughter burst from my mouth! When I could breathe again, I said, "I need to start looking for a new job if you can read my mind *that* good!"

He smiled and replied, "Oh, it isn't hard. I was eighteen once, too, remember."

I made up my mind—no matter how carnivorous these butterflies got, I was going to see Lexi. It didn't help that we still had another hour till we finished. Luckily, Scott could see my distress, and as soon as we nailed on the last shingle, he said, "I'm going to put the tools away. You GET OUT OF HERE!" He swung his hammer at me, and I jumped back. "And tell her I want my employee back!" he yelled over his shoulder as I got into my truck.

My hands were shaking so bad I had to put them in my pockets as soon as I stepped through the main entry. The nurse was pleasantly surprised when I told her I would like to see Lexi Dupree. She enthusiastically pointed out room number 107.

I paused in front of her door as my knees joined the party of shaking body parts. *Am I crazy? I guess I'm about to find out!* I willed a sweaty hand into a fist and knocked three times.

There was only a slight moment of hesitation, and a girl's voice responded, "Come on in." I slowly opened the door to see a wall of curtain and not much else. The voice started to speak again, this time with more life. "You know, you don't need to knock. I don't mind you . . ."

I pulled the curtain aside.

The only thing that registered in my mind was a pretty face, topped with disheveled hair, in pure shock. I couldn't help smiling nervously at her reaction. I was glad I wasn't the only one who seemed surprised by my visit. "Hey, Lexi." My vocal cords actually worked! "Sorry about the knock, but I figured you probably wouldn't want me to just walk in."

This snapped her out of it. "Hey. No it's fine, it's just . . . I wasn't expecting anyone." She seemed to suddenly become aware of herself and quickly tried to straighten out her hair. Self-consciously, she examined herself down to her feet, which were nestled protectively in T-Rex slippers. Looking up, she asked, "It's David, isn't it?"

Now it was my turn to be shocked. "Yeah! How'd ya know?"

She smiled and said, "I remember you from all those text messages I got a few weeks ago at school."

"Oh, those," I said in dismay. She let out a sweet giggle. I shook my head and said, "I never should've let Frank talk me into that one."

She smoothed the wrinkles out of her plaid pajama pants as she said, "I thought it was hilarious. I've never liked all the high school gossip, and I think what you guys did was awesome."

Air began to flow again. "Well, if I'd known they were *that* good, I would've put them on Facebook."

She smiled. "You'd probably get a million likes!" We laughed again. Relieved to have broken through the ice so easily, I didn't care if the water was hot or cold. As my fear released other senses, slowly my brain began sending me information again. She was sitting in a wheelchair on the far side of the room. Between us was a big hospital bed. The sheets and blanket were tightly stretched and on it sat a lunch tray with an uneaten sandwich and a small container of medication. Most of the normal hospital stuff was gone. A large bathroom was to my left with the door slightly ajar.

She must've noticed me looking around, because she said, "Sorry about the mess. I'm still trying to get used to this small space." She rolled the wheelchair closer to a couch under the window and pushed a pile of clothes to one side. "Would you like to sit down?"

As I walked by a table stacked with what looked like school work, I remembered the M&Ms and pulled them from my pocket. "Here, these are for you," I said handing them to her as I sat down. We were only a few feet apart.

"For me?" she asked in surprise. "Thank you! Peanut M&Ms are my favorite!" She looked at me quizzically. "How'd you know?"

"Well . . . I kind of *owe* them to you. You may not remember, but I was the guy who plowed you over after the football game that one night."

After a brief second her eyes lit up. "Oh yeah, I remember!" But as the memory flashed across her mind a deep sadness came over her, and she looked down. "I was going to see Zack." I didn't realize till then that her pain was much more than broken bones.

"I'm so sorry, Lexi." I didn't know what else to say.

Tears started down her face as her shoulders began to tremble. She tried to control the sobs, but it was hard. Vivid memories of Zack dancing on the benches in the locker room cut fresh wounds across my heart. My eyes burned as my own tears began to fall. He was such a fun, crazy guy.

Seeing her cry awakened something inside me; a desire to rush over and hold her! Fear quickly countered with, *But David, you don't even know her.* The conflict kept me frozen in place. Not knowing what to do, I sent up a silent plea for help.

A calming thought came into my mind: *Remember the good.*

"You know, the last time I saw Zack, he cornered me in Rent-a-Flick." I sniffed, then let out a quiet chuckle. "I thought he was going to pummel me for quitting the football team. But he wasn't mad. He told me all about the awesome game against Mingus. He even reenacted the game-saving touchdown pass he threw to Brett England! He was one funny, talented guy." I looked at her. She had stopped crying and was staring intensely at me. I looked back down and said, "And we all miss him."

I saw a box of tissue on the chair by her bed and grabbed it. As I picked it up, I noticed the small trash can full of used tissue by her bed. My heart sank. That's a lot of suffering. I walked back over and offered her one and took one for myself.

"Yeah, he was one funny goober," she said with a tender laugh. The tears had all gone for the moment. "I miss him, too."

We sat in silence for a while longer. A nurse popped her head in to remind Lexi her physical therapy would be starting soon. I took that as a good cue it was time to go. Standing up, I said, "I hear you've been recovering fast! I hope it continues to go well for you."

"Thanks, David, I hope so, too." She looked up at me and held my gaze for a moment. "Thank you . . . for coming to see me today." Her emotions almost brought back the tears, but she suppressed them quickly. "It meant more than you'll ever know."

I looked away embarrassed. "Well, all I brought were some M&Ms and a few tears." Jokingly, I continued, "I didn't realize they were *that* good."

She laughed and opened the bag. "Here, see for yourself!" and she poured me a small handful.

I smiled and popped one into my mouth. Trying to mimic the intensity of those food tasters I'd seen on TV, I chewed slowly. After a long swallow I said, "Yep, that's by far the best M&M I've ever tasted."

She grinned, and after a moment, her face became serious—almost desperate. "I hope you'll come back and see me sometime. I really enjoyed your visit."

"Of course!" Grinning, I lifted my handful of candy and added, "Especially if you have more of these!"

She smiled wide and said, "I'll make sure to save some for next time, then."

I returned the smile and said, "You've got a deal."

What was I THINKING? I still can't believe I actually did that. But what's even *crazier* is, I really enjoyed it! I mean, as soon as the ice cracked, I felt . . . comfortable. We laughed and joked and cried, and I was myself. Not a socially awkward nerd. And she sincerely asked me to come back! Yeah, I guess I might go back. ☺ HA! I probably won't stop thinking about her till I do. And that leads to the part that scares me—I wasn't scared. I mean, at first I was but not for very long. I'll need to be careful. Maybe she's just luring me in for the kill!

David . . . she's in a WHEELCHAIR! What is she going to DO? Wrestle me down and steal my virtue? Oh, gee whiz. I need to grow up. Not that I shouldn't be on my toes, but Lexi really needs a friend. That much I could see easily enough. And who am I kidding, I could really use a friend myself.

Tuesday, 13 December 2011

You know what? In all my spontaneous, extracurricular activities last week, I forgot to tell you that Elli stood me up! I don't know what happened, but I wasn't too worried about it. And when I felt us connect again tonight, I knew everything was going to be all right.

Let me guess, I thought first. You got busy talking with a boy and lost track of time. Am I right?

She was happy. Good. And I'm glad she could tell I was joking. She replied with a bit of spunk, *Not a boy, David . . . a man.*

I busted out laughing! Mom asked from the front room. "You okay, David?"

"Yeah, Mom, I'm fine." It's a good thing Josh was busy in the kitchen doing homework. I thought to Elli, Oh, I see. Well, I hope this "man" is treating you good, or I might have to do something about it!

What do you mean? she asked innocently. *Will you want to have words with Jared?*

Yes . . . words. I chuckled a bit. So was I right?

Actually, David, you were exactly right! Feeling guilty, she added, *I do apologize for not keeping track of the time. Will you please forgive me?*

Oh, of course, I caved in pretty easily. I didn't want to waste any more time when I had so much to tell! But first, I wanted to hear from her. Well, how did it go? What did you guys talk about?

Her emotions soured slightly. *We talked a long time about the Salvation Side yesterday . . .*

And?

She replied a guiltily, *And . . . he has some very convincing points.*

Like what? I asked in surprise.

228

She continued hesitantly, *The whole foundation for their proposed plan is that salvation will be given to all. Honestly, part of me likes the idea of not losing a single one of my brothers and sisters.*

What? I asked in shock. Are you supporting *him* now?

Oh, please don't be cross with me. No, I'm not supporting their plan. However, I can see why it's appealing to many people.

I sat back hard against the wall by my bed. I'd never thought about it like that before. I knew I personally chose Christ's plan, but I never thought about why one third of my spirit siblings would have been persuaded to follow Satan's. The idea she presented made sense. I asked, kind of to myself, Okay . . . but at what cost?

The question seemed to embolden her. *That is EXACTLY why I still disagree with them! They say, in order for everyone to be saved, someone would have to take agency away. Instead of everyone having freedom to overcome the bad by choosing the good, one person would conquer all evil. BUT, the glory and strength that comes from overcoming opposition would only go to that one person!*

I don't quite follow, I said in confusion. Why would that be?

She paused for a moment. I could tell her wheels where churning when she thought, *Is this too much to say? No, I don't feel like it is. Oh, sorry! That was me thinking too loudly.* Her comment made me smile. She continued, *You know about the three degrees of glory, correct?*

Yes, the Telestial, Terrestrial, and the Celestial.

If we take away opposition, there would be no degrees of glory. Everyone would be saved to the same, lesser level, all except the chosen one, that is. The purifying and sanctifying process that lifts us to a Celestial status can only take place by passing **through** *opposition.*

The shady curtains in my mind seemed to be peeling back for a second as I contemplated this idea. That makes so much sense!

Yes! she stated emphatically. *And the cost of selecting the Salvation Side is this: only the* **one** *person who is chosen to save* *us all will be glorified like Father!* She paused before continuing, for which I am grateful. This deeper understanding of concepts I already knew was like a warm ray of sunlight on my soul.

David, The Freedom Side allows opposition and agency so we all have a fair and equal chance to find our own way to Celestial Glory—for ourselves. There will still need to be a Savior, but instead of taking away opposition, He will take upon himself the consequences of choosing evil over good. This will allow any who have faith in their Savior to be lifted up by Him through obedience to covenants and the performing of ordinances. The Savior in return gives His Glory to the Father, who shares all He has with those who make it home!

Her light literally radiated *through* the Airlis! For a brief moment, it gave off a bright glimmer of light! Not only was it dazzling to see, but I *felt* her sweet . . . intelligence! That's as close as I can describe it.

Wow! Did you feel that? I know it was a silly question, but it's all that came to mind, okay! And, yes, she laughed at me.

Ha! Yes, I felt it, as well!

It makes so much more sense now, I said, ignoring the giggles. I don't see how it could be any other way.

Her enthusiasm and light was still great, but now it was tinged with sadness. *Yes, I also feel it's the right way. I only hope I can get Jared to see it.* Changing the subject, and in a happier mood, she asked, *So, what have you been up to for the past . . . two weeks is it?* It suddenly registered, *Oh, the stars! It's been fourteen days?*

I laughed at her. Yep, fourteen days. Are you sitting down?

I am! she replied anxiously. I opened the gates and let my story go. After I emptied the corral of every detail, she paused for a moment, and asked, *Have you been back to see her?*

No. Not yet, I replied sheepishly. I didn't want her to think I'm a stalker or something.

A stalker? she asked in confusion. *Sorry, but I'm not familiar with that word.*

I should've known it wasn't a heavenly term. I thought a moment and tried again. I mean, I didn't want to make her uncomfortable by coming back too quickly, and I didn't want to be bothersome.

I understand now, but I think you're wrong. She did not beat around the bush. *If she is in pain and without friends, and if she's a girl, I think I can tell you without reserve she has been waiting for your return.*

Really? I hadn't thought of it that way. I just didn't want to creep her out . . . and perhaps I was a little bit scared.

Elli giggled again. *I can feel your nervousness! Don't worry about it, David. Just be yourself and be honest! There is nothing to be afraid of. Will you promise to go back soon?*

Yeah, I promise, I smiled again. What would I ever do without Elli.

Thursday, 15 December 2011

I wasn't able to get away yesterday, because we had our Christmas Choir Concert, but as soon as Scott gave me the okay today, I raced for home! Because Scott says he can fix anything, sometimes we end up with the craziest jobs. Today we built a chicken coop, and yes, part of the job description was to catch all the loose chickens and put them inside. So I chased chickens today! I love my job. Who else do you know that gets paid to do that? The down side is, I absolutely *had* to shower before I went anywhere.

Mom arrived home as I was heading out the door. "David, are you going somewhere? I plan to have dinner ready in about thirty minutes."

Do I tell her? I wondered. "I was uh . . . planning on running to Show Low for a while. Don't worry, though. I'll grab something to eat on the way."

"Oh, okay. Why are you going to Show Low on a school night?" Mom has never been the nosy type, but she's still a mom. I think she was more curious than concerned, but I decided to tell her the truth anyway.

"I'm, uh, going to see Lexi." If I'd been smart I would've had my phone out! The look on her face—even though it was brief—was hilarious!

"OH! Okay . . . well, tell her I said hello!" She was shocked, surprised, and nearly speechless, but she was also grinning mischievously.

"I will!" I said as I bolted out the door.

The nurse gave a friendly scowl when I walked up to the front desk. "It's about time you came back!" she said teasingly. "I think someone has been expecting you for a few days now."

I felt embarrassed but also a bit excited. Elli was right! I'm glad I didn't wait for more than a week like I originally thought I should. I knocked loudly on room 107.

"Come in!" said a hopeful voice. I opened the door and saw Lexi sitting at the table, the privacy curtain was pulled aside this time. "David! You came back!" She quickly set down her pen and closed her history book. "I was beginning to worry I'd scared you off!"

"No . . . well, maybe a little." Smiling, I held my hand up to show her it was only like an inch of fear.

She got a look of mock pain and said, "I know I looked atrocious, but I didn't realize it was *that* bad."

I hadn't intended the comment to be aimed at her looks, but I realize now there was probably no other way to take it. I quickly held out my hands. "No, no. That's not it at all! It's just—well if I'm being honest . . ." I thought about Elli. *Okay, here it goes.* I scrunched up my face as if I was about to eat a sour lemon and said, "I'm kinda scared of girls."

After a brief look of disbelief, Lexi threw her head back and started laughing! Quickly, she doubled back over and gasped, *"Oh, that hurts."* But she kept giggling and snorting, trying her hardest to keep it ladylike but failing in her attempt.

It felt good to see her smile, and I couldn't help but to start chuckling at her reaction. After a moment, I painted on a hurt expression and said, "Go ahead and laugh! You have no idea what kind of torture I've been through."

This only made the giggles worse. Wincing in pain, she tried desperately to get it under control. "Well then," she said with flushed cheeks, "that's a story you absolutely MUST tell!"

I pulled out the chair next to her and sat down at the table. With my eyes squinted in suspicion, I said, "I don't know. The last time I told my story, I got *laughed* at."

She placed her hands over her mouth to stifle another burst, and after a quick second, she crossed her heart and said, "I promise not to laugh. Cross my heart and hope to die."

By the look on her face, I honestly didn't think she could do it. She was about to burst at the seams! I raised an eyebrow, and after a moment of supposed contemplation, I said, "Okay. But you have to SWEAR this never leaves the room!"

She held up her right hand and said with a solemn smile, "I swear."

I accepted her promise and for the next thirty minutes, opened the gates to my soul. What was I thinking? I'm not sure, but unlike before when these stories felt like mental bullheads of shame and pain, this time it felt good to pull them out.

She tried hard not to giggle when I told about the stolen kiss in first grade, but when I confessed the botched love note to Andrea Marks, she couldn't hold it in anymore. She had both hands clasped to her mouth and was choking on muffled snorts. I pointed my finger at her and jokingly yelled, "HEY, you promised not to LAUGH!"

With her shoulders still heaving, she dropped her hands and shook her head side to side as she tried to say, "I'm not," but no sound came out.

I began to tell her about the date with Ashley and how we climbed the High Hills to watch the sunset. She leaned forward, giggles gone and watched me with genuine interest. "So there we were enjoying the sunset, when all of a sudden I turned to her—and she was staring at me. I felt a pull of evil super powers, and I KNEW she was getting ready to pounce." Lexi snorted again, but I pressed on, animating the story as best I could. "Like a lion stalking a grazing antelope, she drew closer. As she crouched to strike . . ." I ducked my head and said in shame, "I gave her a pretty rock."

Lexi lost it. Bent forward in painful throbs of laugher, she started crying. I stood up and teasingly stomped to the door. "That's it. I'm OUTTA here!"

She squeaked out between breaths, "No—No, please don't go. I'm sorry, but it's SO *funny!*"

"Go ahead, mock my pain!" I said with exaggerated anger.

This time, she was the one holding up her hands to stop the words. "Okay, okay. I think it's only fair that I give you some blackmail, too. Will that get you to stay?"

I pondered her proposal for a second. "Okay. But it better be good, or I'm gone!"

"All right, it's a deal." I walked over and sat back down. She straightened her white button-up blouse as if she were getting ready for a speech. She really looked beautiful today. She had her blonde hair pulled up in a simple pony tail, her long bangs swept behind her right ear. I didn't notice till today, she also has a darker color of brown layered stylishly underneath. Having her hair up made it stand out more. It was really cute!

She cleared her throat. "Hi, my name is Lexi Dupree. I am five foot eleven inches tall. I like long walks on the beach, roses, and desserts in a cup!"

I gave her an unimpressed look, and said, "Not quite what I'd call blackmail material."

She shushed me and went on. "I was born in San Diego, California on Christmas Eve in 1994. I am an only child, and I'm spoiled rotten."

"Well, at least she admits it!" I said under my breath, but obviously loud enough for her to hear.

She got an angry look on her face and pulled her hand back to hit me, but she was too far away, so instead, she grabbed her pen and threw it at me! "QUIT interrupting me, or this is all you'll get!"

"All right, all right." I threw my hands up in surrender. "I'll be nice. I promise," crossing my heart as she had done.

She glared at me, cleared her throat, and continued, "I grew up in San Diego playing volleyball, but when Dad got a job offer to manage the TEP power plant here in the White Mountains, he couldn't pass it up. So me, being the spoiled brat that I am, made a deal with him. I would only move if I could pick the town with the best volleyball team, and after some research, I decided on Snowflake."

I was about to give some sarcastic comment, but she held up her finger and cut me off saying, "I'm not finished! I'll get to the good stuff, I promise." She put her hand back down. I smiled and leaned back in my chair. "My first kiss . . ." she raised her eyebrows at me like she was saying, *See, I told you it was coming.* ". . . happened in fourth grade. I was at a friend's birthday party, and I trapped Joey Martinez behind the swing set. I told him if he let me kiss him, we would be the coolest kids in school. He was hesitant, but I convinced him."

My eyes got wide, and I was about to point at her and accuse her of being evil Jodi Burrow, but she reached her hand up and cut me off like a conductor. "Shhh!"

I dramatically flopped back in my chair like a scolded two year-old and crossed my arms. She ignored the tantrum and kept going. "But my most embarrassing boy moment, by far, happened my freshman year. I got a ride back to school from lunch with my boyfriend Jack Taylor. He was a *good*-looking Junior with one of those jacked up Chevys! Oh, it was nice." I wasn't liking this story anymore. "We got back early and were able to find a spot in the second row, right behind the teacher's spots. I scooted over and started making out with him, but neither of us realized he hadn't put his truck in park yet! My foot hit the gas pedal, and the truck shot forward! It hit the Vice Principal's car, climbed up the trunk, and landed on the hood! It was smashed clear down to the seats!"

I didn't laugh. I didn't say anything. For some reason, this story snapped me back to how things were before. She was the hot, popular girl again, and I was the socially backward choir boy. I felt very self-conscious and even defensive—and she noticed. "David, what's wrong?"

"Oh, nothing," I said, and looked away. I didn't know how to explain a conflict of emotions I didn't understand myself. Lexi looked confused, too. *Just be honest*, I tried to tell myself.

"Was it something I said?" she asked, concerned.

"No. Well . . . maybe." *What do I say?*

"Oh, I'm sorry," she said subdued. She thought for a minute, then looked down. Somehow, she figured it out. "It bothers you that we live such different lives, doesn't it. That you're a good guy, and I'm a bad girl?"

"No! I mean . . . I don't know." *Oh how to explain.* "It's just that . . . I really have been scared of girls like you my whole life. And for some reason, I didn't think about it until your story reminded me . . . that you're like that." Her shoulders sagged as my words seemed to suck the life right out of her. *Oops. David, you IDIOT!*

She started to tear up. *Why didn't I keep my mouth shut?* "Yeah, I know," she sniffed. "I don't deserve a friend like you. I've really screwed up a lot of things in life. I see that now. I'll understand if you decide not to come back."

If I had melted into a pile of poop and been hit by a car, I think I would've felt better than I did at that moment. I said a silent prayer and begged God to please help me! She sat with her head down, deflated; 180 degree turn from moments before. Then God *did* help me. He hit me upside the head with a hard SMACK!

I knew what type of girl Lexi used to be, but for some reason the accident clouded all that for a time. I say clouded, but what it *really* did was take away all my preconceived judgments. In an unlikely set of circumstances, we met on equal ground. But when she told me about her past, I let our level field of friendship begin to split again. It was like I turned the binoculars around after seeing clearly, and forced her far away and out of focus.

Until this moment, I never realized I had gotten it completely backward! I had viewed her as a person living a promiscuous life of sin, someone who I *thought* should be shunned. Instantly, God opened my eyes and showed me how "He" sees her: A beautiful young woman, humbled and broken, searching for answers and friendship; a girl wishing with all her might to find a shred of hope to get her through another day. I saw a precious daughter of God, whom He loves *very* much—and I hurt her.

I've never felt more horrible in my entire life.

Guilt tore through my chest. "Lexi?" She looked up at me, her face twisted with turmoil. My heart shattered. "I'm *sorry*."

This shocked her, and her eyebrows scrunched in confusion. "Sorry for what?"

"For judging you." The truth hurt, but it would've been more damaging to us both if I'd kept it in. "Lexi, what have you ever done to me except be a friend? I've done nothing but judge you . . . a judgment that is wrong and not even mine to give . . . *and I am so sorry.*"

She shook her head, still not understanding. "It's okay, David. I deserved it."

"No, you didn't." I shot back. "You deserve a friend who will like you for who you are and be there for you no matter what."

She wiped her tears with the back of her hand, and after a few seconds, her countenance calmed. She even got a slight smile right before she asked, "So . . . do you know where I might *find* a friend like that?"

Relief flooded over me. "Maybe,"—I smiled—"but you might need to forgive him first. He's kinda hard-headed."

She smiled the sweetest smile and said, "I think I might be able to do that."

We shared a tender look, and I could feel the temperature in the room begin to rise. It took me a second to realize she was tractor beaming me in, and I quickly broke the stare by forcing my eyes to the wall. There happened to be a clock there, and I said with surprise, "Oh, wow, it's already past 8:00! I probably better be heading home." When I looked back, one side of her mouth was turned up in mischievous half grin. I think she was delighting in my discomfort! I nervously stood to leave.

That wiped the smirk right off. In a desperate tone, she asked, "You'll come back to see me, won't you?"

This time I got to give the grin. After waiting a second longer than I should've, I smiled and said, "Yeah, I guess so."

She relaxed. "Good." Suddenly those blue eyes flared with sassiness. "I need someone to have a good cry with every now and again."

"Oh, ha ha," I answered flatly as I rolled my eyes. With a smile I joked, "I *might* come back, but only if next time you have some of those M&Ms."

Her eyes lit up. "I forgot!" She pulled a bag out from under her books on the table and tossed it to me. "Here. Maybe this will help you remember me this time."

I laughed as I cradled the Peanut M&Ms. "Oh, I don't think I'd forget about you, but thanks."

"And you might want to put my number in your phone. Sometimes they take me out for appointments, and sometimes I get to go home for the weekends! I wouldn't want you to drive all this way and miss me." She told me her number as I punched it into my cell.

"Thank you," I said. "I'll definitely keep in touch." I walked to the door and stepped out into the hall. "I hope you have a good night, Lexi."

"I think I will. You too, David."

Well, it isn't exactly how I thought the evening would go, and besides the few moments when I almost destroyed her heart and crushed her soul, I think things turned out okay. Oh, the stupid things I say sometimes. Surprisingly, in spite of all my idiocy, things ended up better in a way. Honesty can be harsh, but it can also be healing. And if I'm truly being honest with myself—I'm starting to care for Lexi a lot more than I ever thought I would.

Tuesday, 20 December 2011

Sometimes it's hard to find a quiet place around here. Josh has been on one all day and won't stop teasing Sarah. Mom finally threatened him to cool it or he wouldn't get his license till he was seventeen. He was still in our room sulking when I got the heck outta Dodge. I didn't have enough time to build a fire, so I decided to park my truck somewhere and run the heater. I drove north toward Holbrook, and right before the Snowflake city limit sign, I took a left onto the Flake ranch. There's a big hill, similar to our High Hills, that they call Four Mile Knoll. People used to be able to drive to the top, but the road has since washed out. I got about halfway before I had to stop. The sun had been asleep for a while. Dusk was fading, and the stars had taken over the watch. I only had to wait about twenty minutes, but I didn't mind the silence.

Hi, David! You seem to be more at peace than usual today. Her words were accompanied with a sweet sensation of joy.

I was about to say the same about you. You seem a lot happier than last time.

Yes, much happier than yesterday. I think something sparked inside Jared today as we discussed the Freedom Side again. He thought long and deep when I explained to him the points we discussed in our last conversation. I don't think he likes the idea of being limited because of others. But he also had a lot of questions I didn't know how to answer. Her emotions brightened. *How did your meeting go with Lexi?*

It went surprisingly well, in spite of the fact I almost killed the whole relationship before it had a chance to start!

She jolted in what I thought was a gasp. *I'm glad I can feel your joy, or I might be very worried. Everything went well?*

There were a few rocky places, but at least ended on a positive note. I took a good forty-five minutes retelling her (in as many details as I could remember) everything that happened. She was very curious, even to the point of asking about colors and sounds. It was funny to me, but I loved her enthusiasm.

When I finally quenched her curiosity, she paused for a second, and with a shade of angelic sassiness, said, *And yes, David, I am a little jealous. A part of me wonders what it would be like to experience all these things with you in more than words and brief emotions, but I know my time will come soon enough.* Her excitement began bubbling to the surface again. *It's only days now instead of what used to be millennia! It's a good thing you cannot remember how difficult it was to wait for this long!*

I tried to imagine how she might feel, but it's hard to comprehend such vast timelines. The anticipation must've been awful.

You have no idea, she said with a shot of humor. (A shot—I doubt an angel would know what that means, but, oh well. Enjoy the irony!) *What else happened to you this week?*

Well, I'm afraid I have some bad news, I said, hating to dampen her good mood.

What is it?

We started our winter break from school on Saturday, and I couldn't handle going all vacation without smoothing things over with Frank.

And were you successful? She was filled with hope, and I hated bursting such a warm bubble

No. I tried going to his house on Saturday, but everyone was gone. I sent him a text to see what he was up to, and he only gave a short, rude reply. He said his family was out of town for the holidays, a fact I would've known if I was a real friend.

What a harsh thing to say, Elli said in disgust.

I laughed in agreement, but in Frank's defense, I knew he was somewhat justified in the comment. I really haven't been a good friend to him, Elli. Between being busy at work, and you, and Lexi—well, I kinda forgot about him for a while.

David, you must not let him continue feeling this way, no matter the cost! I can't bear the thought of someone having so much hatred in their heart. Please try to make things right!

I will, I promise, I smiled. Besides, I don't think I can handle another second of the silent treatment.

Thanks, David. It means a lot to me. We sat for a moment before she asked, *And what about Lexi?* her bubble re-inflating with the question.

Well, you'll be happy to know, I didn't wait to talk to her again. But the down side is, when I texted her the next day, she told me she was packing up to go to California for the holidays. She'll be gone for more than a week.

Oh, was all she replied, and down the bubble went again. Luckily, it wasn't as far this time. *But you can still contact her right? Didn't you say your phone works like the Airlis?*

Yeah, kinda. And yes, I'll keep in touch with her while she's gone.

Good! She's probably going to need it.

My heart filled with appreciation, and I wanted her to know it. Thanks for all your advice, Elli. I'm so grateful for all your help.

You're quite welcome. She smiled warmly. *I'm glad I could return the favor!*

It had been over an hour by then, so we said our goodbyes. Sometimes, Frank, I think you act like a girl, and sometimes, I wanna deck you! But, Frank, if you ever read this, I want you to know you're still my best friend, and I'm going to do better at showing it. Besides, if I don't try to mend this, I think I might make a certain young lady pretty upset, and I'd really hate to see what kind of shotgun her Dad carries! ☺

Monday, 26 December 2011

Lexi is finally coming home! Not that I've been waiting or anything. ☺ I tell you what, my texting skills have improved dramatically over the last week.

Christmas was bittersweet. Sarah woke up late and very depressed, which was a shock to us all. When we finally coaxed her out of bed, she dragged her stuffed horse into the living room and flopped on the couch.

"What's wrong, honey?" Mom asked with deep concern.

Sarah folded her arms, scowled, then barked, "Santa's NOT REAL!" The words were venomous.

Mom sat down next to her and tried to put her arms around her, but Sarah twisted away. Mom asked, "Why do you say that, honey?"

She whirled on Mom with tears in her eyes, "Because I saw YOU put the presents under the tree!" She jabbed her finger at Mom like she was pointing out the bad guy in a line up. "I cracked open my door and waited, because I wanted to prove to all my friends that they were WRONG!" She started sobbing.

I caught Josh's eye, and we were about to start chuckling, but Mom must've sensed our intentions and gave us The Look. We shut it down immediately. Mom grabbed Sarah's crying face in both hands. After a moment, Sarah finally caved in and looked up at her. Mom said tenderly, "Sarah, you're wrong. Santa IS real!" Sarah looked at her confused. Mom continued, "You just haven't known who 'he' is until last night!" Sarah's eyes narrowed in anger again, but she didn't pull away. Mom leaned in closer and whispered, "*YOU are Santa now!*"

More confused, Sarah pulled away slowly and asked, "What do you mean? I saw YOU!"

The anger faded as she tried desperately to understand. Mom smiled and said, "One day, not too many years from now, you'll have a little girl of your own who will absolutely *adore* Santa Clause. *You* are now the Secret Santa who will make all her dreams come true!" Sarah's eyes widened in wonder. "And now that you know the truth about who Santa *really* is, we can spend

242

the next few years turning you into the *best* Santa who has ever delivered presents from the North Pole!"

Sarah sat up straight. All anger and malice were gone. In its place burned a new fire. It was the flame of potential, and she was ready for the new adventure! I looked at Mom in wonder. I saw her with different eyes this Christmas morning. She has such a natural ability to love and console, and with a single kiss, she has the power to heal a broken heart. I can't think of another person in the world who has that kind of power. Mom, you're my hero!

Josh, on the other hand, saw things differently. "Well, you never gave ME that talk!" he smirked jokingly.

Mom squeezed Sarah, and said, "That's because you're not my special girl!" She kissed Sarah on the head and asked her, "So, do you want to see what 'Santa' brought you?"

Sarah jumped off the couch with an emphatic, "YES!" and the craziness of Christmas morning continued as usual.

I have long since grown out of getting cool toys for Christmas, but that doesn't mean I don't try to convince "Santa" otherwise. I'm not complaining, though. I looked briefly at suits online a few Sundays ago. I was curious how much it'll cost to get the clothes I need for a mission, and was SHOCKED to see how expensive they are. When I calculated the cost of my mission, I didn't realize it would be so expensive to look like one. Because of the added expenses, I was planning to work a lot of extra hours to cover it, but to my surprise, Grandma and Grandpa got me two suits for Christmas! I made sure to run over as soon as I could to thank them. Mom also got me a bunch of small things: a few ties, a belt, and a nice duffle bag. I'm very grateful for getting a bunch of things I needed. It could've been worse. I could have gotten a remote controlled car that I ruined the next day . . . like Josh. Ha! Sorry, I shouldn't laugh, but the ding dong tried to jump it off the trampoline! When it landed hard, one of the front wheels snapped off. Josh got humbled for Christmas, and it was great!

Lexi will get back from California today sometime! Her father had to come back for work. I plan to see her tomorrow as soon as Scott lets me go. Even though she was in another state, I learned a lot of things about her through our text messages.

Her dad's name is Steve, and he was in the military for four years and became a mechanical engineer because of his service.

His education, coupled with leadership skills and a head for business, paved a quick road up the ranks and landed him the job at Tucson Electric Power.

Her mom, Nancy, was diagnosed with multiple sclerosis shortly before Lexi was born. She was only able to have one child due to the illness. Over the years, she grew steadily worse and now is mostly confined to a wheelchair. Lexi told me this on Thursday. I remember, because once again, I was stabbed with guilt for judging her without getting to know her first. I think most of the kids in school did the same thing. Lexi was always on her phone because she was checking on her mom! She does have a few friends she keeps in contact with in California, but most of the time it was her mother.

Before the accident, her mom would fall or get herself in some kind of bind almost daily. Lexi would get a text and have to excuse herself from class to go help. Her Dad works a lot, and they really didn't have anyone else who could help. Sometimes, when Lexi was away for volleyball games and something would happen, she'd ask their neighbor Cathy to help, but that was a rare occasion. Talk about feeling two inches tall. I'm glad this was all through texts, because I wouldn't have been able to hide my shame had we talked face to face.

So that's the reason Lexi stays at The Cottage. After the accident, her dad took nearly three weeks off work, but he couldn't stay away forever. Nancy is barely able to fend for herself, let alone give Lexi the care she needs, and luckily, Cathy offered to check on her periodically. Lexi goes home whenever her dad is off work, but he has a busy schedule. Until she can care for herself, Lexi is stuck in a 20' x 20' cell with a cranky neighbor called Mean Jean and a roaming old flirt in a wheelchair called Crazy Dan.

Somehow, through all that, her spirits are up! She had a great Christmas, and even the trip to Cali wasn't too bad. They were able to remove the seats of their Escalade and put in a comfortable mattress for her to lie on. I'm glad she's finally coming home. I can't wait to see her tomorrow!

Tuesday, 27 December 2011

Today we had to work later than usual—to my great dismay. Scott wants to take advantage of Christmas break this week and plans to finish a full-kitchen remodel before I go back. I've been trying not to "zone out" on him like before, so instead I work harder in hopes it'll make the time go by faster. It doesn't help much.

By the time I got home and showered, it was after 7:00. My fingers struggled with the laces as my mind battled—*Lexi or Elli?* As the absurdity of me having two dates with different girls sank in, I laughed out loud. Shaking my head, I said to myself, "Elli, I hope you're still here when I get back!" Grabbing an apple and the sandwich mom made me, I ran out the door.

107!

"Come in." It was not the voice I was expecting. It was sad and sounded as if it had been weeping.

I opened the door hesitantly. Lexi was sitting between the foot of her bed and the couch, facing the window. She wiped her face with a tissue before she turned around.

"Hey, David." Even though she had to force a smile past the tears, it was genuine and sweet.

"Lexi, what's wrong?"

She waved a hand dismissively. "Oh nothing. Just a bad day. I have them every now and then." Her slightly puffy eyes did not prevent a mischievous grin. "Well, are you going to come in? Or are you still scared of me?"

I realized I was still standing in the doorway. "Oh, no. Not really," I replied with a smile. "But I'm leaving this open, just in case." I pushed the door against the wall, and it stayed there. "That way they can hear me if I start screaming."

She laughed and shook her head. "Yeah, you'd hate to be attacked by a helpless girl in a wheelchair."

Raising a hand in self-defense, I said, "Hey, I've seen the super powers you girls possess, and I don't think a wheelchair would slow them at all!" She blushed at the comment. "So, if you don't mind, I think I'll leave the door open for now."

She shook her head in wonder. I think she can't believe a guy like me exists. She's probably right. Looking down at my hands, she asked, "So what's that? Did you bring something for Mean Jean?"

I glanced at the gift bag in my other hand. "Oh, this?" I held it up. "Yeah, I was thinking about it, but when I stopped by, she was sleeping." I walked over and held it out, "So I figured I'd give it to you instead."

"Oh, you're too kind." Her eyes were narrowed, but she couldn't hide a smile. She wheeled her chair back to allow me room to sit on the couch. As I sat, she hefted the bag questioningly. "I didn't realize you had such strong feelings for Mean Jean!" She grinned wide.

It was my turn to blush. Trying to change the subject, I asked, "Did you have a good birthday?"

"Much better now, thanks to Mean Jean!" I rolled my eyes. She smiled and finally let me off the hook. "Actually, I'm surprised you remembered. Thanks, David." She opened the bag and pulled out a small shoe box. Twisting it, she noticed a picture on the side that showed Sarah's latest Dora shoes. "I think they might be a few sizes too small, but at least they're cute!"

Chuckling, I said, "You'll have to wrestle Sarah for them. She wears them every day!"

"In my physical state, she'd probably win," she smiled.

She tore off the scotch tape and opened the lid hesitantly. All she saw was a wad of newspaper and looked up questioningly. "It's not *alive,*" I laughed. "But it *is* fragile, so be careful."

She gently peeled off the layers until she unwrapped a single, glass rose. I had looked all over town for some kind of rose, but the dollar stores didn't have much of a selection. Finally, I decided to try a small thrift store, and hidden toward the back of the glass section I found a stunning red rose!

She held it worshipfully. "OH! It's *beautiful!*" She twirled it slowly, soaking up every angle. After admiring it for a while she pressed it to her heart. "Mean Jean will be so sad she didn't get this . . . I promise I won't tell her." She grinned. "Thanks, David. I love it!" Peering in the bag, she gasped as she pulled out a small container. "AH! You got me BEN AND JERRY'S! And one of my favorite flavors, too." She looked at me curiously. "How'd you know?"

I shrugged. "I figured it was a pretty safe guess. Most people like cookie dough."

"Well, you guessed right," she declared with a smile. "Would you like some?"

"Sure! I wouldn't mind a bite or two." I forgot spoons, so she buzzed a nurse and asked if she would grab us a couple. While the nurse was searching, I told Lexi, "There's one more part to this gift, but I couldn't put it in the bag."

She looked at me curiously, "Oh, and what's that?"

I smiled and said, "I owe you a walk on the beach."

Tilting her head back, she laughed as it dawned on her what I'd done. Her eyes sparkled as she held up each object. "A rose . . . a dessert in a cup . . ."—a huge grin lit up her face—"and a walk on the beach. You remembered!" Smiling, I nodded my head.

She held my gaze for a long second. "Okay, David, it's a deal. But you might have to wait a while." Her demeanor changed suddenly, and her face became sad. "They said I might not be able to walk for five or six months."

"I don't mind waiting," I said with a grin. This brought a smile back to her face as well.

The nurse came in with some spoons, and we started on our cup of goodness. After a few bites, Lexi handed me the ice cream and held up a finger as if to say, "wait a second." She wheeled over to a small closet next to the door and pulled out a wrapped box. Glowing with excitement, she came back and handed it to me. "And this was supposed to be for Crazy Dan, but I'd like you to have it instead."

I laughed and replied teasingly, "Well, thank you for being thoughtful."

Shrugging, she said, "No problem." Then she rolled back to my side and picked up the ice cream from where I'd set it on the couch.

It was small, about the size of a tissue box. And when I un-wrapped it, I saw that it WAS a tissue box. I held it up and said flatly, "Really."

She looked at me in confusion for a second before it registered. Had she not quickly clamped her hands over her mouth, she probably would've spewed ice cream all over the room! Snorting a few times before she could get it under control, she briskly waved her hands and said, "No, no! I wasn't implying . . . Ha! No you goober, look inside!" I rolled my eyes with exaggeration as her snickers subsided, then I reached in and pulled out . . . a small, hand-held Taser? My look of confusion prompted her to explain, "I had Dad get that for you so you can protect yourself from girls!"

I lost it. We both lost it! We laughed till the tears came and she was begging me to stop because it hurt too much. After a while, I was finally able to say in a mocking tone, "Well, I feel SO much safer now!" Wiping my eyes, I smiled and added, "Maybe I won't have to yell for help after all."

She laughed and said, "You never know when someone might catch you unaware." Her eyes flickered ever so slightly.

I stared at her for a moment, wondering if I saw what I thought I saw, then said hesitantly, "Yeah . . . better to be safe than sorry, I guess."

We laughed and visited a while longer. It was almost nine before I realized what time it was. We said goodbye, and I hurried home, but I was too late. Sometime after 11:00, I put the Airlis back in the ammo box and slid it under my bed. I'm sad I missed Elli tonight, but I'm going to bed with a smile. It's about time Elli feels what it's like to get stood up!

Sunday, 1 January 2012

You know the term, "working your tail off"? Yeah, I think I lost mine sometime Thursday. Scott would've kept me till 9:00 every night if I hadn't asked to go home early on Friday to see Lexi. She'd been giving me a hard time about not coming back to see her, but I think she was mostly teasing. It's hard to tell sometimes in a text. After reminding him for the third time, Scott grudgingly let me go at 7:00. Lexi complained the day before that no one had asked her out in over a month. Her subliminal message was not very camouflaged, and I don't think she was intending it to be. Ha! So I told her to make it up to her I'd bring a movie Friday night and we'd watch it together. She texted a lot of exclamation points and smiley faces. ☺

When I asked her what movie she'd like to watch, she said to surprise her. Oh, she shouldn't have done that. I brought three movies, but I made her believe I only brought one, at first: *The Swan Princess*. By the way she was cracking up, I knew *The Lord of the Rings* and *Star Wars—The Phantom Menace* wouldn't have a chance. Insisting adamantly that we watch the cartoon, I think she was hoping my joke would backfire. Little did she know, I can quote *The Swan Princess*, too. I would blame it on Sarah, but honestly, I've watched it a time or two without her. Don't tell anyone, though.

The only bad part about seeing it before—many times before—is that I couldn't keep my eyes open. I was so worn out from working multiple twelve-hour days, it was impossible to stay awake. She kept teasing me about being a poor excuse for a date and started throwing stuff at me on the couch, but in the end, I don't think she was too upset. When I asked her if she wanted to try again sometime she said, "You know, I'm probably going to be busy washing my hair, so why don't you wait till I call you." I knew she was teasing, and before I got halfway home, she called to make sure I was still awake then asked *me* to ask *her* out again. She's so full of it! I marvel at how she can keep such a happy outlook on life while sitting in a wheelchair. It was a fun night even if I did sleep through most of it.

Lexi got to spend New Year's with her family. Her grandparents on her dad's side flew in for the weekend, so I told her I'd catch up with her sometime next week. I decided against going to the Church's New Year's dance. Besides not really caring to see anyone from school, I was so tired I fell asleep before ten! I thought it was a *great* way to welcome in the New Year. ☺

Frank didn't come to church today, but his family did. His mom didn't say much except he has been really depressed lately. Something is going on with him. When I texted, he didn't reply, and when I went by his house, he wasn't there. I'm really starting to worry about him now. I'm not sure what in the heck's going on.

Monday, 2 January 2012

"Frank, STOP!" I cornered him by his car on the way to Honor Choir, and instead of putting his books inside and going to class, he jumped in the driver seat! He cranked the car over and started to pull away, but before he could get up to speed, I was able to open the passenger door and dive in.

"What in the HELL is GOING ON?" I yelled as I slammed the door. We were already a half a block away from the school by then. (Sorry, Mom. I really have been doing better with my cussing, but my emotions kind of overwhelmed me at the moment.)

"Like YOU care!" Frank shot back.

"Frank, I DO care! Dude, you almost *ran* me over, but that didn't stop me from trying to talk to you! It's YOU who doesn't seem to care anymore." He slammed on the brakes as we came to the Main Street stop sign and then gunned the car to the left. "Frank—I've been calling, and texting, and driving all around FLIPPIN' town to try and FIND you!" Frank stared down the road, his face full of pain and anger. I'm sure he was speeding, but neither of us cared at the moment.

"Well, you found me. Are you happy?" His words were dripping with disdain.

"Dude, what's going on? If you're still mad at me for not waving and for missing your date, I'm SORRY, man!" I tried not to sound sarcastic, but I couldn't help it. Why was he filled with so much hate over such a small problem? Wheels screeched as he took a hard right at the stop light.

Shaking his head, like I was missing the whole picture, he hissed through gritted teeth, "If you *just* would've come on that **stupid** date." To my surprise, tears started rolling down his face. By this time, we'd crossed the creek, and without touching the brakes, he whipped the car to the left, and we shot down Old Woodruff Road.

"The DATE? Really?" I asked in astonishment. "This is all because I didn't go on a stupid date?"

He slammed on his brakes. The car slid sideways down the road until it came to rest at a weird angle. He jerked his head toward me, glaring with bloodshot eyes. "YES, David! Yes! If you would've been on that date with me, I wouldn't have messed up with Tracy!"

Understanding hit like a tsunami. As the words left his mouth, I watched his anger melt away to reveal crushing guilt and shame. He started to cry again. This completely blind-sided me at first, but as I thought about it, I wasn't really that surprised. I'd always wondered how smooth-talking lady killers like Frank could get away unaffected from their frivolity. He was always so confident! I figured his ability to control his feelings was much stronger than mine. I see now, at least for Frank, it was all for show.

"Frank, . . . I'm *sorry*, man." His head bobbed slightly as tears soaked his shirt and jeans. I didn't know what else to say, so I let him cry. He worked hard to get his emotions under control and finally was able to dam up the tear ducts. Finding my voice and some courage, I asked, "Is she pregnant?"

Sniffing, he said, "No. We don't think so. At least all the tests have come back negative so far."

"Is she alive?"

He looked at me with a funny expression. "Yes, David, she's alive." His eyebrows furrowed in confusion.

"Are you alive?"

His head drooped as he sunk into the seat. "Sometimes it doesn't feel like it, but yeah, I'm still alive." After a moment he looked at me curiously. "Why?"

I smiled and said, "Because it's a whole lot easier to make things right if you're still alive."

Turning, he stared blankly out the window. In a resigned tone he said, "I don't think I can make this right."

"Well, you won't know till you try, Frank." I tried to sound encouraging.

He shrugged his shoulders and held his palms up in a pleading gesture. "What do I do, David?"

I thought about it for a moment. "I'm not sure, Frank, but I know someone who does." His eyes clouded over as he contemplated my suggestion. "Look, *I* need to talk to the Bishop on Wednesday, anyway." He glanced at me in surprise, but I kept talking. "Why don't you come with me and see him, too?"

He thought about it for a minute, and something shifted in his far-off gaze. For the first time in weeks, I saw a small spark of hope in his eyes as he nodded in acceptance. So I did what any other guy would've done in the situation . . . and punched him as HARD as I COULD!

"OW!" he yelled in pain as he grabbed his shoulder. "What was THAT for?"

"THAT," I replied, as I poked him hard on his fresh injury, "is for almost RUNNING ME OVER in front of the WHOLE SCHOOL!" Frank couldn't keep the smile from taking over his face. It was good to see it there again. I sat back hard and said, "Well, let's go!" and pointed down the road.

"Where?" he asked confused.

Smiling, I said, "Not back to school, that's for DANG sure."

Wednesday, 4 January 2012

Frank and I sat on the soft couch in the foyer of the church waiting for our turn to see Bishop Call. I told him I thought it'd be better if we came in shirt and tie, so there he sat, elbows on knees, nervously rolling his tie up to his neck and letting it fall—over and over again.

"Don't worry, Frank." I pushed him hard on the shoulder, trying to shake him out of his trance. "You're doing the right thing, man."

Bishop walked out of his office right after that and asked, "All right, who's next?"

I pointed to Frank. The blood seemed to drain from his already pale face. I was afraid if I went first and left him out here alone, he might disappear. "Come on in Brother Owens. We missed you at church last week!"

Frank gave me one last look that said, *You better be right about this*! I gave him a slight nod and a thumbs up. He was in there for a good half hour, but I was expecting it and didn't care. I'm still so proud of him for being brave enough to face this.

Eventually, the door opened, and they stepped back out. To my surprise, they both were shedding tears. Bishop gave Frank a big, fatherly hug then pushed him to arm's length and said in a hushed voice, "I'm proud of you, Frank. I *know* you can do this."

Frank nodded his head in agreement. His whole countenance had changed. He was—lighter! Not only did his face emanate peace again, but his whole essence seemed relieved of a heavy, heavy burden. I know what that feels like. That night on the loft, when everything was crashing down around me, God lifted a ton of bitterness from my smothered soul. Standing here, looking at Frank, I was reminded of those sweet, sweet feelings once again.

Tears fell from my own eyes as he walked over and gave me a big hug, slapping me hard on the back like brothers do. We pulled apart, but before I could say anything, he doubled up his fist and gave me a dead arm I'll never forget!

"WHAT THE . . . ?" I yelled as I backed away wounded. I'm just glad I didn't cuss in front of Bishop.

Jabbing a finger stiffly into my fresh bruise, he mocked, "And THAT'S for not telling me the WHOLE TRUTH!"

Failing to hide a guilty smile, I said with a chuckle, "What are you talking about?" But I knew he knew.

"You're not here to CONFESS anything! You're here to start your mission papers!"

Still laughing, I looked at Bishop. He shrugged his shoulders and said, "Sorry. I didn't know it was a secret." But it was okay. My ploy had worked.

In my defense I said, "Well, you never asked, did you?" He narrowed his eyes at me. I continued, "And maybe I *do* have something to confess!"

Bishop cleared his throat, "Well, Brother Thorn, maybe we should continue this conversation in my office." He smiled and stepped to the side of his office door, motioning for me to come in.

I moved toward him, but before walking inside, I heard Frank say, "Hey, David." Turning around, I looked at him standing there in his shirt and tie, face radiating new hope, and for a brief moment I could see a hazy outline of a stripling warrior. "Thanks, man."

I nodded and stepped through the door.

"Brother Thorn, if I had any doubts about you becoming a great missionary, they're all gone now." I couldn't hold his gaze. I wasn't expecting a compliment. "What you did for Frank, as small as it may seem to you, will not only affect his mortal existence, David, it'll change his eternal destiny."

As the immensity of what he was saying began to sink in, I felt the Holy Spirit pour into my soul! But it was different this time. It wasn't liberating or inspirational like I'd experienced before. No, this time it was simply undiluted, *pure* love. It consumed me! It reached into every cell, penetrated every space— and it was more than my soul could contain. Tears of joy streamed down my cheeks, and I noticed Bishop's joy was overflowing, too. We sat in silence for a long time, relishing the feeling of being wrapped in the arms of God's great love.

As the emotion eventually began to subside, I said to Bishop, "If that's what it feels like to share the gospel, sign me up!" Both our grins went from ear to ear.

We didn't spend much more time. He asked me the interview questions, and I answered as honestly as I could.

"Well, David, it's with great pleasure that I will recommend your name to the Stake President as one worthy and ready to serve a mission for the Lord. Please contact the Stake Secretary to set up an interview with President Smith. It should take place the second Wednesday of next month. Your papers of recommendation will then be emailed to President Monson, and hopefully, within two more weeks, you'll receive a call to serve from an authorized prophet of God!" He paused for a moment, eyes glistening. "What an amazing opportunity this is, David. A call to serve from a true prophet of God. I'd like you to ponder that, because I have a feeling you'll get a chance to share your thoughts about it in church soon." He gave me a wink, and I accepted with a smile.

"David, before you go, I'd like to commit you to something." I was getting up to leave and quickly sat back down. "I committed Frank to the same thing, and maybe you can help each other be successful. Please tell him I said that. I want you to read again the *For The Strength of Youth* pamphlet, and I challenge you to live it as closely as you can. If you do, I promise that Satan will not be able to tempt you away from making it on your mission. Will you commit to doing that?"

"Yes," I said as I nodded in agreement.

"Good. I'm going to follow up with you two as often as I can, so you better be ready."

I smiled and said, "Okay, I will."

"And one more thing, before you leave on your mission, I would encourage you to re-read the Book of Mormon from cover to cover. If you haven't yet received a testimony of that book— GET one! It'll be the difference between success and failure. And I'm not just talking about your mission."

I understood. "I'll do it, Bishop. I promise."

Saturday, 7 January, 2012

Sorry, but with all the craziness going on with Frank, I forgot to tell you about Elli! When I talked to her on Tuesday, disappointingly, she was not upset about being stood up. Once she found out it was because I was talking to "a girl," she quickly forgave me and wanted all the details in full color, Braille, and Spanish! But when the recap of the last two weeks got to Frank, her bubbly comments were quickly subdued.

Oh David, does he realize how horrible a sin that is?! The consequences for such actions continue for eternities! I admit, the gravity of her comment seemed silly to me at first. The worldly acceptance of such things as common and okay made it difficult for me to see her perspective. But the next day when Bishop looked me in the eyes and told me I helped change Frank's eternal destiny!—suddenly Elli's words didn't seem so extreme. I can't wait to tell her the rest of the story!

Frank's road is going to be hard. When he told Tracy he couldn't steady date her anymore, she flipped out! I guess she was viewing their relationship through marriage goggles, but Frank's telescope is set on a mission now. It's still a ways out there for him, but at least it's a possibility. He's absolutely determined not to mess it up again.

I was surprised at Tracy's reaction, though. I thought she'd be more supportive. If their love was great enough to drive them over the edge of self-control, wouldn't it be big enough to support Frank through a two-year mission? But instead, Tracy got bitter. Poor Frank. It was bad enough having him mad at me for weeks, but I'd take ten furious Franks over one ticked-off Tracy any day! One day after school, all his tires were flat. Another day, someone keyed both sides of his car! No, it's not going to be easy.

On a happier note—sort of—Lexi was able to stay at her own house all week. Grandma and Grandpa Dupree decided to prolong their stay to keep Lexi from having to go back to "prison," as they called it. I probably could've pushed a bit harder to see her during the week, but honestly, I'm scared to death to meet her family. But fate wouldn't allow me to wallow in cowardice. Lexi invited me to dinner with her family tonight.

When I told Lexi I was going to be busy finishing *The Swan Princess*, she texted a laughing face and threatened:

~If you DON'T come, I'm going to tell every girl in school about your favorite movie!

`-Ooo, low blow. Low blow. Fine. I'll come over.`

It took me nearly twenty minutes to get to the Dupree residence. They live south of Taylor on Bourdon Ranch Road. Taylor is the neighboring town. After taking a right and driving through an old farm that'd been cut up into housing lots, I wound my way up a steep ridge to a big, beautiful house. When I got out of my truck, I turned and noticed the High Hills directly to the north of us. As I scanned the horizon, I could make out most of the landmarks on Grandpa's ranch. It was strange to see my secret life of adventure from someone else's front door step.

Steve Dupree answered the door. "Hello, David. Come on in." If he hadn't used such a welcoming tone, I think I might've wet my pants on the door mat. Steve is a BIG man. His hand swallowed mine, and with every firm shake, I swear he grew another inch. You can tell not long ago he was in good enough shape to pull the horns off a bull, but a few years behind a desk has given him a bit of a gut. Even so, I realized if he wanted to rip my arms off, my Taser would be useless. It would take a lot more than a few volts to stop that train! I had it in the pocket of my jacket as a reminder to thank Steve, but I found myself grasping it like a life line.

He led me through the entry and into a spacious living room area. There was a huge flat-screen TV on the left wall, circled by leather couches. On the far side of the room was a beautiful fireplace with a nice-size fire burning.

The house was amazing, but what captured my attention when I first walked in was the giant moose head hanging above the mantel. The room was filled with hunting trophies, some of them obviously from different countries.

I gawked.

Steve smiled and said, "Come, sit down. The girls will be out in a minute."

The plush sofa sucked me in as I surveyed the room. Finally making use of my open mouth, I said, "Your house is awesome!"

258

Steve chuckled. "Thank you." He looked around the room. "Perhaps I enjoy hunting a little too much. But," he let out a sigh, "it's an addiction I can't shake."

Gratefully, Lexi appeared and saved me from saying anything else stupid. "Yes, a disgusting addiction if you ask me." She wheeled her chair from down the hall that disappeared around the left side of the fireplace. "I used to have nightmares all the time of bears and cougars sneaking into my bedroom at night."

Steve laughed, "Yes, yes. And that's exactly why bears and cougars are no longer *in* our house."

Lexi's cheeks turned a light-red and she smiled guiltily. She looked stunning in her dark-purple, V-neck sweater. The long sleeves were pushed up slightly revealing a simple gold bracelet on her left arm. She was wearing nice, black dress pants and black pull-on shoes, the flat kind with no laces. Her shoulder-length hair was down tonight, curled out slightly on the bottom, and once again, her bangs were pulled behind her right ear. But I couldn't stop staring at her eyes! They seemed darker blue for some reason. I must've gawked a little too long, because she glanced down at her lap and tried brushing her hair behind her ear, even though it was already there.

I didn't have time to notice if Steve saw my trance, because her grandparents walked through the front door carrying what looked like a sack of ice cream. Her grandmother was talking as they came in, ". . . it took me forever waiting in line, and I . . ." Her face brightened as she saw me sitting on the couch. "OH! And this must be the David we've heard *so* much about!"

She stepped quickly toward me. I stood and extended my hand. Instead of shaking, she held it firmly in both of hers as she scrutinized my face. Right before the awkwardness melted into a puddle of embarrassment, she looked at Lexi with a mischievous Grandma Grin and said, "Ooo, he IS handsome, just like you said."

The only thing that kept me from squirming a hole in the floor was the look on Lexi's face. Her cheeks went instantly crimson as her eyes widened in disbelief. She let out a soft groan and covered her eyes with her hand. This brought a smile to an otherwise dreadful situation. By then her grandpa had walked over and said, "Oh, leave the poor chap alone. We'd hate to scare him outta here before dessert!" He reached forward, and we briskly shook hands as he said, "I'm Greg Dupree, and this is my wife Anne. It's a pleasure to meet you, son."

"Thank you," I squeaked out. "It's a pleasure to meet all of you."

Steve said, "You'll have to excuse Nancy. She got worn out preparing the food and is resting a while. I don't think she'll be much longer."

Lexi spoke up from behind her hand, "Yeah, she'll be right out." She looked up, her red cheeks almost back to normal. "She was fixing her hair when I came in."

"Good! Because I'm starving," Greg huffed in a grandpa tone.

Anne swatted his arm and said, "Oh, Dear, you're *always* starving."

"It's cause I don't get fed enough around here!" he replied teasingly.

Anne rolled her eyes, and they walked to the kitchen to put the food away. A large, open kitchen was to our right behind a counter lined with stools. All the appliances were stainless steel. As I found myself looking around again, I couldn't help but ask Steve about his trophies. "So where did you get all these?"

He took a deep breath, and with a look of delight said, "The moose I got in '98 on a big-game hunting trip in Northern Canada!"

Lexi rolled her eyes playfully and said, "Here we go again."

Steve waved a dismissive hand at her, like he was swatting at a fly. "Oh, you hush. The boy asked an honest question."

But before he could say another word, we heard Nancy from down the hall. "Don't believe a word he says, David! His stories get taller with each telling."

Lexi laughed in agreement. Nancy appeared around the same corner Lexi had. I instantly knew where Lexi got her looks. The only real difference between them, besides a few extra wrinkles, was Nancy's hair. It was chopped rather short, and she had it spiked up in the back. Her bangs were barely long enough to pull to the side and pin out of her face.

She wheeled her chair around Lexi to shake my hand, saying, "We're so grateful Lexi has finally found a half-decent boyfriend!"

Lexi gasped in shock, "MOM!" I think she was starting to regret inviting me over. Her distress made me chuckle.

Nancy looked at Lexi innocently. "What? If half the things you've told us about David are true, I hope you keep him around a while." She looked at me and winked as Lexi groaned. I decided I really liked Nancy. She nodded toward the kitchen. "Come on over, kids. Let's get the food on the table."

The open space of the living room and kitchen flowed to the right of the fireplace, and into a huge dining room. They had a long table surrounded by tall chairs, all made out of a beautiful dark wood. The table was set with fancy dishes.

Steve pushed Nancy the rest of the way to the dining room. Lexi came up beside me and said, "I'm sorry, David." Then loud enough for all to hear, she added, "Sometimes my family doesn't know when to keep their MOUTHS SHUT!"

Her mom shot back. "I don't think we're the ones with THAT problem!"

We all laughed. Out of the corner of my mouth, and only loud enough for Lexi to hear, I said, "Boyfriend, huh?" She looked at me with a guilty smile. I turned so only she could see me pull out the Taser, and whispered threateningly, *"Okay. But you better watch it!"*

She laughed out loud and raised her hands in surrender. "Okay, okay! I promise."

I nodded, then got behind her and pushed her to the table. Her grandmother was smiling at us.

The ribs, potatoes, steamed vegetables, and hand-made rolls were delicious. And the Mandarin Jell-O—amazing! Whatever tension I had coming through the front door, melted away completely by the time Anne brought dessert to the table. It was her famous apple dumplings, and they were still hot. When she topped it with vanilla ice cream, I thought I'd died and gone to heaven!

As Anne finished serving dessert, Greg and Steve began comparing military stories, at least until Nancy threatened to swap childbirth stories with Anne if they didn't stop! That caused an abrupt change in topic. The focus turned back to me, and they asked about school and what I liked to do. Anne was very interested in the farm since she grew up on one back in Nebraska. Then Steve asked me about football.

"Lexi told us you're quite the football star. I was able to make a few of the Lobo's games toward the end of the season, but I can't remember many of the guys' names. What position do you play?"

I cleared my throat. Steve didn't seem like the kind of man who took kindly to "deserters," and I didn't really want to explain all the religious and spiritual reasons for quitting, either. I wasn't sure which would be harder for him to understand. It would be so easy to make up some grand story, but I didn't want to lie. In the end, I decided to give him a condensed version and hope it would be enough.

"I was a tight end at the beginning of the season, but I didn't play the last few games." He looked at me with the searching eyes of a judge about to pass a verdict. Hesitantly, I continued, "I uh . . . had an injury that kept bothering me . . . along with some other personal reasons . . . and decided to quit."

It was brief, but I saw a slight expression of disappointment on Steve's face. It hurt, but I knew a lie would be a lot worse. Looking over at Lexi, I was surprised to see her staring at me curiously. I could tell she had something she wanted to ask but graciously decided to rescue me from the awkward moment instead.

"You should've seen him against Winslow, Dad. He's the reason the Lobos won that game!" It wasn't *exactly* true, but it was by far the best game I'd ever played. I was surprised she remembered.

Steve shrugged his shoulders. "Oh, it's just a sport. When it's all said and done, you don't get much out of it except a few bad injuries and a handful of memories." There was pain behind his eyes as he took his last bite of ice cream, and when I looked at Lexi, her head was down. There was pain there, too.

We didn't dwell on it much longer. Nancy quickly funneled us to the couches where we sat and visited till it got late. For the most part, I really enjoyed the evening; Lexi has a great family. When I told them I should be going, Lexi followed me outside and closed the door.

"Thank you for coming over tonight, David. I'm sorry about all the embarrassing comments." She gritted her teeth. "I hope it wasn't too much torture."

"I'm still alive, so no harm done," I smiled. "And I didn't even have to tase anyone." I snapped my fingers. "Which reminds me. Will you please tell your dad thanks for the gift? I can't wait to see what it does to Frank!"

She laughed. "Well, let me know when you decide to try. I'd love to see that."

What an evening. Lexi has awesome parents, and I love her sweet Granny Anne. That's what she preferred I call her toward the end. But the best part was when Lexi said I was her boyfriend! She called *me* her **boyfriend**!

Sorry. It's so crazy, I had to say it twice. And yep, it feels just as good the second time! I know I need to be careful. Frank's situation is a stark warning to the dangers of relationships, but I also can't help the fact that I'm beginning to like Lexi, a lot.

Tuesday, 10 January 2012

Lexi's grandparents left Monday morning, and her dad started a night shift Tuesday, so it was back to room 107. She kept asking when I was coming to see her, but after church on Sunday, I had a family dinner and my Mission Prep class. On Monday, Mom insisted I stay home for Family Home Evening, so Lexi was adamant I come see her as soon as I got off work today.

I was hoping to make it to Show Low and back by 8:00 so I wouldn't miss Elli, but it was already past 7:00 when I left. Lexi's door was open, but her privacy curtain was pulled closed. I knocked on the door frame. "Hello?"

"Hey, David. Come on in, I'm decent." I pulled the curtain aside and saw her sitting by the couch, staring out the window.

"Hey, how's the cell? Did Crazy Dan miss you?"

She didn't smile. "Oh, he isn't here anymore." She turned back to the window and said longingly, "He got to go home."

"What? Did he die?" I was mostly kidding, but didn't doubt it might've happened.

Her forehead crinkled as she smirked. "No, goober, he got to go *home!*" But the comment lacked her usual spunk. Stoically, she looked back out the window.

I came in and sat next to her on the couch. "Hey, are you okay?"

Turning, her eyes locked on mine. Squinting slightly, she tilted her head as she searched deep for something she couldn't quite grasp. I began to squirm.

"David, why did you quit football?"

Flinching, I sat back on the sofa. Her question stabbed home like a dagger to the heart. Apparently, it had been on her mind a while.

"Well, that came out of nowhere," I chuckled nervously. Looking down I watched as my hands began fidgeting. "Do you want me to make up an awesome lie about how I was looking for a cure for cancer? Or do you want the truth?"

"I want the truth, David, and no sugar coating."

Glancing up, her face showed she was all business. "And what if I'm just a lazy quitter?" *What was she looking for?* This was a heavy topic, and I worried the truth might tip the scale of friendship.

She lowered her eyebrows in a scowl. "Well, I know those are both not true, so .·. . are you going to tell me or not?"

Sinking into the couch, I contemplated the consequences. *She's going to find out sooner or later—might as well get this over with.* Shrugging my shoulders in resignation, I looked at her and said, "All right. But you probably won't look at me the same afterward."

She replied straight-faced, "I guess I'll have to be the judge of that."

Forcing the air out in a long breath, I paused—took a deep one back in—and began.

Sitting cross legged in her wheelchair, she never flinched. Her hands were clasped in her lap as tight as her lips, and her piercing gaze scrutinized every action as I spilled my guts. I told her everything (except Elli, of course) starting from the fateful day I broke my arm. When I got to the part where I wanted to maim Josh, I hesitated. *If Lexi really wanted the truth, I would have to tell her about Bo.* I let out a long sigh with a silent prayer and unlocked that cell door.

I didn't dance around anything, there was no dancing at all. With shame, I told her about my childhood and how it led to a broken window and a broken heart. Miraculously, a few days later I found myself at a foggy lake where I watched a new sun rise on a new David Thorn.

"So I decided to serve a mission, get a job, . . . and quit football. It was the hardest thing I've ever done, but I survived. Somehow, through all the pain, I found a dream that made me so much happier than football ever did." I looked down at my sweaty hands clenched together, grateful to finally be at the end of this painful journey.

Silence was my only reward for opening my soul, and it hung thick in the room. This was the make-or-break moment, and I *hated* not being able to feel what she was thinking. So I sat there . . . and waited.

Finally, she spoke, "And this 'mission'—is that what'll make you happy?"

I glanced up to see if I could read her emotions, but still couldn't. I thought about Frank and replied, "I *know* it will, Lexi, but it isn't my end goal."

"Then what is?" Her eyes searched mine with all the strength of a lost orphan looking for home . . . *for home.*

I returned her stare with a new-found conviction. "Lexi, I want to go home. I mean to our *real* home. I want to go back and live with Heavenly Father again, and I want to be there with my wife, my kids, and my family." Warm, peaceful feelings filled my chest. It was the Spirit confirming these truths again with an assurance that leaves no doubt. Lexi's eyes widened as her face softened, and I knew she felt it, too.

Eyes glistening as tears began to from, she whispered, "*I wish I had that dream.*"

Instinctively, I took her hand. All fear was lost in the tenderness I felt for her. I smiled and said, "You can, Lexi! You just have to believe you can! Faith will open doors you never dreamed would budge." Her eyes peered into mine with such hopeful longing, I forgot about everything else.

For a moment, we shared something deeper than a mere spark. Unlike previous fire starters, this was driven by something much more powerful than lust or desire. As my mind struggled to find answers, I suddenly became aware that my hands were holding hers! Before I could stop myself, I flinched in shock—my hands opening stiffly.

Without letting go, Lexi began laughing hysterically! Only when the pain forced her to grab her stomach did her hands finally relinquish their prisoners. She fought hard to control it, but every time she looked up to see me staring dumbfounded at my hands, she lost it all over again.

Finally, I was able to gather my wits enough to speak. Holding my hands up, I said in a surprised voice, "I didn't know they could do that!" We couldn't help it. We both laughed until it hurt. After a long time, when we could finally breathe again, she cocked her head and gazed intensely into my eyes once more.

"You were right," she said softly. "I *do* see you differently now."

Thursday, 12 January 2012

Needless to say, I stood up my angel, again. I didn't get home till after 9:00 and was never able to connect to Elli. I think it was worth it, though. I HELD HANDS WITH A GIRL!!! I'm still dizzy with shock about it. Lexi has been the only thing on my mind the last few days. I can't deny there's something between us I've never experienced before—a feeling I can't describe, but I don't dare say *that* four letter word. What do I know about love anyway? And if it's not, . . . I can sure see it transforming into that, real easy.

On Wednesday, we had a Church basketball game for our Young Men's activity, so I didn't get to see her. I'm glad I had another day, though. I needed time to think things over—and to keep my promise to Bishop.

I realized last night, as I read the *For The Strength of Youth Pamphlet*, I've been lowering my guard around girls again. (Well, at least around one. ☺) Because Lexi lives in a compound, I justified seeing her with the fact that she's surrounded by people—when actually we were quite alone most of the time. I know, I know. This is all too familiar territory. What am I thinking!? Frank definitely wasn't thinking, either. But unlike Frank, I've decided to do something about it. I've gotta talk to Lexi. I need to set up some boundaries, and I hope she'll be supportive, . . . and I'm scared to death.

107

"Hey, David! Come in!" Her voice was much more joyful than a few days ago. She was sitting at the table she'd cleared off, and a chair was pulled out in front of her. She waved me over.

Because of my spontaneous maiden voyage to the land of holding hands last time, I didn't realize till after I got home that Lexi never said anything about my story. *Does she think I'm crazy? Will she still like me?* It drove me nuts not knowing.

I couldn't wait another minute. "So, now that you've had time to think about what I said, do you still want to be friends?"

She smiled deeply. "I promise, the things you said were *exactly* what I needed to hear." I looked at her in confusion. I hadn't said those words thinking she "needed" to hear them at all. It was just my story. She must've understood my confused look because she explained, "I've been doing a lot of thinking the last few days, and if you don't mind, I'd like to share MY story with you."

I tensed. I could tell this would be another loaded conversation. Squinting my eyes in scrutiny, I asked, "What kind of stories?" Teasingly, I added, "Are you going to tell me more about your boyfriends?" Maybe it wasn't all in jest. I really didn't want to know how many boys she kissed or how many times.

"Of course there'll be boys!" She was not able to conceal the mischief on her face. "It wouldn't be my story without them." I got up and acted like I was about to leave. She reached for me and said, "I'm KIDDING! Please don't go." I paused for a moment, then timidly returned to the chair. "I promise to leave out the mushy parts, *okay*?" I raised one eyebrow questioningly, but she shook her head and ignored it.

Now that I wasn't fleeing, she leaned back in her chair, but her relaxed demeanor did not remain long. Folding her arms across her chest as if the temperature in the room had plummeted, she gazed out the window.

"When I regained consciousness after the accident, I couldn't feel anything, and I couldn't move. The first thing that registered in my mind was the taste of dirt in my mouth. Slowly, I concluded I must be lying face down somewhere, but I couldn't remember where or why. I stayed there for what seemed like eternity. I was completely and utterly alone. After a time, I began to feel hot, burning pain all over my body. The sensation came slowly at first, like when you lower yourself into an icy swimming pool, but instead of cold it was burning hot! The pain focused on parts of my body—my legs and back specifically. It was at this time I remembered I'd been in the truck with Zack. I tried calling his name—but it was eerily quiet."

Tears started to form, and her gaze went from the window to the tissue clasped tightly in her hands on her lap. Quietly, she continued, "They said he went instantly, and for that I'm very grateful. The thought of anyone else having to endure pain like this . . . it makes my whole body quake thinking about it." She paused again, her pale face grimacing.

"The pain became unbearable! And just as it reached a boiling climax, I heard a woman's voice. It was a kind voice, asking if I was all right. She told me I had been in an accident and not to move, that everything was going to be fine. I remember thinking it was funny, because I couldn't move if I wanted to. She placed a warm blanket over my body, and I could feel her hands gently cleaning my face. Wonderfully, the pain started to subside. I couldn't open my eyes, because they were full of dirt, so she got some water and a rag from somewhere and gently cleaned me off, making sure not to move me at all.

"She sat down next to me and talked calmly as she gently stroked my hair. Even though she'd cleaned my eyes as best she could, my vision was blurry when I tried to look at her. All I saw was a silhouette against the night sky. The pain of the dirt under my eyelids was so great, I decided not to open them again. She talked about peculiar things, and as she spoke, the pain continued to decrease.

"I must've fallen asleep because the next thing I remember was an officer saying, 'She's still alive!' From that point until I made it to the hospital in Phoenix, I was in and out of consciousness. When I finally woke up completely, it was midway through the next day. The surgeries to put plates on top of both tibias had already taken place, but they told me my back would have to heal on its own.

"I wasn't wearing my seatbelt and was thrown from the truck. They think I must've landed feet first. My femurs impacted the tops of my tibias with enough force to crush them and shorten my legs over an inch. My right leg was worse than the left. When the rest of my body collided with the ground, a few of the vertebrae in my back were literally smashed together and shattered."

Lexi paused after this. Her teary eyes squeezed shut. I couldn't believe what I was hearing, shocked by the horror she had lived through.

Finally, after gathering her thoughts, she turned to me and said, "David, I'm part of the 1% of people who actually survive being ejected from a vehicle. And the fact that my spinal cord was not severed is a miracle in itself. You'd think, with all these things,

I'd be more grateful." Tears flowed down her cheeks again. "When I got in a wheelchair, I thought things would get better. I was so depressed. But the wheelchair didn't fix it, and coming back didn't fix it, because I had to come here."

She looked up and gestured to the room and said, "But in all this, do you know the straw that finally broke the camel's back?" She wiped her tears and smiled. "Sorry, no pun intended."

Laughing in relief, I realized my knuckles were turning white and relaxed my vice grip on the chair. To see her smile in the middle of such an awful story was comforting. Perhaps there was a silver lining on this horrible cyclone, but sensing the ugly climax was yet to hit land, I braced myself again.

Her smile dissipated and she continued, "The tipping point was when I finally accepted the fact that I'll *never* be the same." She bowed her head as the tears cut paths down her beautiful cheeks. "I'll never be able to jump, or climb, or surf . . . or play volleyball." She sniffed and fought to regain control, and after a few more seconds, she continued, "I finally decided it wasn't worth it anymore. I gave up, David."

She looked at me, the most tender expression filled her face, and she whispered, *"Then you knocked on my door."* I looked at her in shock! I had no idea. "Yes, David, when you walked in, I was sitting right there trying to come up with a way to end my life." She pointed across the room, and her chin started quivering. I couldn't handle it and had to look away, my own tears began blurring my vision.

She grabbed my face with both hands and turned it gently back to look at hers. Those blue eyes held me motionless. Her painful tears were replaced now with the sweetest glow of love and gratitude. Tenderly, she said, *"You* changed my mind." A warm, beautiful smile radiated from her tear-soaked face. "You brought laughter, and jokes, and life back into me. You and your *crazy* story—girl phobia and all." She giggled sweetly, then leaned in and whispered, *"You brought me hope!"*

Pulling me forward, she gently kissed my lips.

There was no resistance, no thought to run and hide. I didn't hand her a pretty rock or try to tase her. (But I should have!) I soaked it up with all the intensity of a burning desert. And that's about how I felt, too. I was on FIRE!

She slowly let me go, and I almost collapsed onto the floor! I literally had to catch myself with a jolt before I completely lost my balance. She covered her mouth and did her best to hold in a chuckle. I rocked back in my chair, stunned to infinity and beyond!

. . . she kissed me . . .

The only word I could form was, "Whoa."

She lost it and started to laugh. Staring at her in a daze, I could hardly contain the fireworks exploding inside.

. . . SHE REALLY KISSED ME . . . !!

Lexi doubled over and would've fallen to the ground if the pain hadn't sat her back up with a jolt, but still she laughed. The sight of her hysteria didn't help my ability to make sense of what in the CRAP just happened!

Wait a minute. Wait a minute! I thought. *This isn't supposed to happen at all! I'm supposed to be putting up barriers, not getting dragged into the deep end!* I shook my head, trying to get my ricocheting thoughts to regain some kind of order.

Wiping away the humor-filled tears as she battled waves of giggles, Lexi surprisingly managed a serious tone as she said, "I wanted to show you how much I truly appreciate all you've done, *before* you go improving your standards on me!"

I looked at her stunned, realization dawning. *She TRICKED ME!* I tried to scrunch my face in anger, but a smile neutralized the attempt. "Why you little . . . sneaky . . . EVIL GIRL!"

Grinning playfully, she chuckled and said, "Sneaky? Yes. Little? Maybe. But evil? Oh, David—you ain't seen evil yet."

I was totally gone. Up, down; north, south—it was all screwed up. Hoping to clear my mind, I stood and began moving around aimlessly. Her giggling just got worse. Finally, I shook my head and put my hands up in surrender. Throwing them in her direction, I said, "Oh . . . I'll . . . talk to you later," and marched out the door, not pausing to close it behind me. I don't remember driving home or climbing in bed with all my clothes on, but I do remember not being able to fall asleep till about three in the morning. I kept thinking over and over in my mind, *What have I gotten myself into?*

Saturday, 14 January 2012

Lexi tried texting and calling all day yesterday, but I deliberately ignored her. My confused thoughts and feelings plowed right through Friday, as I struggled to make sense of her ambush. I know I'm not supposed to go steady, but something is happening between us that I don't want to end! Besides, she really needs a friend right now . . . and so do I. Finally, after another sleepless night, I came up with a plan. Besides, I thoroughly enjoyed watching her texts go from cocky and teasing, to repentant and worried.

I texted her back this morning:

-I have a proposition.

~WHAT?!

-To avoid being attacked again unaware, U need to promise me something!

~Attacked huh...what do I need to promise?

-I want you to read something, a pamphlet that explains all the standards I'm trying to live, and then PROMISE you'll help me keep them!

~...hum...okay, I promise. But you have to promise me something too!

-oh...and what's that? You sneaky snake!

~Ooh I LIKE that! Yes, a sneaky promise, but these are my terms. At LEAST once, before you leave on your mission, YOU have to kiss ME!

-...let me think about it...

~OH!!! You have to think about it?! Maybe I retract my offer and you can find some other poor girl to play your Jedi mind tricks on!!!

-You know what a Jedi is!!!! You changed my mind, I ACCEPT!

~what is it with guys and Star Wars?...okay it's a DEAL!

There were a lot of smiley faces, and devil faces, and all sorts of things that I don't know how to do. The fireworks started up again, but they were off in the distance this time. Not like it felt the other night. But the thought alone of what I agreed to do got my heart rate speeding up. Wow, it's hard to believe how much power a girl can have on a guy. Don't you dare tell anyone I said that. If they ever find out we're helpless against them, they'll be ruling the whole world in a matter of days!

107

Palms sweaty, I knocked on the door.

"Come in!" The sweet and innocent tone seemed slightly exaggerated. Cracking open the door, I peered inside. Lexi was sitting on the bed with books spread all around. To avoid further seduction and manipulation, I'd planned a hit and run approach: Get close enough to hit her with the For the Strength of Youth pamphlet, and then run away! Brave, I know, but besides still feeling awkward and embarrassed at my reaction to "the kiss," I really did have a ton of homework I needed to do.

Holding up my Taser in seemingly shaky hands, I walked timidly into the room. Lexi laughed and rolled her eyes. "Oh, *please!*" She said shaking her head. "What am I gonna do? Dive off my bed and tackle you?" A smile sat softly on her face.

"I wouldn't doubt it!" I shot back with a grin and lowered the Taser slightly.

"Besides," her eyes twinkled, "I *know* you liked it."

My face grew hot, and I tried to hide it by feigning innocence, "What makes you say that?"

"Oh, just the way you stumbled out of here Thursday . . . and how your cheeks are getting all red again thinking about it." She started to giggle.

Narrowing my eyes, I held the Taser back up, "I WILL use this."

She raised her hands in surrender. "Okay, I'll stop. It's just so cute when you get all embarrassed."

Oh, the mockery! Not letting her out of my crosshairs, I flung the pamphlet at her from the doorway. It landed on some papers by her feet. "The contract," I said, changing the subject. "Do you remember the promise you made a few hours ago? Or has it slipped your mind?"

She picked it up and began flipping through it. With her eyes curiously following the pages, she said, "I remember." She smiled a sardonic grin and cocked her head to the side, "Do you remember *yours?*"

Before I could think, I said, "Oh, I won't be forgetting *that* very easily." Her eyes brightened as she giggled sweetly. I started backing away. "Let me know when you finish, and *maybe* I'll come back, and we can talk about it."

She nodded, "Okay, I will." Then her smile drooped. "You're not going to stay?"

I shook my head. "Not until the deal is signed!" A flash of hurt reflected behind her eyes, and I didn't want that, so I broke character slightly and said, ". . . and I have a ton of homework I need to get finished." Glaring accusingly, I added, "I've been too 'side tracked' the last few days to focus on anything!"

She looked down briefly in embarrassment, but it was chased away quickly as a new thought seemed to enter her mind. "David, perhaps as part of our new 'deal,' you could help me *focus* on my school work? I am so far behind, I'm afraid I'm going to be held back next year."

I dropped the Taser along with the Mr. Tough Guy act. I liked the idea. It would give us something to concentrate on and give me an excuse to see her more often. "Yeah, I think that'd be a good idea!"

"Thanks, David." Holding up the pamphlet she said, "I'm actually looking forward to this! I've always wondered why you Mormons are so weird." She was teasing me again, but I couldn't help feeling, at least at one time in her life, she probably truly thought of us that way. I can only imagine what we look like from the outside. Pretty peculiar to say the least.

Tuesday, 17 January 2012

Elli! Have I got some stories to tell you! My excitement was hard to contain.

David—the Airlis is BEAMING! What has happened to you?

The sensation of Elli's excitement was warm and soothing. It made me realize how much I missed her. Embarrassed she might have felt that, I quickly dove into my latest adventures in life. She was ecstatic to hear about our interviews with Bishop, and praised me for helping Frank come back into the light. I told her about meeting Lexi's family, the house, the food, the conversations; she wouldn't allow me to leave out a single detail. But as I began to tell about the accident, her questions stopped. As I reached the painful pinnacle of the story, I was brought up short. It felt like the Airlis was going to shatter from pain! Elli was weeping.

Hey, are you okay?

Sorry, David. I've never felt such strong emotions of pain before. It's shocking and—horrible!

Then let me finish the story, I said consolingly. I think you'll feel better in a moment.

Yes, please continue. I could sense her immediate relief in knowing there was a happy ending.

Elli gasped when I told her about Lexi's confession of suicidal plans, so I quickly continued. When I described how Lexi looked me in the eyes and said I had basically saved her life without knowing it, a sensation of wonder flowed into me. Elli's emotions leapt for joy when I told her Lexi grabbed me gently by the face—and kissed me!

Oh, David. Her mood became reverent. The sudden change confused me. *A kiss is such a sacred thing. We reserve them for the most intimate relationships.* I was about to laugh at her view of what a kiss means, but she said, *She must cherish you more than you have portrayed.*

This shocked all humor from the conversation. I hoped Lexi might have feelings for me, and the thought of it being true got my heart fluttering.

Focusing back on the Airlis, I saw no words, but I could sense a giggle.

Apparently, David, she's not alone in these feelings!

My inner confession of love did not go unnoticed. Ears burning, I didn't know what to say.

In a very sisterly way, Elli advised, *It's a precious thing, David, to care deeply for someone else. Remember to keep it precious.*

She was absolutely right. Thank you, Elli. I promise I will. I decided it was a good time to change the subject. What about you, Elli? How have your discussions been going with Jared?

They're going well, thank you. It was an unemotional reply. *Things are about the same. We both remain strongly rooted in our ideas, and it's difficult to gain any ground.* The Airlis flowed with gratitude as she said, *You don't know how much I rely on you to keep me anchored, David. Your life and experiences—your joy and growth—they are reminders that I have made the correct decision. Thank you for being my friend.*

After she was gone, I lay on my bed for a long time.

How strange. This is so FLIPPIN' CRAZY! Sometimes it's still hard to wrap my mind around the whole idea that I'm literally communicating with an angel. How I wish I could see beyond tomorrow. Why was I blessed to have Elli brought into my life? How long will she stay? Losing her now would be like losing my best friend. But I don't see how this can last forever, and the thought of losing her is . . . it's unbearable. There has to be a way. I keep hoping and praying that someday, somehow, I'll be able to thank her in person.

<u>Saturday, 28 January 2012</u>

Wow, has it been over a week? How are you holding in the suspense? Ha! Well, hang on to something while I give you the highlights of the David Thorn Show. Actually, there isn't a whole lot to report. Between the lack of life-altering, mountain-moving first kisses and a shortage of evil villains to subdue in Snowflake, life has been plugging along.

I do have info about the Lexi saga, though. I believe it was a day or two after my last entry when she called to tell me she had finished the booklet and was ready to discuss our friendship contract. Yeah, I thought she was joking at first, too, but to my surprise, she handed me a two-page document that we debated, changed, and signed! It was a laughter-filled evening. Basically, she agreed to help me keep my standards. She also promised: *I, Lexi Dupree, will not attack, lure, or seduce David Thorne in any manner that I would not feel comfortable doing in front of my mother.* I knew by the way she smirked she was being overly-dramatic to give me a hard time. I, on the other hand, had to promise: *Before leaving on my mission, I, David Thorn, will give Lexi Dupree at least one kiss.* Ironically, I think we're both determined to see it through. As curious as I am to see how this all ends, I can't help but think I got the better end of this bargain. ☺

Her response to the *For the Strength of Youth* pamphlet was interesting. She didn't mock or tease like I thought she would, but told me she totally understood the importance of the standards and was happy to support me in keeping them! Then she laughed at the surprised look on my face.

It's kinda funny when she quickly turns the channel if something inappropriate comes on TV now, but I'm grateful she does. Surprisingly, she also changed the way she dresses! She quit wearing her tight-fitting, low-cut outfits, and I instantly noticed how much easier it was to keep my thoughts and eyes focused on good things. It wasn't just her change of clothes; I noticed a change in her, and it made me want to be a better person, too. The sacrifices she's made mean more than she could ever imagine.

Speaking of amazing, her health has also improved by leaps and bounds! They're saying she's ahead of schedule and recovering much faster than expected. She stood for the first time today, and it hasn't been three months since the accident! I went over this afternoon for a few hours, and with her dad and me by her side, she scrunched her face in pain and FINALLY got those feet beneath her where they belong. We were all shedding tears of joy! Well, I think hers were laced with pain, but that didn't stop her from shouting, "I DID IT!" It was awesome to be a part of such a momentous occasion. I'm so proud of her for what she's done, for the mountains she's climbed in a wheelchair! If you want to be humbled, try *that* someday.

We decided to meet, at least, on Thursday and Friday evenings to do our school work. Yeah, not the most exciting of activities, but after she showed me the amount of work she has to turn in before the end of the school year, I wondered if we were spending *enough* time on it. I told her I needed Monday through Wednesdays for family and Church activities. (I guess I kind of threw Elli in with family but couldn't come up with a better excuse.)

Most weekends she gets to go home. Luckily, her dad's schedule is usually Monday through Friday. She told me, "I'll go see my family, and you can have the weekend to chase girls!" She meant it jokingly, but I could sense a hint of jealousy in the comment. I honestly, and rather shamefully, confessed I had no other friends. She smiled and said, "Well, if you can't choose between all the girls waiting in line to see you, I guess you can come hang out with the Dupree family if you want." I liked the idea very much!

Now for the soap opera I call "Poor Frank." Actually, I'm not really sure what a soap opera is, but if it's full of drama and torture, it fits the description. In spite of the rumors, texts, and bad rap he's been mercilessly pounded with at school, his spirits have remained high. It's been inspiring to see how he handles this. Tracy treats him like dirt, and sadly, she's fallen off the wagon. She's hanging with a different crowd now, won't talk to Ashley anymore, and has quit coming to Seminary.

It's no wonder Frank has sworn off girls completely, but his hopes are high and his motivation to achieve new goals is strong. He even picks me up for the Mission Prep class! It's amazing to watch him change. I love having Frank back; a new and improved

Frank if you ask me. Now we laugh and joke like old times and curse high school with all its melodramatic mediocrity. During one of these conversations, we hatched a wonderful plan!

You see, MORP is coming up before too long. (I think everyone knows what that is—PROM backwards—a girl-ask-guy dance. Moving on.) Truthfully, we aren't even sure we'll get asked with all the crap being flung around, and we both think that's GREAT! We don't WANT to be asked by anyone in *our* high school ANYWAY! (Sorry. I've got a lot of bitterness boiling beneath the surface if you can't tell.) So we came up with the genius idea to ask my cousin Meagan if she would find a friend, and *they* ask *us* to *our* MORP! You see where I'm going with this? Take that SNOWFLAKE!

I called Meagan, and of course, she was all bubbles and excited, incoherent phrases—especially when I told her how handsome Frank is. He was standing next to me snickering. I told her we'd get the tickets and arrange the date if they would find a way to get up here on March tenth. She hung up with a squeal, and I gave Frank a high five!

Having something positive to look forward to was good for Frank. I could see this whole experience lift him out of a stagnant melancholy. It was then I decided it was time to tell him my secret.

Now don't go speculating, people. You know I'm talking about Lexi. Stay with me. You see, the only people who knew about us were her parents, grandparents, and my mom. Well, maybe a nurse or two, but you get my drift.

With Operation M.O.R.P. successfully deployed and our high-fiving celebration accomplished, the room got quiet as we mentally reveled in our success. Lying on my bed, I looked at Frank sitting at my desk and said, "Frank, . . . I have a confession to make."

He gasped and said, "It was YOU who killed Miss Scarlet in the dining room!"

I shook my head and cracked a smile, but I kept it serious. "Well . . . I don't think I *killed* her, and it wasn't in her dining room . . . but something sure happened in her apartment."

His jaw hit the floor. The look was priceless! Why do I always miss those with my phone? He picked up his teeth and asked, "What are you talking about? Have you been seeing Ashley again?" He was shocked and confused.

I sat up and mischievously said, "No, not Ashley."

His eyes got big. "Who then?"

"Frank, you have to promise not to tell a SOUL! You know better than anyone what gossip can do, and the last thing I want to do is hurt Le . . . this girl."

He stumbled, "Who? Yes, of course, I swear! Now you better tell me who you're talking about before I beat it out of you!"

I leaned forward and said conspiratorially, "Lexi Dupree!"

He reared back in his chair and literally fell to the floor! I don't think he meant for his reaction to be so dramatic, but he underestimated the flimsy chair and landed with a thump on his back. With his legs still tangled in the upturned seat, Frank grabbed his head and yelled, "WHAT? Are you KIDDING ME?" Dropping his hands, he glared. "You're pulling my leg . . . you better not be pulling my leg—Lexi Dupree?"

So I told him to lie there for a second while I finished the whole story; that way he wouldn't fall over again. He remained frozen in total shock and amazement—until I told him about the kiss. He exploded off the ground, kicking the chair across the room! Dancing in a tight circle, he started whooping and hollering!

"FRANK! FRANK, calm DOWN! Gramps is going to hear and come over with a shotgun!"

Frank kept yelling, "YOU DID IT! YOU DID IT! I can't believe it. You DID IT!" I got to laughing so hard, when Mom came in and asked what was going on, I couldn't answer her. She gave us a curious look, shook her head, and closed the door with a smile.

I swear it took Frank fifteen minutes to calm down. I had to keep reminding him what he promised, and he reassured me he had locked it away. He kept congratulating me as if it was my greatest accomplishment in life! He must not have understood that it was SHE who kissed ME, not the other way around. That sheer cliff is yet to be climbed.

Finally, as his excitement died down, I was surprised to see a seriousness overcome his exuberant activities. He looked at me with a maturity I hadn't seen before and said, "Just promise me, David, you won't make the same mistake I did."

I nodded in solemn agreement. "I promise, Frank."

The only downside to the whole evening was, after he left, Mom caught me crossing the living room and asked, "So . . . what was all the commotion about?"

Guilt hit hard, and I felt horrible for leaving her out. It was all so new—and embarrassing—I chickened out every time I tried to say something. But now I *had* to tell. It wasn't right for Frank to know and not Mom. She definitely deserved to know.

"Well Mom . . ." I looked around, worried Josh and Sarah might be within earshot. "Can I talk to you in your room?"

"Sure, David." She got a worried look on her face.

For the second time in one night, I revealed my hidden love life. Okay, so that's probably too strong of a term, but it fits, all right? Mom listened stoically. She didn't fall over or start dancing, but toward the end, she could not contain a huge grin. When I finished my story, to my surprise her chin began to quiver, and she quickly covered her mouth.

When her emotions were again in control, she said, "Oh David, you've grown up so much in the past few months." Tears welled up in her eyes. "Remember to not grow up too fast." She reached for me, and I gave her a big hug. When we pulled apart, she grinned wide. "And try not to get this one pregnant, okay!?"

I almost fell over from laughing so hard! Catching my breath and wiping away the tears, I said, "I promise to be careful."

Her smile filled with unconditional love. "I know you will be. I love you, son."

I should never have kept her out of the loop. I decided from then on I would be more open with her. She deserves that much *at least*—she deserves so much more.

The final chapter of the week is Elli, but sadly, there isn't much to say. Not only does her time move much slower than ours, it also seems when you have eternity to accomplish things you aren't in a rush to get it done. Most often she asks a million questions, and I talk and talk. Before I know it, we're out of time. Things are much the same for her. She's still worried about Jared. She cares deeply for him, more than I think she admits, and the thought of losing him is something she hates to consider. She asks a lot of questions, because I think it helps to get her mind off things for a while, and I like telling my story, especially when I have such a perfect audience. One of many things I've learned from our unusual friendship is a best friend is someone who listens.

Friday, 10 February 2012

Time is the weirdest thing. How is it possible for days to drag along so painfully slow, but every time you look at the calendar, a week has disappeared without a trace? That's how life is getting for me. School and work are monotonies that kill time and drag its dead carcass behind them. But my moments with Lexi, Elli, and Frank skip past like a white rabbit in some crazy dream! I wish time were reversed and it would drag the good and skip the bad. Wouldn't life be wonderful then? I don't mean to complain. The brief, good moments far outweigh the bad, and the substance in them is much more fulfilling, for which I am very grateful.

Don't let my wandering thoughts confuse you. Life is **most** excellent! Lexi took her first steps today! She's been working relentlessly at strengthening her legs and learning to keep her balance. She started taking steps holding onto the back of her wheelchair this evening, and she just wouldn't stop! The pain was etched in her face, but her determination and joy silenced it. Her friends in The Cottage gave her a standing ovation. It was one of the best days of my life! To see her go from a girl who had given up to a fighting warrior who conquers her foes has been awe inspiring, to say the least. I can't think of one superhero who compares. Sorry, Mom, but I think you have a contender for first place. Lexi's expression of pure joy, in spite of the pain, will be forever held in my memory as one of my most prized possessions.

We're also conquering school! I haven't had as far to go, but at this point, she's only a few weeks behind the rest of the junior class. We're confident she'll be able to move on to her senior year without a hitch. Shoot, at this rate I wouldn't be surprised if she'll finish the last month actually going to school! She's one amazing girl.

As far as "us" goes, well, I'd be lying if I said things haven't been improving, but we're definitely not a normal couple. If I had to compare our relationship to an animal, I'd have to say we're more like a sloth than a cheetah, but as interesting as a chameleon in a hippie shop. Does that help? You might be proud to know we actually hold hands occasionally! Yeah, I know, you'd probably prefer the chameleon, but it works for us, okay? Cut me some slack. I can see I try her patience sometimes, but most often, I think she views my social handicaps as an entertaining break from ALL her previous experiences. She's always laughing at me, but I don't mind. I love seeing her smile!

It's interesting how, as I've gotten more comfortable around her, we've changed roles in my goal to not be alone together. I seem to fight the rules more now, and she's the one who won't let us bend our boundaries. Sometimes we really get to laughing over it.

We've started approaching this new conundrum by asking her parents to join us for movies, and then we try to sneak holding hands where they can't see us! I know, these are *exactly* the kinds of things I used to make fun of, but I can't help it! I'm flat-out twitterpated, and I like it! It's moments like this that go by *way* too fast.

I do have a funny story about holding hands. After I amazingly hurdled that first experience, I got clotheslined hard by fear. That, coupled with extreme ignorance, combined to make another awkward learning experience.

We were watching *Just Like Heaven* with Nancy, but her mom had fallen asleep. Lexi was sitting to my left with her right hand on her knee, which was close to my leg. Not long into the movie, she started drumming her fingers and wouldn't stop! I glanced at her to see if she was nervous or something, but she acted like she didn't see me, so I went back to the movie. A little while later, the finger drumming stopped, and she began rubbing her hands together and blowing into them. I thought, *It isn't cold in here.* Then she started tapping her fingers again. **Finally**, I realized what she was doing! Remember what I was said about a sloth? It's all me. I smiled and leaned over to whisper, "Um . . . would you like me to hold that for you?"

She rolled her eyes and let out an exasperated breath. "Oh, I thought you were *never* going to ask!"

We both laughed, and I had no problems staying awake for the rest of the movie. Sorry, I can't help that I'm socially backward, but I'm getting over it in leaps and bounds. I find myself surprising myself all the time! (That sounds weird. Oh well.) This is another one of the thousand reasons I'm glad Lexi's my girlfriend. Yeah, I said it, now you can quit whining and get back to reading. She's blessed my life in so many more ways than I feel I ever have hers. Sometimes I catch myself staring at her and wonder, *Did this really happen to me?* Out of all the guys in school—in the world!—why me? Don't get me wrong, I'm absolutely ecstatic it IS me, I just wonder sometimes how long this will last.

Will we make it through high school? Through my mission? And what happens if we do? She's not a Mormon. Can eternal friendships still happen if they aren't sealed together? It's these kind of question that give me a headache—and a heartache. I can't imagine losing my best friend. Sorry Frank, but you had to realize you'd get demoted someday.

Speaking of Frank, that guy is spiritually on fire! He changed his music, his language, his clothes; HE has changed. He acts more mature now and seems to see life more clearly. It's been inspiring to watch his transformation.

Tracy, on the other hand, got dark—and I'm not talking about a tan. You can actually see in her countenance how her decisions have affected her. The contrast between the two is black and white. It kills me to see a girl full of spunk and life suffocated by her own bitterness and guilt. If she would *just* turn to God. Frank told me right before they broke up, Tracy wanted to get married, because it would solve everything. Frank told her he was trying to set things right first and how good it felt to get the guilt off his chest! When he pled with her to try it, she got angry.

I'm not sure which is harder, dealing with a friend's death, going with a friend through extreme pain and suffering, or watching one spiritually killing herself. Of the three, I think the worst experience is the last. What makes it more difficult is knowing it doesn't have to be this way. There is a way out, but it has to be her choice. Frank's taking it really hard. Of course, he still feels responsible, but no matter how many times he talks to her and apologizes, he can't *make* her forgive him. It tears him up. I'm proud of him, though, because he doesn't lose faith. However, having faith doesn't mean you won't have to deal with the consequences.

I know you're wondering, *Well, what about Ashley?* What? Are you craving some sick, "Twilight" love triangle? Well, I hate to disappoint you on that one. (And don't ask me how I know about that book. I lost a bet, okay? End of story.) But to ease your worried mind, I'm happy to inform you Ashley has been hanging around Joe Carter lately. I even heard she asked him to MORP. So you see: *Where once love dies in all its pain, through ash of death it grows again!* Do you like that? I made it up for you. She moved on. I moved on. Moving on.

I had an interview with President Smith on Wednesday to complete my mission papers. He said I can't go.

I'm sorry. I don't know why I'm feeling full of crap today! I think it has something to do with Lexi. I am still so happy for her. And I like her! And she's hot! Okay I confessed it. Do you forgive me now? For what you might ask? For lying to you about my interview. Hee hee. President *really* said he's absolutely delighted to email my recommendation! Sorry, I couldn't resist. Perhaps to regain your trust, and if you're still looking for a "triangle," I'll tell about the battle I had during my interview. It wasn't between two girls, just one girl . . . and God.

I know God wants me on a mission. I know I want to go! I know what it feels like to help people come to Christ, and I *know* what Christ has done for me. He changed my whole life, my whole existence! I want to share that with people, . . . but I'm in love with Lexi. I can't deny it anymore. I'm not sure what it means completely, but I know what I *feel*. I never dreamed I'd have to make this decision, but somehow, quite unexpectedly, she wheeled herself right into the middle of my life and stole my heart! And now I'm not sure I can make it two years without her.

President Smith's face paled as I told him about Lexi. When I first entered his office, I sat myself in one of two chairs that faced a large desk. To my surprise, instead of sitting in his plush office chair, he turned the one next to me and sat nearly knee to knee. The cozy feeling was fine—until now.

"David . . . do you have any idea how many young men are unable to go on missions because of mistakes made in serious relationships?" His face showed a pain, the depth of which was beyond my understanding. "Love is real, even at such a tender age, but if uncontrolled it becomes one of Satan's greatest tools in destroying lives." The intensity in his eyes pierced my soul, and I melted a little further into my seat. "Your destiny teeters on this very moment and keeping the standards given by our prophets is the only thing that will lead to true happiness!"

I was about to climb under the desk when his face softened. "David, there's nothing wrong with falling in love before you leave, *unless* it keeps you from going." With the precision of a surgeon removing a tumor, he cut right to the point. "Now, expecting you will do everything in your power to remain worthy, would you still serve if you knew you'd lose Lexi?"

It felt like my heart was being dissected. He waited for me to answer and wasn't concerned about how long it took. I stared at my hands and pondered for a long time. Finally, I said, "Yeah, I think so."

"And if she doesn't wait for you and you find some other beautiful girl to marry for time and all eternity, will you really have lost anything in the end?"

It didn't take me as long this time. "No, sir. I guess not."

A heavy hand rested on my shoulder, and I looked up into eyes now full of love. "Have faith in God, David—not your girlfriend." It wasn't the words I wanted to hear, but I knew it was what I needed to hear. I nodded my head in solemn agreement. He smiled and continued, "Besides, if she is 'the one,' I believe God will not leave her unprotected, and you'll have a chance to win her heart again when you return—a man worthy of that relationship."

His words resonated with truth, and my resolve to serve a mission has never been stronger. He's absolutely right! The outcome of my relationship with Lexi isn't something I can control. She'll have to choose for herself, and there's also that small problem of her not being a member of the church that throws a wrench in this whole crazy idea! Even if the stars align and she loves me and is willing to wait for me, we won't be able to get sealed in the temple for eternity. Marriage? I'm only eighteen!!! President is right. I need to quit worrying and have faith. If it works out later, it works out. I guess that's part of the excitement of not being able to see tomorrow. It would be like spoiling Christmas every day, and where's the fun in that?

<u>Monday, 27 February 2012</u>

IT CAME!! I've been waiting, planning, and preparing for *so* long, and today I FINALLY got my mission call! The postmaster in town is an awesome guy, and he probably knows everybody, so the moment he saw that big, white envelope from The Church of Jesus Christ of Latter-Day Saints, he immediately picked up the phone.

Mom shot me a text as soon as she heard. My first instinct was to ditch Miss Spencer's class, but it's the one I struggle the most in. (English . . . go figure.) Not that it did any good to stay. I don't remember a thing she said!

After the bell, I grabbed Frank and marched him to my truck. He was concerned for a second until I yelled, "My CALL is here! Now MOVE IT!" I didn't have to drag him after that. Sure enough, as I burst into the Post Office, I saw a large, 9x12, white envelope sitting on the counter. The postmaster looked up from his computer and handed it to me with a smile. "My guess is London, England! That's where I served twenty years ago. It's the best mission in the world!"

"I'll let you know!" I laughed, as I bolted out the door.

Frank and I made a unanimous decision—he wasn't going back to school, and I wasn't going to work. I called Scott to let him know I'd be late, but Frank didn't care if he ditched. He's been practicing for years. I called Lexi to make sure she wasn't at an appointment, and then I called Mom and told her to meet us at The Cottage as soon as she could!

Mom was already there when we arrived. They were sitting on the couch laughing when Frank and I ran through the door. It was odd; as close as Lexi and I had become, this was the first time she and Mom really talked. Usually, I would either meet Lexi here or at her house. It was difficult when she had to maneuver that wheelchair around. Now Lexi won't go anywhere unless she can struggle there on crutches. I don't think she'll *ever* get back in a wheelchair *again*!

A few weekends ago, Steve had to work so Lexi stayed at The Cottage. That Saturday I invited Frank to come play games with us. He was more than excited to meet Lexi for the first time. I think part of it was, deep down he wanted to see with his own eyes that I truly had a girlfriend. If you ever want to jazz up a game of UNO, bring Frank along.

On the way home that night, he leaned over, slugged me on the shoulder, and said, "Dude, I don't know what you did right in the pre-existence, but DANG! She still looks SMOKIN' HOT!" Oh, Frank.

MY CALL! Sorry, got sidetracked, again. Frank squeezed onto the couch next to Lexi so they could have a clear view of my face. I sat nervously on the bed. With hands shaking, I tore open the envelope and pulled out a packet of papers. On the top sat a letter addressed to Elder Thorn. Sending the three of them a nervous smile, I held up the quivering pages and began to read.

"Dear Elder Thorn: You are hereby called to serve as a missionary of the Church of Jesus Christ of Latter-day Saints. You are assigned to labor in—the **Australia, Adelaide Mission!**"

Frank shot off the couch. "AUSTRALIA!! Are you KIDDING ME?!" As he did a victory dance around the room my emotions collided into a state of shock, and I flopped limply on the bed.

Australia . . . so that's where I'm going. I felt a peaceful confirmation flow through me, and I knew it was where God wanted me to go.

The sound of Lexi's laughter brought me to my senses. When I sat back up, Mom had tears rolling down her face. Standing unsteadily, she reached for me. Jumping to my feet, we squeezed out a few more tears. It felt so good! As I was holding Mom, I saw over her shoulder that Lexi was crying now, too, both hands over her face. I gently released Mom and sat down next to her. She immediately threw her arms around my neck. Holding me as tight as she could, she whispered in my ear, "I'm *proud* of you, David."

Frank cleared his throat, "Huh hum . . . we're still *here,* David. Save that for later, man! When do you *report?*"

"Oh!" As our embrace released, Lexi snatched my hand. Blinking some focus back to my vision, I continued, "It is anticipated that you will serve for twenty-four months." At this I felt a slight twitch in Lexi's grip. I knew exactly what it meant, because I also felt it in my heart. Quickly pressing on, I read, "You should report to the Provo Missionary Training Center on Wednesday, May 30, 2012!"

Mom and Lexi gasped at the same time. Lexi's grip tightened tremendously. Frank stuttered, "M-May thirtieth? That's right after graduation!" The excitement was still hanging in the room, but it suddenly felt a lot heavier.

After a moment, Mom spoke quietly, "Well, it's probably better this way." She gave me a loving smile. "I bet God doesn't want to hold you back a *second* longer than necessary." Though her words were filled with pride, her sweet smile could not hide the turmoil in her eyes.

It hit me as well, like a fist to the gut. *My days are numbered!* The nervous discomfort we both were feeling was the pain of change. It reminded me of when I jumped off Brad's Rock at Clear Creek. Oh, what a THRILL! But once you leave that ledge—your life is never the same again. Lexi leaned her head on my shoulder as she clung to my arm. She could feel it, too.

Thursday, 1 March 2012

Tuesday evening I sat with anticipation on the front swing. The chilly spring air did little to cool my excitement to talk to Elli. By then I had already researched Australia for hours. Do you have any idea how many deadly poisonous snakes are found Down Under? (Gotta start using the lingo.) I think I quit reading after the fifteenth one. Talk about fear. I hate snakes! I hate them worse than high school! That's pretty bad. I guess this adventure will be a test of faith in more ways than I thought.

Elli was surprised about the poison. I guess snakes aren't that bad in heaven. Hearing about my call to serve sparked a conversation about similar assignments she's received from her Father. It was amazing to hear her describe the first time she was asked to co-organize a flower! I didn't understand much of what she said, but I didn't want to disrupt her story with stupid questions.

To organize your own flower; wouldn't that be something. I bet Lexi would love her own personal flower!

Oh, but we don't "own" anything, David. Once again I was caught thinking out loud. *Everything's available to everyone! You simply have to prepare yourself to receive it.*

Confused, I said jokingly, Heaven and Hell must be pretty different.

David, you're not in Hell. You're probably in the most crucial period of your eternity!

Her comment startled me. Once again, our differing perspectives collided, and it felt like a sumo wrestler sat on my ability to comprehend. Elli—you have no idea how hard it is to keep that perspective. Even when you know the purpose of life, you get caught up in the stupid day-to-day things, and sometimes you forget. My mind was chugging hard as my train of thought derailed into a pile of ponderation. (Am I trying too hard to impress you with my literary locomotion? Hee hee. Sorry, I'll stop it.)

A wave of the sweetest love and adoration flowed through my hands and into my heart. *Oh, David. You truly are a miracle in my life.*

This abrupt change in our conversation brushed the toy train wreck right off my mind and into the waste basket. Like being drawn to a firefly, the pure glow of friendship suddenly made everything else seem inconsequential. Mentally holding this simple illuminance in gentle hands, I said, Elli—I think the real miracle is you.

It was a great way to end my Tuesday. Now I'll jump back to Thursday. Going from Elli to Lexi in the same journal entry is like enjoying a rose and then grabbing its thorns! You'll understand in a moment.

Lexi was uncharacteristically subdued when I walked into her room late this afternoon.

"Hey, Lexi. What's on your mind?" I didn't knock because the door was open, and she was waiting. "You look like a lost puppy!" She cocked an eyebrow at me warningly. "A very *cute* puppy . . . oh stop it. You know what I mean."

She laughed, but didn't follow up with any sarcastic jabs. That's when I began to worry. With a *little* more excitement she asked, "Do you mind if we go for a walk?" This was becoming a ritual in our relationship. She absolutely loves her new-found freedom of motion!

We headed out the front door and took a left down the sidewalk.

Watching her steps carefully, I noticed her confidence had improved since last time, as well as her balance. Though she no longer needed help to stay upright, I stayed vigilant just in case.

"David, there's something I need to tell you." Her eyes were down and her voice serious. At first glance I feared the worse, then she looked up grinning from ear to ear.

Stopping dead in my tracks, I stared at her in disbelief. Realizing what she might be implying, I asked hesitantly, "Can you go home?"

Her eyes lit up, and she nodded adamantly.

"YOU CAN GO HOME!"

Squealing something unintelligible, the crutches hit the walkway as she stumbled, laughing, into my arms. Momentarily lost in blissful celebration, I pulled her in tight . . . too tight. She gasped and stiffened! I froze in horror. A wave of guilt hit me like I'd broken Grandma's china, again.

To my relief, I felt her relax. Folds of my shirt released from her grip, and she slid her arms around my neck. A look of serene joy returned to her face. "YES, David! I *finally* get to go home!" Tilting her head back, she yelled triumphantly, "I'M GOING HOME!"

When she looked at me again, she had the smile of the warmest sunrise dancing on her lips. Leaning in, I gently kissed them. I couldn't resist!

Large, shock-filled eyes greeted me when I returned to earth. Grinning at the unusual sight, I teased, "So *that's* what I looked like!"

Shoving herself to arm's length, she tried to slug me but lost her balance and grabbed for me instead. Laughing at her failed attempt was the wrong thing to do. Before she was steady on her feet, I caught a stiff jab to the gut! Not hard enough to knock the wind out of me, but she got her point across.

Chuckling quietly, I let her hold onto one arm while I picked up her crutches.

As we began to walk, she said, "You know you deserved that."

"What, the kiss?" I asked sheepishly.

"No! You *stole* that from me you little thief. I'm talking about punching you, and I should've hit you harder!"

The tone in her voice was playful, but the fire in her eyes told me this wasn't over yet. I began to fidget by rubbing my wound, and as I did, I asked in confusion, "What are you talking about?"

I thought her demeanor changed to teasing anger until the words started coming out. "Oh, I don't know. Maybe it has something to do with the fact that you're *seeing* someone *else*!" She glared at me with knowing eyes.

Guilt struck before I had a chance to hide it. *How did she know about Elli?* Struggling to find something to say, she jabbed her finger in my face and exclaimed, "Ha! It IS true!"

I was completely dumbfounded. No one knew about Elli . . . I thought. Was Mom able to figure it out? I was about to explain the whole situation when her countenance contorted into pain. "Why didn't you *tell* me about your MORP date?"

Morp . . . it took me a minute to compute this new data. *MORP! I didn't tell LEXI! Oh crap.*

Her stare of death was hammered back and ready to fire. Raising my hands in surrender, I stuttered, "Lexi, . . . I uh . . . c-can explain! It's not what you think, I swear!"

Folding her arms stiffly over her crutches, she glared. Her face was stern as stone. How do girls do it? A 180-degree flip in less than three seconds! It should be impossible, but it happens all the time! I continued stumbling over my excuses. "I . . . I wanted to do something with Frank and . . . and we set it up a long time ago and . . . hey, I don't even know the girl, it's a blind date with my cousin!" I was groveling, and it wasn't getting me anywhere. Finally, I lowered my head in defeat. "Sorry, Lexi. I should've asked, or told you, or whatever a boyfriend is supposed to do."

"How about NOT GO OUT WITH HER!" She yelled, but her voice cracked at the end. She was silent for a second, and then I heard a snicker. Looking up, she was covering her mouth with eyes watering, and her cheeks were turning red. *She did it AGAIN!*

When I could finally compress my shocked expression into a fake scowl, I growled, "Why you *sorry* bounder."

Her dam broke, and the laughter came pouring out! I stomped off down the street until I could find a patch of grass to pout on. Sitting down hard, I slumped over, letting my hands hang limp by my sides. I was trying for the most pathetic look possible. Maybe, just maybe, I could get her to feel a fraction of remorse for torturing me ruthlessly. After a few minutes, I heard the thumping of her crutches along with giggling. I stared at the ground.

She stopped in front of me and said, "I'm sorry David, but your mom asked me to do that."

I looked up at her befuddled. "My mom? When have you ever . . . oh." *The day I opened my call . . . they were giggling when we came in!* It all made sense. Forcing a pain-filled face, I pled, "Why on EARTH would she ask you to TORTURE me like this?" I realized Mom *really* must have done that! But why?

Lexi started laughing again. Grabbing the bottom of a crutch, I carefully but forcefully pulled it from her grip, making sure she didn't lose her balance. She didn't put up much resistance, and I finally had some leverage in this whole rotten deal!

Standing up, I backed away as I shook her crutch at her. "Now you come clean, young lady, or you'll be hopping home with one crutch!"

She was laughing so hard she was having a hard time standing. Begging between gasps of air, she said, "Will you— please help me—sit before I fall over?"

Lending her a hand, I gently lowered her to the grass. Right as she touched the lawn I snatched her other crutch. "Ha ha! Now you'll *have* to talk, or these crutches will never again see the light of day!"

Shaking both hands in surrender, it took a few more seconds before she could speak. "When your mom came in my room the other day, she had just gotten off the phone with her sister. Your aunt told her how excited Meagan was to go to MORP with you! Well, your mom knew nothing about it! When she got to my room, she *obviously* thought you were going with me and thought I might know more details!" Lexi folded her arms with attitude. "But she thought wrong! When I didn't know anything either, she called your Aunt back and got all the juicy information. Your mom was pretty peeved—you keep leaving her out of things—and she could tell I felt the same way, . . . so we decided to teach you a lesson."

She held her chin up and got a smug look on her face. I couldn't resist grinning at her sassiness. "And do you still feel the same way considering the circumstances?" I asked, dangling the crutches in front of her.

Without cracking a smile, she said, "YES, and until you sincerely apologize to me AND your mom," she dropped her hands and yelled "I think you should be punched EVERY DAY!" but then she couldn't suppress the smile anymore.

Smiling back, I surrendered her crutches. In a cowed voice I said, "You're right. You're both right. And I'm sorry."

Grinning, she snatched them. "You BETTER be!"

Helping her stand, we began walking back to The Cottage. After a few steps in silence, she chuckled and said, "You almost started crying!"

"I did NOT!" I shot back in defense. Smiling, I nodded as I admitted, "But you sure got me. You're a very good actress!"

Looking at me seriously, she said, "Oh, that wasn't acting. Don't you EVER do that again!" Her threatening stare broke apart after a few seconds and remolded into a teasing grin.

"So do you *really* get to go home?" I asked as we neared The Cottage. "Or was that part of the trap?"

Gleefully, she replied, "Nope, it was all real! I get released from prison tomorrow!" As fast as the joy covered her face, it was replaced by devilish intentions. "Well, at least *most* of it was real. I'm not so sure about that kiss."

"OH, REALLY!" I shot back, wounded. "Well, maybe I'll have to give one to Meagan's friend and see if SHE thinks they're real!"

Lexi's jaw dropped, and she tried to hit me again, but I was quicker this time. Taking a step back, I put my hands on my hips and glared at her threateningly. She met my glare with attitude, but after a short stalemate, she cracked. "Okay. Maybe it wasn't *that* bad."

I huffed at her in response.

She smiled teasingly at first, but then her face got serious. "There is one thing I want to point out, though."

We were at the front door, and she stopped and leaned her crutches against the wall. She reached for me, and like a bug to a zapper, I fell for it. Wrapping her arms around my neck, she looked into my eyes and said, "It doesn't count."

My jaw dropped in disbelief. *Are you kidding me?* As if anticipating an attempt to leave, her arms squeezed tighter. Narrowing my eyes, I realized, *She sucked me in on purpose!* Smiling like the little demon she is, she continued, "Nope. It doesn't count. It clearly states in our contract our next kiss you will *give* me, not *steal* from me."

I should've left her standing there. I should've told her I already "gave" it my best shot, and it wasn't good enough. But instead, I pulled her in close and asked mockingly, "May I *give* you one now?"

Compressing her lips and twisting them to one side, she pondered the question with calculating eyes. Shaking my head, I thought, *What a crazy, beautiful girl!*

In a soft, sweet, innocent voice, she said, "No."

My face must've expressed my stupor-of-thought, because she started giggling.

Pushing me gently away, she said again, "No. Not yet, David. When I finally get *that* kiss from you, it better be a whole lot more romantic than on the doorstep of hell."

See! She IS crazy! Yeah, I know what you're thinking: Who's crazier, the girl or the guy who falls for her? Well, I've definitely fallen—and it's definitely making *me* crazy. Oh, how I want to STRANGLE her sometimes! Then she smiles and those feelings begin to melt; she laughs and they disappear. And as her happiness chases away the shadows, I can see, growing in the unhindered light, the most beautiful relationship I have ever had. A friendship I don't ever want to end.

Saturday, 10 March 2012

MORP!

Even though Lexi was mostly teasing me about my date (I think), it's interesting how much it changed my view on things. I've always liked girls, but within the last few years, that animal has been awakening like a cold lizard under the summer sun. My response to this startling discovery was to quickly stuff it in a shoe box and poke a few holes in the top. Some guys, like Frank, would rather run around and show it off. Either way you handle the critter, I believe most guys have a universal moto: *You see a girl, you check her out*! Then you rate her from one to ten on your scale of hotness and secretly daydream a world of what ifs.

Guys have wandering minds, okay! They're easily distracted and manipulated by a long set of legs or a beautiful pair of . . . eyes . . . This is getting awkward. My whole point being, guys have to learn how to control that. A true man, a man who I look up to anyway, is one who has wrestled his inner beast and won! I love the phrase "to bridle all your passions," because I can relate. Not as a confession, but because I know what a bridle is and what it does.

Once, when I was first breaking Dallas, Josh and I decided to take our horses out for a long ride on the ranch. Dallas is a spooky critter, and you never know when a passing rock or tree stump will suddenly turn into a wild mountain lion and attack!

On this particular day, we had only gone a mile or two when out of nowhere, Dallas jumped sideways ten feet! I wasn't paying attention, but luckily I was able to grab the saddle horn and pull myself back in the seat. Only when I saw both reins dragging in the dirt did I realize how high a price I paid for that horn. The spook turned into a jump, which sparked a crow hop, and the rodeo was ON!

With no way to control, guide, or slow him down, Dallas was as free as a bird. And that's exactly what he wanted to be. After about the third buck, I knew I was doomed. Quickly calculating my choices, I decided I could try to stay on, get pummeled to death, and *then* get thrown off, OR I could cut my losses and aim for a soft spot. It wasn't a hard decision, but it did end up being a hard landing. I'm lucky it didn't happen in the Prickly Pear Flat!

The point of all this is when I lost my reins, I was at the mercy of an uncontrollable demon on crack. Being in a relationship with Lexi has shown me how my inner demon is a lot less controlled than I thought it was.

When Frank and I first planned MORP, I was excited about a blind date. *What will she look like? Will she be one of Meagan's hot friends? What if she likes me?* My inner beast had the reins and was doing as it pleased with my thoughts. Lexi pointed this out very clearly and made sure to dot the exclamation point with a right hook! I need to respect her and our relationship by getting the reins back in my hands and guiding not only my actions, but more importantly, my thoughts. I can no longer lustfully scan, grade, and fantasize over every girl that walks by. Probably shouldn't have been doing it in the first place. I don't like the idea of Lexi drooling over every hunk of meat that struts down the hall, so why should I act that way with girls?

I didn't have to convince Frank; it was like preaching to the preacher. Instead of planning our whole date around "making a move" like he used to, we decided to have as much fun as we could. I knew Meagan wanted to ride horses, so when the girls showed up, Frosty and Lucky were saddled and waiting.

"Hi, Meagan! Hey, Brianna! It's good to see you again!" An interesting conflict of emotions sparked inside when she stepped out of the car. It was a three-hour drive, but the girls were spruced up and ready to go. "Hi, Aunt Rose, thanks for bringing them up here."

She chuckled and said, "I didn't have much of a choice, but I'm glad I got to come. I haven't spent a whole day with Mom and Dad in a long time."

Turning back to the girls, I said, "This is my friend, Frank."

Meagan shook his hand. "Hi, Frank! So *this* is the face behind all those stories David told me."

Frank shot me a worried glance as Meagan started laughing. He turned back to her with an appreciative grin. He likes a girl who can tease. "Well, I sure hope he didn't tell you about the *last* time we took girls on a horseback ride."

Meagan got a mischievous grin, "Oh, does this happen a lot?"

Frank reddened slightly, "No, it's just that . . . well, let's just say I didn't quite have the 'landing' I was looking for."

I couldn't keep it in and started laughing out loud. Meagan smiled and looked at me pleadingly, "You can't leave us hanging like THAT!" Frank promised to tell them the whole story as soon as we got on the trail. This pacified them for the moment.

As we walked around the barn, Frank began to explain our plan. "Well, Meagan, as you probably know, David and I are getting ready to go on missions soon, so we have kind of a weird proposition for you ladies."

Meagan glared at me and scolded, "No, he DIDN'T tell me!"

Frank turned on me, too, "You haven't told her?"

Meagan's face quickly shifted to excitement. "WHERE?" I couldn't help the smile as I revealed my upcoming adventure. "Australia! That's awesome, David!" She gave me a quick hug. "When do you leave?"

"May thirtieth!"

"Wow! That's right after school!" Meagan turned to Frank and asked, "How about you?"

Frank looked down for a second, then facing them again, said, "I still have to wait a while, but I'm getting ready."

I think Meagan understood what Frank meant, but I only saw respect in her eyes. "Well, I am proud of you both. So, what's your proposition?"

Frank looked at me as if to say, *Are you sure?* I think he was having second thoughts, so I turned to the girls and asked, "We were wondering if you guys wouldn't mind riding double on Frosty, and Frank and I will ride double on Lucky?"

They both giggled at the idea but accepted without hesitation. We helped them on first, then Frank jumped on behind me. He immediately snuggled his head into my back and snaked his arms around my waist!

"HEY!" I yelled and smacked his hands, but he wouldn't let go!

In a purring voice, he said, "Oh, yeah, I like this better."

The girls busted out laughing, and Meagan pulled out her phone. Before I could cause enough pain to get Frank to let go, she'd already taken a handful of pictures. Laughing, she said, "Yep, I think this was a *great* idea!"

We had a fun ride around Grandpa's farm as Frank told all about his amazing belly flop. Then he threw me under the bus and told how I gave Ashley a rock instead of a kiss. This is when we started wrestling and ended up both falling off the horse! Lucky stood there staring as if he was completely confused. Giggling, the girls got a whole new round of photos.

For lunch, we had a cookout at Grandma's house. The weather was nice for spring; barely a breeze and not too cold. The grass was perking up after a long hibernation. Gramps grilled some burgers on the back lawn for everyone—Mom, Josh, Sarah, and Aunt Rose, included. It was a fun meal of swapping stories and enjoying each other's company.

After lunch we borrowed Gramps truck and a couple .22 rifles. He said he wouldn't mind us taking the girls out on the ranch as long as we threw in a few bags of salt and a couple bales of hay.

"You might as well check on the cows if you're already going out there." Just like Gramps to get as much use out of the situation as possible. I don't think his generation would have thrown away a half-used tissue paper! The girls were actually excited to do some "real" ranch work.

I "coincidentally" placed the .22's in the middle of the front seat to avoid any snuggling situations, but the girls had no objection to riding in the back seat when I told them about the cowboy code. Once again, Frank was the designated gate opener. We grabbed a couple candy bars and a soda at Maverick on our way out of town.

The cows were lazily hanging around when we drove up to Jay Tank. We showed the girls how to fill the salt boxes, and Frank had the *great* idea to teach them the correct technique for cow tipping! They immediately whipped out their phones. I'm glad they did, too.

What Frank miscalculated was how friendly the cows and calves had gotten since Gramps started feeding them hay. The herd was bedded down about 400 yards away under some small cottonwood trees by the tank, so Frank, very sneaky like, tried to walk over unnoticed. When they eventually saw him, he was only fifty yards away. Instead of bolting in fear, they stood up and started trotting right at him, thinking he was Grandpa!

Frank SCREAMED like a girl and came sprinting back to the truck! Well, this only made matters worse. Now excited, the herd bolted after him. By the time he reached the truck, the cows were running and bucking all around him! The girls were laughing so hard they didn't realize their own dilemma until the last second. They let out a blood-curdling scream and dove in the truck, landing on top of each other while Frank did a swan dive into the bed! I just stood out in the open, laughing my guts out! I knew the cows were full of it and not trying to hurt anyone. Sure enough, they bucked and played all around me and the truck for a minute and then calmly awaited their lunch.

The best part of the whole experience was the priceless photo Brianna captured right before she pancaked Meagan in the truck. There was Frank, held motionless in mid stride, his head cranked over his shoulder. The rest of the dust-filled background was crammed with a ferocious-looking stampede! The cows and calves were bucking, kicking, slobbering—it gave the impression that Frank was about to be consumed by a herd of rabid bovines! We put it on all our phones, and Frank sent out a mass text to his other friends. Before we got back home, Frank's small-town fame was restored in full. Oh what a memory!

The girls insisted we show them the scene of Frank's "accident," so we drove out to Lost Lake for the rest of the afternoon. They loved the swing, but no one got in the water this time. We threw some dried cow pies on the lake and taught them how to shoot the floating targets. Neither girl had fired a gun before, but we found out that Meagan, with all her uncoordinated motor skills, is actually a dead shot! Of course, we had to hike to the top of the High Hills where we watched the sun set and all exchanged rocks . . . ha ha, very funny Frank. I never should have told him that story, but the girls seemed to enjoy it immensely. The view from up there never gets old.

It would've been a great date if it hadn't been for the guilt. Whenever we started to have fun, I found myself thinking, *I wish Lexi were here.* I vowed to myself I would make it up to her someday.

We made it home after dark and decided to treat the girls to McDonalds as a finale to their Snowflake experience. Even though I'd prefer Mexican any day, you can't come to Snowflake and miss

McDonalds; it's our only major fast food joint! (Our Hometown restaurants are the BEST, though!)

We dropped the girls off at Grandma's so they could get cleaned up, and we headed across the street. Frank brought a change of clothes with him, so he wouldn't have to go home.

"Dude, if I hadn't sworn off girls a few weeks ago, I would be fighting tooth and nail right now to win your cousin's heart. She's pretty awesome!"

I smiled at this. Throughout the day, I noticed his stare lingering on her when he thought no one was looking, and surprisingly, she did the same! They actually make a pretty good pair. Their personalities seem to really mesh, but he was determined to keep his goals, and I could see the battle within him. It's a war I'm all too familiar with.

"I think she likes you too, Frank, but don't worry about it. What will be, will be." The words felt hypocritical coming from my mouth, but still I hoped they were true. "I promise I'll hook you two up when you get home if she's still single. Deal?"

He whirled on me with a little more excitement than I was expecting. "DEAL!" And we shook on it.

We picked up the girls and headed to the dance. Frank and Meagan had a great time, but I don't think my forced smile fooled Brianna one bit. Or maybe it was when I stiffly held her at arm's length as we danced. Either way, I could tell she got the picture. I think we were both relieved when Meagan told us it was time to go. Aunt Rose wanted to leave at 10:30 because of the long drive. I kinda felt bad for Brianna. When we hung out before, things were more playful, there was a mutual attraction, but not anymore. Hopefully it wasn't a complete waste of her time. We all laughed enough to be sore for days! She really is a great girl, and I have no doubt she'll find her prince someday—it just won't be me.

Sunday, 11 March 2012

Last night, after I finished writing in my journal, I got into a texting battle with Lexi. She kept grilling me for information, but I told her I would rather give it in person. She couldn't understand why, unless I was hiding something, and she accused me of all sorts of things. We joked back and forth, but eventually, I convinced her I was only waiting because I wanted to see the reaction on her face when I *showed* her what happened. She gave in and invited me over for Sunday dinner with her parents, but not without one final threat. I believe her exact words were, "I WILL get the truth out of you one way or another!"

When Lexi opened her front door, I was stunned speechless. She looked gorgeous! She wore a beautiful spring dress that went slightly past her knees. It was sleeveless with a deep, V neckline, but a white, long-sleeve undershirt covered her modestly—one of the many things she's changed as we started growing closer. I don't think she realizes how much it means to me. Self— remember to tell her next time!

Her hair was pulled back in a ponytail, her bangs hanging loose across her right eye. However, the best part of the whole ensemble was those T-rex house slippers. They summed up her personality in one glance: Stunning to behold, but watch out for those teeth!

She leaned on her crutches, brushing the stray strands behind her ear. When I remained unmoving in the doorway, caught in a trance, she blushed slightly and said, "What? Can a girl not wear a dress in her own house?"

I shook my head and walked in, "No, I'm glad you did! You look beautiful!"

She tried to cover her delight in the compliment by grabbing the side of her dress and saying, "Oh this old thing? I wanted to be more comfortable today is all."

"Well, you should be comfortable more often, then!"

She smiled in gratitude, and just like that, a smirk returned. "Don't try to distract me with your forked tongue, Mr. Thorn. You're not getting out of it THAT easy!"

I let out a huff.

"Hello, David! So glad you could come over!" Lexi's mom wheeled herself into the living room.

"Hi, Nancy!" As she rolled toward the door, I got a mischievous idea. "You sure look *nice* today!" I complimented, and she did. She was wearing a dark-green blouse with black dress pants, and her hair was spiky as usual.

"Why, thank you, David! You're looking pretty handsome yourself!"

I turned to Lexi and said, "You see! That's how *nice* people usually accept HONEST compliments!"

Lexi rolled her eyes and said, "Mom, don't let him fool you. He's good at snatching the hearts of unsuspecting maidens!"

I glared at her, and she gave me that devilish grin. Luckily, Nancy came to my rescue. "Well, he's captured MINE! And if you're not careful, I might steal him from you!"

In victory I stuck out my tongue . . . so Lexi punched me.

Just then, Steve walked in through the big French doors that lead out back. "Hey, no fighting you two. Dinner's ready." Lexi waited till her dad wasn't looking and stuck her tongue back at me. We both started laughing at each other.

Before the pork chops could make it around the table, Lexi sassed, "So are you going to *show* me what happened or not?"

For a good portion of the meal, I retold our date and passed my phone around. Nancy got a good laugh at the riding-double picture, but Lexi only gave a half smile. Steve grinned and shook his head, not believing two guys would do such a thing. Next, I showed the stampede picture. Steve started laughing so hard I thought he might rupture something! Lexi let out a soft chuckle, and then her face went solemn. This wasn't what I was expecting, at all. Something was clearly bothering her.

After dinner, Nancy excused herself to go rest. Lexi and I started quietly clearing the table. Steve said he wanted to finish the game in his office and also left. I think he could tell there was something going on between us and respectfully gave us some space.

"So . . . you had a pretty good time with this Brianna, huh?" I was carrying a stack of plates to the sink, but turned around to glare. Lexi tried to give me her innocent look and said, "What?"

I sat the dishes in the sink and turned on her. "I'm sorry, okay? I am SORRY!" I threw my hands in the air. "How many times do I have to tell you? And NO, I didn't have a good time with BRI-AN-NA. Do you want to know why?"

She looked at me seriously and said, "Yes, actually, I do."

I walked over to her and playfully yanked the cup out of her hand. "It was all YOUR fault! The whole time I was on that *stupid* date, the only person I could think about was YOU!" I roughly gathered up the rest of the dishes and marched over to the sink, acting like I was mad. Lexi didn't reply. When I looked back, she was facing away from me, staring through the big glass doors into the yard.

Dropping the act, I leaned on the counter and asked, "Hey, are you okay?" That's when I heard her sniff. "Lexi, what's wrong?" Worried, I walked up behind her and grabbed her gently by both shoulders. When she didn't turn, I leaned my head around. She glanced away.

With a shaky voice, she said, "Oh, *nothing*." Her right hand was up to her mouth, trying to keep the sobs in.

"I know it's not 'nothing'. Will you please tell me?" I stepped in front of her and softly grabbed her chin, lifting it gently till she looked me in the eyes. *"Please?"*

Tears began to roll down her grief-stricken face. I let go of her chin, and she dropped her gaze to the ground. *What was going on?* I was incredibly confused. While contemplating whether or not to shake it out of her, she said quietly, "David, . . . I don't deserve you."

Her words shocked me like an electric fence. "What are you talking about, Lexi? What does *this*"—I gestured to her and back to me—"have to do with deserving anything?" She shook her head like I was missing the whole point, but she wouldn't speak.

A terrible feeling began to twist in my gut. I tried to bring in some comic relief, hoping it would help make things better. "I *promise* I won't date any more girls."

That was the wrong thing to say. Her face filled with pain, and she turned away, hobbling toward the kitchen. As she walked she exclaimed without looking back, "That's *exactly* what I'm talking about, David! You *should* be dating other girls, not stuck with me." She stopped and lowered her head as her shoulders started quivering. It took a second for her to regain enough control to speak. Without turning, she quietly said, "I'll never be able to give you what you want, David. I could never make you truly happy." As soft and final as a gravestone, she whispered. "*I can't do this anymore . . . I'm sorry.*" Her shoulders heaved as she bent forward in great sobs of pain.

Something ripped in half. Surprisingly, no tears fell. I think all emotions died with my heart—leaving me cold and lifeless. Steve stepped around the corner carrying an empty cup. His look of confusion flared to anger when he saw Lexi's tears. "What in the *world* is going on?"

I didn't know what to do or say. My body seemed robbed of its senses. Finally, I fumbled out the words, "Sorry, Steve. I was just leaving." The last thing I saw before I numbly walked through the door was Steve hurrying to his daughter's side and Lexi burying her face in his chest. That's when the pain hit, and shock blacked out all memory.

<u>Friday, 30 March 2012</u>

Have you ever experienced hell? In the last three weeks, it feels like I've been there and back again. But unlike a hobbit, I would've preferred to have been eaten by a dragon. Darkness crept in like a leech and drained every last drop of light from my twitching body. Sorry, that may be too graphic for children, but I don't know how else to explain it. I would take 100 broken arms over another broken heart *any* day.

I must've entered some kind of emotional coma, because my memory becomes hazy for quite a few days. Mom instantly knew something was wrong when I walked into the house, and I remember saying Lexi broke up with me, but then the nightmares took over. They faded in and out till the next morning when I vaguely recall telling Mom I wasn't going to school or work. She told the school I was ill, and ironically, I really did get sick the next day. I think it was my body's physical reaction to all the emotional damage I'd incurred.

Lexi never texted or called. I considered trying, but the pain of thinking about her was unbearable. The days began running together as my suffering festered and then stagnated. I crawled into a very dark hole and didn't plan to ever come out. Mom was the only thing that kept me alive for a week and a half.

Grandma ended up being my lifeline, believe it or not. Last Thursday evening she came over and shocked a spark of life back into me when she suggested I get out of town—get out of the State! She'd already called Uncle John who runs a fishing boat in Alaska and arranged all the details. The thought of leaving everything behind was so alluring, immediately I began to feel better. I left two days later.

Back home it's spring break, but there's nowhere in the world I'd rather be than sitting on a bench in Sitka, Alaska. I'm freezing my butt off, but I don't mind the cold. It's the first thing that's eased the pain of my pulverized heart.

My great uncle is a hermit of a man. His two kids are grown with kids of their own, and his wife Tammy passed away before I was born. A thirty-foot fishing boat called *Lady Luck* is his only family within a thousand miles, and his passion is his daily fishing trips; it doesn't matter if he has paying guests or not. It makes him happy as a seagull in a fish hatchery! He lives a block from the marina in a small two-bedroom apartment, which he never cleans, but that's okay. I'd rather be outside in the cold, anyway.

Surprisingly, in the course of a few days, this Arizona cowboy has really grown to love the sea as well. Once I learned to stay above deck and keep my eyes on the horizon, the seasickness went away. That's when, for the first time in weeks, I started to have a little fun.

It's amazing to me the different types of fish people reel in. Uncle John showed me how to bait the lines for his guests, and after a few days, I could even help him gut and clean fish, although it's not a part of the job I'd ever enjoy. My favorite time of day, though, is when the work is done, and I come out here by the dock to watch the sunset. It's very peaceful.

When I first arrived and began unpacking my duffle bag, to my surprise I found a Book of Mormon. Mom must've slipped it in when my back was turned. For some reason, as I held it in my hands, I remembered with guilty conscience the commitment I'd made—and failed to keep—to Bishop Call. I decided, if I was going to get my life back on track, keeping my promises was a good place to start.

From the very first moment I cracked the cover, I felt something stir inside me. The darkness didn't like it, but the flicker of light that came from reading didn't only burn the shadows away, it began to heal the wounds the blackness left behind. I couldn't stop! Late at night, I wasn't able to put it down. When it got too cold on the dock, I would read on my bed till I fell asleep.

It's my last day in Sitka now. From my bench, I soak up a tranquil scene; warm rays of a brilliant setting sun reflect a thousand colors across the bay. It's been good to get this all out. Writing truly is a balm to my wounded soul. But better than extracting my pains and fears with ink, I find joy in capturing my life-altering experiences.

Moments ago, things were not as serene. Having finished reading the Book of Mormon, I sat here leaning forward, book grasped tightly in both hands, at war with myself. My unsettled mind kept echoing Bishop's challenge: *If you haven't yet received a testimony of that book—GET one! It'll be the difference between success and failure. And I'm not just talking about your mission.*

Words have never seemed fuller of eternal consequences. I *wanted* to know, but the more I battled to form the words, the harder it was to ask. I tried and tried again, and eventually realized, they *couldn't* come. That's when I closed my eyes and whispered, "Father, I *can't* ask if this book is true because . . . I already know."

Warm, familiar arms wrapped around my soul as the Spirit filled my heart. The remaining tentacles of darkness dissipated like fog in a morning breeze. My view of eternal truths became crystal clear once again, and I *remembered*!

Snap shots of reading in bed and as a family flashed through my mind, bringing with them the tender feelings of assurance I had felt many times. I *knew* the Book of Mormon was true. I KNOW the Book of Mormon is true.

As if finally able to connect after being starved away, the Spirit continued pouring out memories hungrily. I remembered sitting with Bishop Call and feeling God's love stronger than words can express. Ignited by the thought, once again I felt His loving arms embrace me. Then, like a concerned father would do, God spiritually pushed me to arm's length and asked, *Would you still go on a mission, if you knew it meant you'd lose Lexi?* I sat back hard as President Smith's words penetrated deeply. I realized, *This is my test! I lost her . . . now what am I going to do?*

"I'll go." The words slid solemnly from my lips, and even though I was physically alone, I knew they were heard. Great relief settled on my broken heart. It soothed much better than the cold. All of a sudden, a familiar sensation came over me. If I hadn't felt it through the Airlis from Elli, I probably would've missed it. As good as my renewed life made me feel, it was nothing compared to when God smiled down on me.

My bags are now packed. I'm leaving Alaska with a rededicated dream and a new goal. I now know I *will* go on my mission, and I'll leave everything in God's hands. No matter what else comes—even if he requires my own life—I will give it knowing He sees the end from the beginning. He'll make it right, somehow. I also know I still have two things left to do before this is set right. I have to apologize to the angel I've stood up . . . and forgive the one who broke my heart.

<u>Sunday, 1 April 2012</u>

Uncle John gave me a hug as he dropped me off Saturday morning for my flight home. He almost shed a tear, but briskly chased it away with his hand. He told me to come back and see him anytime. "And if you ever want a job, you have one waiting in Sitka." It felt good to be wanted, and I promised him I would come back as soon as I got off my mission.

My plane touched down on Arizona tarmac last night, and Mom was there waiting. As we got in the car to leave, she handed me my phone. I'd left it in Arizona with all my other worries. If Mom needed me, she could call Uncle John.

"You got quite a few text messages while you were gone," she said as we pulled onto the freeway. "I didn't read them . . . but I did notice you had a few from Lexi."

Jerking my head up, I looked at Mom stunned. *How dare she use* that *four letter word!* Turning, she gave me a soft smile. I didn't understand. She knew what happened, and it was nothing to smile about. With shaking hands, I held up my phone. Next to my messages icon was the number sixteen. My heart quivered as if longing to live again. Ten of them were from Frank (go figure), two were from Tyler Sorenson, and sure enough, four of them were from Lexi Dupree.

I swiped a trembling finger over her name to pull up the messages and began to read:

-Wed, Mar 28, 3:44 PM- I know I don't deserve this, but David, I need to talk to you. Will you please text me?-

-Wed, Mar 28, 6:57 PM- David, I really need to talk. PLEASE text me back!-

-Thu, Mar 29, 7:50 AM- . . . please David . . . -

-Thu, Mar 29, 5:34 PM- I just got off the phone with your mom. She said you're in Alaska? Please call me when you get home. It's important. Thanks, David.-

I looked at mom, still extremely confused, and asked, "What does she want?" I tried hard not to let myself feel hope, but it was like trying to stop a ray of sunlight with a baseball glove. It hit me everywhere at once and no amount of padding could stop it from penetrating. My heart thumped to life, but I quickly silenced it. I didn't want to go through *that* again . . . but . . . what if? My head started to hurt.

Mom stared at me with a look of deep concern, then silently looked back down the road. I read Lexi's messages again and was about to start them a third time when Mom said, "David, do you think your father loved me?"

This caught me by surprise. *No,* was my initial response, but I didn't say it out loud because I didn't want to hurt Mom's feelings. Instead, I fumbled with my phone and said, "Um . . . I don't know."

"He did, David." She glanced at me, her eyes were full of longing. "I know you don't think he ever showed it, but I promise you the years weren't always bad." Her eyes looked down the freeway, but her mind seemed to be on a different road. "Bo had his weaknesses all right, but the worse one he faced was not alcohol. No, his biggest problem was he let things fester. He never tried to fix anything wrong in his life. He simply buried it, and before long, it drove him down the road that took his life." She paused and let me stew over this a while.

"David, he dealt with his pain with alcohol. *You* dealt with your pain by fleeing the state!" I looked at her, and she was smiling. One crept onto my own face, and I let it stay a while. "Lexi has had pain too, son. A lot more than I think you realize. Perhaps she thought the only way to deal with it was to push you away."

Before now, I had tried and tried but could never come up with a logical reason why Lexi dumped me. It was a main source of the extreme suffering I went through, but the things Mom said made sense. It was a concept I hadn't thought about, and it shook the foundations of my justified resentment. I stared out the window as new understanding slowly began loosening the tight knots in my heart.

"David, if you want to get rid of your pain, you have to forgive. Even if Lexi never wants to see you again, you'll stay bitter your whole life if you don't learn how to let go. Believe me. I know that for a fact."

I looked at her in wonder. She was at peace, the sweet smile on her face confirmed that once again, but it still astounded me. Reflecting on her miracle reminded me of the night in my room when God took that anger from my heart, too. The hatred that had festered for so long was replaced with God's love. It didn't make Bo's wrongs right, but it did make my heart right from his wrongs. I thought about it as we drove through the night. Mom was content with the silence, and I didn't mind it either.

Finally, as we neared Payson and I could get cell service again, I picked up my phone.

-hey Lexi. I'm back in Arizona now. I'll be home late tonight.-

It was a start. I know my text sounded drab, but I had no emotions to give. Hey, it's better than what I would've texted last week. I promise, you don't want to know.

The phone buzzed to life almost immediately! My heart jumped.

-David!! I am so glad you didn't stay in Alaska! ☺ Can I see you tomorrow?-

-sure-

-When?-

-I guess any time after church.-

-When is that?-

-from 9 to 12-

-OK. See you tomorrow. Thank you David!-

My heart tried fluttering to life. It wanted to, so bad! But I kept it in check. I had no idea what she wanted. Maybe she would pull an Ashley and throw a soda at me then run away crying. Maybe she just wants to be "friends." Could I accept that? I wasn't sure yet.

My mind churned all the way home. Exhausted after such a long, emotional day, I dropped on my bed, fully dressed—but sleep wouldn't come. I still hadn't forgiven Lexi, and I knew I could never face her if I continued harboring such bitter feelings. Sliding to my knees, I pled once again for a miracle.

It wasn't what I expected. My heart didn't completely heal on the spot, but slowly I did feel peace settle in the cracks. Come rain or shine, I knew tomorrow I *could* forgive Lexi and mean it.

My family usually sits on the right side of the chapel, near the back row. Today I was nearest the isle with my elbow propped on the arm rest. The meeting was about to start, and I found myself staring at the wooden frame on the wall behind the Bishopric that shows the hymn numbers, wondering why they were always

312

wrong, when I felt a tap on my shoulder. I looked up and froze. It was Lexi!

She said quietly, "Is there room here for one more?"

I stared in shock, mouth agape. My hand was frozen in midair like it got lost on its way *somewhere.* She blushed slightly and smiled. I didn't snap out of it until I heard the rest of my family sliding over. Somehow, my body moved without having a brain connected to it, and I slid over to make room. She moved her crutches to one arm and gingerly sat down. Quietly, she leaned them on the bench next to her and clasped her hands in her lap.

She was wearing a long, purple dress that rustled slightly as her hands fidgeted. Her hair was down and curled out at the bottom, and she was wearing a simple gold necklace. I did a double take—it had a CTR on it! *Was I dreaming?* My brain struggled hard to make sense of things, but all the gears were jammed together. It was probably very distracting to the people behind us, but I couldn't stop looking at her! I think I expected her to disappear any moment, and then I'd wake up with cold sweats. But she was very real. I could see her and feel her shoulder against mine, and the slight smell of vanilla was as familiar and intoxicating as I remembered. About my fourth awkward glance, she gave me a crooked grin and nodded toward the pulpit as if to say, *Pay attention*!

As soon as the "Amen" concluded the meeting, I turned on her in disbelief. "What are you *doing* here?"

She looked down and blushed again, but her face remained rather serious. "A lot of things have happened in the past three weeks, David." She looked up from her clasped hands. "Would you like to go to Sunday School? Or would you rather go somewhere and talk?"

Wait . . . how does she know about Sunday School? No, there was NO WAY I was doing ANYTHING until I got to the bottom of this. "No, I think I'd rather talk." I glared at Mom to see if she knew about this, but her look of shock was a good enough alibi. As we were about to stand up to leave, Frank grabbed both sides of our pew and blocked us in. His face showed a battle of emotions. Anger and surprise collided into bewilderment. "What—is going on?" He wasn't letting us go without an answer.

Lexi looked at me as if to say, *What do I do?* I turned to Frank and said threateningly, "When I find out . . . I'll let you know."

He got the hint and stepped out of the way. He didn't say another word.

Lexi led me outside to her car and placed her crutches in the back seat. It didn't click until she gingerly placed herself behind the wheel that she was well enough to drive, but I was still too stunned to comment. "Do you mind if we go find a peaceful place to talk?" Lexi asked as I slid into the passenger seat.

I thought it was a weird question, but replied, "No, I don't mind." Looking out my window, I half said to myself, "A little peace would be helpful right now."

"Good! I know just the place." She almost sounded . . . happy? I was utterly confused. It got quiet as we headed north on Main Street. My mind was all jumbled from being shell shocked. I couldn't get my thoughts to congeal on anything, so I blankly stared out my window.

Lexi never liked awkward silence. Before we went much farther, she cleared her throat and said, "After you left—I couldn't stop crying. Dad was mad at you at first, but when I explained what happened, he put his guns away."

I huffed, but didn't look at her. I tried to use comedy once, too, and it didn't help at all. She cleared her throat again and went on. "Dad asked me why I would chase you away like that. He couldn't understand. In his eyes, there's no guy in the world good enough for me . . . except you. He really said that, David."

A big chunk fell off the iceberg around my heart, and my shoulders slumped. I tried to look at her, but my glance couldn't make it past my shoes. Finally, to have a sliver of hope! But it was *so* fragile I was afraid it'd break if I breathed too hard. Holding as still as I could—I stared at my feet. She took a left at the light and headed west toward Heber.

"But that only made it hurt worse! I left Dad stunned in the kitchen and went crying to Mom. By that time, she had heard the commotion and was calling for me down the hall. I threw myself on her bed and wept while she stroked my hair. I told her the whole story and the reasons why. When I was done, she grabbed my face and said, 'Oh, my poor dear. You can't run from this!' It was not what I wanted to hear, but I needed to hear it. She said,

'Lexi, do you want to know what true love is? Honey . . . *love* is *sacrifice!*'

"This caught me by surprise! I didn't understand, and so I asked Mom what she meant. She explained that when she first met Dad, she fell head over heels in love, but he was planning to join the military soon. When he asked her to marry him, she knew her life would be uprooted, and he would be gone for months at a time. There would also be weeks of torture, not knowing if he was alive or dead as he undoubtedly would face enemies. She had a choice to make. Was she willing to sacrifice all this to be with the man she loved?"

Lexi got a far off look and said, "Her words weighed on me for days."

We were a few miles out of town when she took a left turn toward the Snowflake temple. Smiling sheepishly, she said, "Isn't it beautiful?" The complete irony of the whole situation was so absurd, for the first time in three weeks a real smile split my face. Shards of that iceberg went flying in all directions.

Still in disbelief, but supported now by weak legs of hope, I stammered, "I still don't understand."

She smiled, and in a reprimanding tone, she said, "Well then, let me finish!" I sat back in the seat, relaxing for the first time since she tapped my shoulder in church. She continued, "I was sitting out in the back yard, contemplating what to do, when I realized it was not fair to you or me if I didn't at least give it an honest try. I remembered seeing a website on the back of your Mormon pamphlet, so I dug it out and turned on the computer.

"Before I knew it, I was chatting with a sister missionary from what she called 'Temple Square.' She told me it was somewhere in Utah, but anyway, we had a long discussion, and she asked if I would like to have the local missionaries come by and teach me more. I said yes!"

The Temple gates were closed, and the parking lot was empty. Lexi pulled into a handicap parking spot right in front and shut off the car. When she turned to finish her story, instead of speaking, she had to quickly grab her mouth to choke back a laugh. I realized my jaw had dropped to the seat and quickly put it back. Still not daring to believe what I was hearing, I asked, "Are you joking with me?"

Her face got serious as she shook her head emphatically. "No. Two sister missionaries showed up the next day. Mom had no problem letting them in, but Dad was hesitant. I could tell he was about to say something, but Mom gave him the glare. He never said another word. Mom listened to all the missionary's lessons with me, and when we went to church again last week, we actually talked Dad into coming with us!

"David, I read the *whole* Book of Mormon; I couldn't put it down! The missionaries taught me about Christ and His Church. They taught me about modern prophets and Joseph Smith! With every new teaching, it felt like I was suddenly understanding. Things were *finally* making sense! There *is* a God in Heaven! I've always thought there was, but to *know* He is real and has a plan for *me*—to know there's a purpose for my life . . ." Her words trailed off as her eyes glistened with tears.

She looked at me, her face beaming! "They taught me how to pray, David. I *talked* to Heavenly Father for the first time—and I *felt* Him answer me! It was the sweetest thing I've ever experienced!"

I knew that feeling, too. She reached over and took my hand, squeezing it gently. "So. I have two questions I need to ask you." Her joyful smile drooped in pain as the tears continued to flow. "David, will you *please* forgive me for how badly I hurt you?"

Overwhelmed by amazement, it took a second to realize— there was nothing to forgive! The miracle I was seeing, the miracle I was *holding*, it wiped away the hurt as if it never happened! The sweet, sweet emotions were more than I could take. Her soft hands in mine again was shock enough, but added with the complete transformation that had taken place . . . I wept with joy!

Reaching up, I gently wiped tears from her beautiful cheeks, even as they ran down my own, and whispered, "*I already have.*"

Her shining smile returned with all its splendor. She let out a long sigh of relief and said, "Good." The peace that flowed from that one word could have filled the Grand Canyon. "I've been praying you'd say that." Her relief morphed into giddy excitement as she began bouncing in her chair. "Now, for question two. David Thorn, will you baptize me?"

Words cannot express the feelings that cascaded through me. I accepted her invitation with a speechless nod, then was given a hug that would've squeezed lemonade out of a coconut, whether I wanted it or not! I accepted that too. ☺

All wounds were healed; bitterness gone. It truly was a miracle.

A wise man once said, *Where once love dies in all its pain, through ash of death it grows again!* Okay, so maybe he wasn't wise at the time, but that doesn't mean there's not some truth in it after all. Isn't wisdom learning from your mistakes, anyway?

Lexi will be baptized next week! She thought it would be fitting to start her new life on Easter Sunday. Her mom feels the church is true as well, but to avoid conflict with Steve, she's decided to wait to get baptized until they feel unified in the decision. Steve has been very supportive of Lexi, though. After we talked at the temple, she raced me to her house—never letting go of my hand—to tell her parents the news. I was nervous to go in, but Steve gave me a warm handshake, and Nancy squeezed a few more tears out of everyone!

Lexi held me hostage until we ate dinner, and I spilled every detail of my sabbatical to Alaska. I told her the whole experience, tears and all. I realize now, as I flip back through these pages, there are quite a few of them wrinkled with water marks. I want you to know I really don't cry ALL the time, only when things hurt really bad or feel really good . . . and today I've *never* felt better!

Sunday, 8 April 2012

I guess it's poetic justice. I completely avoided Elli for three weeks, and now I can't reach her! I know I shouldn't have locked her out with everyone else, but how do you talk to an angel when you feel like sh—outing? I'm glad it's only three days for her and not weeks. Besides, she's an angel! Don't they have to forgive no matter what? I hope so.

Besides that small downer, this week has been the best of my entire life! I clawed my way out of the "pit of despair" to gain a mended relationship with Lexi and a strengthened faith in God! Even my mountain of homework could not restrain the joyful feelings of my heart! In fact, the homework ended up being extra rocket fuel, because it became another excuse to spend more time with Lexi. So God *can* help your trials become blessings, but you might have to die a little before you really start living. Don't get discouraged, though, God revives people who are "mostly dead" all the time! (You can't have a love story without quoting *The Princess Bride* at least a few times. ☺)

Lexi's baptism was the pinnacle of this amazing week. It took place in the Taylor Stake Center, and the building was packed till there was standing room only! I wouldn't be surprised if the whole school was there. It didn't matter what religion you were, when people heard Lexi was getting baptized *and* walking again, it was a reason for celebration. She has overcome so much to get this far. If angels could be seen, I doubt they'd shine brighter than Lexi did today.

Steve held her crutches in one hand and steadied her with the other. The sight of Lexi Dupree standing there in white unexpectedly stripped my body of its ability to move. She was radiant! As she reached for the handrail I shook myself and forced my legs to act. Climbing the few stairs, I carefully guided her into the warm water. Her plain, white jumpsuit did nothing to diminish her glowing smile! She held my arm firmly as we moved to the center of the font.

"Can you believe this is happening?" she whispered excitedly.

"Not really," I chuckled quietly. "Can you?"

"YES!" I think people may have heard that one. "I've been *dreaming* of this day ever since you told me what makes *you* truly happy!" I remember that day perfectly. She moved closer and looked deep into my eyes. Almost inaudibly she said, "I can *feel* it now!"

Holding her close as familiar feelings swelled inside my chest, I whispered, "Yeah . . . me too."

Raising my arm to the square, I recited those sacred words. With a resounding "Amen!" from her family and friends, I gently submerged her in the water. When I pulled her from the depths of the font, the look on her face galvanized the moment in my memory forever. Her head was tilted slightly back. Her eyes peacefully closed. Small beads of water trickled over a joyous smile. For an instant I saw, glowing in her beautiful face, praises only the heart can sing: *I AM CLEAN!*

Holding that sacred moment protectively in mental hands, I opened the vault of my most prized possessions and placed it safely inside. Before closing the door, I scanned that hallowed room. Of all the memories I could see, there was nothing else quite as precious to me.

Tuesday, 10 April 2012

Pain shot down both arms, and I threw the Airlis on the bed! Turning my hand over, I half expected to see burns, but it wasn't a physical pain. It was a weeping, crushing pain. Steeling my courage, I clamped the stone in both hands and gasped in shock!

Elli! What HAPPENED?

HE'S GONE! I jerked as the exclamation stabbed deep. *"David . . . Jared is gone!"*

What do you mean, he's gone?

The searing discomfort continued to increase. *It started two days ago. He began to change! I could sense he was leaning toward the Salvation Side, but as his mind got more and more convinced, his countenance darkened! When I pointed the change out to him in great alarm, he got very defensive and began to yell! Then . . . he left.*

An overpowering wave of pain slammed into me. It was too much to handle, and I jerked my hands from the Airlis as if it were a red-hot piece of metal. After attempting to rub the hurt from my palms without success, I took a deep breath and grabbed the stone again.

This time, the pain was not as sharp. I think when I broke contact, it helped bring Elli to her senses, and she was a little more in control now. But still, WOW! If it had been physical pain instead of emotional, I think my hands would've been permanently damaged!

I'm so sorry, David. It's just . . . the pain is more than I can bear, and it felt good to share the load—if only for a moment.

That was only a **moment**? Elli, that's some SERIOUS pain! What do you think happened? What made him *do* that?

I'm not sure, David. I know their governing ones have been pressuring him to commit, and they ridiculed him harshly for even contemplating our side. He also hinted something about promising his soul? I didn't understand. David, what do I do?

Do you mind if let go so I can think a moment? It's hard to focus when I feel your suffering like this!

Of course, David. I apologize for hurting you, too. She deflated into an abyss of depression. I was losing her!

Elli don't leave! Please—I'm not letting go! I don't want to lose you. I feared she was about to sever our link!

She didn't, but I felt her indecision. Quickly, I tried to clear my mind of words. As I did, images and emotions of the past three weeks began flashing by. Pain. I also had endured great pain, but oh how sweet the joy once the pain was gone!

At this thought, I felt Elli relax slightly, so anxiously I continued. With fondness I revisited my reunion with Lexi and the precious change that came to us both as we individually turned to God, finding healing in HIS love, not in ours. Sacredly, I reviewed the moment when I lifted Lexi from the water, gazing once again on her beautiful, peaceful face.

I felt a gasp—then nothing.

Elli, but my thoughts didn't leave my mind. The Airlis was blank.

"ELLI!" I yelled in desperation, but her name only bounced off the walls and jolted Josh out of bed.

"H-hey, what's going on?" His voice was groggy. "David, are you okay?"

After a few more numb seconds, I said, "I think—I just had a very bad dream."

It's been hours now. Josh eventually went back to sleep. However, rancid fear prevents me from following him. Something is horribly wrong, and I'm not letting go of this Airlis until I find out.

<u>Monday, 16 April 2012</u>

Every night I've gone to bed with the Airlis clenched in my hand and still no word from Elli. The worry and stress has ignited a series of horrible nightmares, most of which end with me racing through a dying garden and falling through a blackened pool of empty space. That's as close as I can describe it. It's like watching all the seasons of your favorite TV show, only to find out they never filmed the final episode. I can't handle this anymore! But I have no choice—*Elli, where are you?*

Lexi quickly noticed something was bothering me. I told her I had a lot on my mind, and I'd explain it to her someday. She wasn't excited about waiting but patiently acquiesced. (I got that word from *Pirates of the Caribbean*! ☺)

What else can I do? I feel so helpless. I've been trying to stay busy with work and school. Gratefully, Scott did not fire me for my three-week vacation. I also spend a lot of time with Lexi and her mom and sometimes Steve. It's funny, because now I'm the one behind in school, and Lexi is helping *me* catch up. It's good, though. It means we don't have too much time for "us," and I think we both agree it's better we keep our hands off each other. Not that we've done anything wrong, but these feelings have only grown since we got back together, and we both recognize the danger of complacency. We're determined to keep the covenants we made to God, and it's been wonderful to have a friend around who isn't afraid to put me in time out!

It's amazing to see how much Lexi's life has changed for the better. Where we used to spend evenings watching TV, now we sit and she asks me a million questions about God, His church, and my experiences with them. Instead of leaving each other at night with playful flirtations, I usually go home with some deep question to think about. Not to say we don't tease—that girl can get on a roll! Which brings me to Prom.

At the beginning of this school year, before I met Lexi, I was determined not to go. Why go to Prom? I hate high school, and I didn't like girls much more, so . . . win, win! Well, I lost that attitude somewhere between twitterpation, annihilation, and restoration. (Do you like my love life analogy?) Another side effect that came from my whirlwind of life experiences was—I completely forgot about Prom! That is, until last Friday during announcements at school when they read the list of nominees for Prom royalty.

You guessed it, David Thorn was second to last.

Where is that gopher hole when I need it!? The drama and gossip of Prom royalty is the last thing I wanted to worry about. A few of the text messages during spring break were about getting me involved in Prom, but I didn't get them till it was too late. Our buddy from church Tyler Sorenson wanted Frank and me to go in his Prom group, but they didn't hear back from me in time. They had to preorder their tickets to some concert in the Valley. I don't blame them at all.

So now Prom is less than two weeks away, and I don't have a date, or a date for my date . . . I mean, something to do with my date . . . on our date . . . oh never mind. You can figure it out. I wish I would've asked Lexi sooner, but, in my defense, life was kind of crazy for a few weeks, and then everything happened with Elli, and I completely forgot about it . . . till now.

I spent all weekend coming up with a plan. First, how to ask her. Last week I happened to overhear Lexi say she had a doctor's appointment Monday, which is today. She mentioned something about an x-ray of her back. Well, Mom and Lexi's Doctor happen to be good friends, and when I went to him with my plan, he was more than happy to help.

Her appointment was early afternoon, and Scott didn't mind if I was an hour late. When I volunteered to take Lexi to the Medical Center in Snowflake, she thought I was being sweet (hee hee). Once she got called out of the waiting room, I ran out to my truck and pulled a red rose from behind my seat. When I came back inside, the nurse let me wait outside Lexi's room. When Doctor Hiatt came back with her x-ray, he purposefully left the door cracked, so I would know when to come in.

"Well, Lexi, I'm afraid I have some bad news."

There was a pause and then a worried, "What is it?"

"Your back is not healing like it's supposed to, and I'm afraid it only leaves you with two options." He paused for dramatic effect.

A much quieter Lexi said, "Oh."

"Your first option is, you can have surgery and return to a wheelchair for five or six months."

I heard sniffling. *Oh no—she's crying!* That was the moment I realized I'd made a mistake. In a quivering voice she squeaked, "Or?"

"Or . . . you can go to Prom with David Thorn."

Dead silence. That was my cue, but suddenly, I became fearful for my life! I heard a very low, very angry, "I'm going to kill him."

Opening the door enough to show my face, I held out the rose with a please-don't-hurt-me grin. Her wet eyes were FURIOUS! She grabbed the rose and threw it at my face! I knew better than to give her more of a target and quickly shut the door for protection.

"DAVID THORN! I'm going to BEAT you with MY CRUTCHES!!" The threat was heard throughout the entire office.

I cracked the door a mere inch this time. Doctor Hiatt must've been trying to hold in a laugh, because I could hear a muffled chuckle. Pushing my mouth close to the slot, I asked, "Do I take that as a 'yes'?"

That's when a crutch hit the door. "NO!! I will NOT go to Prom with you! You can go with someone else, for all I care. Go find BRIANNA!"

Okay, maybe I deserved that one. But you know as well as I, it was CLEARLY her turn to be the blunt end of a joke . . . just maybe not such a harsh one.

Doctor Hiatt said he had other patients to see and fled the scene. It took Lexi five minutes to calm down enough for me to open the door. I won't repeat any of the threats she made in that time. Luckily, I escaped with my life and only minor injuries. In the truck, she finally admitted I had gotten her good. When she told her mom what happened, Nancy lost it! Lexi even cracked a smile, but it was followed by a piercing stare. Later this evening, Lexi sent me a text. When her Dad heard about it, I guess he laughed so hard he started crying! The message was followed by a skull and cross bones. I think I earned some points with Steve, but I'm afraid it might cost me more than I want to pay. It's not a question of *if* she'll seek revenge, but *when*.

Saturday, 28 April 2012

PROM!

Before I melt hearts and bring tears, maybe it'd be better to get the bad news over with first. Still no word from Elli. I flipped back a few pages and did some calculating, and I think last Tuesday, the twenty-fourth, was supposed to be Elli's big day. You remember, the day her whole spirit family would decide which plan they choose for their mortal experience. I'm worried sick. I feel like I've abandoned my closest friend, and I can only pray that God can help her . . . in some way. I've tried to have faith, but it's been a struggle. If I ask *my* Father in Heaven, could He reach out to *her* Father and work out a way to help Elli in the future? I don't know how that all works in the spectrum of time. It doesn't make sense, but I cling to hope. It's all I have.

I would love to jump from a "downer" right to Prom, but first I have a confession to make. Well, it's more like a statement. I will NEVER pull a prank like that on Lexi, EVER again!

She remained stoic all week, like the friendly face of a ticking atom bomb. I couldn't help but want to see her, but I found myself staying at least a crutch length away. Friday morning of last week rolled around, and the anticipation was killing me! She would never bring it up. The one time I alluded to Prom, I got a stare that would've treed her T-rex slippers! I didn't breech the subject again.

So I was sitting in Seminary Friday, waiting for morning announcements, when over the intercom, I get a school-wide summon: "Will David Thorn please come to the office?" The blood drained from my face . . . this was it.

That was a very long walk. I almost executed three different "escape plans" before I got there, but I knew I couldn't run forever, and I didn't want to live in suspense another day. Resignedly, I opened the office door and stepped into my fate.

The office lady, Mrs. Evans, was already chuckling. Not a good sign. "Well, David, it seems you have angered the wrong young lady!"

I lowered my head in shameful acceptance. In a dry, monotone voice, I asked, "How bad is it?"

She started laughing and handed me a letter:

Dear, Sweet, David.

After suffering for days from the traumatic experience of my latest doctor's appointment, I have come to one conclusion. The only way to make this insatiable pain begin to diminish, you must read the following statement over the intercom—to the WHOLE SCHOOL!

"I, David Thorn, on Monday, April sixteenth, maliciously tortured Lexi Dupree in a heartless attempt to ask her to Prom. Not only did I inflict incalculable pain, but I waited till the very last minute, making it IMPOSSIBLE for her to get a dress!

I am a lowdown, dirty rotten scoundrel, and I deserve to be punched today by everyone who sees me! IF I am sufficiently humbled by tonight, maybe, just *maybe* Lexi Dupree will say, yes. Please help me be worthy of my date. Don't hold back! The bruises will need to be visible.

Sincerely, the scum of the earth: David Thorn."

Have a good day! ☺

~Lexi~

Needless to say, I earned a "yes" and much, much more. I was literally running for my life everywhere I went! EVERYONE offered *graciously* to "help" me earn a yes. Most saw it as a contest to see who could hit me the hardest. Five minutes before the lunch bell rang, I picked up my books and bolted out of Miss Spencer's class—not caring if it landed me in detention. I've never been more grateful for only having a half day of school.

I had plenty of proof my suffering was sufficient when I saw Lexi that evening. She kindly had an icepack waiting, wrapped in a small hand towel with a beautiful "YES" written in permanent marker. When I told Mom what happened, she got the giggles like I've never seen! She liked Lexi before, but now her heart is sold.

Holding my fingers up as if pinching a frog hair, I told Lexi I was this close to bagging the whole date! I think she did feel bad, especially when she saw the purple and blue spot the McCray kid left me, but she was too happy to admit it. I was hoping to make her feel worse, but I think she knew I'd still go even if my eyes were swollen shut. She knows she has all the leverage, and she relishes it!

That brings us to today. I told Lexi to be ready by 10 am, and to her surprise, when I walked in her house, I asked if Steve and Nancy were ready as well. They had graciously accepted to double with us.

Steve drove his nice truck, and we headed south. It was a beautiful, clear day, for which I was very grateful. I didn't really have a backup if the weather turned bad. We drove through Show Low, then Pinetop-Lakeside, and began to wind our way into the mountains.

"So where are we going? Or will you keep it a surprise FOREVER?" Lexi was sitting next to me in the back seat, holding my hand.

"Just wait. It wouldn't be a surprise if I tell you before we get there!"

She huffed impatiently and smiled. "Okay . . . I'll *wait*."

We'd already driven for over an hour, and we were pushing her limits. It wasn't much farther till we came to a turnoff and took a right toward the Sunrise Ski Resort.

"Skiing? But there's no snow." She kept looking at the mountain ahead of us in confusion.

"We don't need snow." I tried to remain straight-faced as I said, "I'm going to take you to the top and push you down the mountain to see if you get more bruises than I've got!"

For the first time since my beating, I actually saw some remorse. Looking at our interlocked fingers, her thumb began rubbing mine consolingly. I guess she was hoping it would help make everything better. "I really *am* sorry about that," she said quietly. Then looking up she shrugged her shoulders. "I didn't realize guys actually *enjoyed* inflicting pain." I snorted in response. Looking at me with pleading eyes, she begged, "Can we call it even?"

Giving her my meanest glare, she countered with a pouting lip. How do you compete with that? I melted like ice cream on a hot summer day. "Yeah, I guess we're even," I consented. She smiled gratefully. "But I don't know what we're going to do now. I guess we'll have to go have a picnic or something."

By this time, we'd pulled into the resort. Lexi looked at me questioningly. "But aren't they closed?" Steve parked the truck right up front. There were only two other cars in the whole lot. I opened the door and got out. It looked like there wasn't a soul around, but as I reached in to help her down, as if by magic, the main lift sprang to life!

"Usually they're getting ready for their summer activities." I smiled wide. "But for *you* they decided to open for the day!"

Turning her amazed look from the lift to me, she said, "You're *serious*!"

Laughing merrily, I handed her the crutches. "Come on, you goober, let's go!" I grabbed the cooler out of the back as Steve helped Nancy into her wheelchair. When we neared the main lift, it stopped. A man with a reflective vest stepped out of the control station. "Miss Dupree, your carriage awaits!" He gestured to the lift chair.

Lexi giggled, her eyes sparkling. Turning to her parents, she asked, "Are you guys coming, too?"

"You better believe it!" Nancy said with a huge grin. I think she was more excited than Lexi!

With a look of pure adoration, Lexi gawked at me. Chuckling, I gently pushed her toward the first chair and said, "Are we going or not?"

Steve lifted Nancy into the chair behind us, and the operator loaded the wheelchair and cooler in the seat behind them and bungeed them down. The lift shuddered to life once again, and we began our ascent. Without thought, Lexi's slender fingers locked smoothly into mine. Looking down at my left hand, for a moment I was baffled at how natural our relationship had become—and how sweet.

We rode in silence for a few minutes, content to absorb the view for a time. From the corner of my eye, I saw Lexi turn and stare at me. I tried to ignore her for a while, but her look was too intense, and eventually, I gave in. Scanning my face with an admiration that made me blush, she said, "David, this is the sweetest thing anyone has done for my mom in a very long time . . ."—her eyes began to glisten—"and for me." She leaned over and kissed my cheek. With a sly grin, she added, "That one doesn't count, either."

The chairs swayed gently side to side as we rose above the pine trees. After gazing around for a while longer, she turned to me again. Brushing her bangs behind her right ear, she studied me quizzically. Gently shaking her head, she asked in wonder, "How in the *world* did you make this happen?"

Contemplating the question as I looked off at the distant horizon, I said, "Well, it helps to know people in high places, for one." Glancing around conspiratorially, I leaned toward her and whispered, "*You have no idea how many people I had to kill to get us here!*"

Before I could blink, she yanked her hand from my grasp and elbowed my biggest bruise! My shriek of pain was followed instantly by her look of horror. "Oh, I'm so sorry!" she gasped. In an attempt to take it back, she tried caressing the wound.

"Don't TOUCH me!" I yelled and briskly pushed her hand away. Her blue eyes sparkled with delight as she giggled. Grabbing my hand more gently this time, she slid back next to me.

"Now,"—her eyebrows wrinkled up—"will you *please* tell me the 'real' story?"

Rubbing my shoulder dramatically with my other hand, I said, "Okay, okay!"

Her pretty hair swished around her shoulders as she shook her head and rolled her eyes. "When Doctor Hiatt and I were uh . . . making plans." She glared at me, but I didn't allow her time to growl. "I also told him about what I *wanted* to do, but *couldn't* because the resort was going to be closed. He told me to give him a few hours, and by that evening, he had called a friend who knew the owner, and Wa La! You have your own personal resort!" I spanned my free arm across the panorama before us.

After slowly surveying our beautiful surroundings again, Lexi gently leaned her head on my shoulder and let out a long sigh. "Well, it's wonderful."

An operator at the top helped us dismount. Lexi opted to leave her crutches at the bottom and use me instead. I thought it was a great idea! She can move around a lot now without them, but she still has to have a wall, or a man, to lean on. (That's right, and don't forget it!)

Nearby were a few picnic tables, so we grabbed the one providing the best view. The whole world was at our feet! I've been snowboarding here a few times, and absolutely love coming to the top. The endless vista of verdant valleys nestled in the arms of forested mountains takes your breath away!

We had an amazing time. Nancy was so excited she didn't realize she kept repeating the word, "wonderful"! The ride, the view, the sandwich—shoot, even the lift operator—were all wonderful! Steve started teasing her about it, and by the time we got to the truck, she was dubbed 'Wonder' Woman!

On our way back through Show Low, we stopped at the bowling alley. Since Nancy was in a wheelchair and Lexi on crutches, we decided—to make it even—Steve and I would bowl wrong handed. We asked for the manager to put the bumpers up, and the contest was on. Surprisingly, Nancy ended up beating all of us! She could lean over enough to get a pretty decent shot. Lexi still can't bend very well, so I would set the ball on the floor, and she would push it with her foot. Even though it moved slowly, she still ended up with two strikes! But my favorite part was watching the girls laugh at us. Yeah, it was a bit embarrassing because we looked so goofy, but everything balanced out to make it the best bowling experience I've ever had.

By the time we got home around 3:30 pm, everyone was beat. We crashed on the couches and fell asleep for a time watching TV. Usually, you have a nice dinner on your Prom date, and I thought about trying to impress the Dupree's with my cooking skills . . . but luckily, for their sakes, I decided to order out instead. After our delicious Trapper's hamburgers, we all shared one of their famous Banana Cream pies! I think Steve and I could've handled it ourselves, but between the four of us, it was gone in minutes.

I left around 6:30 pm. Lexi insisted she have at least an hour and a half to get ready. We agreed I should pick her up at 8:00.

Lexi and her mom had made a mad dash to the Valley last weekend to pick out a dress, and they grabbed me a dark-blue tie to match. I didn't have time to order a wrist thingy, so Mom used her amazing talents to make two small rose pins. On her final inspection, Mom attached one to the lapel of my new mission suit.

"Now, don't forget to stop by before you go to the dance! I want to see Lexi's dress and get a few pictures." Mom finished with the pin and stood back to look at me. Her face filled with emotion and she said softly, "You've grown up, son." Tears welled up in her eyes. "You're no longer my little David." She stepped in close and wrapped me in a warm embrace. Before letting go, she whispered, "I'm proud of the man you've become."

Steve was the one to greet me when I knocked on the door. "Come in, David. Lexi's just about ready."

I chuckled softly as I thought about the Brad Paisley song, *Waitin' on a Woman*. We sat down on the couches, and Steve leaned forward, resting his arms on his knees. He looked down for a moment before he said, "I want to thank you, David, . . . for what you did for my girls today." Looking up, I could see his eyes were starting to get watery. "I haven't seen them this happy in *years,*" his voice cracked. He looked down again, trying to rub the tears back. I felt the awesome strength of his love for them, and my emotions got away from me for a second, too.

Standing quickly, he walked to the kitchen. As I wiped my eyes, he cleared his throat and asked, "Can I get you a soda or something? I've got Root Beer, Pepsi, and Diet Dr. Pepper."

"A Root Beer would be great."

As he fumbled around for a cup and some ice, Lexi walked around the corner by the fireplace. My legs involuntarily brought me to my feet, and for a moment . . . the rest of the room fuzzed out of focus.

She . . . was . . . *stunning!*

I must've been gawking slightly, because her cheeks reddened, and she began fumbling with her dress. It was a deep-blue, floor-length dress that shimmered when she moved. Seamless and creaseless, the top fit snug to her body with the bottom hanging loose in soft, rolling curves. The sleeves were barely wide enough to cover her shoulders, and they were connected with small bows to the top of the dress. Even after being mutilated and broken, Lexi is still the most attractive girl I have ever seen.

Steve stepped beside me with a drink in each hand. "Honey, you sure look beautiful," he said admiringly. He looked over at me and began to chuckle. "But I don't think David feels the same way."

I closed my mouth and tried to speak, "No. I mean YES! I DO feel the same way."

In a joking tone, he said, "Oh, I couldn't tell." He smiled and handed me a cup.

Nancy rolled in behind her and said to Lexi, "Well, give them a turn, dear."

Looking down, slightly embarrassed, Lexi removed her hand from the wall and turned slowly in a circle. Even though she struggled, to me she looked as graceful as a princess. The hand-width sash around her waist was tied in a big bow, and down her back, the fabric was laced together in a delicate crisscross pattern.

A sweet smile of giddy delight beamed from her face, and suddenly, her dress was bland in comparison to the young woman it was holding. Her hair was braided into a finely-knit band that circled the crown of her head. It appeared to be on an unending journey. That alone must've taken an hour! Her makeup was mellow, and that was fine with me. She usually never wears it, except for some mascara, and she doesn't need any. It was nice, though, to see her lips with a dash of red. It helped them stand out and gave them the volume they deserved. Of all the things that coalesced to create the most *beautiful* girl I've ever seen, what finally grabbed my attention—with enough potency to paralyze helplessly—was those sparkling blue eyes. Held completely captive, I felt a deep longing for them to never let me go.

We stopped at my house for a brief photo shoot, and it was almost 9:00 by the time we reached the Highland Primary gym. Lexi's dad was kind enough to chauffer us in his sweet truck. Nancy was clearly the motivation behind the deed. She did *not* want Lexi soiling her dress in my beat-up ranch truck. Lexi would've requested a double date, anyway. She doesn't just follow her new standards, she loves them! And I'm *so* grateful she does.

When I went to get Lexi's crutches out of the back, she grabbed my shoulder and said teasingly, "You know, if I could find *someone* to hold me a little tighter tonight, I could leave those things behind!"

Grinning widely, I helped her to the ground. "Okay. But on one condition."

The corner of her mouth slid effortlessly into that mischievous grin. "Oh, and what might that be?" She took a half step closer.

Leaning in, I squinted my eyes and threatened, "NO punching OR elbowing tonight! I *still* can't feel my left arm!"

Tilting her head back, she laughed with delight as her arm slid through mine.

When we got around the truck, Steve called out, "Well, have fun you two. I'll be back to pick you up about 11:45."

"Thank you, Daddy!" Lexi waved as he drove away. Turning to walk toward the gym, she said, "All right. I promise not to swing." But as we neared the open door, she added with a smirk, "*Unless*—it's absolutely necessary."

Laughing out loud, I pulled her close, and we stepped through a huge curtain of stars!

The room was already crowded. At barely half the size of the high school gym, there was no possible way to sneak in quietly. Dates stopped dancing and groups stopped chatting as it seemed every face turned to gawk at us.

Lexi hadn't been back to school yet, and as shocking as it might've been to see her walk into the room, I know it's not the only reason people were stunned. (And no, it wasn't because of me.)

We meandered around until we ran into Frank. He stood up from where he sat by his date and motioned us over. "Hey, Lexi! Wow, you look *really* nice!"

His date, Amanda Schneider, looked down as she rubbed her eyebrow. I couldn't resist a quiet chuckle as I realized it probably wasn't the first time Frank had made her feel uncomfortable.

"Thanks—Frank. You too!" Lexi said slightly embarrassed. Trying to direct the awkward attention elsewhere, she looked at Amanda and gasped with genuine delight. "Amanda, your dress is absolutely gorgeous! Where did you find that?"

This opened the flood gates as all the girls began to chitter back and forth. So of course, we guys began discussing the far more important topic of the current state of the Arizona Diamondbacks!

We stayed with their group for a while, dancing and swapping stories. When Lexi told them, animatedly, about our date, all the other girls began to ooh and ah. Suddenly, Tina Gardner whirled on Jeff Phillips, slugging him hard as she said, "Why didn't YOU think of that?" Everyone started cracking up, but the best part was seeing how much Lexi was enjoying herself.

After dancing another slow song, we headed to the refreshment table for a drink. The evening was going perfectly—until I turned to see Ashley and Joe walking toward us.

Glancing nervously at Lexi, I tried quickly to calculate my options. Before I had time to organize an escape plan, though, they were standing by our side. My legs wanted to run, but when I couldn't get them to move, my mind decided to leave instead.

"Hey, David! Hi, Lexi! Wow, your dress is stunning!" Ashley smiled warmly.

Lexi looked up in surprise. "Oh, hey, Ashley! Thank you! Yours too!" It's a good thing I wasn't included in the conversation, because I know nothing intelligent would've come out of my mouth. Ashley was all compliments as she and Lexi chatted like old friends. I let out a long breath with a silent prayer of thanks. Ashley is a great person. I should've known she'd only have kind things to say. Well, kind things to Lexi, anyway.

After congratulating Lexi again on getting baptized, Ashley glanced at me from the corner of her eye and said, "I'm so sorry for the horrible way David asked you to Prom!" She laughed and added, "But that's the *coolest* way to answer someone I've *ever* heard!"

From out of nowhere, something smashed into my left arm with bone-cracking force! Sucking air hard through gritted teeth, it took all my control to keep un-pleasantries from flying out my mouth. Joe chuckled as he dropped his fist. "Yeah, Thorn, I *sure* enjoyed it!"

It's a good thing my cup was empty, or punch would've been all over everyone. It was everything my limp arm could do to drop it in the trash by the table. Trying to rub the sharp stab of pain away, I replied sarcastically, "Yeah, thanks for *all* your help." Lexi started giggling, but quickly covered her mouth when she saw my glare of death.

Ashley and Joe sure got a kick out of that. Laughing, they linked arms and turned to leave. Calling over her shoulder, Ashley said, "It's good to see you, Lexi!" Then they disappeared into the crowd.

Shuffling our way to some chairs, Lexi couldn't help but start giggling again as I tenderly caressed my very re-injured bruise. Before I could verbally thrash her for mocking me, a drum roll played over the speakers as the DJ's booming voice reverberated around the gym.

"Now it's time to crown this year's PRO-O-OM ROYALTY!" *Oh how embarrassing.* "Could I please have all nominees come to the center of the room!" Grudgingly, I helped Lexi sit down and dragged myself onto the dance floor.

After introducing us again, the DJ yelled with exaggerated enthusiasm, "And the NEW, 2012, Prom King and Queen of Snowflake High IS?—Hunter Farr and Makenzie Solomon!"

Oh the relief! I clapped gratefully as they stepped to their thrones to receive their robes and crowns. They were smiling ear to ear, and I was very happy for them both. I walked back to my seat with a bounce in my step. Shaking her head, Lexi fumed, "Those votes were rigged! You're easily the better-looking guy."

Embarrassed, I said, "Well, I'm glad at least someone thinks that way."

"Oh, believe me, David, your mom isn't the only one." My mouth dropped. She was absolutely full of—something—tonight!

Jabbing my finger at her pretty face, I threatened, "I think I'm going to ask FRANK to take you HOME TONIGHT!"

"Oh, please don't!" She laughed and shook her head. "I take it back!"

"You better!" I plopped myself down next to her and folded my arms.

Lexi scooted closer and forcibly pulled my arm out till she could hold my hand in both of hers. "Oh, stop your pouting." Resting her head on my shoulder, she added in a tired voice, "Besides, I wasn't the one who hit you."

There was no staying mad at her now. How suddenly they can change your whole world! I leaned my head onto hers and willed time to stand still.

We watched as the King and Queen finished their victory dance, then the call went out for last song. Squeezing Lexi's hand gently, I asked, "So . . . will it *shame* you to dance with second best?"

Pulling her head off my shoulder, she looked up at me with that devilish grin. "How do you know it wasn't third?"

I threw my hands in the air and stood to leave. She grabbed the bottom of my suit coat, laughing, and said out of breath, "I'm sorry, I couldn't resist! I'll stop."

Turning, I looked down at this witty, beautiful, *amazing* girl, and I couldn't help but feel in my heart, *I never want this to end.* Reaching for her hand I pulled her gently to her feet. "Come here, you—before I change my mind!"

We walked arm in arm onto the dance floor. I could feel the strain of her steps as she leaned into my shoulder. As I thought about all she'd been through to get to this point in her life—to get to this Prom—emotions gripped my heart, and my vision began to blur. I hoped the lights were low enough to hide my struggle. She turned and placed her arms around my neck as I wrapped mine gently around her waist. We began to move slowly, and with every turn, the world faded further and further away.

Leaning in till her check pressed against mine, she whispered, "Thank you, David. Thank you for a *wonderful* day." The thought of Nancy and her undiluted excitement brought a wide grin to my face. It truly was a wonderful day! Lexi pulled back far enough to look into my eyes, her face surprisingly serious. The dreamy starlight of the room began to shimmer from soft tears. "It's been one of the *best* days of my life!"

For a moment, lost in her arms, something bigger than I'd ever felt swelled in my chest till I thought it would burst!

"*Yeah. Mine, too,*" I whispered back.

A beautiful smile spread across her face, brushing up small wrinkles near her eyes.

"Lexi, . . . I'd like to *give* you that kiss now."

For a brief moment I felt her tense as if she would pull me in close, but then the smile faded. Something began to churn inside those pools of blue. Heavy things were weighed and balanced, causing them to shimmer and deepen. Leaning back slightly, her face showed the smooth, emotion-free seriousness of a woman about to make a life changing decision.

"David, I want to promise you something." I nodded for her to go on, not able to look away if I wanted to. "If you can wait to give me 'that' kiss for two more years . . . I promise, I'll wait for it."

This *was* heavy. As I contemplated what she said, the gravity of her words began to increase. The more I thought about what she would be giving up, the more I worried it was not right to ask it of her.

"No, Lexi." She leaned back, her eyebrows furrowed. Shaking my head, I continued, "No, I don't accept. I'm going to leave for two years, and if you want to wait for me, well, that's up to you. But, I'm not going to make you promise that."

Confused, and slightly angered, Lexi scowled, "Why not?"

How do I explain this? Fumbling for words, I said, "Because . . . well, two years is an awfully long time, Lexi and . . ."—my shoulders sagged—"what if your knight in shining armor shows up, and you miss him because of me?"

Her arms relaxed around my neck, and I felt the tension leave her stiffened back. Smiling calmly, she melted into a close embrace. With her head nestled softly on my shoulder, she sighed and said, "Oh, David, . . . I've already found mine."

Pulling her in a little tighter, I held her till my worries began to drift away. "I tell you what, Lexi. I'll wait for two years, and IF it works out—and you still want it—I'll give you that kiss when I return."

Breathing softly, she said in surrender, "Okay." We swayed, locked in each other's arms and wished the night would never end. As the music began to fade, I heard her whisper, "*I love you, David Thorn.*"

I leaned my head down onto hers and said softly, "I love you, too."

3:30 am – ish

"David? Can you hear me, David?" The vaguely familiar voice drifted lazily through the deep fog of my wandering dreams.

Lexi and I floated home after the dance. As much as I would've loved it, I did *not* give her a kiss on the door step. Even so, it was a night to top all nights. She said she LOVES ME! Even though the words were barely audible—Oh words, thy power shaketh my very soul, and lifteth me to eternity!

Why do confessions of love make you want to quote Shakespeare? Don't have an answer for that one. And no, that wasn't Shakespeare. That was all me, baby! ☺

I ran to my bedside and pulled out the ammunition box. Elli HAD to be there! I sat on my bed and tried with all my mental capacity to reach her . . . but she was still gone. Letting out an exasperated breath, I fell on my bed, holding the Airlis to my chest. Despondent feelings slowly melted as a deep-blue-eyed girl danced me away in a cloud.

"Elli! Is that you?" It seemed like I was crying out, but the words fell at my feet. The emotions had been so familiar, and like a relapsed addict, I *knew* it was Elli . . . but that voice? I clearly heard a voice—and yet, it was familiar, too!

The swirling mists of dreams and reality churned in my view; shades of light and dark coalesced into colors of the warmest sunset. As the fog began to dissipate, a beautiful garden came into focus. There, sitting on a simple stone bench under a beautiful tree, was a girl. Her light shone brighter than the rest of the vision, and when she turned to look at me, I *knew* that face!

"LEXI?"

A pure, undiluted smile warmed my soul. She motioned for me to sit next to her, but I stood paralyzed. How could this be? I *knew* I felt the emotions of Elli, but my eyes and ears were telling me otherwise.

She patted the seat next to her. "Come here, silly," she giggled. "I promise I will not bite . . . too hard."

The words were Elli's, but the playful teasing and the voice was clearly Lexi. Were my dreams colliding with reality? This felt so real! I shuffled over and sat as far away from her as possible.

She placed her hands in her lap and laughed gently. "Well, at least this is a start," she said with a tender smile. "I know how confused and shocked you must be, because I felt the same way the last time we spoke."

"What are you talking about?" I shook my head in confusion. "*Who* are you?"

Her smile remained as she looked at me with great love. Tilting her head to the side slightly, in a very familiar way, she teased, "If you promise not to leave, I'll explain the whole thing. Deal?"

I could only nod my head in acceptance.

"Good! Now, let's see—I should probably start at the beginning. David, when we first connected through the Airlis, and I found out you were in a mortal world, I made a profound mistake. I *assumed* you were from the past, and I was in the future. I did not look both ways down the eternal scope of time.

"But in our last conversation, something happened to the Airlis. Perhaps it was sparked by my surge of uncontrolled feelings, but no need to speculate. As you began to mentally review the experiences of your previous weeks, an astonishing thing happened. I began to *see* them with you! They played across the window of my mind as if I were looking through *your* eyes! Things were unfocused at first, but as the connection strengthened, they quickly became clear. I saw a girl being pulled from the water, and as her face came into view . . . it was ME!"

I shook my head in disbelief. How was *she* . . . Lexi? The thought was like a slippery fish. Every time I tried to grasp it, it wriggled free. Elli pressed on, "I realized then, I was not in the future at all. *You* were the one in the future, and I was in the past. Not just any past, I was in *your* past! David . . . you are Jared, and I am Lexi."

It's a good thing I was in some kind of dream/spirit . . . place, because, otherwise, it might've hurt when I fell off the bench! She reached out to grab me but was too late. When I looked up from lying on my back, she was covering her mouth, and her cheeks were turning red. I had seen that look many times before.

"You ARE Lexi!" I exclaimed. "And I'm . . . Jared?" I was halfway there.

She nodded her head as she fought to hold back the laughter. I struggled to gather myself up, mentally and physically, and sat—unsteady—on the bench.

She dropped her hands and exclaimed, "YES! Is it not absolutely *amazing*!?"

"Yeah, it's . . . *crazy*." My thoughts were still trying to connect like an old dial-up computer. There was lots of "beeping," but no information was being passed yet. "Elli, how in the *world* is this possible?"

"I don't know!" she giggled in excitement. "But somehow you and I, as Jared and Elli, will get sent to earth and become David and Lexi! And by some miracle from Father, we have been able to connect our separate time and existence through the Airlis, further aiding one another on our journey of eternal progression!"

It finally sank in! A smile burst from my lips with enough ambition I was afraid it'd leap from my face! Warm, pure feelings blanketed me, and for the first time, I realized the sensation came not only from *my* Heavenly Father, but *our* Heavenly Father.

For a moment, we were both content to let my mind try to catch up. As I pondered the past few months from this new perspective, some things, once hard to fathom, became clear, while others only got more confusing.

"So I don't live long ago, in a galaxy far away," I stated in acceptance. Furrowing my brow, I thought about loose ends that didn't match up. "But Elli, when we spoke last, you said that Jared . . . that I . . . had gone to the Salvation Side—to Satan's side!" The realization of what really happened struck me like a Polynesian linebacker.

"Yes, that's right. You chose Lucifer's side. When I saw my face in your thoughts and realized I was in your world, in that instant, my heart *knew* you were Jared. I concluded, in order for both of us to soon have a mortal experience with a Plan of Agency, you *had* to come back! I absolutely could not fail to convince you otherwise.

"Immediately, I ran to find you, searching an entire day before I was successful. Lucifer and his followers had become distanced and elusive, retreating to dark places. Eventually, my investigating led me to a council upon which you were seated. As I burst through the door, at first your face lit up with shocked delight that I had turned sides, but when I began to beg with tears for you to come with me, your countenance became grey. Your face was creased with confusion as you pulled your hand from my grasp. Others began to scold and ridicule me, and I saw conflict in your eyes. Every part of me was pleading for you to return, but before I could reach you again, angry hands grabbed me and threw me from the room. I landed hard in the hallway outside."

Elli turned and gazed into the distance. Her eyes reflected a painful memory, but her face was still calm and serene. "I'd lost you forever! My soul was *crushed*. You thought my pain was strong before, but it was nothing compared to how I felt at that moment. I cried out in agony as my heart tore in two."

I knew that pain. It's the worst pain you can *ever* experience, but as I looked at her, I was comforted. Those familiar blue eyes were shimmering with a peace larger than oceans.

She smiled and continued, "But then I felt tender hands lift me from the ground. In shock, I looked up—and it was *you*! Tears were falling from your tortured face. You cradled me gently in your arms and pled for my forgiveness. I'd never heard words more sweet! I threw my hands around your neck and exclaimed, 'Oh YES, Jared! YES!' Turning your back on the crowd of angry voices, you carried me from that evil place. All the darkness, without and within, we left behind forever."

Tears were dripping from my eyes, and I didn't care; they had never felt so good on my face. Elli smiled sweetly, and her radiance reflected like diamonds through the tears on her cheeks. She giggled softly and said, "So you see, David, I pulled Jared away from the darkness, and you brought Lexi into the light!" I smiled at the beautiful irony and closed my eyes as a feeling of perfect love permeated my whole soul. I realized—this did not happen by chance! As if to read my thoughts once more, Elli laughed and said, "That's right! By Father's grace, we have saved each other!"

For some reason, my gaze was drawn away, and briefly, I thought I could make out a small lake surrounded by Cottonwood trees; a rope swing hanging peacefully in the air. God *really* loves me. He has **always** loved me! He was aware of my path and concerned for my outcome long before I even came to this earth.

Somehow, amazingly, He continues showing His love in a very intimate and individual way. Oh how *great* is our God!

I turned back to Elli and said, "Well, I guess there's just one more question."

She gave me that mischievous grin and asked, "Oh, and what is that?"

"What happens to *us* now?"

Her head tilted back, laughing merrily. She looked at me with those perfect eyes and said, "My sweet David. It wouldn't be a surprise if I told you the ending, now would it?"

I smiled at the familiar sound of her words. How strange. Things seem to go round and round in an eternal journey. She reached up and gently placed her warm hand on my face. I could *feel* her! Closing my eyes, I grabbed her hand and held it firmly in place, not wanting it to leave. My emotions could no longer be contained, and I wept joyously!

"I will not be able to talk to you again, David. Not as Elli, anyway." A wave of concern tumbled me back to reality. Looking up, I found her precious tears were now mixed with sorrow. "My time is now short. The plan has been chosen, and there is much to be done. Father told me where to place the Airlis, so you will find it someday, and . . . I must bid you *farewell*."

In spite of the sadness of losing a friend, her eyes glistened with joy. "Remember David, as much as you'll desire to share these things with me—with Lexi—you must refrain until the Spirit tells you the moment is right. Be patient, and the day will come to share your story, not only with her, but with the whole world. There's more Father desires from you than you know."

Her eyes seemed to suddenly shine bright with understanding, and a peaceful smile caressed her face. "Father was right! What once was mine, will return to me again!" She leaned in and gently kissed my cheek as the vision began to fade. "I *love* you, Jared, . . . and I can't wait to fall in love with you again."

I sat up on my bed with a jolt! Tears were streaming down my cheeks. Lifting my hand in the darkness, I watched as the Airlis slowly dimmed . . . for the last time.

<u>Friday, 6 June, 2014</u>

I can't help it. If I find a way to surprise a smile out of my sweet Lexi, I'm not going to pass it up!

Yes, it's been over two years since my last entry. In compiling my story, I've decided to skip ahead to the juicy stuff. I did finish high school, and I did leave on my mission. And yes, I also kept my word to not kiss the girl I love. It got rather comical at times when I could tell she was wondering why in the WORLD she asked me to wait! Like the moment we hugged goodbye. As hard as it was for both of us, it was better in the end.

I can testify now to the fact a mission is the best thing for a guy to do if he truly desires to become a man. Not that it's the only way, but if that man wants to become a man of God, there is no better way. I could fill volumes of books with the experiences I had, but that's a different story. Perhaps, someday I'll share it as well.

What was my greatest achievement? Well, I found this knot-headed, love-struck teenager and was able to convert him to the Lord. His name was David Thorn, and even though he thought he knew God before, he was only breaking the surface of that relationship. What an eternal blessing it is to know the Lord in deeper and stronger ways.

Even though many guys gave a valiant effort to derail Lexi from her goal, she never faltered in her desire to wait for me. She began her senior year of high school at the same time she started college! I guess a lot of her classes qualified for both objectives. After I left, she had a few soul-searching months. She wants to become a therapist and counselor for troubled young people. I have no doubt she'll accomplish great things.

She graduated a few weeks ago from our local community college and is ready to move on to complete her Bachelor's degree. She told me in emails that she enjoyed having something to take her mind off things. I'm so proud of her.

And that brings me back to my latest cruel joke. "Cruel" is not the way I would've described it, but Lexi's fist argued otherwise. Under a garb of secrecy, Mom and Nancy gleefully accepted my awesome plan! Except for my partners in crime, I told everyone back home I'd be ending my mission on June eleventh, when actually, my service completed on June fourth! Do you see where this is going?

I flew into Phoenix early this morning, and Mom met me at the airport. It was hard for her not to tell Josh and Sarah, but I convinced her the surprise would be worth it. When I neared Snowflake, I texted Nancy to see where Lexi was. She told me Lexi was home and sitting outside, working on a project. PERFECT! The kids were still in school, so I dropped Mom off and raced to the Dupree's.

Without knocking, I gently opened the door and peeked inside. Nancy was sitting at the table and waved me in conspiratorially. I ran over and gave her a long embrace. She started to cry, and after wiping away her tears, she gestured out the big French doors. I walked over and peered outside.

Before today, I hadn't explored the back yard much. I helped Steve grill a few things on the back patio, but that was the extent of it. Lexi wasn't on the lawn. Looking back I shrugged my shoulders. Nancy pointed to the left and mouthed the word, "Garden!"

Quietly stepping through the door, I noticed a white gate standing ajar at the corner of the house. Walking in stealth mode, I crossed the yard like a ninja. After stepping silently through the gate, I paused in wonder. The garden was immaculate! I remember hearing Nancy allude to her work out here, but I never realized how deep her passion was until today. The garden sloped gently toward the north. It was surrounded on three sides with a large hedge of lilacs and honeysuckles. That's why you can't see the garden from the driveway. The north side was open to reveal a breathtaking view of the valley, spread out for miles! A stone path wound its way from the gate, through raised flower beds, to a stunning tree in a beautifully manicured lawn.

I tip-toed my way through amazing flowers of varying types and colors, keeping the magnificent weeping willow between me and the small bench on the far side. Leaning around the trunk, I gazed at the beautiful woman who sat with her back toward me . . . and I froze in SHOCK!

I *knew* this garden. It was the *same* garden from my vision of Elli! She wasn't glowing but was dressed rather plainly with a

344

white t-shirt, blue jeans, and no shoes—but it *was* her! In her hands she held a pad of paper. She was in the middle of doodling some kind of flower on the edge of her notes. Her face was completely at ease as she focused on her work. A quiet and uncontrolled exclamation escaped my mouth:

"*Elli.*"

Lexi whirled. Her expression of shock and surprise was so extreme I couldn't resist a soft chuckle.

Smiling wide I asked, "May I sit down?" gesturing to the same spot I had sat in my dream.

Devoid of emotion and speech, she nodded almost imperceptibly. Sitting hesitantly, I began to worry I had just cornered a wild she-lion. Looking away for a moment, she clasped her hands tightly in her lap. Then from out of nowhere, she turned and PUNCHED me as hard as she could!

The fierceness of her attack, mixed with my reaction to flee for my life, caused me to topple over backward! Laughing too hard to get off the ground, I finally sputtered, "Ww-what was THAT for?"

Smiling broadly, she jabbed a finger at me and yelled, "I DON'T KNOW . . . but I BET you DESERVED IT!"

Still laughing, I rolled to my hands and knees and stood. As I brushed the dry grass blades from my suit, I mumbled, "This is like a bad version of dèjà vu."

She looked at me accusingly and asked, "What does *that* mean?" But before I could reply, her face grew serious. "And why did you call me Elli?"

Judging by the ferocity of her first attack, I thought there'd be more fire behind that question. Or at least be followed by some sassy accusation about me chasing some Australian girl, but she only had the most curious look of bewilderment I'd ever seen. This is NOT what I was expecting. I was hoping for a big hug and a long kiss. That's how I envisioned this reunion during more daydreams than I care to admit. Sitting back down a little heavier this time, I contemplated how to answer her question. After a few long arguments with myself, I suddenly felt a sweet peace that whispered—*This is the moment!*

Gazing out at the horizon, my attention was drawn to a place my heart had longed to see. There stood The High Hills, the guardians of my childhood memories. And as my eyes wandered through the valley to the east, I was able to find a small patch of green in the middle of a sea of brown.

"Do you see that dark spot just to the east of those large hills?"

Lexi followed my pointing finger and after a few seconds replied, "Yeah, I see it. Why?" She looked back confused.

"That's where I went after I broke my arm and life was falling apart." This was it. This was the moment I either lose her or keep her forever. I let out a long breath and leapt with only faith to catch me. "And that's when I met a girl named Elli." Tilting her head, I could see big questions behind her curious eyes, but she held her tongue. I figured she didn't want to interrupt, because she wanted as much evidence as possible before she called the nut house.

I told it all; the whole CRAZY story. Well, as much as I could remember, anyway. I've found my journal holds a lot more detail than my memory, and for that I'll be forever grateful. I finally finished with my dream after Prom and how I sat on this exact bench, falling on that exact spot when I said goodbye to my angel, Elli.

Everything was on the table. Cringing, I awaited the verdict. She didn't run, and she didn't laugh or mock in disbelief—instead, she looked back to that small green smudge and remained silent for a long time.

"David, I haven't been exactly truthful with you, either." Now it was my turn to be bewildered. Once again, I was shocked at a reply I was *not* expecting. Her eyes went to her sketch of a flower, and she slowly rubbed her fingers over it.

Hesitantly, she continued, "After the accident, do you remember me telling you about the woman who helped me?" I did remember and nodded. "I've never told anyone this, David. I thought, perhaps, I made it up, and it would eventually fade away, but to this day, I can hear her voice as *clearly* as if it happened yesterday." Lexi looked at me with eyes full of wonder, and said, "David, she called *me*—Elli."

A smile of utter amazement lit up her face as truth burst through the clouds of unanswered questions that hung over her for years. To *finally* tell her—and to have our separate experiences align perfectly—it was the evidence we had both searched years to find.

It was all REAL!

My tension immediately disappeared. The weight of holding my secret for years was much heavier than I realized. The miracle was so liberating, I thought I might float right off the bench! But as I was about to leap in the air and shout for joy, I looked back. She was crying.

Why was she crying?

Talk about bursting a bubble.

"Lexi? What's wrong?"

She held her face with both hands as the tears poured through her fingers. Her body shuddered in agony. As much as she tried, the sobs wouldn't stop. When her struggle to regain control failed, she had to force her words out through gritted teeth. "David, I love you. I know I do. And now I know I even loved you before, but— *oh, this* hurts—David, I **still** can't give you the happiness you want."

No. Not true! I seized her by the shoulders with both hands and forced her to turn and face me. The shock of my physical reaction jarred her lose from her anguish, and she looked at me with stunned eyes.

"NO, Lexi. There's *nothing* that would keep you from making me the happiest man on earth!" My intense stare tried desperately to embed these words in her heart.

She didn't look away, and for a second, I thought she'd believe me, but then her eyes became dull. Shaking her head weakly, she whispered, *"David, I can never have children."*

My grip loosened slightly as my mind fought to grasp the meaning of her words. With painful resignation, she continued, "The whole reason Zack and I got in that *stupid* accident is because on the way home from his game, I told him I was . . . *pregnant.*" The word nearly choked off her throat. Though spoken in nearly a whisper, it resounded in my head like the blow from an anvil. My hands released her shoulders involuntarily as my mind struggled for comprehension. Slowly, I sat back on the bench and stared blankly at the ground.

"I'm sorry, David, but I *have* to tell you. Zack had some alcohol in his truck. He was planning on celebrating after a win. It was bad timing on my part, and before we got to Heber, he was in a drunken rage."

I could sense her relief to finally remove this from her conscience. I know the process well. The only bad thing is the weight lifted from her and landed squarely on me.

She continued dejectedly, "Because of the violent way I was thrown from the truck, not only did I lose the *baby,*"—her face cringed as if someone slugged her in the gut, and her chin began to quiver—"but, my organs were so damaged, they had to perform a hysterectomy." She slumped as the tears returned. "So not only am I not a virgin, but I will **never** *be able to have children.*"

Grabbing her stomach as if she'd been kicked, she doubled over. Bitter tears of agony fell like petals of a dying flower. *Was this the end?* My heart began to strain, and I knew it was moments away from breaking forever.

No. We've come too far. We've been through too much to have it all crash like this. I will NOT lose her again!

Sliding off the bench, I knelt in her tears. Placing my hands softly on her knees, I said quietly, "Lexi?"

Her crying began to subside, but her head remained bowed in defeat. Cupping her quivering chin gently in one hand, I raised her face till she looked me in the eyes.

"I don't care."

Startled, she sniffed as the tears began to slow.

"I don't *care* that you were pregnant. I don't *care* that you can never have children. I don't!" At this declaration, something in my mind shifted. In a split moment I was able to look back on our lives as if from a higher perspective—and I smiled!

"You know what, Lexi? Actually, I'm glad!" Slowly, she lifted her face from my hand, deep wrinkles creased between her eyebrows. Grabbing her gently by the shoulders this time, I held her firmly. I wasn't through, and she wasn't going anywhere.

"I'm *glad* you got pregnant. I'm **glad** you got in that horrible accident. And yes, I'm even GLAD you can't have kids! Do you know why?"

The pain was almost gone from her face now, replaced with a deep curiosity. She tilted her head and begged for clarity with pleading eyes.

"Lexi, if you had not gone through *all* of that . . . I would never have met you."

Her gaze searched my face desperately for a moment longer, then her expression softened.

Continuing with more confidence, I said, "If all of that had never happened, I wouldn't have come to The Cottage, we never would have shared M&Ms, and you never would have seduced me and stole my first kiss." A smile struggled briefly on her lips and then broke free. It warmed her face like the morning sun after an Arctic winter. It was absolutely beautiful!

Releasing her shoulders, I grabbed both her hands as I sat back on my feet. Squeezing gently, I continued, "Now, it might be really selfish of me to think this way, but there's not a single thing in your life, or mine, I would change if it meant losing you."

Her frame sagged as she let out a long breath and closed her eyes. The worry wrinkles were gone, leaving her face peacefully smooth. What was bound moments ago in unyielding chains, was now free! Leaning forward, I whispered, "*I want you, Lexi Dupree. All of you. Boy crazy past and everything.*"

Looking into my eyes, she blushed and glanced away. It was the first time I'd ever seen her embarrassed on my account. But I wasn't finished.

"I love you, Lexi!"

Her eyes suddenly locked on mine with shocking intensity. Those perfectly trimmed eyebrows bunched up as she desperately scrutinized my soul. Returning her intense stare ounce for ounce with my conviction, I assured her calmly, "And I promise, if worlds and time can't keep us apart, there's nothing we won't be able to overcome. Lexi, will you be my eternity?"

Pure tears spilt from her eyes as a sweet laugh born of relief pushed up that crooked grin.

Wiping her cheeks as she sniffed, she giggled merrily and said, "No!"

Tilting my head back, I let out a burst of laughter! I should've been expecting this, but once again, she caught me by surprise.

"Would you like me go back to Australia and ask again next week?" I smirked as I moved to stand, but before I got more than an inch, she grabbed the front of my suit and yanked me down hard. And this time *she* wasn't letting go.

"Don't you DARE!" she yelled and pulled me in close. My heart started racing. When we were only inches apart, she said in a soft but very threatening voice, "You are not leaving me *ever* again!"

Trying to match her deadly tone, I replied, "Well, that sounds like eternity to me!"

"No, David." Tilting her head slightly, she pushed her lips cutely to one side as she calculated a counter offer. "We'll start with three hundred million years, and then, IF you're a good husband, we'll discuss further contracts."

Oh, how I love this girl! Reaching up, I took her face tenderly in both hands and said with a grin, "I accept!"

An amazing new sensation began to fill my chest. This was more than love now. As my intentions of commitment, honesty, sacrifice, and loyalty began to wrap their way around our love, a sense of endless possibilities began to expand!

Slowly leaning in—I paused. On my lips I held the kiss that would begin our eternal adventure, but I knew it was now up to her. She threw her arms around my neck, and with a GREAT exclamation point, we placed the title on *our* first chapter: THAT Kiss!

<u>Saturday, 6 February 2016</u>

The sun is setting over an Alaskan ocean in one of those picture-perfect moments. Life has been crunchy, as my brother Josh used to say. (He was referring to his cereal then, but the analogy fits.) I can now shuffle through a much fuller vault of my most valuable memories, but the one that takes the cake happened on Friday, August 11, 2014 when I took my beautiful Lexi to the Snowflake Temple and was sealed to her for time and all eternity! I can tell you, with all the certainty of a man who has lived it, there's nothing in this world that can bring you more happiness than that!

We had an absolutely wonderful honeymoon in Sitka, Alaska. Uncle John was more than happy to help plan it all out. We found a beautiful bed and breakfast inn right on the ocean, just outside of town. It was there I FINALLY made good on my promise to take Lexi for a walk on the beach. She never let me forget!

The plane ride was long, so even though darkness was reclaiming the world when we arrived at the inn, we both wanted to stretch our legs and headed to the beach. Her long fingers felt good intertwined with mine, like they were formed to fit there. Fading light still illuminated an almost-glass-covered ocean. Soft waves lapped on rounded stones, seducing us to silence with their quiet melodies.

"I have something for you!" I said, breaking the ocean's spell.

"Is it alive?" she asked with that crooked grin.

I smiled as I thought about it. "Well, it used to be."

She turned and tried to pull her hand free, but wasn't fast enough. I yanked her in close and wrapped her in an anaconda squeeze. Struggling playfully for a moment, she gave in. "Okay. If you promise not to *throw* it at me, I promise not to run!"

"Deal!" I pecked her on the neck before letting go.

Her slender fingers laced through mine again as she leaned in flirtatiously and kissed me solidly on the lips. "There, that's better." Returning to our walk, she asked, "Now, what poor creature have you tortured to death?"

"Oh, it's two things, actually." Grinning, I pulled out a bag of Peanut M&Ms.

Squealing in delight, she exclaimed, "You DO love me!"

"You better believe it!" I said with a chuckle.

She opened the bag and tossed a few in her mouth. After relishing the flavor for a moment, she asked with a smirk, "Oh, did you want some?"

"Only if *you* love *me,* too?" I teased. She rolled her eyes and poured me a handful.

We'd reached some boulders, and happy to take a moment to relax, Lexi sat down and crossed her legs. Pulling the Airlis from my pocket, I held it out to her.

She looked at it with one eyebrow raised, but before the smart-aleck comment could escape her mouth, realization struck, and she reverently took it from my palm.

With excitement dripping from her smile, she asked, "Is this what I think it is?" Grinning wide, I affirmed her conclusion with an emphatic nod.

She rolled it over in her hands, scrutinizing every detail. Her eyebrows knit together in concentration. After a moment, she asked, "So how does it work?"

I shrugged and said, "It doesn't anymore. But it used to read my thoughts and text them across the heavens, whether I wanted it to or not!"

Disappointed at first, she looked at it again. Then her expression softened.

In a quieter voice, she said reverently, "What an amazing experience we have *both* had." And I knew she was referring to her accident. Her eyes glistened as she looked up at me. "It was a *miracle!*"

Mountains of emotions stirred as tears came to my eyes. I nodded in agreement, not trusting myself to speak.

"So what are you going to do with it now?" Lexi's question was one I'd thought long and hard about.

"Actually, I was hoping you'd throw it in the ocean."

Her jaw dropped, and I couldn't help but chuckle. She stuttered, "B-but it's special!"

I shook my head. "It was only special, Lexi, because God used it to help me understand . . . *you* are my eternity now."

The intensity of my heart reflected in those azure eyes as she soaked up my words and sent them back with a smile. Lexi tilted her head as she stared adoringly. Standing abruptly, she walked to the water's edge and skipped the Airlis into the sea.

After watching the ripples for a moment, she turned and sauntered back, moving her hips more intensely than usual. My heart began to pound and immediately I pulled back. It had become my natural response after years of fighting for control. Chuckling to myself, I released the pressure on the reins. The time had finally come to see how fast this inner beast could run! Her warm arms wrapped around my neck as I pulled her in till there was nothing between us. The same mischievous grin that stole my heart so many years ago spread across her pretty face. Squinting seductive eyes, she threatened in her sweetest voice, "And don't you forget it!"

We kissed with all the passion we possessed! Now it was the ocean who paused breathless, held spellbound by us!

*   *   *   *

So, it was there on the beaches of Sitka, Alaska that Lexi finally fell in love . . . with a town. Ha! (Believe me, our love was strong long before that!) The streets, the marinas, and of course the nice bed and breakfast accommodations on the beach (wink wink) stole her heart over and over again.

Speaking of bed and breakfast, I do have a very funny—and quite embarrassing—story to tell about our first night together as a married couple when we stopped in Payson on our way to the airport. To back up . . . in my defense, it's all *her* fault for not explaining herself clearly that day in the garden—but I'm sure you could hear her laughter throughout the hotel when, to my great surprise and extreme relief, I found out that when she said she couldn't *have* children, she wasn't referring to the *process* but the organs necessary to create them! How was I supposed to know what a hysterectomy was? But I have NOW learned, it does NOT prevent the process! That would've been nice to know a few months earlier. You have no idea how wonderful it feels to be freed from celibacy! I probably won't live THAT one down for a million years.

Back to Sitka—we made all the arrangements, and as soon as Lexi graduated from ASU with her bachelor degree, we had jobs and a house waiting! Our top priority, then, was to fill our home with joy. God must have been in a rush, because before we lived here a month, we were able to miraculously adopt not one, but two bundles of that joy we were looking for.

A brother and sister! Our precious Elli is one and a half, and Jared is five months old. It has been a shock to adjust abruptly to parenthood. Life has never been harder, but it also has never been sweeter!

I really enjoy working with Uncle John. Business has picked up since I took over the paperwork. First, I had to find it in his house and organize it. That took days! Now I run things from an office in our home. It's amazing what a bit of online advertising can do. I help fish when I can, but Uncle John doesn't mind taking the boat out on his own. That's his passion, and it works well for both of us.

Lexi found part-time work as a school counselor, but she's happy with only twenty hours a week. We're not wealthy in the eyes of most, but we have much more than most eyes can see. Though money is tight, she'd much rather be home. It's such a sweet joy to watch this beautiful woman turn into a beautiful mother. I couldn't be more proud of her! Even though I don't get much done as a businessman when she's gone, my days are much more rewarding when filled with story books, toys, and Peter Pan-like adventures! I *love* being a dad!

Gramps was supportive of my decision to leave. Josh really stepped up while I was gone on my mission, and it wasn't hard to see he has a passion for ranching and farming I would never have. He returns home from his mission soon, and he's already planning on running the place. Grandma and Gramps were even discussing a mission of their own the last time we visited. I'm so happy for them all!

As a side note, you will be excited to know I kept my promise to Frank! He left on his mission eight months after I did, and Meagan was still single when he returned home. After a very fun and explosive courtship, he and Meagan were sealed in the Mesa Temple two months later in April! Frank is going into the insurance realm as an agent and financial advisor. They had their first child a few weeks ago, a cute baby girl they named Berlin! Frank swears it has nothing to do with the fact that he served in

Germany, but we all know better. You can still read him like a book.

We miss Arizona some days, but when we get sad we turn up the heater to ninety for a few minutes and remember why we love it here. Besides, the views are fantastic! Looking out my office window, across the bay I can see large mountain islands standing as sentinels, protecting us from the harsh, unforgiving ocean. The rugged majesty takes your breath away. But for all the beauty I have out my window—the sunsets in all their stunning glory—my favorite view is not looking out.

The house is unusually quiet for this early in the evening. A few steps down the hall, the house opens up to a messy living room. Soggy graham crackers are smashed in the carpet, toys strewn across the floor, but amid all the chaos, you cannot help but be drawn to a Celestial site. Asleep on the couch is the most beautiful daughter of God I have ever seen! She is worn out and ruffled from a long day as mommy, and asleep in her arms are two of the sweetest creations God has ever made!

So you see, I *have* held eternity in my hands . . . and my favorite part is when *they* hold it back. I found the things that make me *truly* happy. It's not the ending, though it may appear to be that way. No, the best part is I *know* without a doubt that this is *not* the end. My eternity—has just begun.

Acknowledgments

It was hard to put my name on this book. In so many ways it does not deserve to be here. If you only knew how many people have sacrificed their time and talents to make this possible. It would take chapters to describe a scant summary of all who helped and what they've done.

So where do you draw the line of who makes the thank you list? The encouraging pat on the back when the days were dreary was just as appreciated as the hundreds of hours of free proofreading and advice. Some gave little, others gave much. *Airlis* wouldn't have made it without each one of you. Thank you. Thank you with all of my heart.

With that being said, there are two people who deserve all the praise and gratitude I can give. First is my amazing wife, Tiffany. Without her years of encouragement and sacrifice this never would've happened. Words cannot express how much I love her. If you get nothing else from this book, know that my love for this beautiful woman was the inspiration for this story—for our story. May the whole world know: Honey, you are *my* eternity!

Eternity *is* real. Tiffany and I *can* be together forever! I have no doubt of this. Our Heavenly Father has a plan that makes it possible for anyone to achieve this most precious of all goals! This is where the praise should be given. His name should be on the cover, not mine.

Often as I wrote, I felt God guide my thoughts. My hands would fly across the keys as words spilled from my heart and tears fell from my eyes. Miracles came too frequently to ignore. Many of them were the people who helped along the way. God is the author of everything good found in these pages—for everything good in our lives! Only through Him is there hope for greater things to come. How great is our God!

brian

Made in the USA
San Bernardino, CA
17 June 2017